FACE THE WIND AND FLY

Jenny Harper

Published by Accent Press Ltd 2014

ISBN 9781783752645

Cover design by Caleb Rutherford, Eidetic Graphic
Design

*In memory of my dear and much-missed
friend and critic,
Jan Fairley 1949-2012*

Acknowledgements

I didn't know much about wind farms when I started writing this book, so I am very grateful to SSE, who took me on a visit to one of their larger sites and gave me many insights into how wind turbines work and how they sit in the landscape. Wind farms are often controversial and there is a long process of education and engagement with local communities prior to planning approval, all of which were explained to me with great clarity.

I'd like to pay tribute to those writers who have supported me through their teaching, in particular Anita Burgh and Katie Fforde, whose experience, patience and belief in my writing abilities have been hugely valuable and much appreciated. Also, this book would certainly not have been published if it had not been for the endless support and encouragement of my writing buddies Jennifer Young and Dianne Haley – thank you so much. Likewise, I owe a great debt to others who have encouraged me. They include many members of the Romantic Novelists' Association, my friends in the e-group writersscotland, and members of a number of other forums. Also to Jan Sprenger, aka Rosie Dean, who has been of particular help during the process of publishing.

Thanks are due to my wonderful daughter-in-law, Sarah Carter, who has given me useful advice on HR matters and long-term encouragement; and to my friend Susan Inch who, like my heroine Kate, loves scarves. I'd like to thank Mrs Jane Burnett, who gave me many insights into life in a small village, and

Elizabeth Garrett, in whose beautiful retreat on the east coast of Scotland many thousands of words of this novel were written.

And finally, I cannot express enough thanks to my long-suffering husband, Robin, who puts up with long absences while I'm at my computer, and is expected to contribute ideas for both plot and character at the drop of a hat – a challenge to which he rises magnificently.

Note

The company AeGen, where Kate Courtenay works, is an imaginary company, and any resemblance to any actual company is completely accidental.

Note: Hailesbank and the Heartlands

The small market town of Hailesbank is born of my imagination, as are the surrounding villages of Forgie and Stoneyford and the Council housing estate known as Summerfield, which together form The Heartlands. I have placed the area, in my mind, to the east of Scotland's capital city, Edinburgh.

The first mention of The Heartlands was made by Agrippa Centorius in AD77, not long after the Romans began their surge north in the hopes of conquering this savage land. 'This is a place of great beauty,' wrote Agrippus, 'and its wildness has clutched my heart.' He makes several mentions thereafter of The Heartlands. There are still signs of Roman occupation in Hailesbank, which has great transport links to the south (and England) and the north, especially to Edinburgh, and its proximity to the sea and the (real) coastal town of Musselburgh made it a great place to settle. The Georgians and Victorians began to develop the small village, its clean air and glorious views, rich farming hinterland and great transport proving highly attractive.

The River Hailes flows through the town. There is a Hailes Castle in East Lothian (it has not yet featured in my novels!), but it sits on the Tyne.

Hailesbank has a Town Hall, a High Street, from which a number of ancient small lanes, or vennels, run down to the river, which once was the lifeblood of the town.

In my novels, characters populate the shops, cafes and pubs in Hailesbank and the pretty adjoining village of Forgie, with Summerfield inhabitants providing another layer of social interaction.

You can meet more inhabitants of the town and area in *Maximum Exposure* and *Loving Susie* – with more titles to follow!

Chapter One

'You're late,' Andrew Courtenay said unnecessarily as his wife Kate hurried into the kitchen, a blur of arms and legs and shopping. He had already changed into his dinner suit and was lounging against the island unit in the middle of the room sipping white wine, a perfect picture of relaxation and readiness.

Kate dropped the bags and stared at him.

'What?' He smoothed down his tie and patted his hair self-consciously. 'Did I spill curry down my front the last time I had this on? Should I have clipped my nose hairs?'

Andrew cut a fine figure, but then, he always had done. When they first met, she had just graduated but he'd been a young-looking forty-one. Sixteen years into their marriage, he inhabited his skin with assuredness. Master and Commander. Her master. At least, the owner of her heart – but not, right now, of her affections. Her mind still whirling with the news she'd been given at work she said, more curtly than she meant to, 'I thought you said you'd drive.'

'Ah.' He studied the glass in his hand and then looked at the clock. 'I forgot. I was in need. Martyne has been particularly difficult today.'

Martyne Noreis was the eponymous hero of Andrew's bestselling medieval murder mysteries.

Martyne Noreis and the Circle of Fire
Martyne Noreis and the Woman in Scarlet
Martyne Noreis and —

Nine of them, the tenth to be published shortly.

'Martyne was difficult?' she echoed, thinking of the

1

project she'd just been handed and wondering what could possibly be so challenging about a character that had never existed.

Andrew wrote his novels in the small room next to the front door of Willow Corner, their home in the pretty conservation village of Forgie. His study overlooked the garden on two sides and had book-covered walls and a leather sofa. In winter, Andrew lit the fire. While Kate scurried into whatever the weather chose to throw at her, frequently with her hard hat in one hand and jacket and boots in the other, Andrew sidled down the comfortably carpeted stairs a civilised hour or so later, put a match to the kindling, and settled to his thoughts without ever having to put a toe out of the door. Where Andrew's life was lived from the study, Kate spent much of hers at the top of some wind-blown hill staring at wind turbines, or where they would shortly appear.

Kate liked wind turbines, which was good, because her job was to build them, whole farms of the things. Now, though, standing in the kitchen in mud-spattered trousers and still with her high-visibility vest over her jacket, she wondered why the hell she'd picked engineering when there must be a hundred other less challenging careers she could have chosen.

'I really could do with a— Oh, never mind.'

Sometimes she felt she had to fight with the fictional Martyne and his perfectly beautiful, perfectly sensible wife Ellyn for Andrew's attention, but she and Andrew had agreed their division of labour years ago. She was to be free to pursue her ambitions as an engineer, he to follow his dream of writing and, because he worked from home, to look after their son Ninian. Somewhere in the small print of that agreement lay all the dull minutiae of daily tasks, negotiated and renegotiated across the years.

She crossed the room to kiss him. The wine on his lips tasted tantalising. 'It's all right,' she said, memories of this morning's difficult meeting fading as his arms came round her, 'I'll have some champagne when we get there. I can survive.'

'No, I'm safe, this is my first. I'll do my duty.'

'Really? I don't mind. He's your son.'

Tonight they were going to her stepson Harry's engagement party. It would be a celebration, of course, but she knew it wouldn't be quite as simple as that. When your stepson is older than you are, nothing is ever straightforward.

'Kate,' Andrew said, his eyes deep brown and burnished, like chestnuts after roasting. Their expression as he looked down at her was at once amused and resigned. 'I'll drive. One drink and you're dangerous.'

He knew her well. She was small and slim and alcohol hit her system quickly. She kissed him again and smiled. 'Okay. Thanks. Is Ninian ready?'

'He's in protest mode.'

'Surely he can wear a tie for once, for his brother?'

'You'd think so. Will you try?'

Kate loved her son, but Ninian was now a teenager and therefore unfathomable. 'Should I be stern or pleading?' As if it would make any difference.

'Jolly?'

'Right. I can do jolly. 'Could you—?' She gestured at the shopping helplessly, thinking of the shower, and choosing a dress, and shoes...

He glanced at his watch.

'I know, I know, I'll be quick.'

She knocked on Ninian's door as she passed it. 'Nearly ready? Ten minutes. Do you want to borrow one of Dad's ties?'

Another grunt.

'Ninian? Did you hear me?'

'Yeah, I heard.' Gruff but not surly. At least that was a bonus. 'You're all right.'

3

She took this to mean 'I'll find a tie', and turned to her own needs.

Short hair was a blessing. It received quick attention as she showered, and a rub with a towel was all it needed afterwards. Kate – slim, energetic and well organised – was mistress of the quick change. All she ever needed was a minute to assess her mood, because her mood dictated which scarf she would wear. In the male-dominated, frenetically busy world she inhabited, the scarf was a small but defiantly feminine gesture and what had started as a quirk had become an addiction. She hoarded scarves with a passion. Her collection nestled in a special section of her wardrobe, outnumbering her clothes by a factor of twenty – she needed nothing more than a couple of well-cut suits and some neat shift dresses in black, or white, or a plain, bold colour, because the chosen scarf set any outfit off to perfection. Draped, wound round and round her neck, knotted, tied, looped through itself or thrown over her shoulders as the mood took her, Kate's scarf was her weather vane and her security blanket.

She wriggled into a black Moschino shift and put on the pearl choker Andrew had given her for their tenth wedding anniversary, because tonight was a special occasion. A pair of improbable heels added height and sophistication. She closed her eyes. Which scarf? The Georgina Von Etzdorf pansy-printed velvet? The Versace with its bold Greek key-pattern half-border and riotous scarlet poppies? The Weston agate silk-satin, all pale blues and browns and white?

Her eyes snapped open. She had it.

Twelve shelves faced her, each stacked neatly and colour-sorted. Kate knew exactly where each scarf was stored. She reached in and pulled out one of her treasures, the fantastic hand-woven Botan Peony silk and cashmere gauze in taupe and black, by legendary Japanese tattoo artist Horiyoshi the Third. For a moment she fingered it lovingly, admiring the subtly-drawn flowers, then she draped it carefully round her neck, rearranging it to ensure that the pearls were visible.

A touch of smoky grey eye colour and a dab of mascara were all that was still needed. Elfin, her best friend Charlotte called her: 'Audrey Hepburn in a hard hat.' Kate surveyed herself in the mirror. No sign of Hard-hat Kate now, the transformation from business diva to soirée siren was complete.

She ran downstairs and opened the front door. It was April and all week the sun had been shining – Edinburgh had been hotter than Palma, Rome or Hawaii. Now, out of the blue, it had started snowing and the garden had turned white. She looked at it with dismay.

'I should be wearing boots,' she called to Andrew.

'Wear boots then,' he responded unsympathetically, then shouted up the stairs, 'Ninian! We're off. Hurry up.'

She knew it was too much to expect understanding, on this issue at least. All Andrew's imaginative empathy was in the Middle Ages, where Ellyn Noreis would be prosaically practical about boots. She threw on a coat, put her handbag over her head to protect it from the spiralling snowflakes, and ran the few yards to the car. She really didn't want to be late, she hated being late and the last thing she wanted was an excuse for Harry to pass judgement on her timekeeping.

Ninian bundled into the back of the car a moment later and slammed the door. She swivelled round to look at him and gave an appreciative whistle. 'Wow.'

'What?' Her fifteen-year-old glowered warningly.

'You look great, that's all.' She turned away, smiling. Ninian never wore a tie outside of the dreaded school uniform – and then usually knotted at half-mast – but tonight smartness was mandatory.

Andrew slid in and started to reverse the car down Willow Corner's short drive. He swung left at the gate, down the hill past the church, and slithered into the outskirts of Hailesbank. Kate, usually talkative, was still thinking about work and besides, she was wound up about tonight's celebration. Andrew's first wife Val would be there. Sixteen years had passed since Kate's affair with Andrew had precipitated a bitter divorce and she was sure that Val had still not forgiven her.

They crossed the River Hailes and headed down to the coast. When they reached the outskirts of Edinburgh, they drove through Portobello towards the city. Here the snow eased.

'So what'll I do all evening?' Ninian asked from the back of the car.

'Talk to people. Be nice. You'll enjoy it.'

He grunted. 'Bet it'll be boring. I won't know anyone.'

'Harry and Jane'll be there. And Charlotte Proctor.'

Another grunt.

Ninian had been a delightful child, whose main challenges were not boisterousness and cheek but shyness and caution. Right now the hormones were kicking in. His voice had broken and his shoulders were getting broad, and the natural, unselfconscious charm of boyhood had been replaced with a gaucheness that Kate sometimes found hard to watch.

'Will there be speeches?'

She swung down the vanity mirror and got out her lipstick. Under the pretence of touching up her make-up, she was able to sneak a look at Ninian without having to swing round. Her sandy-haired, gangly boy was growing private. Once, she used to delight in hopping into the bath with him, her special treat to both of them after she got home from a long day at work, her chance to catch up on 'Mum' time. That stopped without either of them really noticing when Ninian reached six or thereabouts and she had never found a way to replace the comfortable affinity of such moments. And now, she sensed, her child was beginning to slip away from her. She swiped the stick across her lips and pursed them together. 'I'm sure Harry will say something.'

'Harry's always got something to say,' Andrew commented as he turned the car into London Road.

She smiled, but was wise enough not to let Andrew see. Experience had taught her to avoid criticising her husband's son.

'Why does he want a party, anyway?' Ninian grumbled. 'We already had dinner out.'

She tried to read his expression in the mirror but he was staring out of the side window. 'It's a chance for our families to meet. Just be happy for your brother. Make it a night to remember. It'll be your turn one day.'

Ninian snorted. 'No way.'

Andrew turned his head to glance at her and she had to work hard to stop herself laughing. So far as she was aware, Ninian hadn't woken up to the lure of girls yet, but he would. And when her handsome, funny, essentially likeable young son sloughed off the gauche trappings of the teenager and recovered his inherent charm – look out world.

She flipped the mirror up and settled back into her seat. Tonight would be another ritual dance in this complicated family of hers, and she needed to be ready.

Chapter Two

Kate knew as soon as they set foot in the smart surroundings of Edinburgh's exclusive Abercrombie Club that it wasn't going to be easy. It was too crowded, too full of people she had never met and had little wish to talk to. She was not generally antisocial – quite the opposite – and her apprehension surprised her. She was used to connecting with strangers. But then, this party was for Harry, and Harry and Kate tiptoed round each other at best.

Her stepson's greeting seemed to confirm her fears. He was waiting at the top of the stairs to greet his guests, but as soon as he saw her she sensed a shadow passing across his face. Would he never forget? His father was happy now, after all. As Harry bent, dutifully, to kiss her cheek, the deep alarm she had felt at his abiding unresponsiveness when she married Andrew came flooding back. He'd made it so hard for her and though she'd understood how he must feel, the memory of those years was bitter. It was a complex cocktail of emotions – easy to mix, impossible to separate.

'Hello Harry,' she said, resolutely cheerful. 'Where is she, this gorgeous woman who has captured your heart?'

She saw him trying not to wince and knew that yet again she'd hit the wrong note. She never got it right, not with Harry. But he smiled and, even through whatever it was he was thinking, pride of possession shone through. 'She was here a second ago. Ah, there she is – Jane!' He reached out and laid a hand on his fiancée's arm. 'Here's Dad and Kate.'

Harry always called her Kate. What else should he call her? The age difference was such an awkward one. How had Andrew ever thought she'd take easily to motherhood? She'd only just finished being a student, for heaven's sake, just graduated from living in messy shared flats, clubbing, drinking, dealing in easy laughter and long lies and endless days of zero responsibility. Then there'd been Andrew Courtenay, and they'd fallen in love, and her life had taken a direction that hadn't been anywhere on the road map she'd drawn for herself.

Jane said, 'Hi!' and air-kissed her. She was effervescent, as sparkling as the bubbles in the champagne she was holding, the perfect foil to Harry's worthiness.

'You're looking beautiful!' Kate exclaimed, and meant it. Her own gamine looks drew compliments but she still envied women with Jane's conventional kind of prettiness.

'Thanks. Got to shine tonight, haven't I?'

For all Jane's vivaciousness, she seemed to Kate to lack warmth. Or maybe she had just picked up on Harry's coolness? Already talking was difficult over the noise of conversation, so she kept it brief. 'I'm so pleased for you both, Jane.'

'Thank you, Mrs Courtenay.'

'Kate,' she corrected automatically, as she had many times already.

'Kate,' Jane repeated and smiled again – but already her gaze was directed behind her, to Andrew.

Kate gave up.

'Champagne, madam?'

The waiter looked little older than Ninian. She picked up a glass and looked round for them both, but they'd already been swallowed up by the crowd. She inched her way towards the window, where there was a magnificent view across the gardens to the Castle.

'Fabulous, isn't it?'

'Amazing.'

10

'How do you know the couple?'

'I'm Harry's stepmother.'

'Really? You don't look nearly old enough.'

The amazement was all too familiar. The nineteen-year age difference between Andrew and herself always took people by surprise and everyone reacted differently. Kate negotiated the conversation on autopilot while her mind flitted back to this morning's meeting. She'd been drawing, she remembered, only half listening because she knew she wasn't involved in the project under discussion. She'd dragged her pencil across her notepad and watched as a fine, flowing line spread itself from edge to edge. She'd drawn another, the exact mirror image. A blade of a wind turbine materialised, as beautiful and symmetrical as a petal on a dahlia. Another flick. Two. A stem for her wind-flower. Her turbine was complete, ready to make its magic of turning God's breath into power. Bold. Ingenious. *Controversial.*

'And finally,' she remembered Mark Matthews saying, 'we come to Summerfield.'

There was a touch on her elbow. Jerked back to the present, Kate focused on the earnest stranger who was talking to her. 'I said, such a happy occasion, isn't it? You must be very proud.'

'Yes. Happy. Proud.'

'Oh, there's Mrs Slater. Will you excuse me, dear? I haven't seen her in an age. Do you mind?'

'Not at all. Nice to meet you.'

She should find Ninian. Still, she hadn't had a moment to think about the meeting. She'd finished her drawing, she remembered, because Summerfield wasn't her project. Hills had appeared, tufts of grass, a cloud. Her pencil had produced a small bee and she'd added a frowning, anthropomorphic face.

'So what do you think, Kate?'

Mark was seated at the head of the table and ten faces

11

were all staring at her expectantly. There'd been something else there too. Surprise? Shock? What had she missed?

'I'm sorry, I didn't catch that. What did you—?'

'Summerfield,' he'd said, weightily.

'Yes?' Summerfield was Jack's project.

'I've decided it would be best if you take this one on. What do you think?'

'Jack's doing Summerfield.' She'd fingered her Burberry scarf like a comfort blanket. It was one of her favourites, in royal blue and turquoise with a section in bold houndstooth check.

'Yes. That was the plan.' Mark had spoken with elaborate patience. 'But I have been discussing it with the senior management team and we've decided to make this change.'

Kate had fought rising concern. Why had the executive been involved in a decision about the project management of a very small-scale wind farm?

'You are familiar with Summerfield?'

She had a degree in environmental science and a Masters in renewable energy technologies – she was not only familiar with the project, she'd done much of the early planning for it. 'Yes of course, you know I am.'

'So I take it there's no problem.'

He'd said it as a statement rather than a question and she'd realised that his earlier 'What do you think?' phrase had been in the same category: rhetorical. 'What do you think?' meant 'starting Monday'.

Jack was avoiding her gaze, studying the table as though the graining on the cheap veneer held all the fascination of sixteenth-century Italian intaglio.

'Summerfield? Me?'

'I know you're used to running things on a rather grander scale, but you know more about it than anyone. It makes sense.'

12

'I couldn't do it. Sorry. We discussed this, Mark. Behind-the-scenes work is one thing, but high visibility involvement is out of the question.'

Don't argue with your boss. Not in public.

Too late.

'Jack's terrific, but we need your experience on this one. Sorry.'

Kate's glass was empty again. How had that happened? She dumped it on a passing tray and picked up a glass of juice. It wouldn't do to get tiddly tonight.

Summerfield! She paraded the difficulties in her head.

Summerfield was a small council estate that sat like a pimple on the forehead of the charming old village of Forgie, east of Edinburgh. Just twelve wind turbines were planned and by the time the public consultation was over, there would probably only be eight. They would sit on the hillside above the council estate. This aspect of the project was hardly problematic – AeGen would ensure that there would be significant community benefits to the estate and the residents of Summerfield would almost certainly be happy to accept the trade-off: a few wind turbines in exchange for a new community leisure and sports centre, additional home insulation or double glazing perhaps. No – the problem would be the residents of the small, pretty, historic and extremely well-heeled village of Forgie itself.

And Forgie was where Kate lived.

Local knowledge. They were anticipating trouble and were expecting her to draw on the bank of goodwill and friendship they assumed she must have in the village. Mark had handed her a briefcase full of toxins and she'd been forced to accept it.

Kate wiped a hand over her forehead. What a day. Someone near her said, 'Isn't that Andrew Courtenay over there? Harry's father? The novelist?'

She followed the gaze and saw that Andrew was with a rather oddly dressed girl, maybe about Jane's age, late

13

twenties. When she drew close she heard Andrew say, 'So he poisoned the woman using a concoction of berries of belladonna, stewed and stirred into hot ale.'

The girl looked rapt. '*Really?*'

Andrew loved to impress. Some novelists hid behind their laptops, but Andrew revelled in an audience. He'd been a teacher before he turned novelist, and the innate showman in him still survived. He took Kate's elbow and drew her in. 'Kate, this is Sophie MacAteer. She's a cousin of Jane's.'

'And a *huge* fan of Mr Courtenay's books. Really. I've read all of them.'

'But that's just the first murder in the latest novel.' Andrew looked at Sophie indolently. Andrew's lazy gaze could be intoxicating, as Kate knew from experience. She could see that Sophie was transfixed. She was wearing a cloche hat – or was it a headscarf? – pulled tightly over her hair and gathered into a knot on one side, just above her ear, completely concealing her hair so that she couldn't be sure what colour it was. The thing was a statement, though quite what it was saying Kate wasn't sure. Her skin was as pale and translucent as a baby's, she had plucked her eyebrows and painted her lips dark red. She was certainly striking.

'Does the woman die?'

'Of course. Would there be a story if she didn't?'

'But does the boy get caught?' she persisted.

Over the years Andrew had learned how to deal with admiring fans. 'Well now,' he temporised. 'That would be telling. The book's out next month. You must come to the launch party.'

He did it so easily. A fan delighted, another book sold. Tick. Job done.

Kate said, 'Darling, I see Charlotte,' and nodded in the direction of the stairwell, where Charlotte Proctor had just appeared.

14

Charlotte was Kate's oldest friend. She'd shared a student flat with Charlotte and studied engineering with her husband, Mike. Kate had gone into renewable energy, Mike into oil and gas.

'I'll be over in a minute,' Andrew smiled.

'Hello Charlotte.'

'Hi! You look fab.'

'Where's Mike?'

'He's offshore. Went yesterday. I've brought Dad instead.'

'Kate!' Frank Griffiths took her hands and kissed her ceremoniously, right cheek, left cheek, right cheek again. A gentleman of the old kind – courteous, affable, and erudite – he wore his dinner jacket and bow tie like a birthright. 'You look supremely elegant, my darling, doesn't she, Charlotte?'

'Kate always looks magnificent.'

Compliments or no compliments, Frank was the chair of Summerfield and Forgie Community Council and an unrepentant opponent of wind farms. Kate foresaw trouble.

He leaned towards her and said, 'This wind farm, Kate—'

Charlotte groaned and rolled her eyes. 'Dad! Not here, please!'

'—We've just been notified about the planning application.'

So I was right, Kate thought, *it's starting already.*

In all their years of animated but affable conversations about renewable energy, Kate had never convinced Frank either of the need for it nor of the merits of new technologies and his reactions now were predictable. 'The application's just for a Met mast.'

'It's the first step to disaster.'

'Hardly.'

Frank's face was growing redder. 'A wind farm above Summerfield would be a catastrophe for the whole

15

neighbourhood.'

'*Dad!*'

Frank stepped back. 'I know it puts you in a difficult position, Kate,' he said in a more conciliatory tone, 'working for AeGen, but I'm sure you must have some kind of inside line that could help us in this consultation process.'

'Inside line?'

'You know, Kate, come on, some stuff on the QT, some facts and figures. Something that'll help us fight the damned proposal. I know it's your job but you can't really want the blessed things hovering above Forgie, be truthful.'

'They'll hardly be visible from Forgie village.' Kate decided to get it over with, risk swift execution rather than death by a thousand cuts. 'Frank, I think you should know that I've been put in charge of the Summerfield project – so we'll have plenty of opportunities to discuss this properly.'

He was clearly thunderstruck. Kate felt nothing but empathy, because his reaction exactly mirrored hers at the meeting that afternoon, but she could hardly show it.

'Now,' she said with forced cheerfulness, 'come and let me introduce you to Jane's parents, they're right over here.'

Kate sat down for dinner and readjusted her scarf. Although the room was hot, the top table was by the window and she could feel a slight draught at her back. She draped it round her shoulders like a shawl, and took stock. Harry and Jane had seated Andrew next to Val, a small piece of manipulation she found unsettling. Andrew and his first wife had learned politeness, but a whole evening was a long time to sustain it. Harry was making a point with this arrangement and rightly or wrongly, Kate took it personally. Across the room, she saw Ninian,

16

hunched over, his shoulders slumped. Was it just because he was finding the tie disagreeable, or had he found no-one to talk to? Harry was so inconsiderate, he should have seated Ninian here, with the rest of the family. She watched her son as he raised a pint glass to his lips. Had he drunk beer before? Not in her presence, certainly. Could he cope with the alcohol? The tables were so tightly packed there was no way of reaching him.

Ninian glanced across at her. She raised her eyebrows and picked up her own glass, tapping it queryingly then pointing at him. Ninian, in return, gave his innocent 'What?' look. She knew it well. 'What me? Would I? As if!' More often than not it concealed mischief of some sort. She frowned at him but he grinned and shrugged, draining his glass. It was impossible to do anything, she was completely boxed in.

After dinner, Harry stood up. 'I'd like to say a few words.' There was laughter, and comments – *A few? That'll be a first!* and *Go, man!*

Across the room, Ninian was looking queasy. She'd find him as soon as she could.

But when the speeches finished and the throng of guests made their way out of the dining room, Ninian and Andrew had both disappeared again. Kate drifted from one group of guests to another, smiling vaguely, then finally spotted her son slipping back into the supper room. From there, glass doors led to a balcony. Perhaps, sensibly, he was looking for some air.

The room was dark. Ninian had crossed to the far side. Kate was about to call out to him when she saw him pull up sharply and stare at the balcony. There was someone out there. She couldn't make out who, she just saw shadowy shapes, half hidden by the blinds at the far end. She started to pad across the carpet towards her son.

'Oh, *fuck!*' Ninian swivelled round and covered his hand with his mouth. It was a futile gesture. He threw up,

17

violently, all over the plush carpet.

'I haven't been so embarrassed since you bared your bottom to the bishop when you were four,' Kate said after the staff had masterminded the clean-up discreetly. 'Do you want me to take you home?'

'No, you're all right,' he muttered, not looking at her.

'Are you ill? Or was it the beer?'

'Mu-um. I've drunk beer before.'

'Well you shouldn't have. Here, drink some water.'

'It's so boring,' Ninian protested, but he drank the water.

'Well being sick was hardly the best way to enliven proceedings. Are you really all right? You're still looking a bit green.' She couldn't just turn off motherly concern even if Ninian's illness was self-inflicted.

'I'm fine. Just let me sit here. Go and chat up whoever you have to chat up.'

An hour later, all chatted out, she went to find him again. They could wait together till Andrew was ready to go home. She spotted him across the large landing lounging on a leather sofa, talking to Harry, and padded across the thick carpet unseen.

'Don't you *dare* tell Kate,' she heard Harry hiss.

Kate shrank back a step.

'But I *saw* them, I tell you!' Ninian muttered, his voice furious.

Skulking was ridiculous. Kate stepped into their line of vision and blazed a smile. 'Saw who, darling?'

'Nobody,' Harry said.

Ninian scowled. 'Nothing,' he said.

'Oh come on. What was it you weren't to tell me?'

But neither was to be drawn.

'Can we go yet, Mum?'

It was nearly midnight. Kate twisted her scarf round her neck.

18

'Find your father, then,' she said, giving up. No doubt their little secret would emerge in time.

Chapter Three

Ibsen Brown loved weather. When friends or clients complained of the wind or the rain, he'd shrug and say, 'It's just weather,' before putting on a jacket, or a sweater, or a waterproof and getting on with the task in hand. At six feet tall, Ibsen was built like an Olympic swimmer, with broad, powerful shoulders, trim waist and neat, muscular legs. Not that he'd ever been inside a gym – he was a gardener and his fitness came from hard physical work. He spent his days digging and hoeing, building small patios and terraces, lopping trees and rooting out unwanted stumps whose roots burrowed obstinately deep into cold earth.

Ibsen never thought about fitness, or six-packs, or bulging biceps. He wasn't vain, far from it – he barely looked in a mirror. His idea of smart dressing was a clean tee shirt and jeans and he refused to have his hair cut. It was dark and thick and irrepressible and he controlled it by pulling it back into a pony tail and securing it with an elastic band – or, if he couldn't find one, with an odd piece of string pulled from some pocket.

No, what Ibsen liked was growing things. He liked the feel of rich brown earth in his hands, but most of all, he loved watching leaves unfurl and strong, questing shoots pushing up through the soil from bulbs he'd buried below months earlier. He'd been a draughtsman, once, qualifying the hard way, head down every evening swotting for his exams while he sat by day in an architect's office. It was what his father wanted him to do – Tam Brown, who was head gardener at Forgie House, was a self-taught man who prized education.

Ibsen had loathed it, but supporting Lynn and—

Say her name. You never stop thinking of her anyway.

—supporting Lynn and his baby daughter, Violet, meant buckling down to 'a proper job'.

Ibsen parked his battered old van in front of Helena Banks's gate and turned off the wipers. The drizzle had almost stopped. The Banks's house was on the outskirts of Hailesbank, on the eastern side, high on a hill. At the back there were spectacular panoramas of the sea, but further down the garden a high wall provided shelter from the prevailing winds and stole the views.

'Come on, boy.' His chocolate Labrador, Wellington, jumped onto the pavement, tail wagging, tongue lolling, delighted to be freed from his prison. 'Let's see what she's got planned for us, eh?'

He grabbed his tools from the back of the van and pushed open the gate. He'd been planning to give the grass its first cut of the year, but yesterday's snow had set that back. The snow had taken everyone by surprise. It shouldn't have been snowing – earlier in the week it had been unseasonably warm. Between jobs, he'd nipped into the garden centre outside Hailesbank to purchase a new pair of secateurs. Mistaking him in his overalls for an assistant, someone had asked him for petunias.

'It's April,' he'd said shortly, 'and we're in Scotland.' He'd left them staring at him, open-mouthed, then apologised to the girl on the till. 'I can't stand idiotic questions,' he admitted, vexed at his own rudeness, 'that's why I squirrel myself away in people's gardens.'

Rain had washed away the scant snow. Cutting the grass was out, but there was a lot of tidying to do.

'Morning Ibsen,' read the note on the nail in the shed, *'I'm out this morning. Please can you build a new compost heap today? The old one really needs to be cleared out. Maybe see you later. Thank you. Helena Banks.'*

He smiled, liking her directness. 'That's Mrs B for you, eh Wellington?' The instruction scuppered his plans for tidying, but she was right – the compost did need attention. There were some planks of wood in the corner of the shed, and he found a ball of string and strolled out, whistling. He was going to enjoy his morning.

Wellington, picking up the smell of a rabbit – or maybe a hedgehog – followed it, nose down, into the undergrowth and disappeared.

They were both happy.

'Ibsen? Ah, you're still here.'

Ibsen straightened up. 'Morning, Mrs Banks. What's the time?'

'Almost one.'

'Is it really? I lost track.'

A strong breeze whipped Helena Banks's dark auburn hair across her face and she pushed it back with slim fingers and laughed. 'So you were enjoying yourself.'

Ibsen thrust his spade into the ground and grinned. 'Guess I must have been.'

'Nearly finished?'

'Just about to tidy up. Want to see?'

She peered round him. 'Looks very neat. Sorry about the lawn, maybe it'll be drier by next week. Time for a coffee?'

'Thanks. Maybe a quick one.'

Ten minutes later, Ibsen had kicked off his boots and washed his hands, and was seated at the large scrubbed pine table in Helena Banks's homely kitchen.

'That smells terrific.'

'There's some soup, if you prefer?'

'Coffee will do me fine, honestly.'

Helena filled two mugs, pulled out a chair and sat down to join him. 'Have a biscuit at least. Alice baked yesterday.'

'I never could resist your daughter's baking.' Ibsen picked up a macadamia and white chocolate cookie the size of his fist and bit into it with relish.

'What do you think of this wind farm, then? We're a little worried we'll see the turbines.'

'Wind farm? What wind farm?'

'Oh, hadn't you heard? The planning application was in the paper a few days ago. They're building it on top of Summerfield Law.'

Ibsen stopped chewing. His hyacinth-blue eyes shaded to ink as they narrowed into slits. '*What?*'

'It's far enough away, of course, and anyway, David and I are firm supporters of renewable energy, but—'

Ibsen laid down the cookie and pushed back his chair. 'I'd better go.'

'Ibsen? You've hardly touched your coffee. And what about Alice's—?'

'I'll be back on Monday as usual. Thanks Mrs B.'

He pulled on his boots, picked up his tools, and strode round the house to his van.

A wind farm? On Summerfield Law?

Not if I can stop it.

The climb to the top of Summerfield Law was not a long one, but it was steep. The track was muddy and uneven, and the grassy verges turned to bracken and heather as it rose to more than a thousand feet. Ibsen started briskly, then instead of slowing as he gained height, took the steepest part of the climb almost at a run, pushing himself to go faster and faster so that he arrived at the summit breathless but invigorated. Wellington bounded ahead, covering twice as much ground as he ran a hundred yards forward, then doubled back to check that his master was still on course for the top.

The last few hundred yards wound through a Sitka plantation, a dark, ugly wood that had been planted in the

24

Sixties for commercial timber. If the wind farm went ahead, these trees would probably be felled, which would be one good outcome at least. Ibsen abhorred the stiff, close-planted trees, for all the world like serried ranks of foreign soldiers. This wasn't wildlife, it was nature on an industrial scale. The path here became narrower and very steep but a wooden stile across a dry stone wall marked the end of the plantation and the beginning of the rough moorland at the top of the Law. Stone and earth made way for moss and heather, and where small songbirds had flitted shyly in the branches, the clear expanse of land became a hunting ground for kestrels and buzzards and sparrowhawks.

At the top, Ibsen sank onto a flat boulder. Summerfield Law was the highest point in this part of the county and the climb was worth the effort. The Firth of Forth made a dark blue slash across the canvas of grass and moor and hill spread out in front of him. He could just glimpse the tiny white triangular sails of a flotilla of yachts, scudding in the wind way out on the deep waters. His stomach knotted. *They can't build a wind farm here. It would be utter sacrilege.*

A figure emerged from the woods into a puddle of sunshine. A woman. A walker, by the looks of her – properly clad. She looked tiny, a couple of hundred feet beneath him, a pinprick in the landscape.

As she neared him, he saw that it wasn't just an illusion, she actually was small, and she was attacking the hill with energy and a step so light she was almost dancing. Nice.

He called, 'There's room for two on this rock,' and patted the space beside him invitingly.

The woman stopped a few feet below him and looked up, frowning. Her eyes were like sloes, dark and shiny, and her hair was cropped so short that it barely ruffled in the wind.

'I don't bite. Neither does Wellington, I promise you.' Ibsen's hair was fanning out behind him, the stiff breeze tugging at the rubber band that held his ponytail in place. 'I've got coffee, by the way.' He patted his shoulder bag, which still had his flask in it, untouched.

The woman's smile transformed her face. The small frown – concentration? irritation? – vanished and she looked eighteen, though the spray of fine lines that trailed from the corners of her eyes marked her as older.

'Is that a bribe?'

'It's an offer.'

She clambered the last few yards and sat down beside him. 'Hi.'

'I don't have milk. Sorry.' He filled the top of his vacuum flask with steaming coffee and handed it to her. 'But there again, I don't have germs either.'

'How do you know?'

He shrugged. 'I'm fit as a fiddle, always have been.'

She accepted the cup. 'Well in that case, Mr Germinator, your tee shirt is lying.'

'Sorry?'

She laughed and looked down. The bottle-green tee shirt he'd pulled on that morning bore the legend THE GERMINATOR! accompanied by a child's drawing of a cheerful plant in a pot.

'Aha. Not germs. Germination. I'm a gardener. Ibsen Brown, nice to meet you.'

'Unusual.'

He was conscious of the warmth of her thigh, pressed close against his as they perched together on the small rock. He groaned. 'No wisecracks, please. I've had a lifetime of ribbing. My father is self educated, and passionate about reading. And if you think Ibsen is an odd name, spare a thought for my sister.'

'Hedda?'

'Good guess. Most people have no idea who Ibsen was

26

– but no, she's called Cassiopeia.'

'Beautiful but arrogant?'

'You *are* well educated. Actually, she was named after the star constellation, not the Greek goddess.' Wellington put an insistent nose in his lap and he fondled the dog's silky ears. 'We call her Cassie.'

'That's a relief. Ibsen's good, though. I like Ibsen.'

He fumbled in his pocket and pulled out an old tennis ball. 'Here boy, fetch!' His arm arced back and he threw the ball as far as he could across the moor. Wellington shot off, a blur of gleaming brown fur. 'Do you have a name?'

'I guess so.'

Ibsen looked down at her. Was she being funny?

She was smiling. 'Kate. Kate Courtenay.'

'Nice to meet you, Kate.' He held out his hand. After a second she transferred the coffee to her left hand and took his. She was small-boned, like a bird. A rush of sweetness filled him, taking him by surprise.

She withdrew her hand and returned the empty cup. 'Great coffee. Thanks.'

'You're welcome.'

They sat for a few minutes in a companionable silence. Ibsen broke it first. 'Spectacular, isn't it?'

'Yes. Yes it is.'

'Did you know they're planning to put a wind farm up here?'

There was a few seconds' silence, then she said, 'Really?'

'Nowhere's sacred any more, is it?'

'Sacred? You mean—'

He gestured at the panorama. 'People like to come here, walk their dogs, enjoy the peace and quiet.'

'I don't think wind turbines are particularly noisy these days.'

'They're hardly likely to blend into the landscape though, are they?'

27

'I think they're only planning a few.' Kate stood up abruptly. 'Thanks for the coffee. I'd better get going.'

She started to pick her way down the stony path.

Was it something he said?

'Bye, Kate Courtenay,' he called at the retreating back, the odd feeling of contentment replaced by something more forlorn.

She turned to look at him. The sloe eyes seemed to have lost their sparkle. Or was it just a trick of the light? 'Goodbye, Ibsen Brown.'

She turned her back and raised one arm in farewell. In a minute she was tinier than ever, just a dark speck on the heather.

Chapter Four

When Kate was just nine she entered a competition to design and build a bridge from a set of specified objects – pipe cleaners, wooden skewers, string, paper clips, no more than four biro pens and a maximum of four bulldog clips. The bridge was to be judged for the size of its span, the weight it could bear without collapsing and its aesthetic appeal ('how nice it looks', the competition blurb said). The competition, part of a local Science Festival, was to take place in a big hall in Exeter and competitors had an hour to complete their bridge. Kate spent a month practising. Every morning when she woke up, she would draw another design, every afternoon when she got home from school, she tried to build it. She was obsessed, and utterly determined to win. On the day, she was the only girl to take part, which only increased her doggedness.

Her bridge was good. It was very good. In her own eyes it was certainly the best – but a boy won.

'Mine was *loads* better!' she wailed to her father, who'd only been able to look on helplessly as she came an honourable second.

'His was a little bigger, darling.'

'But it looked *rubbish*.'

'Sadly, the judges didn't think so. Come on love, let's go and get an ice cream and celebrate. You did come second!'

Later, she wondered if the judges had assumed that her father had designed the bridge and penalised her for it. He was a professor of engineering and she found everything he did beautiful. That bridge had been all her own work,

29

though, and the unfairness of the decision had been devastating. She was upset and bitter for months, but the episode taught her two things: first, that as a girl in a male-dominated field, you need to try not just harder, but ten times harder than the boys in order to succeed – and second, that she did not like losing. These lessons had stayed with her over the years and coloured her entire career.

Now, looking at the chart Jack Bailey was spreading out in front of her, she knew she had to call on those lessons yet again.

'We need to put the access road up to the wind farm *here*.' Jack pointed at a line he'd drawn.

Jack had been in charge of the Summerfield project and now he was her assistant. If he harboured resentment, then he might challenge her authority. Besides, he didn't know the area as she did. One glance at the map was enough to tell Kate his proposed route wouldn't work. 'We can't, Jack.'

'Can't? It's the obvious place.'

'I know. But that will drive right through a small patch of ancient oak wood and the locals won't stand for it.'

'Then we need to do some PR work with the locals and get it sorted.'

'Sorry. No. I did look at that early on. That's why I drew the access the other way, round the back of Summerfield Boggs.'

'But it'll almost double the cost,' Jack protested.

He didn't like having to answer to her, she could see that. She'd have to be tactful, but it was important to stamp her authority on this. She understood now why Mark wanted her to head up the job – making the right choices now would be much easier and more cost-effective in the long run, and local knowledge would certainly help. She held firm. 'I know. But trust me, Jack, it's going to be the only way. Once we go into the consultation stage we'll need to keep the community on side as much as possible, it's going to be hard enough to win some of them round as it is.'

She refrained from saying, *That's why I'm project-managing and you're not*, but she knew from Jack's ill-concealed scowl that he wasn't happy. She moved the discussion on. 'How are the land lease negotiations coming on?'

'The two farmers whose land we need for the turbines are happy. They're going to make shedloads of money, so they should be. The Forgie House Trust might be a stumbling block though. The access road will need to pass the House whichever route we take further up.'

'Keep at it, Jack, you're doing a great job.' Kate doubted that the praise would mollify him, but cumulative compliments might help over the long haul. 'Have you got any meetings set up yet? We'll need to start with the Community Council, of course, and the heritage and environment bodies. Plus, we'll have to put some real thought into how we tackle things locally if we're going to avoid confrontation.'

Jack consulted his notes. 'There's a meeting with Forgie and Summerfield Community Council in the diary. I've heard that someone's already organising a petition against the project, but there's not much we can do about that.'

'No. All we can do is give the positive arguments for this wind farm and be prepared to answer questions as honestly as we can. And Jack—'

'Yes?'

'Leave out the direct access route on the plans, will you?'

Kate was so immersed in Summerfield that she got home late.

'Did you remember my burgers?' Ninian demanded as

31

soon as she got through the door.

She dropped her bulging briefcase on the kitchen floor, tired. The start of a project was the most demanding stage – all builds had disasters and needed firefighting, but thinking the task through properly at the beginning made life much easier. 'I forgot to go to the supermarket,' she confessed.

'Mu-um!'

'It's no big deal, Ninian, there's enough food in the house for a month.'

'I was looking forward to my burgers,' Ninian said, glowering.

'Really Ninian! There's pasta and rice and plenty of basics like cheese and eggs. And the freezer's well enough stocked to see us through a siege.'

'But—'

'And stop sounding like a five-year-old. We can manage for one night.' She filled a saucepan with water and stuck it on the stove. 'Where's your father?'

Ninian shrugged. 'I dunno.'

Kate glanced over at the kitchen clock. It was seven thirty. 'Is he out?'

'I dunno.'

The wall calendar in the kitchen doubled as the family engagement diary. Kate studied it. 'There's nothing in for tonight. Did he go out after you came home from school?'

'I *dunno,* Mum, I told you.' Ninian jerked open the fridge door angrily and muttered, 'He's been acting weirdly recently.'

'What? Stop mumbling, Ninian. What did you say?' What was *wrong* with him?

Ninian slammed the fridge door shut. 'There's no bloody cheese. I said he's been acting weirdly. Hadn't you noticed?'

'Don't swear. And no, I hadn't noticed. What do you mean, weirdly?'

The water was bubbling. She opened the spaghetti jar and shoved a couple of handfuls into the saucepan. She'd no real idea of how much to cook, hopefully she'd got it about right.

There was a slam of a door and Andrew called, 'Hi! I'm home! Sorry I'm so late.'

'We're in here.'

Andrew appeared at the kitchen door, casual in rust-coloured chinos and a soft white shirt, open at the neck.

'Where've you been?'

'In Edinburgh. I had a meeting with my agent, he's up from London. Didn't I tell you?'

'No, you didn't. Or Ninian. The poor boy's been wondering where you were.'

He was unruffled. 'Sorry. I thought I'd said. Anyway, I brought you some flowers to make up for it.'

He produced a bunch of sorry-looking petrol forecourt chrysanthemums. Kate took them doubtfully. Andrew was not given to buying flowers, not even third-rate ones and judging by the quality of these, that was perhaps a good thing. 'Thanks.'

'And I called in for a Chinese at the Yangtse Palace, which held me up even more – I hope you haven't eaten yet?' He hoisted two white carrier bags onto the breakfast bar and started to unload a stack of hot foil cartons.

'You could have called. I've just put on some pasta.'

'I wasn't thinking, sorry. We can have pasta salad tomorrow, let's eat this while it's hot. Ninian, get some plates, would you?'

Whatever Ninian had meant by 'acting weirdly', Kate thought, he was surely mistaken. Everything Andrew was doing seemed quite normal to her. But Ninian, who had been fiddling with his place mat during this explanation, slammed it down on the table. 'You're such a bloody convincing storyteller, Dad, you could tell fucking lies to the Pope and get him to believe you.'

33

Kate said, '*Ninian!*' but to her astonishment, Andrew ignored his son's outburst. He merely said, calmly, 'No lie, Ninian. Why don't you settle down and just enjoy some Singapore noodles and king prawns?'

But Ninian, who adored Chinese food, stood up and walked out.

Kate fell in love with Andrew one rainy afternoon sixteen years ago. They'd met in a cinema café, forced to share a table by a swift, torrential shower that drove people indoors. The attraction had been instant. Coffee turned into a drink, a drink turned into dinner, dinner somehow led to Kate's flat and, with her boyfriend away, to bed.

It wasn't behaviour she condoned, she was fiercely loyal and by principle monogamous, but never in her lifetime had Kate experienced such monumental, uncontrollable lust. Had they slept that night? Perhaps dozed, briefly, entwined round each other like columbine, arms and legs turned into tendrils. Between dozing, they explored each other's bodies in childlike delight before, inevitably, joining once more in a sweet union that led to utter ecstasy.

As light dawned, Kate confessed, 'I have a boyfriend.'

Andrew, gazing at her with the lazy, sleepy eyes that had captivated her from that first encounter, said, 'And I'm married.'

'What?' She sat up abruptly.

He pulled her back down and rolled half over her, pinning her to the sheet with gentle force. 'It's not working. It hasn't been working for a long time. But it took me till tonight to understand that it's over.'

It was a great line, and she fell for it. Who wouldn't? How silly of her, though, not to have considered that he might be married. She'd only ever dated schoolboys and students, she had no experience at all of older men.

It was the first hiccup. The path of true love, Kate discovered by way of another cliché, never did run

34

smooth. Andrew was not only older than she was, she discovered that he was *nineteen years* older, a gap that required a series of adaptations and compromises that weren't entirely easy. Soon she discovered that he not only had a wife, he also had a son – and that brought a further shock. Andrew had married Val when he was only nineteen and Harry had arrived soon afterwards. Kate did quick sums in her head and was horrified.

'That makes him older than me!'

'You'll love him,' Andrew assured her.

Kate had a feeling it might not be quite straightforward, but she was an engineer. She liked order and structure. If a job had to be done, she first planned the process required for efficient results. She started to pave the way for Harry liking her, but soon discovered that people don't obey flow charts and systems quite so neatly as building bridges or wind turbines.

She thought about that a lot in the early days. 'How,' she demanded of Charlotte one morning some months later, when she was desperately trying to calm a howling baby Ninian and feeling horribly out of control, 'did this happen? How am I here? Tell me.'

'Lust,' Charlotte answered honestly and they both burst out laughing. Charlotte's hair had still been naturally golden then, her face smooth and fresh, while all Kate was conscious of in those days was the dark rings under her own eyes from lack of sleep.

Now Andrew was so much a part of her life that a new order had been constructed that no longer felt odd, or difficult, or anything other than completely natural. Kate had never dissected her marriage, never taken it apart and examined the bones of it, nor felt the need to. Yet for some reason she could feel the sands shifting under her, the infinitesimal rearranging of a million grains as the sea drains back. Ninian's comment rattled round her head. *You could tell fucking lies to the Pope and get him to believe*

35

you. Why hadn't Andrew reprimanded him? And what the hell had he been talking about? The muttered conversation between Ninian and Harry at the party played again in her mind. *'Don't you dare tell Kate,'* Harry had said, and Ninian had answered, *'But I saw them, I tell you!'*

Tell her what? Saw who? Small doubts, but they wormed their way into Kate's brain and she couldn't stop thinking about them.

Chapter Five

Forgie village hall was a stone-built Victorian building, functional but shabby. The whole place begged for redecoration. There was a corner where the roof leaked and damp had leached in. It needed to be sorted but money, as ever, was the issue. The main hall was big enough for a badminton court and there was a small stage at one end. Tonight it was the venue for the launch of *Martyne Noreis and the Body in the Belfry* – despite the fact that Andrew had become something of a celebrity, he still unveiled each novel locally. Rows of chairs were set out facing the stage, where Andrew and an interviewer would sit. Kate, who hated being late for anything, had made a particular effort to be here in good time because she hadn't yet broken the news to Andrew that she couldn't stay on afterwards. Instead, she had to make an after-dinner speech at a conference for renewables engineers – in fact, she should be there now.

The room was already busy. Kate, feeling self-conscious in her little black dress and Chan Luu slate-to-white ombré scarf, spied Ninian waving at her and made her way down to the front.

'Saved you a seat.'

'Thanks, darling.' She gave him a hug although she was never quite sure these days how he would respond to that.

Tonight he hugged her back. 'You look neat.'

'Afraid I've got to rush off right after. I'm giving a speech at a dinner.' Ninian's face fell. 'I know, I am sorry, love. I should be there now.'

He was clearly upset. He shoved his hand abruptly through his thick hair so that it stood on end and his eyebrows drew together alarmingly. 'Mum, for fuck's sake—'

'What? Don't swear.'

'It's Dad's *launch*. If you're not there for him he's going to—.'

'Going to do what?' Why was he looking so dismayed? 'Anyway, I am here now, aren't I? Where *is* Dad?' She glanced at her watch, itching for the reading to start so that it finished on time, because otherwise she'd need to slip out while it was still taking place and that would be embarrassing.

'Round the back somewhere.' He kicked at the leg of the chair in front of him, scowling. 'The Maneater's come.'

'What are you talking about?'

He nudged her and she looked along the row. Harry and Jane were on Ninian's left and on the far side of them was Jane's cousin, Sophie MacAteer, wearing what seemed to be a vintage dress and Fifties-style hat. She was perched on the edge of her chair in a pose of eager anticipation. Ninian's scowl deepened into a glare.

'Sophie bleep MacAteer,' he muttered, 'alias the Maneater.'

'Why do you say that?' Ninian's dislike was clear – but what could have sparked such strong antipathy? He could only have met her once, surely?

There was no time for explanations because Andrew and the interviewer, a local journalist, arrived on stage. The audience settled, eagerly.

'So, Andrew, tell us about Martyne Noreis.'

Kate had seen Andrew do this dozens of times and she had a speech to prepare. She fumbled in her bag for her notebook. She felt Harry glaring at her, but her fingers sensed the sharp edges of the book, so she slipped it out.

38

Myth and reality, she scribbled. *Why renewable energy is important. NB Joke here.*

Andrew was filling in the background to his medieval detective. 'Martyne Noreis started life as a ploughboy in Athelstaneford, in East Lothian. It's AD735.'

He was a natural-born storyteller and his audience was rapt. Distracted, Kate's pen hovered. Andrew could be magnetic and tonight he was really on form.

'I've always thought there was something magical about Athelstaneford. I dreamed about a ploughboy there who had special skills. Some locals thought he belonged to the occult, but although Martyne runs up against people who want to burn him as a warlock, he always manages to escape.'

'Luckily for us readers,' the journalist said. 'So, Andrew, are his skills supernatural?'

'Not at all. He's very human, with many human frailties. Martyne is just very observant. He's an eighth-century Sherlock Holmes or Hercule Poirot.'

'There seems to be a lot of murder in Athelstaneford.'

'Fraid so. Fortunately, Martyne always manages to solve it. He looks at little signs, tracks or beaten down grass, or some hair caught in a wooden fence post, puts the clues together and finds the culprit.'

The journalist cleared her throat and moved things along. 'Thank you, Andrew, for explaining that. Now, the moment everyone's been waiting for – a reading from your new novel.'

There was a ripple of applause and Andrew stood up and moved across to where a lectern had been set up with a microphone. He found a marker in the book and opened it at the page.

'*He caught a faint muffled sound of horses hooves in the distance. Martyne lifted his head to listen. He was no longer a ploughboy. He was married to Ellyn, the chieftain's daughter, and was a farmer with land of his own. Aye, there it was, three fields away, heading along the track to the kirkyard. He could spy it through the early morning mist, where the pale, low sun loomed through the haze like a forgotten night lantern in the grey sky. The rumble of the cart over the stones reached him now as well. The cart bearing Alys Rolland's body. There was a mystery there. He could smell it.'*

There was collective intake of breath and a ripple of applause. Kate glanced surreptitiously at her watch. To her left, Sophie MacAteer was wide-eyed and excited. Her face was shining, the pale skin like some deep-sea creature's, almost translucent.

Andrew said, 'Martyne has been talking to some of the villagers about how Alys came to die. The fact that she was in the belfry of the church has put him off the scent, but a discovery when he's out walking one day gives him his first real clue.

'The path through the woods was dank. Syme, his dog, felt the glumness of the place and trotted dolefully by his side, tail down, head drooping. The sheep he was searching for must have come this way, Martyne thought, spying a wisp of wool snagged on a low clump of bog myrtle. He stopped. Bog myrtle? Here? He'd never seen it growing deep in the woods. Surely the soil was all wrong. Syme sniffed at the plant with interest as Martyne squatted down to examine it. As he thought. It was not bog myrtle at all, it was dwale. And there were signs that someone had been disturbing the soil around the base of the plant in recent months. It was possible – nay, likely – that someone had even set the shrub to grow here, in this secret place, to avoid its detection.'

Someone behind Kate called, 'Dwale? Is that a made up name?'

The voice sounded familiar. She peered over her shoulder. It was Ibsen Brown, her acquaintance from the top of Summerfield Law, his blue eyes brilliant under the artificial light, his long hair again pulled tightly back from his face.

'No. It's the Anglo Saxon word for something we know by a completely different name, deadly nightshade, or belladonna. There is quite an Anglo Saxon influence in southern parts of Scotland, so it's not unlikely that Martyne would have known it by this common name.'

'And calling it dwale keeps the secret from the reader just a little longer,' Ibsen grinned.

Kate turned back to the stage, smiling. He'd put his finger on Andrew's technique precisely.

'Exactly. And now I've let the cat out of the bag. But,' he snapped the book shut and held it up, cover side to the audience, 'there are plenty more cats in here, and a few bags too, and if you want to know any more, can I suggest you buy the book?'

As the applause started, Kate tossed her notebook into her handbag and stood up. 'I've got to go. Sorry.'

Harry said, 'Not going for dinner?'

'I'm sorry, but it's impossible tonight. I've a really unfortunate diary clash. I'm giving a speech—'

She had to go but with her stepson's gaze on her she put the moment off.

Andrew appeared by her side, looking pleased with himself. 'Well? What did you think? That go well?'

'Brilliant, Dad.'

'Loved it. Another triumph.'

'Are we all set for dinner?'

'Kate's got to rush off,' Harry said.

She looked apologetically at Andrew. 'Sorry, love. I forgot to tell you.' Guilt pressed down on her but she pushed back at it by remembering how she'd rushed home early to change so that she could be here at all, and that she hadn't eaten and would miss dinner at both functions. She was about to point this out to him so that he could appreciate the lengths she'd gone to but she knew that was just defensiveness. If necessary she could explain later.

Harry said, 'Actually, we won't be able to make it this time ourselves. Jane's flying down to London in the morning and she's got to get up at four. In fact, we'd better head off soon too.'

So Harry couldn't go either! Kate pursed her lips in annoyance. How dare he be so critical of her when he was ducking out himself?

Andrew's face grew longer. A family dinner after the local launch was all part of the ritual. He turned to Ninian. 'Looks like it'll be you and me then, Ninian.'

'Fine.'

'I can come.' Sophie MacAteer had been standing on the fringes of the family group, Kate realised, hanging on like a limpet. 'I'm not in a hurry to go anywhere tonight.'

'Just the three of us then.'

Ninian scowled. He scuffed one toe against the floor, kicking at some imaginary spot. 'Actually, I've just remembered, I told Cuzzer we could finish the game we're playing on the X Box.'

It didn't seem like an ideal solution, but Kate really had to go. She kissed Andrew briefly. 'Right then. Sorry love. Must dash.'

She hurried towards the door, but was caught by Frank Griffiths.

'About Summerfield,' he growled, blocking her path, 'you do realise, don't you, how disastrous the project will be for us all?'

She was late. She was put out by Harry's hypocrisy. Under these pressures, diplomacy deserted her. 'I'm sorry, Frank,' she said, her voice crisp, 'I don't have time to discuss this right now, but you're absolutely wrong.'

'AeGen absolutely cannot be allowed to go forward with this plan.'

'We're just putting a mast in, that's all.'

'We'll be opposing it.' He leaned forward, his face so

42

close to hers for a moment that their noses almost touched. His face was ruddy with pent-up anger but she didn't retreat by an inch and it was Frank who gave ground first. He gained control of himself, swivelled on his heel, and marched off. Kate drew a breath and felt her body soften, as if a moment of danger had passed. She turned to the door for the second time, but just as she did so, someone stepped in front of her. It was Ibsen Brown. 'The Germinator'.

He grinned. 'Oops.'

She stepped the other way. So did he. She frowned in exasperation and his grin widened.

'Sorry.' She moved again. He mirrored her move.

'Dear me,' he said with a smile that split his face. Despite her irritation, she couldn't help liking the effect. 'We'll have to sort this out, won't we?' He took her firmly by the elbows and her arms tensed like springs at his touch. He moved her to one side. 'There. I wait, you move. Right?'

'Thank you.' She said it coolly, though she was finding the intense blue of his eyes extremely disconcerting.

'What did you say your name was?'

Had he really forgotten? Her ego punctured, she said, 'Kate. Kate Courtenay.'

'Suits you. Short and spiky.'

She was taken aback at the judgement and couldn't help showing it.

'No offence meant. Sorry to get in your way.' Again, the grin flashed. Each line in his face, she suspected, told a story. Not one of his features was quite even, but there was something about its liveliness that was definitely interesting.

'No problem.' She swung away. Now she really was short of time.

'Kate,' he said.

She turned, puzzled. 'Yes?'

'Nothing.' There was a gleam in his eyes. 'Nice to meet you again, Kate.'

Kate and Andrew's bedroom had the elegant proportions typical of early Georgian architecture. It was roughly square, which she liked, but its best feature was the floor-to-ceiling windows overlooking the garden. There was one on either side of Kate's dressing table, where she kept the miniature gargoyle Andrew had brought her from Melrose Abbey (his first gift), her grandmother's scent bottle – a treasured relic of her childhood – and the small box with Ninian's first baby tooth. The room was perhaps looking a little shabby now because it hadn't been redecorated for years, not since she'd blitzed the place with the enthusiasm of a new owner, but the deep pile cream carpet and pale blue silk curtains still pleased her. It was a calming room – and calm was what she needed by the time her long days drew to a close.

When she got back from the dinner, Andrew was already in bed, reading. He was wearing a black tee shirt. For his age, he was still enormously attractive.

'Interesting book?'

He angled it towards himself and showed her the cover. It was a history tome. Nothing new there. 'You look tired.'

'Mm. But I must read these papers.' She held up her briefcase. 'I've got a meeting first thing and what with your book launch and that damned dinner—'

'Oh, right,' he mumbled, immersing himself once more in his book.

Kate blinked. Things had changed and she hadn't noticed. Once she would have thought it impossible to get into a bed with Andrew Courtenay to *read.* Once he would have considered bringing a book into bed insulting. Ninian's cryptic comments swirled back into her head. *Sophie Maneater. If you're not there for him he's going to—*

She dropped the briefcase. Andrew didn't even look up at the thud, just tutted at some small irritation in the text and turned a page. Kate peeled her clothes off. Andrew turned another page. Kate glanced down at her naked body, realising that she had never examined it critically. So long as it functioned well, she was comfortable with it. Now she squinted down at it objectively. She was slim and fit, her skin was still taut, there were no unsightly love handles – but Andrew was still reading. Had she stopped being desirable? The duvet cover was cream with a blue fleur-de-lys pattern. Like the decor, it had aged. It was functional, but hardly sexy. Perhaps she should buy some new bed linen, and maybe some silk lingerie? She slipped into bed and gently removed the book from his hands.

'What—?'

'Cuddle?'

'I thought you were going to read.'

'I am. I will. But not till you've given me some attention.'

He took his glasses off and rolled towards her. His hand started to stroke her breast obediently and she felt desire quicken. It was ... comfortable. Nice. She was annoyed at this because she wanted fireworks.

'You're beautiful,' he whispered afterwards, as he always did.

Habit can be reassuring, but it can also be worrying. Andrew's breathing deepened and he started to snore gently. *Sophie Maneater.* The tiny question mark Ninian had planted inside Kate glowed briefly, then curled in on itself and went to sleep.

She extracted her briefing papers from her bag and started to read. Soon she was absorbed in a report on new developments in nacelle construction.

Chapter Six

When Ibsen and Lynn were married they lived in a small new-build in Summerfield, close to the primary school, where she was a teacher. Lynn kept it pin neat yet homely – his ex wife had a knack for homemaking.

They'd still be together if Violet hadn't died.

Ibsen lay with his arm round Melanie McGillivray's slumbering form and despite its seductive softness was filled only with sadness at the memory of what had happened.

Would he never get over it? Waking that morning, going into Violet's little room, ready to pick her up, finding her—

Bugger it!

He blinked as his eyes welled up. It had been five years now. In those terrible hours and days after their baby died in her cot, he and Lynn had pulled together as a team, but over time grief had taken them down different routes and being together only reminded them all the more of what they had made, and lost.

Melanie stirred and Ibsen extricated his arm and slid out of bed. He had maybe another half hour before she'd wake and the day would start. He padded noiselessly across to the window of the small cottage where he now lived – alone, except for Wellington and the occasional company of whoever he happened to be dating – and glanced out of the window, set deep in the thick stone wall. From here he could just see Forgie House, the modest mansion that had been built by some minor member of the Scottish royal family in the seventeenth-century. The house was simple and absolutely symmetrical, almost like a child's drawing. Its main door was set on the first floor and was accessed by a curved staircase leading up to it on either side, which added a touch of elegance. As he watched, the sun rose above the nearby trees and splashed onto the walls. Ibsen smiled. The building was harled – faced with small pebbles mixed with lime – and painted ochre, so that in the sun it looked like a fat satsuma sitting in the verdant green of the lawns.

He pulled on his jeans and a tee shirt and went through to the kitchen. Wellington leapt to his feet, tail flapping, and looked up at him with round brown eyes.

'Morning old thing. Yes, yes, it'll be breakfast time shortly. Off you go now, do your business.'

He opened the door to the garden and the dog trotted out obediently. Ibsen filled the kettle.

After he and Lynn had finally acknowledged they could no longer hold their marriage together, he'd given up on draughtsmanship and embarked on a diploma in horticulture. Tam, his father, was head gardener on the Forgie House estate and when Ibsen qualified he was lucky enough to land a job as his seasonal assistant. The post came, miraculously, with the tenancy of the cottage next door to his parents and here, in the perfect tranquillity of the estate, he at last began to find his own peace.

With tea in his hand, Ibsen walked out into the small garden where he cultivated the dahlias that were his pride and joy. The early morning sun had just reached this small patch and he tilted his face towards it. There was real warmth there already. Good. As he thought, the snow had been a freak blip. All his instincts told him that in another week or so he'd be able to pinch out the tubers and plant them. He had twelve different varieties this year and he was eager to see which did best.

'Morning, Ibs.'

Melanie emerged from the kitchen door, her endless

legs disappearing finally under one of his old checked shirts, her strawberry-blonde mane tumbling messily down her back, both attributes reminding Ibsen just why he'd been so attracted to her in the first place.

'Hi. You okay?'

'Mmm.' She yawned luxuriously and slid an arm round his neck. 'I'd be better if you came back to bed for a bit.'

'Tempting.' He buried his face in her hair, which smelled vaguely of wood smoke. They'd lit a fire in the living room last night to ward off the last of the chill from the snow.

He felt the vibration of the phone in his pocket a couple of seconds before it rang.

Melanie pulled away, pouting.

He didn't recognise the number and was tempted to ignore it. 'Hello?' he said reluctantly.

'Mr Brown? This is the Edinburgh Royal Infirmary. Your sister has asked us to call you—'

Ibsen's heart jump-started in alarm. 'Cassie? Is she all right? Her baby's not due for another month.'

'There've been a few problems—'

'I'm on my way.' He shoved the phone back in his pocket. 'I'll have to run. It's Cassie.'

Melanie's mouth was still puckered in a sulk, but she recovered herself quickly. 'Can you wait five minutes,' she pleaded, 'and drop me in Hailesbank?'

Every instinct urged Ibsen to head off now, this very second, but he could hardly abandon Melanie here with no transport. 'Hurry, then, love. I've really got to go.'

He whistled for Wellington and saw him racing across the huge expanse of grass, ears back, tail streaming. 'Good boy, we'd better get you fed quickly.'

Cassie and Ian had been trying for years to start a family. Twice his sister had miscarried, a third time she'd gone to term, but the baby was stillborn. Watching her mourn each tiny passing of life had torn him apart though it wasn't till Violet died that he fully understood what she'd gone through. She was nearly forty now and this baby might be Cassie's last chance. Ian was working offshore and his parents had gone off for a week in the sun planning to be back in plenty of time to support her. If something had gone wrong—

He raced to the van and turned the engine over. Thank goodness it started this morning, sometimes it could be contrary.

'Here, boy, up you go.' He opened the back doors for Wellington.

Why hadn't they called him earlier? Who'd taken Cassie in? It was too early, by a long way. Surely that was bad news?

Melanie jumped in beside him.

'That was quick. Thanks, love.'

'No bother. I know how much it means to you. Just drop me off at the end of the High Street, okay?'

Ibsen swung the van out of the estate gates and down towards Hailesbank. 'You'll be hellish early.' Melanie worked as a hairdresser in the town. It was barely seven thirty and she wasn't due at work till nine. 'Sorry.'

'I'll survive. I'll go get a bacon buttie.'

'I'll make it up to you, honest.'

In Hailesbank, Melanie turned her face to his for a kiss. 'Hope everything's okay. Call me later?'

Ibsen cursed as the van hiccupped away. Time he looked for a new one. *Don't let me down now*. At least it was still early. He'd miss the worst of the rush hour traffic.

Later, he called Melanie.

'Is she all right?'

Ibsen, still lightheaded with relief, said, 'She's had the baby. A girl. She has eclampsia.'

'That's dangerous, isn't it?'

'Very. But she's okay.'

'Great.' There was a pause. 'Can I see you tonight? Take up where we left off?'

It had taken Ibsen five years to get through the grief, then the divorce. When the decree nisi finally came though, he'd taken a vow never to get serious again.

'I don't do commitment,' he now told each new girlfriend, maybe not on the first date, but on the second, because a second date was, in its own way, a kind of commitment.

'Great, I like it that way myself,' they'd say, or, 'Suits me.' But in his experience that attitude quickly changed. After a few dates they'd be on the phone, texting to ask where he was or why he hadn't called, or when they'd see him next.

Melanie McGillivray was perilously close to becoming possessive and with every emotion stretched tight and quivering from the dramatic birth of his niece and Cassie's brush with death, he had no room to spare for her demands right now.

'Sorry, love, I can't. I've got to get back here to see Cass, there's a hundred people to call and anyway, I'm picking the parents up from the airport at midnight. Do you mind?'

'Oh. Okay. When, then?'

'I'll call you.'

On any other day Ibsen might have been tempted to linger around the hospital and pop in to see Cassie again in the afternoon, but this morning he had his first appointment with a new client. Frank Griffiths lived in one of the houses on the main street in Forgie, one of the pretty, painted cottages near the old corner shop. He remembered going in there as a boy, cycling down from Summerfield and spending his pocket money on sweets and pop. There was no shop there nowadays, though, it had closed years ago – no need for a corner shop in a village where everyone has posh cars and likes to buy

51

uniformly shaped courgettes and tomatoes that have no taste. Ibsen hated shopping, disliked supermarkets and was, in any case, spoiled by having garden-fresh vegetables on hand and on demand.

He found a bell hidden under a climbing rose and pushed it, while Wellington sniffed around the roots and relieved himself to establish his presence.

No-one answered.

He was just about to push it again when a lean figure in blood-red corduroys and a richly patterned sweater strolled out from an arched gateway beside the cottage.

'Morning Ibsen, good to see you. No-one ever uses the front door.'

'Morning Mr Griffiths.' Ibsen took the outstretched hand and shook it.

'Call me Frank. Hello boy, what's your name?' He bent and patted Wellington's head. 'Lovely coat, you keep him in good condition.'

'That's Wellington.'

Frank laughed. 'Don't you need two of them, then? Come on in, we'll go round this way.' He turned back the way he'd come, under the arch. It was the first view Ibsen had had of it and he stopped, astonished.

'Like it?' Frank Griffiths looked at him, obviously pleased by his reaction.

'It looks amazing. Not what I expected at all.'

Amusement was evident on the elderly man's face. 'What did you expect?'

'Something much smaller, for a start. I didn't realise these old cottages had such big gardens.'

'Put you off?'

'Not at all.'

'I've done it myself for years, but I'm getting older. Myra – my wife – tells me it's time to get help, and there's only so long you can put up a fight against the wife, isn't that right?'

'I wouldn't know, sir, I'm not married,' Ibsen admitted.

Frank laughed. 'Don't know how lucky you are. Want a tour?'

All Ibsen's work was by word-of-mouth recommendation. He'd met Frank Griffiths at another client's house one day and although fitting in an extra four hours a week was going to stretch him, he'd taken to the man. The garden was semi formal, with well-trimmed low box hedges arranged geometrically to make an abstract pattern in the shape of a rose. At the centre was a large stone planter. Soon, he could see, it would be brimming over with trailing lobelia – white, he suspected, maybe the dark purple variety as well, because that was clearly the theme of this garden. Filling one box-hedged 'petal' he could see glorious white peonies, their heads bowed under the weight of their own abundance. Another was a blaze of purple and lavender and white tulips. A third contained heavy-headed hellebores and early-flowering white roses.

Ibsen let out a low whistle. 'This has taken some work – and a great deal of planning.'

'Years. I get a bit obsessive about it, I do admit.'

Round the outside of the garden, formality gave way to a more relaxed style. Magnolia candles dripped their wax to set a riot of azaleas ablaze. The bleeding blooms on a large flowering currant contrasted with the green and red flames of a pieris. Ibsen was in heaven. Wellington, sniffing his way along the bottom of the high wall, was in heaven too.

Frank said, 'I hate to admit it, but the work's getting a bit too much for me.'

'Happy to help. Where do you want me to start?'

'This rose.' Frank stopped by a large bush that had grown woody. 'It needs to be rooted out. Think you can manage it?'

'No problem. I'll get started right away.'

Ibsen never minded heavy work. Heavy work cleared

his mind and flattened out the lumps and bumps in whatever emotional path he was on at the time – and today the bumps felt more like mountains.

Two hours later, though, he was thankful when Frank offered him tea.

'Take a break, Ibsen. Myra's made a cuppa, come and sit in the conservatory and we'll talk grafting and pruning.'

Ibsen's clients were usually out at work and most of the time he drank tea from his flask or just gulped water. Frank Griffiths was clearly going to be a client of a different sort – he was zealous about his garden and wanted to share his passion. Ibsen didn't get many chances to share his love of plants with someone knowledgeable and he followed Frank eagerly.

The conservatory faced the garden and was essentially a glassed-in courtyard between the oldest part of the cottage and a later extension. Ibsen sank onto a wooden bench, grateful for a break. Wellington, exhausted by his own busy explorations, sank at his feet, yawned, stretched and fell asleep.

'How are you getting on?'

'I've managed to hack the rose bush back, but getting the roots out is a bit of a challenge.'

'It's an old bush. Well rooted.'

'So I've discovered.' Ibsen ran his fingers across the palm of his hand. Used as he was to hard work, he was going to have a new blister.

'You've heard about this damned wind farm, I take it?' Frank handed him a mug of tea and held out a plate of shortbread.

'On Summerfield Law?' Ibsen bit into the shortbread. Very good and obviously homemade. 'I've heard about it.'

'What do you think?'

Ibsen hesitated, unsure about what Frank wanted him to say and unwilling to alienate a new client. He said cautiously, 'I'd like to know a bit more about it.'

54

'Ghastly things. Blight on our landscape. You're going to be staring at it, aren't you? From that cottage of yours in the Forgie House grounds? Shouldn't have thought you'd be keen. They're useless things anyway, they don't even work half the time.'

'I've never been able to understand – if they don't work, why build them?'

'Subsidies,' Frank growled. 'Bloody Labour government thought it was a good idea, people jumped on the bandwagon to make a killing, and the damn things have sprouted up everywhere. Well, not in my neighbourhood, not if I can help it. Someone has to take a stand.'

'Oh, I absolutely agree.' Ibsen had his own reasons for not wanting a wind farm on Summerfield Law, but it was one only his family would understand, and Lynn. 'But—' he tried to be fair, '—we need energy, I guess, and no-one wants a new nuclear plant on their doorstep, they're so dangerous.'

'Nuclear's not dangerous! Not in the civilised world. We know how to handle our nuclear reactors, not like the bloody stupid Russians. There'll be no Chernobyl in Europe. No, no, lad, nuclear is clean technology. Electricity without pollution, and that's what we need.'

Although his gut reaction was to resist the Summerfield wind farm, Ibsen still wanted to understand the arguments against it. 'You said wind farms don't work—'

'Stands to reason. Think about it. If the wind isn't blowing, the turbine can't produce electricity. And on top of that,' he leaned forwards as if about to share some important secret, 'they have to switch them off when the wind's too strong as well. *And*—' he leaned so far forward that Ibsen thought he was going to topple over completely, '—there's no way of storing the electricity they make.' He leant back finally, slumping into his chair as though his passion had exhausted him.

'That does sound ridiculous.'

'Do you like birds? You must see a lot from your place. What do you get there, hey? Woodpeckers? Waxwings? Redstarts? Birds of prey?'

Ibsen finished his tea and set his mug down. 'Aye. All of those from time to time. The trees round the cottage are hopping with birds.'

'These turbines kill them, you know.'

'Really?'

'Stone dead. They can't see the blades when they're turning. They're a damned nuisance, however you look at them.'

It was a strong argument. Ibsen loved to watch birds. As a boy, he'd spent many a happy day with Tam, binoculars round his neck, watching the ducks on the loch up the hill, or the sea birds along the coast. 'Well,' he said, storing the argument away, 'humans have no right to kill birds just because we want electricity – or a quick profit.'

Frank smiled. 'Knew you were a sympathiser. Bloody project's got to be stopped. There's a meeting in a couple of days in the village hall. Fancy coming?'

'What time?'

'Half past seven. Come along. Chance to question the blighters.'

'I'll do what I can.' Ibsen glanced at his watch. 'Better get back to work now though. I must get those roots out before I go.'

Chapter Seven

'It's started already,' said Kate, absorbed in today's edition of *Scotland Daily* on her iPad.

'What's that?'

Crossly, she read out the headline. ' "SUMMERFIELD WIND FARM WILL BE AN EYESORE, CLAIM LOCALS". I've never understood why people seem to dislike turbines so much, Andrew, have you? To me they're like beautiful swans, with long necks and graceful wings.'

Andrew, who was reading *The Times* – paper version – looked at her over his reading glasses and poured himself a second coffee. 'Some people find them threatening.'

'Threatening? For heaven's sake, why?'

'They're very big. They loom up at you out of the mist like the dementors in Harry Potter, sucking out your life blood.'

'What nonsense.'

'You asked.'

'Why are you looking so smart, by the way?' Andrew was not a morning person. He usually wore an open-necked shirt, with a sweater when it was cold, but today he had donned a jacket and tie. She caught a whiff of aftershave. He'd shaved already too. 'And why are you up at this time, anyway?'

'I'm going into Edinburgh.'

'Oh. I'm working at home and it's such a lovely day, I thought we might manage a salad on the patio at lunchtime.'

'Sorry. I'm meeting the Bishop.'

'The Bishop? For heaven's sake, why?'

'He's a keen medievalist. I've discovered that he knows a great deal about church history of the period and there's a few plot points I'd like to discuss with him for *Martyne Noreis and the Witch of Lothian.*' Although his last novel had just been published, Andrew was already far into writing the next in the series. 'Kate—'

'Mmm?' Kate was getting cross about the myriad inaccuracies peddled in the *Scotland Daily* article.

'You're going to have to tread carefully with this Summerfield thing. There's a lot of bad feeling around already.'

'Do you think I don't know that? AeGen have put me in charge because they believe I have a bank of goodwill locally. They obviously think it will help.'

When Andrew said nothing she prompted him. 'Andrew? Make sense?'

He stood up. 'Maybe. If you do have a bank of goodwill.'

She frowned. 'What are you saying?'

He laid his plate and cup by the sink. 'Well, you must admit, you're hardly the life and soul of the village.'

'What the hell do you mean by that?'

'You're away so much. Off on business trips, away at conferences, out early in the morning, back late at night, too tired to do anything half the time other than plough through papers for the next morning's meeting and shuffle off to bed.'

'Is it that bad?' she tried to laugh, but hurt overtook her. 'You're away a fair bit yourself, on talks and tours.'

'I was the one who did all the school runs, remember. I'm the one who goes to parent evenings and fund raisers.'

Kate's astonishment grew. It felt as if they were having an argument, yet all she'd done this morning was comment on a headline in the newspaper. But in fairness to Andrew, why had she never wondered if he resented her long hours?

'Talking of being here,' he shrugged on a jacket, 'I've invited Andreas Bertolini and his wife for dinner.'

'The film director? Heavens. Why?'

'He's optioned *Circle of Fire*.'

'Optioned it?'

'With a view to making a movie.'

'Oh, Andrew.' Their tiff forgotten, she jumped up impulsively and hugged him.

She had her ambitions, this was Andrew's. He didn't just want to write yet another novel, he also wanted to see his work on the big screen. They'd talked about it, from time to time, as some distant fantasy. Who will play Martyne? Who Ellyn? He saw James McAvoy and Anne Hathaway, she pictured Euan McGregor and Rachel Weisz.

'It's just an option.' He smiled, the old alluring slow curl of the lips.

'But he'll do it? He'll make a film?'

'Maybe. Maybe not. But he's going to be in Scotland and I'd like to entertain him here. He's keen to see where I work – and to meet you. You will make yourself free, won't you?'

Kate hurried to reassure him. 'Of course! When is it?'

'Not for a couple of months. I'm giving you plenty of notice.'

She reached for her mobile and entered the date in her diary. 'There. Done.'

'Thanks. Will you be late tonight?'

Kate grimaced. 'It's the first meeting with Forgie and Summerfield Community Council this evening.'

He spread his hands as if to say 'See?' and the corners of his mouth tightened. Vexed by the coincidence she opened her mouth to justify herself, but he turned and strode out.

Kate heard the front door close, the car door open, the engine turn over. She thumped her fist down on the

59

worktop. 'Damn, damn, damn!'

It was an odd moment of role reversal. Andrew had gone out, jacket and tie on and briefcase in hand while she was here, in jeans and a tee shirt, amid the debris of the breakfast table.

No point in brooding, she had to work. Their housekeeper, Mrs Gillies, was due shortly. Kate and Andrew had always split the domestic chores – Andrew was childcare and cooking, Kate was supermarket supplies and accounts – but once Andrew's novels began to take off, they'd hired a housekeeper as well. Mrs Gillies had for years run the house with a proprietary command that would probably worry her, except that she was so seldom around to witness it. *You forgot to water the geraniums*, Mrs G would write, the note on the kitchen table tangible reproof of omission. Or, *We are clean out of bleach, I asked last week.* Andrew and Kate sometimes laughed at her tone – after all, whose house was this? – and Kate was sure that Andrew saved the notes for inspiration. No character, for him, was ever wasted.

Kate looked around at the mess in the kitchen with a vague feeling that she should tidy it. Her mouth curled into a small smile – tidy up for the cleaner? What was the point of that? She looked around for her briefcase before recalling that she'd taken it upstairs last night to do some work. On the landing, a notice on Ninian's door caught her eye. 'KEEP OUT ON PAIN OF DEATH!' A few weeks ago, she'd have found it funny, but Ninian had grown short-tempered and increasingly reclusive since Harry's party and she was beginning to worry that these traits were growing extreme.

Eight o'clock. She rapped sharply on the door and opened it. The room was in complete darkness and she could only just make out his hunched shape under the covers. 'Ninian? Shouldn't you be up?'

An irritated groan split the darkness. 'Mu-um! Bloody

60

hell! Don't you *know*? I don't go in till eleven on Wednesdays!' He pulled a pillow over his head and she heard another roar of anger, this time muffled.

She pulled the door closed, realising that actually no, she did not know he didn't go in until eleven on Wednesdays, that in fact she didn't know much about his timetable at all.

An unmistakeable whiff of cigarette smoke followed Mrs Gillies into the kitchen on the dot of nine. She must have stubbed her cigarette out on the doorstep. Well, that was something. Kate knew she often lit up in the house, in defiance of orders, she could still smell the nicotine smoke hours later when she got home from work.

'Morning Mrs Gillies.'

'Oh! You're there, are you Kate?'

Jean Gillies had a knack of making Kate feel like an intruder in her own home. She bit back a smart retort. Sarcasm would be lost on Mrs G and besides, she didn't usually have to put up with this, she was out at work. The housekeeper, she reminded herself, was an essential element in the smooth running of Willow Corner – she could allow her the odd irritable habit.

'I'm working at home this morning.'

'I see.' On went the kettle. 'Cup of tea?'

'No, I'm fine thanks. Mrs Gillies, Ninian's still in bed and Andrew's gone to a meeting.' Kate itched to ask her about Ninian but it seemed odd to have to ask the cleaner about her own son's habits.

Mrs G rinsed a cloth under the tap and wrung it out. An impressive array of gold and jewelled rings sparkled and flashed, one on her pinkie, three on her wedding finger, two on her middle finger. They'd come down, she'd explained to Kate once, from grandmother and mother and auntie, like a dowry. The skin on her hands was aged and work-worn, but the rings were clearly some kind of badge

61

of status and she was not to be parted from them.

'Mind if I—?' She gestured at the table, where Kate had started to lay out her papers.

Working in the kitchen was going to be impossible. Kate gathered them up. 'Ninian muttered something about a lie-in—' she made a joke of her ignorance and laughed, 'but I want to make sure he's not having me on.'

'Oh Wednesdays he's got a free period first thing. I'll make sure he's up in half an hour and gets some breakfast in his tum. He's a growing lad.'

That, at least, she did know about. 'And eats like one,' she smiled. Yet the disquiet of earlier turned around like a cat in her stomach, stretched and settled. 'Listen. I'll take myself off to Andrew's study, give you some room.'

Andrew kept his study immaculately tidy. He worked mostly on his computer. His research notes and history books were stored in box files on the shelf at his right hand, but there was room for her papers on the table where he liked to spread the post-its and wallpaper he used for plotting in the early stages of a new novel. Outside, a light breeze ruffled the climbing roses by the front door and sent dappled shadows across the desk. Her hands, full of papers, hovered for a moment as her mind hopped over stepping stones, making connections: roses – garden – gardener – Ibsen. Why had she thought of him?

The telephone on Andrew's desk rang and she answered it at once. 'Willow Corner, hello?'

Silence.

'Hello? Can you hear me?'

There was still silence, though she thought she could hear breathing.

Life is too short to hold conversations with yourself. She cut the call and dialled 1471. Number withheld. Some aborted sales call probably.

She had a stack of estimates to go through and a financial viability report to compile. It had been done before, of course, but by Jack Bailey. She needed to make sure for herself that everything was up-to-date and in order, which was why she'd opted for the peace of home rather than the hurly burly of the office.

Twenty minutes later, she was deep into a complex calculation when the telephone rang again. She had instructed the office not to call her, and in any case, they would use her mobile for anything urgent. It must be for Andrew. Irritated, she picked it up. 'Hello?'

Silence.

'Hello? This is Kate Courtenay at Willow Corner. Is there anyone there?'

The phone went dead and she went through the 1471 performance again, with the same result.

When it happened for the third time, she didn't bother, she just picked the phone up and marched through to the kitchen with it. 'Mrs Gillies,' she mouthed over the noise of the food grinder in the sink. 'The phone keeps ringing but there's no-one there.'

'What?' The grinding stopped and the loose orangey-brown bun scraped up onto the top of Mrs Gillies's head bobbed with annoyance at the interruption.

'Sorry. The phone keeps ringing but there's no-one there. Does it happen a lot? We're ex-directory so there shouldn't be nuisance calls.'

'No idea, Kate, sorry. Andrew usually answers it.' The deafening grinding resumed. Mrs G had her routines.

Kate dropped the phone onto the kitchen table, where at least it would be out of earshot, and returned to the study, pondering the oddity of why the cleaner should use their first names while they addressed her formally.

Andrew didn't appear for supper. At six thirty Kate changed from her jeans into a dark business suit – neat straight skirt, well-cut waisted jacket – and cream silk blouse. She slipped on a pair of commanding heels. She

63

was happiest out on site in jeans and protective boots, but the illusion of height gave her a greater sense of control, and besides, she liked to confound expectation. People never expected a wind farm project manager to be a woman, and a diminutive one at that. The mood tonight was going to be confrontational so it would be great if she could establish an air of authority. Tonight was not a night to fade into the background. So – which scarf? Red. Red was assertive. She opened her eyes and her hand went straight to her treasured Weston Petrified Wood silk print. Its fabulous bold reds and oranges made her feel invincible.

The Council meeting was due to start at seven thirty and she hadn't eaten yet. She knocked on Ninian's door as she passed. 'You hungry?'

'Yeah.' The response was muffled.

'Dad's not home. What do you want?'

Ninian's dishevelled head appeared. 'Christ, does that mean you're cooking?'

Kate was a terrible cook. Where Andrew could conjure up a gourmet meal out of nothing, she could ruin a fillet steak in an instant. She ignored Ninian's remark. 'Beans on toast or eggs and sausage?'

'Okay to feed Cuzzer and Banksy too?' He opened the door a little wider and across a carpet littered with paper and socks and discarded wrappers, she saw Ninian's two friends lounging on the bed.

'Hi! I didn't realise you were here.'

Cuzzer – Stephen Cousins – was a sharp-featured lad with what she knew to be an equally sharp tongue. Elliott Banks had a mop of dark auburn hair and an open, pleasant face. He rose now. 'You're all right, thanks,' he said, 'I'd best be going.'

'Me too.' Cuzzer unwound his skinny legs and stood up. His head was shaved almost to the bone. 'Get you down the road, Banksy.'

Ninian scowled. 'You don't have to go,' he said, 'she's going out.'

'Nah. Ta.' Cuzz squeezed past her, eyes averted, head down. He looked shifty, but then he always did.

'Mum'll be expecting me,' Banksy said, smiling at Kate as he waited for her to step aside. 'See you tomorrow, Nins.'

'Okay. See you.'

'Bye,' Kate called as the two lads disappeared down the stairs. The front door closed behind them.

'Where's Dad?'

'He had a meeting with the Bishop.' But that had been this morning—

Ninian grunted. 'Seems like he's been having a lot of meetings recently.'

'He's researching his new book.'

Another grunt.

'So what would you like to eat?'

'Everything.'

She managed to produce the meal more or less without mishap – the eggs were hard and the toast slightly burnt, but things could have been much worse. Kate cleared the plates into the dishwasher and tidied her scarf. 'I've got to go, love. I'm sure Dad'll be back soon. You all right?'

'Course.'

She picked up her briefcase and kissed the top of his head. Ninian flicked on the television and grabbed a banana from the fruit bowl. Kate said, 'Bye, then.'

There was no response, not even a grunt.

Chapter Eight

When Kate arrived at the village hall, the table was already set up for the Council meeting. She hadn't expected the additional rows of chairs behind the table, though, at the back of the hall. There were going to be observers and the chairs were already filling up. She spotted a woman from the tennis club and May and Jerry Nesbitt, the current tenants of Forgie House, among other familiar faces.

'What do you think?' she hissed at AeGen's community liaison officer, Gail.

'Shows interest.'

Kate disliked public speaking, even though she had to do it all the time. She looked around for clues about how the evening might go. There were three members of the Community Council already seated at the table. Frank Griffiths (who was chairing), a local farmer, and a lawyer, who she knew was on the board of the Forgie House Trust. As she took her place, two more women appeared.

One of them said, 'Good evening,' and smiled. 'I'm Nicola Arnott. I'm head teacher at Summerfield Primary School.'

It was a warm smile. Kate shook her hand. 'Hi. Nice to meet you.'

'And this is Mary Tolen.' Nicola drew the other woman forward.

'Evenin'.'

Kate understood the importance of these committees. They might have no real decision-making powers, but she'd learned the lesson long ago that all politics is local and that an active Community Council had a strong influence, particularly on planning matters. Would the women be allies or foes? The next hour or so would tell.

'Mrs Courtenay,' Frank started formally when they were seated at the table, 'why don't you take a few minutes to address the Council?'

The manner of address unnerved her, so she sprang to her feet, sending her papers flying across the table. She had to spend an embarrassing minute collecting them again, and started shakily. She fingered her scarf and launched her speech, 'Mr Chairman, members of Council—'

Then she was on home ground, sure of herself and her arguments, and everything began to flow.

'What we are proposing is, of course, just our thoughts at the moment. This is the start of a consultation process in which you will be completely involved and your concerns discussed and, where possible, addressed ...'

Half way through her speech, she became aware of movement at the back of the hall. Distracted, she glanced across to the disturbance. It was Ibsen Brown, of all people, and Wellington, his paws sliding and scraping on the polished wood floor. She bit her lip. There was no hiding now.

'... and where possible addressed,' she continued as the nudging of chairs and the shuffling of feet died down again. 'I'd like to outline our early thoughts for this site, then discuss some of the issues with which you might be concerned.'

She held the floor for ten minutes, then cut the talk dead. Better to allow time for questions and discussion than preach at people.

'This proposal,' Frank said, looking at her with ferocious intensity, 'is an utter outrage. These turbines will be a blight on our landscape, they'll kill our birdlife, ruin our moorland habitat and pollute our communities with the kind of noise you can't turn off and can't hide from. Every time we open our front doors, we'll be staring at the things, and if it happens we can't see them, we'll still be able to hear them.'

'It's really a myth that—'

'Don't try to tell me they're not noisy, because they most certainly are. I've heard of people whose lives have been made an utter misery with their whining and grinding.'

Stay calm and quote the science. She needed to establish her authority. All her training kicked into play.

'It may have been the case,' she said, putting both her hands on the table and leaning forward, 'thirty years ago or so when wind turbines were in their infancy, that some were noisy. That is absolutely not true now. Gear boxes are next to silent—'

'They still do that whoosh, whoosh.'

'There is a small sound from the blades when you are close, if they are turning fast,' Kate admitted, 'but it's generally much less than the noise of the wind itself. In any case, these turbines will be sited too far from any human habitation for the sound to be significant.'

She tried to read their faces. The Tolen woman was nodding. Frank was so flushed she began to worry whether he might have a seizure. Nicola Arnott was smiling slightly. The other faces were unreadable.

The lawyer said, 'I understand these turbines are extremely inefficient.' He glanced down at his notes. Trust a lawyer to have prepared. 'According to my information, they only produce around thirty per cent of the power the manufacturers claim.'

'A turbine labelled as one megawatt describes its optimum capacity – in other words, what it can produce when the wind is blowing strongly and steadily.'

'But half the time they're not turning at all.'

'Sure, that's why people think they're inefficient. But we measure output over a year, not minute by minute, and

69

a turbine's annual output is entirely predictable.'

'So—'

She had to be less technical. 'Let's use your car as an analogy, shall we? I'm guessing it's capable of going at, what, a hundred and thirty miles an hour?'

'Yes, but—'

'But of course, you seldom drive it at that speed. Well, *never*, I hope, in Britain.' This got a small laugh, as she'd hoped. 'So your car is *capable* of going at that speed, but you probably drive it at speeds between thirty and seventy miles an hour normally. Does this mean it's inefficient at doing what it's designed to do? No. It gets you from A to B in the time you expect, given variables such as traffic and weather conditions, of course. And sometimes it stays in the garage.

'Wind turbines are the same. We expect them to generate a certain amount of power over a year and that amount is what we plan for.'

The lawyer looked at his notes again. 'But you can't store the electricity either.'

'No, you're right, turbines don't store electricity. What they do is feed power into the network.'

'But surely, if it's not windy when we need power most there's no point, is there?'

Kate said patiently, 'Ever since we established a national grid for our electricity, engineers have been managing what we call "spikes". We can predict when some of these are going to come.'

'The advertising breaks in the middle of the soaps,' said Nicola Arnott with her ready smile.

'Exactly.' Kate flashed her a grin in return. 'And half time in the big football matches and so on. Engineers have always managed these spikes very efficiently. I'll be very happy to go through this with you, and we do have a leaflet—' she picked one up and waved it, '—but briefly, there are certain kinds of power, like hydro and nuclear,

70

we can feed in very quickly into the grid. But the point about *renewable* energy,' she paused, to underline the importance of this point, 'is that we need to feed it into the grid whenever we can to save our finite fuels.'

Kate paused and looked round. Time to wrap up. She drew a deep breath. 'To put it at its most simple, we use renewable energy in the grid when it's available and top it up with other kinds of power when we need to.'

She could see that Frank was getting more and more wound up. She needed this Council – or a majority – to get behind her, or the Summerfield wind farm project was going to be extremely difficult to manage. She said, 'Could I suggest that we ask Council members for their views?'

The farmer broke in eagerly, his ruddy face even ruddier. 'I'm all for it. Could you tell us, Mrs Courtenay, a bit more about the Community Benefit Fund you mentioned earlier on?'

'It's exactly what it says on the tin. The Fund will be set up by AeGen for community projects. You'll need a committee to manage and co-ordinate proposals and apply for the funding, but most sensible proposals are likely to benefit.'

'How much money is there?'

'Two and a half thousand pounds per megawatt hour of installed capacity.'

Mary Tolen whistled. 'I've nae idea what that means, but it sounds like a lot of money tae me,' she said.

'It's very generous. It could mean hundreds of thousands of pounds a year for your communities to spend.'

'Blood money,' Frank growled. 'If you think you can buy us off by—'

'Don't be too hasty, Frank,' said the lawyer. 'Let's hear all sides of the argument. Is this Fund just for the first year, Mrs Courtenay?'

71

Kate shook her head. 'The Fund is for every year that the wind farm is operating. If we get planning permission for twenty-five years, the Fund will run for the same length of time. I have to say,' she smiled warmly round the table, 'that most communities are simply unable to spend all the money available to them.'

'We'd be selling our birthright for a mess of pottage,' Frank boomed.

'I don't think we should dismiss it,' said the farmer.

Mary Tolen said, 'What aboot we tak a wee vote, eh Frank? Get a feeling o' the meetin', like?'

'I think it would be best if we take this evening as a sounding meeting only.'

'Still, it wud be helpful to the lassie if she had some notion o' our feelings,' Mary persisted.

'Very well,' Frank agreed reluctantly. 'In favour?'

Mary Tolen, Nicola Arnott and the farmer raised their hands. The lawyer sat on the fence by abstaining. Frank slammed shut his notebook. 'I declare this meeting closed,' he barked.

There were no thanks to Kate for her time. She started to bundle up her papers and glanced towards the back of the hall. Ibsen must have left because she couldn't see him at all.

'That was some performance.'

'Oh!' The voice right behind her made her jump. She whirled round. 'Thanks, Ibsen.'

'You certainly had me fooled.'

'I'm sorry?'

'You weren't exactly honest with me, were you? You never told me you'd come up to Summerfield Law prospecting on behalf of AeGen.'

'I came up for a walk. That was all.'

'Hardly.' Wellington stopped sniffing her and sat at his heels. Tonight's tee shirt read, DON'T FOLLOW ME, I'M LOST TOO. Ibsen crossed his arms across the words so that

72

all she could see was I'M LOST. . She almost smiled. He said, 'You seem very sure of yourself. About wind farms.'

'I'm an engineer. This is my field. I *am* sure of myself.'

'Pity you're wrong.'

'I beg your pardon?'

'You make it sound like putting monstrosities on top of Summerfield Law would be a good thing.'

'This wind farm will generate enough—'

'I know. You said. Enough electricity to power the homes in Summerfield and Forgie and half of Hailesbank. But you skipped a lot of pretty crucial questions.'

Kate fingered her scarf, trying to relax as the silk slid across her hand. So much for pre-empting attack by wearing red. 'If I can help— Any questions you have, I'd be delighted to answer.' She turned away and started shovelling her papers into her briefcase in untidy wads.

'There really is no answer, is there? The simple fact is they'll wreck the natural landscape. No matter what you say about how efficient the damn things are or how you'll plough money back into replanting, or make sure birds aren't affected, they'll still be there, ruining it all.'

'Yes.' Kate snapped her briefcase shut and turned to face him. 'They'll be there. But you're wrong about the natural landscape, you know. Summerfield Law has been shaped by man for centuries. There's the quarry on the north side. There's the thick conifer plantation over half the hill. There's the destruction of the natural habitat that's been caused by sheep grazing on the other side. Not a lot is "natural".'

'That's different.'

'Is it? Why?'

He shook his head, his hyacinth-blue eyes glinting in the hard glare of the fluorescent lights. 'You're very good with words. But you're still wrong.'

Kate's cheeks burned. He might be subversively attractive, but Ibsen Brown's views were entrenched and

73

uninformed.

'I'm sorry you think so,' she snapped. 'Any time you'd like more information, please do get in touch.' She reached into her pocket and handed him her business card.

As she opened the front door of Willow Corner, she heard Andrew's voice in his study. When the door banged closed, his voice stopped abruptly and a second later he appeared, smiling.

'Hi darling, how did it go?'

'Where've you been?' It sounded petulant, but she was bruised and exhausted – not from talking about wind power, which was easy, but from the effort of having to keep control of her temper. 'And who was that on the phone?'

He scooped her into his arms and her mood shifted a shade, from pitch black to merely inky. 'Sorry I wasn't home in time to cook,' he murmured into her hair, his hand on the hollow of her back in the way that always stirred her.

She pulled away and headed for the kitchen. 'I need a drink.'

He caught up with her and steered her solicitously towards a chair. 'I'll get it. You must be bushed. Wine?'

'Whisky.'

'Was it that bad?'

'The usual kind of blinkered idiocy.'

'Are you talking about Frank Griffiths, by any chance?'

Blue eyes performed a tango in her mind. *Not just Frank, no.* 'I know he's Charlotte's father, but honestly—' Her voice tailed off in weary frustration. 'Frank's attitude is the worst kind of ignorance – a deliberate rejection of the facts. And sadly, there's a lot of people round here ready to simply believe him.'

Like Ibsen Brown.

Andrew's sleepy eyes were looking her, but she

wondered if he was seeing her at all. 'Andrew?'

The deep lids blinked and the eyes focused again. 'People believe what it suits them to believe, Kate, you know that.' So he had been listening. 'Don't worry too much. This is only the beginning. If you start fretting now you'll be a mess by the time the consultation period's finished.'

'I suppose you're right. Where were you, by the way? You didn't say.'

'I told you, I met with the Bishop. We spent the morning together and had lunch. He left me in his library, deep in piles of books. I'm sorry I wasn't home for supper.'

'But that was hours ago. You surely weren't there all that time?'

'Ah Kate – libraries,' he smiled, as if the one word explained everything.

Exhaustion fought back as the quick kick of the whisky faded. She couldn't think about anything any more. Her shoulders hunched and her hands tightened round her glass. This morning Andrew had more or less told her she was an outsider in her own village. After this evening's meeting, she believed he might be right. It was not a pleasant feeling.

'I got you a present.'

'Really? Why?'

'Wait there.'

When he came back, he was holding a small box. She stared at it. Once, many years ago, he held out his hand like that and on it had been a ring, winking and blinking at her in shades of heliotrope and crimson, silver, apple and cerulean – the diamond that bound them together, in love. Now she opened the box curiously and found a brooch, a sixteen-pointed star in gold, embellished with tiny pearls, and amethysts, and emeralds.

He took it out. 'Do you like it? I dropped into an

75

antiques fair and it spoke to me. It's a piece of suffragette jewellery.'

'How do you know?'

'The woman on the stall explained. They're the suffragette colours – purple, white and green. I thought of you, that's why I bought it.'

'I don't see the connection.'

'The suffragettes had beliefs. They fought for a cause and they fought with passion. Got it?'

That brought a smile to Kate's lips. 'Oh, Andrew.'

'Here. Let me pin it on.'

She could smell his Paco Rabanne aftershave as he leant closer, concentrating on the catch. She liked it on him, though it did strike her as odd, because he only usually shaved once a day.

'Thank you, darling.' Her arm curled round his neck and she pulled him to her, her finger tracing the outline of his cheek. The high, sculpted bones still defined his face as beguilingly as they had sixteen years ago. Age cannot wither him. 'I love—' she started to whisper, before he stopped her with a kiss.

Chapter Nine

'Charlotte? Did I wake you?'

'Hi Kate.'

She could hear Charlotte yawn. She was clearly stepping lazily into Saturday morning.

'I did wake you. Sorry.'

'What time is it?'

'Half past nine.'

'Christ, really? That's what happens when Georgie's on a sleepover and Ian's offshore. Bliss.'

'You're making me feel even more guilty.'

'Don't. Something up?'

Kate played with the brooch Andrew'd given her last night and thought of the aftershave. Flowers … unexplained absences … phone calls that ended abruptly … 'I'm not sure. Can we talk?'

Charlotte yawned again. 'Why don't you come round? Just give me time to shower and dress.'

'Thanks, Charl. Half an hour?'

The Herons was just down the road from Willow Corner, but it was an era apart in architecture and in spirit. Willow Corner was Georgian and The Herons, Victorian. The outside of The Herons was gray stone, Willow Corner was painted a delectable dark rose. The rooms in The Herons were bigger and were rectangular rather than square. The ceilings were higher and had elaborate cornices. Charlotte had a taste for the contemporary – with carefully conserved period features, naturally – while Kate felt that a more traditional look was right for her older property. For all the differences, though, The Herons was like a second home to her. When Ninian was little, he'd played with Georgie Proctor all the time. There was something comfortable about the familiarity of it all, just as there was something vital about the solidity of her friendship with Charlotte.

Kate reached the front door of The Herons at ten precisely, full of restless energy. 'Hi. I brought biscuits.' She held out a tin.

'You didn't need to—'

Charlotte knew what a bad cook she was. It was a standing joke between them. 'Mrs Gillies made them.'

'Aha. Then how can I refuse.' Charlotte stood aside. 'Come on in, I've got the kettle on. What's up? Has Dad caught up with you? I've been trying to hold him back.'

Kate laughed. 'Your Dad? I knew he didn't like wind farms, but my goodness, he's certainly determined this one won't go ahead. I had to face the Community Council last night.'

'Oh Kate, *sorry*.' Charlotte apologised, as if she was personally responsible for her father's views. 'Was it hellish?'

'I can handle your father, Char.' Kate twisted the old cotton scarf she'd pulled on, a favourite dusky pink with cream polka dots. 'Oh Lord, sorry, I didn't mean that to sound so dismissive. I just meant, it's all in a day's work.'

'I know. You're Miss Competence personified.'

'You make it sound like a bad thing.'

'Don't mind me, I'm just jealous. My organisational skills are nil. Here—' Charlotte handed her a mug, '—and for goodness sake, sit down, you're driving me nuts walking round and round the kitchen like a blue-arsed fly.'

Kate sat. She looked around at the bright kitchen with its pure white walls, enlivened by the one in lime green. Everything was chrome and glass and white granite, so unlike her homely kitchen with its small windows and Aga and traditional oak units. 'You've known Andrew and me

78

a long time.'

'Oh.'

'Oh what?'

'It's *that* kind of chat. I thought it would be about the Summerfield project. What's wrong?'

'Do you think it's likely that he would have an affair?'

Charlotte startled Kate by laughing.

'What? What's so funny?'

'He had an affair with *you*, ducky.'

'Yes, but that was different.' She waited. Charlotte said nothing. 'I mean, we fell in love,' she added, surprised by the silence.

'Yeah, I know. Prince Charming and Snow White all rolled into one.'

Kate put down her coffee and stared at Charlotte. Was she being sarcastic? 'It was a bit like a fairy tale. I remember pinching myself a hundred times to check I wasn't dreaming.'

'And found you weren't.'

'What *is* wrong with you, Char?' Kate frowned.

'Wrong? Nothing. Why? Were you expecting me to sit back and reassure you and say that of course Andy's not having an affair? I can't do that. Not because he *is*, but because I'd hardly be likely to know about it if he was screwing the entire Scottish membership of the WRI.'

'I suppose not.'

'What's sparked this off, anyway?'

'Initially, something Ninian said.'

'Yes?'

'He said Andrew's been acting weirdly.'

'And has he?'

'I hadn't noticed, no.'

'And what does Andy say?' Charlotte was the only person Kate knew who called her husband Andy.

'I haven't mentioned it.'

'I thought you guys talked about everything.'

79

'We do, we—' *We used to,* she corrected herself in surprise. When had they last had any kind of frank discussion? 'Don't look at me like that.'

'Like what?' Charlotte lowered her raised eyebrow and sipped her coffee. 'You're worrying about Andy because of something Ninian said. Is that reasonable?'

She said slowly, 'Ninian has been rather difficult recently. He may just be looking for attention.'

'Well then.'

Kate said nothing. She thought of the silent phone calls. She'd assumed they were something to do with the Summerfield project. Yet Andrew had missed the Council meeting – he'd been out all day, he'd put on aftershave. *He'd bought her a gift.*

No. Surely not. He wouldn't …

He wouldn't do to her what she'd done to Val.

Charlotte lifted the biscuits and thrust them out at her. 'It sounds to me like an issue of trust. Do you trust Andy or don't you?'

'Of course I trust him.' Doubt made the assertion emerge with force.

'Have a biscuit.'

Kate ignored Mrs Gillies's irresistible cherry and macadamia cookies. She didn't even look at the tin, she looked at Charlotte. 'What do you think, Char? Truly?'

Charlotte, who ate voraciously and always stayed thin, lifted a biscuit out of the tin and bit into it. 'These are terrific,' she said through a mouthful of crumbs. 'She's a treasure, your Mrs G.'

'*Char.*'

Charlotte's slim shoulders lifted in a shrug.

Kate wanted reassurance, not uncertainty. Charlotte's opinion had so well and truly communicated itself to her that she left The Herons feeling more unsettled than she'd been when she arrived.

Forgie was just a dozen miles from Edinburgh. Its location – on a hill overlooking the Firth of Forth – was spectacular, as settlers across the centuries had discovered. There were Pictish remains and traces of Roman occupation, though most of the surviving buildings were Georgian or Victorian. They stood, foursquare and gracious, behind high walls, protected from casual curiosity and shielded from traffic along the one main street.

Willow Corner was one of the oldest houses in the village. It was harled and colourwashed in a traditional deep rose and the small burn that ran through the garden provided the water source for the thirsty willows after which the house had been named. Kate loved her home. She thought of it as much more than a home – it was a precious link through the years to the people of the past who had the money, the vision and the aesthetic good sense to build for elegance and pleasure, and for posterity.

Pleasure and posterity. What kind of posterity was she creating? Kate trudged back to Willow Corner the long way round so that she could gather some composure. Her conversation with Charlotte had left her disturbed. Surely the edifice she'd constructed half a lifetime ago with such passion and optimism could not possibly crumble around her?

'Mrs Courtenay?'

Kate stopped abruptly. 'Hello.'

Nicola Arnott, the head teacher she'd met last night, was desperately trying to restrain a frisky West Highland terrier. Its nose to the ground, it strained and tugged, lured by some scent too enticing to resist.

'Darcy! Behave!' She looked at Kate and laughed. 'I know. Stupid name for a dog. It was my daughter's idea. How funny to meet you again so soon. I've been thinking about you.'

'Nothing too awful, I hope. I just do my job.'

'I thought you did very well last night. It won't be an easy ride, though.'

'I know,' Kate smiled in rueful acknowledgement of this. 'I'm prepared for that.'

'Are you? Well, you have my vote, but there's going to be a lot of resistance. I guess I'm not telling you anything new. Anyway, enough of that – I need some advice.'

'Oh yes?'

'How well do you know Summerfield?'

'A little.'

'There's a piece of waste land next to the school. *Darcy!*' She tugged at the lead.

'I know it, yes.'

'I must have complained about it to the Council a dozen times. It's a mess. The children throw their sweet wrappers there, and heaven knows what other rubbish is lurking among the weeds and rubble. Sadly, I've only ever met indifference.'

'Oh yes?' Kate, who'd had many dealings with the local Council, was not surprised.

'On the last occasion, though, I finally spoke to a young man who showed some intelligence and interest. He promised to do something.'

'That's good.'

'He called me back last night, just before I left for the meeting. Apparently it belongs to the school.'

'Really? How come?'

'The school was built on a plot of land that included this area, but it was never turned into a playground or, indeed, anything useful at all.'

'That could be good news, couldn't it? I imagine it'll take some tidying, though.'

'Sure.'

There was a pause. Kate waited, curious.

'The thing is, well, I was wondering – do you have any ideas about what we might do with it? After it's cleaned up?'

'Me?'

'I've been led to believe you have expertise in this area. Ways of using bits of land, planning applications, project management, all that kind of thing.'

'I've never been involved in a school project, or anything like what you're describing.'

'There's a first for everything.' Nicola smiled her ready smile. 'Your experience would be hugely appreciated.'

'Who did you say gave you my name?'

'Mark Matthews? He works at AeGen.'

Kate shook her head in amused exasperation. *Local knowledge.* He'd set her up. 'Well, I have no ideas off the top of my head, but I'll certainly give it some consideration.'

'Thanks.'

There was a low growl as Darcy's solid behind waggled deep in the weeds beside the pavement. 'What *have* you got there? I'd better get going.' She smiled apologetically. 'He needs a walk. I don't usually come this way but my daughter was going to a friend's near here. I guess Darcy's excited by all the new smells. Will you give it some thought? Can I phone you in a few days?'

Kate took Nicola's outstretched hand. 'Of course.'

The encounter cheered her up. It was a change to come across someone who valued her opinion.

A few days later, a heatwave catapulted Forgie into an early summer. Kate, on her way home from work, pulled up in front of The Herons to return a book she'd borrowed from Charlotte months ago. She'd never finished it – in truth, novels weren't her thing and now she was too busy to read for pleasure in any case. It would be a good excuse to have another chat with Charlotte, clear up some of the comments she'd made.

She smelled the barbecue the moment she climbed out

of her car.

'Hi Kate! Good to see you.' Mike Proctor, ultra casual in shorts and a baggy tee shirt, was brandishing barbecue tongs in one hand. He held them away from her and bent to kiss her cheek. 'Come on in. Drink?'

Kate grinned at his well-padded figure, remembering him as he was during the brief period they'd dated at uni, so skinny she'd felt compelled to feed him up on pasta. She tugged playfully at the shorts, which were smeared with oil and flour and what was almost certainly charcoal.

'Great look, Mike.'

'Less sarcasm, missy. Charlotte's out the back. I've got a jug of Pimms in the fridge, let me get you a glass. I was heading there anyway, we need more burgers.'

'I just came to drop this off.' Kate waved the book.

Charlotte and Georgie, who was fourteen now and looking sweet in tiny shorts and a crop top, were lounging on cushioned deck chairs, reading. Charlotte's toenails were a vivid green, Georgie's purple. The pretty floral tones made Kate feel horrendously overdressed in dark business suit and tights.

'Hi, Kate!' Charlotte waved and touched the arm of the recliner next to her. 'Great to see you. Come and sit down.'

'I mustn't stay. I need to get home to convince Andrew he has a real wife and not an absentee one.'

Charlotte squinted sideways at her. 'Call him. Mike'll throw some more chops on the barbecue.'

'Nice thought. Thanks. But there's Ninian—'

'Get him along here too. We haven't seen him for ages, have we Georgie?'

Ninian and Georgie used to play doctors and nurses, but those days of innocence were long gone. Now her teenage son was embarrassed in the presence of the girls. 'I don't know if he'll come. I suppose I could ask.'

'Not even for a barbied sausage?' Mike handed Kate a

84

glass of amber liquid, decorated with sprigs of mint and slices of cucumber.

'Do call,' Charlotte urged.

One grateful gulp of Pimms and Kate succumbed and called home on her mobile. 'Andrew? Mike and Charlotte are asking us to join them in the garden. Mike's got his chef's pinafore on and the smell's pretty tempting. ... Right. ... Okay.'

'He'll be round in ten minutes,' she said in answer to Charlotte's unspoken question, 'but he doesn't think Ninian will come.'

'Fine either way. Listen, you're looking roasted, why don't you nip in and raid my wardrobe? There's a pair of flip-flops on the floor in our room, and you can grab a tee shirt, you know where they are. Go on, you'll be a lot more comfortable.'

By the time Andrew arrived, cool in cropped trousers and a polo shirt, Kate felt considerably more relaxed.

'Hello Andy.' Charlotte rose from her lounger and raised her face for a kiss. 'You're looking gorgeous, as usual.'

Andrew obliged, laughing. 'Flatterer.'

'Shorts maketh the man.'

'That's not what you said to me,' Mike grumbled from behind the barbecue.

Charlotte always flirted with Andrew, she'd done it for years. 'Fetch Andy a drink, Mike, why don't you?

As they all settled with drinks, Kate said, 'You know Summerfield Primary? They've discovered that that bit of land next to the building actually belongs to the school.'

'Really? What are they going to do with it?'

Kate closed her eyes and felt the warmth of the evening sun on her face. 'The head teacher wondered if I could suggest anything. Anyone got any ideas?'

Andrew said, 'A new school library.'

'It's all computers these days,' Charlotte teased him.

'By the time those kids grow up, no-one will be reading your books, Andy. Not as books, anyway.'

Andrew grunted. Although he wrote on a computer, his knowledge of how to use them was basic. He had an almost pathological dislike of modern technology, particularly e-books.

Mike suggested, 'A music room? School hall? Gym? Some of those kids look as though they could do with some exercise.'

'Look who's talking,' Charlotte said. 'What about a community space?'

'That's it!' Kate exclaimed.

'What's it?'

'A community space. Something everyone can get involved in. But not a building. A garden.'

'A garden? It would get trashed.'

Kate shook her head. 'Not if the whole community was involved in creating it. There'd be pride of ownership. Bet you.'

Mike was doubtful. 'Good in theory, Kate.'

'A garden's something everyone can get involved in. The kids themselves, of course, but you could get the Summerfield residents engaged too – not just clearing the land, but planning what to do with it as well. And you wouldn't need planning permission.'

'I suppose it could be used as a teaching tool,' Andrew said, his old training emerging. 'They could learn about plants and the environment, maybe have a pond, and frogs and fish.'

'You could have a maze,' Charlotte contributed. 'A summerhouse. A pergola. Use it for projects, like art and creative writing. Growing food and herbs.'

'Hang on, Kate,' Mike said. 'Put the brakes on. I hate to be a spoilsport, but surely this would all cost money, however willing people might be.'

Kate said, 'Yes – and I know where I could get my

hands on some.'

Charlotte laughed. 'Won the lottery, have you?'

'The Summerfield Wind Farm Community Benefit Fund.'

'The what?'

'It's not just the farmers who get rent from the land when we build a wind farm, AeGen always gives money back to the local communities the site might affect – in this case, Summerfield, primarily. The school would have to apply for it, of course, but I'm sure it would get funding. A scheme like this would be just the kind of thing they'd kill to put money into, something that benefits children and locals alike.'

Mike stood up. 'Food for thought. And talking of food, time to eat.'

As the sun finally dipped behind the trees at the far end of Charlotte's garden, Kate felt more content than she had for weeks. All projects have their challenges and Summerfield, perhaps, would have more than most, but good things would come out of it too. And she had her family, and her friends. What was there to complain about?

Chapter Ten

Frank Griffiths' living room was packed – which wasn't difficult, because it was quite small. Nevertheless, there were – Ibsen did a swift head count – eighteen people crammed into the space. Five on the sofa (three on the seat and one on each well-padded arm), three on each of the matching chairs (one on the seat and one on each arm), one on a footstool, one on a piano stool and five standing.

There wasn't a single face he recognised, except Frank himself.

'Good evening, everyone,' Frank boomed above the hubbub.

A hush fell.

'It's great that you've all turned out tonight. Thank you. It shows, I think, how strongly we all feel about this.'

There was a mutter of approval and nods all round. A wiry-looking woman with a frizz of grey hair and a hard mouth, called, 'Right on.'

Ibsen shifted from one foot to the other. 'Feel free to bring Wellington,' Frank had said when he'd invited him to the meeting, but he was glad now that he'd left the dog with Tam. Wellington liked space.

'Right, first of all, I have to make it clear that I'm not acting tonight as Chair of the Community Council. The Council has not yet defined its official position but you all know I'm personally opposed. Clear?'

'Absolutely.'

'Sure.'

'Good. So let's assess where we're at. AeGen have put in a planning application for a Met mast on Summerfield Law. We've been told they're planning to build twelve wind turbines on top of this wild beauty spot. My first question is, what do people think? Are you for or against?'

There wasn't a single person here from Summerfield, Ibsen noted. Perhaps later, when they understood the impact more fully, the council estate would rally – or perhaps, like Mary Tolen at the meeting, they'd be seduced by AeGen's promise of hard cash.

But money could never make up for the ugliness of the turbines.

'Outrageous—'

'Spoil everything—'

'We don't want turbines here—'

'It'd never be the same again—'

This crowd, at least, was firmly opposed to the plans. Ibsen scanned their faces. Well-heeled, middle class to a man and woman, people his father would call 'Nimbys' – the Not In My Back Yard brigade. *Is that what I am?* But his objections weren't because the wind farm was near him, they were about protecting an area of outstanding natural beauty.

Ibsen shivered, though the room was warm to the point of stifling. One day, five years ago, he'd climbed Summerfield Law with Lynn and her family, with his own parents, and with Cassie and Ian. The small lead canister in his arms weighed as heavy as the world and his legs had dragged unwillingly to a place he normally loved. It would have been fitting if the weather had been stormy, or icy, but there'd been no synchronicity – it had been a flawless day.

They scattered Violet's ashes on the heather with a poem and a prayer. He'd put his arm round Lynn as they watched a playful breeze waft all that was left of their baby up to the heavens.

And now they wanted to plant a crop of turbines there, dig vast holes in the earth and pour in concrete, desecrate the loveliness of place with ugly machines.

'Our task is to do all we possibly can to prevent them. Agreed?'

Ibsen tried to concentrate. The people at this meeting, at least, were behind Frank Griffiths.

'What do we have to do, Frank?' someone said above the chatter.

'Okay, let's talk about that. I suppose the first thing is to campaign against the planning application for the mast. If that gets turned down, end of story.'

'What's the importance of the mast?'

'They need to test the suitability of the site, weather-wise.'

'So it mightn't be suitable at all?'

'It's a formality in the case of Summerfield Law, I fear.'

'If they get planning permission for the mast, is there anything we can do? Like interfere with the readings, for example?' This from the hippy woman.

Frank laughed. 'Well, at some point we'll need to decide how far we want to go in terms of direct action, but we're not at that point yet. No, I'd say we concentrate on lobbying the planners. They're the ones who'll give permission for the mast.'

'How?'

'There's several things we could do. Make a formal objection, laying out our case. Get up a petition, to back up our objection. Maybe have a march through Hailesbank, or stage some sort of protest at the Council offices. Lobby individuals too. Sandy Armstrong, for starters, the farmer who owns the land. He's key.'

Ibsen wasn't used to this at all. He'd only come along at Frank's insistence and because he objected so viscerally to the plans for the wind farm. He took stock. Most of those present were middle-aged going on elderly and he'd guess that most of them were well heeled. The hippy woman looked as though she'd been at this kind of

91

meeting a dozen times before. There was a teenager with her – her son, by the looks of him – who kept his mouth shut. He looked as though he'd be up for a bit of direct action, though.

Am I?

Someone opened the door to the hall, and a cold draught blew in. He was going to sneeze. He fumbled in his pocket for a handkerchief, found one, and blew his nose just in time.

'You dropped this.'

A woman in a tweed skirt and loafers was handing him a scrap of paper.

'Thanks.' He took it from her. It wasn't paper, it was a business card.

KATE COURTENAY, PROJECT MANAGER, AEGEN.

It was the card Kate had given him the other night, at the end of the Council meeting. She was quite something, that woman. He hated what she did, but by Christ, she was sexy. He'd seen her in hiking boots and a rain jacket and he'd thought so then. He'd seen her in a tight black shift dress and high heels, and wow, that was quite something. What would he give to see her in nothing at all?

Ibsen blinked at the card. It was the first time, he realised with a jolt, that he'd felt this way about any woman since the divorce. Why the hell did he have to pick someone so completely unsuitable? See Kate naked in bed? *It's never going to happen. Especially as your involvement with a protest group will put you and Kate on a collision course.*

He shoved the card back in his pocket and tried to put shiny black eyes and a sweet, heart-shaped face out of his mind.

Ibsen might be emotionally scarred, but he was no monk. He'd had a succession of girlfriends since he and Lynn had split up, and every time he found a new one he could see

92

hope in his mother's eyes – hope that he might find love again, hope that he might settle down, hope that he might have another child to help heal the pain of losing Violet. But it hadn't happened. He wasn't capable of making it happen. Perhaps he never would be.

Maybe part of the problem was that he was still close to Lynn – even though they found it impossible to live together, no-one else understood the hurt in his heart the way she did. Sometimes he wondered if they might try again, then he thought maybe this was what was getting in the way of a new relationship.

So he did try to make a new start. Several times over the past couple of years he'd begun dating. Attracting women wasn't the problem – they swarmed to him like bees to pollen. And they were nice women, though each had a flaw. Jackie had been pretty, but so clearly desperate, at thirty-eight, to bag a man, that she clung like a leech and drained his life blood. Karen fussed over him like a mother hen, obviously worried about him. It had been an unequal balance, and couldn't last. Shelley was too young, their interests didn't overlap at all.

Melanie was a girl for evenings in the pub and a nice bit of leg-entwining under the duvet. She was the most attractive of the lot, and when it came to bed-warming she was a real treat – which made it harder, of course, to do what he was going to have to do before too long.

He turned onto his back and stared at the ceiling. Beside him, Melanie stirred, sleepily. He hooked an arm under her shoulders and rolled her towards him.

'You awake?'

'Mmm,' she muttered sleepily.

She nestled close to him, her head on his chest, her shoulder under his armpit. After a moment he abandoned his examination of the ceiling and laid his cheek on her hair. Sometimes any body was better than nobody, but this wasn't fair. Ibsen decided, with exasperation, that life

93

would be a whole lot simpler if Tam hadn't brought him up with an exaggerated sense of fairness. Mel's expectations were growing, and that couldn't be allowed to go on.

'Shall I bring you breakfast in bed, Ibs?' she whispered, her voice half drugged with drowsiness.

It was seven o'clock in the morning, and Ibsen knew what this offer cost her, because Melanie was not a morning girl and today was Sunday. It was another sign of the lengths she was prepared to go in order to keep him.

Reluctantly, he eased her away. 'You're all right, love. You stay there. I'll bring you a cuppa and some toast.'

He let Wellington out and brewed tea. Melanie was half sitting up by the time he returned to the bedroom, her auburn hair tumbling round her shoulders like a bedjacket.

'Fancy a quiet day, Ibs, just the two of us?' She accepted the tea and placed it on the chair beside the bed, then patted the covers. 'Coming back in?'

He shook his head and perched on the side of the bed. 'I promised Frank Griffiths I'd do a bit of homework for him.'

The meeting at Frank's house had begun by sounding people out, but ended like a military operation, with Frank allocating tasks to anyone who'd shown willing.

'Check it out, Ibsen, would you?' he'd tossed the request in Ibsen's direction. 'Have a look around, see where the turbines might go, have a think about access routes, and where we might have a sit-in, if we end up having to do something like that.'

Ibsen, still feeling like a foreigner in a strange land, nodded an acknowledgement. Outdoor reconnaissance he could manage.

Melanie pulled a face at his announcement. 'Must you?'

'You can come with me if you like. You'll need boots though.'

94

'I've got boots.'

An hour later, Melanie appeared in the kitchen dressed in ripped jeans, an off-the-shoulder tee shirt in luminous orange, and skin-tight boots in tan suede with four-inch heels.

Ibsen grinned. 'When I said boots, I didn't mean boots like that.'

'I haven't got any others.'

'Well, you can't walk in those. I'll see if Ma can lend you something.'

Melanie looked horrified. 'You want me to wear your mother's boots?'

'Mel, we're climbing a hill, not going to a fashion show. You look totally gorgeous—' he said quickly, seeing her face fall, '—just impractical. Listen, don't worry, I can go on my own.'

'No, you're all right. I want to come.'

'Right. If you're sure. Wait there a minute then.'

Five minutes later, he returned with a pair of wellies. 'Not ideal, but I couldn't find her outdoor boots and she's out somewhere.'

In fairness, Melanie was fitter than he'd imagined her to be. Her long legs ate up the yards and she strode with him, pace for pace, up the hill, with Wellington bounding ahead. She even seemed to be quite enjoying herself.

'What's this, Ibsen?' she called, stopping by a tiny orchid almost hidden by heather.

He squatted down and felt its delicate flowers gently. 'Looks like a Heath Spotted-orchid. Likes acid soil. You did well to spot that one, Mel.'

'It's pretty.'

'It is. And if they build a road this way, that'll be the end of it.'

'They won't, will they?'

'Not if I can help it, no.'

95

The June sun was already warm and he was glad he'd only pulled on a tee shirt. It was good to be up here so early, there wasn't another walker in sight.

'What's that bird?'

Mel was looking up in the sky, where a kestrel hovered like a moth.

'A kestrel—'

Because he was looking up, he saw Kate before she saw him. She looked like a slip of a girl from here, jumping from boulder to boulder on the rockiest bit of the summit. What the hell was she doing up here on a Sunday?

Then Wellington sprang across the last twenty yards to where she was standing and did the obligatory ten-circles-round-a-new-friend dance before burying his nose in her crotch.

'Does he know her?' Melanie said, flicking her hair back from her eyes.

'They've met.'

His eyes were on Kate because he couldn't help it. He wanted to pick the woman up in his arms and carry her to his bed, but he knew that was never going to happen. Was that why he wanted her so much? *I want doesn't get*, his mother used to say. But in this case, even asking with a 'please, pretty please', as Lynn used to put it wouldn't do either. She was married and she was a bloody wind farm engineer. Two massive no-no's.

'Who is she, Ibs?'

Melanie's gaze was boring into him, as if she could read his mind. Ibsen blinked and grinned at her. 'No-one that matters,' he said, and slung his arm across her shoulders in a gesture of togetherness as they crossed the last few yards to where Kate stood.

'I knew if Wellington was here you wouldn't be far behind,' Kate said, smiling. She turned to Melanie. 'Hi.'

Melanie ignored the outstretched hand. Instead she swung her arms round Ibsen's waist, the gesture possessive. 'Hi.'

'Up here prospecting?' Ibsen said, not bothering to introduce her.

'Just needed some air. I like it up here.'

'So do I. Just now,' he added meaningfully.

Kate said nothing.

'Did you know they're going to build a wind farm up here?' Melanie said. 'Ibsen's hopping mad, aren't you Ibs? They're planning a major protest.'

Kate didn't look at Melanie, she stared at Ibsen, her dark eyes unwinking. 'Is that right?'

'Well, you knew we would,' Ibsen said softly.

'Yes,' she said. She seemed to be scarcely breathing. 'I knew.'

'Christ,' Melanie said as Kate swung round and began to pick her way down the hill. 'What was that all about?'

Ibsen thought, *If only I understood.*

Chapter Eleven

Willow Corner was the last Georgian house at the northern end of Forgie and the road was a cul-de-sac.

There was no reason for a car to be parked outside the house. Kate saw it from the upstairs landing, squatting low on the road like an iridescent beetle, on the exact same spot it had been a dozen times in recent weeks. She could make out a figure hunched over the steering wheel. She couldn't even tell if it was male or female. Twice she had gone to the front door and started down towards the gate, determined to find out who it was, but as soon as she'd passed the rose arch half way down the path, she heard the engine turn over and saw the car drive off.

She was being watched, she was certain of it. It was a threat, nothing more. AeGen were big on personal safety and there were strict guidelines. House visits should never be made alone, no-one should leave a meeting alone. Kate had experience of protests and knew that when feelings ran high people could get vicious. Protestors might congregate in car parks, cluster round cars, bang on the windows or the bodywork. It could be frightening. Yet what could she do? There was nothing concrete to report.

Frank was certainly becoming a nuisance, phoning Kate every day, sometimes several times a day. Kate's patience – never her strongest suit – was beginning to wear thin. *I can handle your father*, she'd told Charlotte. She could, she was sure, but she was beginning to wish fervently that she didn't have to.

Eight weeks after the application, planning permission was

granted for the Met mast on Summerfield Law.

'Brilliant!' Kate high-fived Jack, who happened to be passing when the news came in.

'First step achieved,' Jack grinned back at her. He'd been on best behaviour recently.

'We'll have to see what the mast records, of course. We shouldn't get too excited,' Kate warned. 'But still, it's into public consultation now. Full steam ahead.'

Mark was pleased with progress. 'The thing about women managers,' he told the Friday wash-up meeting with a broad grin, 'is that they can juggle a dozen balls in the air because they don't have to use their hands to protect the other two.'

Everyone laughed dutifully. It was a small compliment, and a joke they'd all heard before, but it would do.

'I told you,' Mark said to her after the meeting, 'that putting you in charge of Summerfield would be a good move. You're doing all right, Kate. Well done.'

Kate smiled her acknowledgement of his praise, but privately, she had her worries. Feelings about the wind farm proposals were already running high in Forgie and this would bring things to a boil.

As Project Manager, Kate's job was a complex one. Every task was vital and Kate knew that her days were about to get a lot busier. Over the weekend she took the decision to put the half-planned summer holiday on hold.

'We'll go somewhere fabulous in the October break,' she promised Ninian.

'Mu-um. This always happens.'

'And we always go somewhere nice some other time. Chill, Ninian,' Kate responded cheerfully. She loved getting her teeth into a complex project. Ninian could visit her mother in Devon for a week or two, he always liked that, and maybe Andrew would take him somewhere. A bit of bonding would do those two no harm – Ninian had been so snappy with Andrew recently, it would be a good time for them to rediscover each other. Seeing his expression, she relented a little. 'I'll try to find a few days at some point Ninian, I promise.'

Ninian stomped out but Kate's thoughts were already jumping ahead to the next task. Spinning plates was a skill that required concentration.

On Monday, when she turned on her computer at work, a wave of new messages rolled in. Some of them were extremely aggressive. None of the addresses was immediately recognisable, though someone in AeGen would have the technical capability of tracking down the computer they'd been sent from. If they got too threatening, the police would be notified.

The threats had been escalating. *Or else?* What did that mean? *We're watching you.* Was that one person, or a lot of people? Was it the person in the iridescent car? Was it a team?

She contemplated telling Jack or Gail, but decided she should cope with this herself. She created a new mail folder and transferred the messages into it. The worst thing was that these were probably from people who lived near her, maybe from people she actually knew. She could no longer trust anybody. She couldn't even walk down the street without wondering whether the woman carrying supermarket bags she had just passed was one of the writers, or the jogger who always nodded, or the mother with the pushchair and the dog.

She stopped by Lisa Tranter's desk. Lisa was fresh out of college, the youngest member of her team. 'How are the environmental studies coming on?'

The slight blonde looked up, eager to make a good impression. 'They're all under way. We've got a bird surveyor up there today, as a matter of fact, Geoff Harkins.'

'Good. He's been briefed, I take it? And he's properly

101

equipped?'

'Yes. I did it myself, yesterday afternoon because he was going up really early this morning, about three o'clock, he said.'

'Make sure he checks out with you, won't you?'

Lisa had reverted to reading her emails, multi-tasking, being busy and being seen to be busy. 'Will do, Kate.'

Andrew caught her in the middle of everything. He sounded buoyant. 'You're remembering that the Bertolinis are here for supper?'

'I hadn't forgotten,' she lied. 'I'm looking forward to it.'

It was good to hear Andrew sounding so positive. She made sure she finished on time. The job was important, but family had to come first, today at any rate.

The smell of lamb pervaded the house. Andrew was in the kitchen and Kate halted on the threshold to watch him. He was reading a recipe in some recipe book – Delia or Jamie or Nigel or Claudia or Elizabeth, he had them all – his glasses half way down his nose as usual, his concentration absolute. She tiptoed up behind him, put her arms round his waist and laid her cheek on soft white cotton.

'I'm so lucky to have you.'

'You're back.' He sounded pleased. He was certainly pleased enough to lay the book down and turn to gather her to him.

'Something smells wonderful. Want me to do anything?'

'All under control.' He released her and waved towards the dining room, where she glimpsed crisp damask and fuschia cotton, the gleam of silver and a bowl full of sumptuous peonies.

'Wow.'

'Not my doing.' His smile was the smile that wooed her and won her. 'Mrs G had a lot of fun.'

'I didn't know she had such a sense of style,' Kate said, surprised.

'There was a magazine or something—' he gesticulated vaguely.

'God, that woman—'

'What's wrong?'

'She's meant to clean and iron, not act the hostess.'

'Well, if you weren't out all the time—'

'Don't start that, Andrew. Just because you work from home.'

'She was just doing you a favour.'

'She makes me feel useless in my own house.' Kate wrinkled her nose. 'Is there nothing I can do?'

In a sudden change of mood, Andrew pulled her into his arms and kissed her. 'Don't be crotchety, darling. Why don't you just go and make yourself look beautiful?'

Kate sighed. 'It might take too long.'

'Silly.' He kissed her again.

What was she so worried about? She smiled. 'Where's Ninian?'

'Out for the evening with Banksy and Cuzz.'

'Oh God, no.'

'What's wrong?'

'I don't like Stephen Cousins. His mother's an aggressive hippie, if you can visualise the type. I imagine she frightened off the father because there isn't one in evidence. She smokes pot too, I'm sure of it, and I think Stephen has soaked up a lot of her attitude.'

'Well I bribed the three of the them to go off to the movies in Edinburgh,' Andrew said cheerfully. 'So we'll have to see if he gets back in one piece, eh?'

'It's just that—'

'Not like you to worry over Ninian.'

She frowned. 'What does that mean?'

'Nothing. Relax. Just go and change, they'll be here in half an hour. Here—' He opened the fridge and poured her a small glass of white wine, then kissed her forehead. 'Leave me to finish in the kitchen, okay?'

'Okay. Thanks, Andrew.'

Kate carried the wine upstairs and peered into her wardrobe. What was the correct attire for film directors? She selected a cream-to-navy dip-dye Coast dress and added navy heels. As she leaned towards the mirror to apply the smokey grey eye shadow she favoured for evenings, her mobile rang.

It was Lisa Tranter, sounding panicky.

'What is it, Lisa?'

'I was just having my supper when – oh God, I hope nothing's happened.'

'Lisa, calm down,' Kate abandoned her mascara, stood up and switched into work mode. 'Tell me what's wrong.'

'Remember I was telling you about that bird surveyor, Geoff Harkins?'

'Yes.'

'His wife just called me. He hasn't come home.'

'Didn't he check in with you when he left?'

She heard Lisa gulp. 'I forgot about him, Kate. I'm sorry.' She sounded on the verge of tears.

'Have you tried his mobile?'

'Of course, but I think he switches it off when he's watching the birds.'

Kate reviewed all the possibilities in her head. The Summerfield site only stretched to a few square kilometers, but some of the terrain was quite inhospitable – bog and heather, areas of scrub and woodland and rocks. Besides, there was a long walk up to the site itself from the road. If he hadn't driven up, if he'd tried to take a shortcut through the woods, he could be anywhere in quite a wide area. Had he fallen? Been taken ill?

'Was he wearing a high-visibility jacket?'

'I don't know, sorry. I did issue one, but he made his own way up and I suspect he likes to camouflage himself

104

so he doesn't scare the birds off.'

'Did he have GPS equipment?' Satellite positioning equipment would make finding him – in theory at least – much easier.

'Again, I did issue it, but to be honest, Kate, he seemed a bit unsure of the technology. I wouldn't be surprised if he didn't switch it on.'

'We need to find him, Lisa. Have you put any action in place?'

'No, I called you as soon as I heard.'

Kate's brain was racing. Locating Geoff Harkins had to be a top priority – but the Bertolinis would be here at any moment and Andrew was relying on her. 'Right. Lisa, here's what I want you to do. Call Ricky and Evan and any other team members you can get hold of. See how many can turn out. Get them to meet you at the site in half an hour. And call me back as soon as you can to let me know what's happening.'

'Aren't you coming?'

Kate slapped her hand against her chiffon-clad hip in frustration. Any other night, any other time at all, and she'd be there in an instant. 'I don't think I can, Lisa. I'll call Jack, though, and he'll take over.'

'Right then.' The girl sounded relieved, making Kate all the more exasperated. A chance like this was all Jack needed to make some kind of point that she was not up to the job.

'Just get started, Lisa. We'll talk in a few minutes, okay?'

Damn, and double damn! She'd have to tell Andrew. Even if she could get the team organised, there were going to be calls interrupting their evening. Any other day—

'Did I hear you talking?' Andrew was pouring mint sauce into a dish. 'Everything's pretty much ready now.' He glanced up. 'You look gorgeous.'

She stood in the doorway, chewing her lip with anxiety.

Something about her stillness must have caught his attention because he looked back at her and stopped pouring. 'What is it?'

'Someone's gone missing at the site. A bird surveyor.'

'Missing? How?'

She explained. 'The thing is, Andrew, I need to get a search organised.'

'Oh no. Not you, Kate. Not tonight. Surely someone else can do it? Other people do work at AeGen, I take it?'

Kate gulped. This was hard. 'Yes. I'm going to phone Jack Bailey.'

Andrew screwed the lid back on the jar of mint sauce and turned away. 'Better get on with it then. They'll be here in a minute.'

It was infuriating, but it had to be done. Kate retreated to Andrew's den and dialled Jack's number. His phone went straight onto voice mail. Shit! What was she going to do? She paused, thought quickly, called Lisa. 'How's it going? Who have you managed to contact?'

'Not great, Kate. I've got three so far, but the others aren't answering their phones.'

'I've tried Jack. He's not answering either.'

'Jack plays five-a-side on Mondays.'

'What? You didn't say earlier.'

'I've just remembered.'

'*Je-sus*, Lisa!'

'Sorry.'

Kate went quiet. She was in an impossible situation. She couldn't leave Lisa and the others on her team unsupervised, not in these circumstances. It was too important. Potentially, there was a man's life at stake – and even in the case of a bad injury, the repercussions if they didn't do this right were serious in the extreme. There was only one other person she could possibly ask to head up the search and that was Mark Matthews, but asking your boss to do your job so that you could enjoy a cosy dinner at home was unthinkable. There was no choice.

'Carry on phoning, Lisa. Get as many people as you can. And head to the site yourself. I'll see you there in twenty minutes.'

Andrew had changed and looked remarkably at ease – considering how important this evening was to him – in a black open-necked shirt. He was wearing the silver cuff links she'd given him last Christmas, a closed book on one cuff, an open book on the other. Guilt engulfed her and she grimaced.

He guessed at once. 'No, Kate. You can't do this to me.'

Outside, she heard a car on the gravel. 'There's no time,' she said quietly, 'to tell you how sorry I am.'

The hooded eyes closed almost to slits and his lips tightened, sure signs of just how angry he was.

The doorbell rang.

'I can stay for five minutes to explain. There's a man's *life* at stake, Andrew.'

His mouth clamped shut and his jaw jutted ominously. He went into the hall to answer the door. 'Andreas!' he greeted his guests smoothly, all signs of anger concealed, 'How wonderful you could make it. And Signora Bertolini, welcome to Willow Corner.'

Kate moved forward, her dip-dyed dress skimming her neat waist and hips, the image of the perfect hostess. In three minutes she would have to go and change into jeans and stout shoes and head for the site. She smiled in welcome, but inside she had never felt so miserable – or so guilty – in her life.

Chapter Twelve

The team – or, at least, the members Kate had been able to muster – met at the gate onto Summerfield Law, donned high-visibility gear and marched off as a phalanx. It was fortunate that it was summer –searching in the dark would have been a nightmare.

'We'll spread out, ten feet apart. Call if you see anything, a bit of equipment, any clothing, even so much as a breadcrumb. Okay?'

There was plenty of warmth still in the sun. Kate, head down, searching the rough grassland for clues, thought only of roast lamb and of Andrew's anger. After twenty minutes they had seen nothing.

'Stop,' Kate ordered. They clustered round her, wanting leadership. Lisa looked white with anxiety. 'We've got to be cleverer about this. We're just walking randomly. Where might he have gone? Where might he settle comfortably for a period, so that he could watch for birds? That's one way we can tackle this. Alternatively, where are the potential hazards up here? Rocks he might have stumbled over, worst part for rabbit holes, gullies?'

'Top end, the ground's really uneven, but there's some shelter at the edge of the wood,' volunteered Evan, a stout, bright young engineer.

'That's where I'd go,' agreed another young member of the team. 'Prop my back up against a tree, fantastic views, bit of shelter.'

'Right. Let's start up there, then, and work our way down. You want to lead, Evan?'

It was a good piece of thinking. They found Geoff

109

Harkins a few minutes later, crumpled awkwardly in a small gully.

'I feel so stupid,' he panted. His face, drained of blood, was almost the colour of his silvery hair. 'I stumbled and hit my head, passed out. And my ankle's really painful.'

'I don't think we should move him, Kate,' Evan said quietly. 'There may be injuries we can't see.'

'You're right. We'll call the paramedics.'

'I didn't have the wretched GPS thingy on,' Geoff apologised feebly. 'Sorry. Such a nuisance. Couldn't remember how to work the damn thing. Sorry. Sorry.'

'Don't apologise, Geoff.' Kate squatted next to him in the gully. She took his hand and was rewarded with an appreciative squeeze. 'We've found you now. Everything's going to be fine.'

They had to summon a helicopter, because access across the rough land would have been impossible for any vehicle. Once the development started, Kate thought, things would change. Ibsen had certainly been right about that.

The helicopter arrived within minutes.

'I feel dreadful,' Lisa muttered as the paramedics checked Geoff over. 'It's my fault.'

Kate couldn't help heaving a sigh. 'Well,' she said, 'perhaps you should have been more insistent that he follow our procedures, but I can see the difficulty. I'm just nervous about press reaction.'

'Will it be bad?' Lisa looked panic-stricken.

'Who knows? They'll seize on anything.'

'My own stupid fault,' Geoff said, over and over again as he was strapped onto a stretcher. 'Lisa did show me how to work this GPS thing but I did something wrong, and my mobile phone was out of juice. I can't believe how stupid I've been. Honestly, I'm so grateful, I can't say thank you enough to everyone.'

It was clear that the press would get nothing out of him

but praise. With luck it would be a small paragraph on an inside page, no more.

It took almost four hours to assemble the team, search for Geoff, locate him, call the paramedics, and get back to the office to do the necessary paperwork. When Kate finally did get back to Willow Corner around eleven thirty, the Bertolinis had already left and Andrew had retreated to bed, leaving a shambles behind him to make a point. Kate tore off pieces of cold, leftover lamb and stuffed them into her mouth gracelessly. Who cared? She was ravenous and the meat was delicious. She scraped a spoonful of gratin dauphinoise potatoes out of the baking dish and consumed it with gusto.

Andrew's wrath – or media excoriation and vilification at the office? Fifteen years ago, would she have weighed out the choices in this way, counterbalanced the evils in the scales to see which side fell more heavily? What had happened to instinct? What had happened to love? Back then, would she have been so much in thrall to her job that she'd have put Andrew's needs below the demands of corporate reputation? As the adrenalin subsided, to be replaced by bone weariness, Kate began to see how much her life had shifted.

It's the price you have to pay for a career. Any man would have made the choice I made tonight.

But she couldn't put another thought to the side: *Andrew needed me and I let him down.*

Ninian arrived home around midnight, on his own. Kate was relieved, because it was not unknown for one or more of Ninian's friends to stay late, bang around the kitchen in the small hours, and crash out on his floor until mid morning.

'Hi Ninian, good film?'

'Okay,' he grunted in his increasingly monosyllabic fashion. 'Anything to eat?'

111

He pulled out all the food Kate had just packed into the fridge and started to guzzle. She was about to suggest a fork and knife, then she remembered her own predatory attack on the meat and held her peace.

'Great nosh. How did the dinner go?'

'I don't know, I wasn't there,' she confessed wearily.

The weirdness of this statement penetrated even Ninian's brain and his hand stopped half way to his mouth, a sizeable slab of lamb dangling from it. 'How come?'

'I was called out to an emergency.' The tensions of the evening had drained her utterly and now all she wanted to do was go to bed.

'Christ, Dad must've been livid.'

'Yes. I suspect he was.'

'Haven't you seen him?'

'No. He'd gone to bed before I got back.'

'Wouldn't like to be in your shoes.'

'I guess not. I'm going to bed, Ninian. Will you please put anything you don't eat back in the fridge?'

'Sure.'

'Night.' She looked at him wistfully, wanting a hug but unsure whether to reach out or not.

Well into the leftover potato, Ninian was oblivious. 'Night, Mum. Good luck in the morning.'

It gave her enough strength to smile at him. 'I have a feeling I'm going to need it.'

In the morning, though, Andrew was asleep – or feigning sleep, she wasn't entirely sure which – depriving her, either way, of the chance to find out how things had gone. And later, when she arrived home from work, Andrew pointedly put on his jacket and headed straight for the door.

'Meeting,' he said briefly, without bothering to explain further.

Kate was still desperately tired. Sleep hadn't come

easily last night and she'd gone to work early to mop up the last of the spillage from the Geoff Harkins episode. Her first inclination was to press him, but the pettiness of his punishment infuriated her. In her own mind, she had already tested her decision-making process and found it to be sound. She'd had no choice, so how dare he be so censorious? With an effort, she smothered her anger and let it pass. 'How did it go last night?'

Andrew picked up his car keys from the hall table. 'As if you care.'

If he'd slapped her in the face she couldn't be more shocked. 'Andrew! Of course I care!'

He turned back, a hard glint in the hooded eyes. 'If you'd cared, Kate, you would have stayed.'

'You know that was impossible. I tried everything. There was no-one else to take charge. I *had* to go.'

'You *had* to stay, but you didn't.'

'That's so unfair! It was—'

'It just shows, doesn't it, where I stand in your hierarchy of importance. I should have known. Work always comes first with you, doesn't it?'

'If I could have found someone else to—'

'And what about Ninian? How do you think the boy feels about his summer holiday being cancelled? Being shunted off to his grandma's?'

Kate blinked. She was unprepared for this onslaught and too tired to deal with it sensibly. 'But I ... we—'

'I'm going out. I have a meeting, and I'm late.'

'Don't run away from me. We should talk.'

The door slammed behind him and she was left in a void.

Ninian was nowhere in evidence. Kate had no appetite and no concentration. Nothing she did or said to Andrew seemed fit to rescue a deteriorating situation. What the hell was happening? They'd had their spats in the past – what marriage never had those? – but they'd always been able to

113

discuss them, then laugh about them, then put them aside. This time, she could not get Andrew to talk.

The thought of dealing with the stack of papers in her briefcase awaiting her attention was dismal. Willow Corner – her pride, her joy, her home – felt empty. She meandered through the rooms. Each held memories, each had seen laughter and love. In the living room she touched the ornate clock Andrew had insisted on buying in an antiques shop years ago. Ninian had been three, Andrew still a teacher, her salary was modest and money was tight. There'd been something about the clock's age and style, though, that he had loved and she'd given in. Back then, she'd deferred to his wishes and been able to laugh, despite the folly of it.

On the small coffee table, a netsuke mouse, beady eyes staring out of sweetly carved ivory, reminded her of a time before they were even married. She'd been out at a special Engineering Department lecture with Mike, leaving Andrew and Charlotte together for the evening. Things with Val had been at their most difficult and she remembered being torn between going to the dinner and staying behind to support Andrew. And yet, the next day, it was Andrew who had presented her with this delightful (and probably stupidly expensive) gift.

In the dining room, Ninian's childhood library still nestled among the Dickens, Austen and reference books on medieval history. Her baby, now all but grown up. Kate picked out one battered book. *Where The Wild Things Are.* It had been thumbed almost to destruction – but how often had she sat with him and read this book? Andrew had been the reader. Andrew had introduced him to words and pictures, dreams and nightmares. A monster stared at her from a crumpled page, toothy and grinning and not really fierce. Had Ninian been frightened, or thrilled? Had Andrew had to comfort him, or had they laughed together?

She had found child-rearing a distraction. Now, she

realised, time had sped past her and she would never again be able to share precious, wild moments with her son.

At the door of Andrew's study, she heard the telephone ring. She stepped in and picked it up.

'Willow Corner, hello?'

There was silence.

Kate was in no mood for patience. 'Look, I've had enough of this! What you're doing is harassment. AeGen knows all about your moronic attempts at intimidation. If you do this one more time, I'll report you to the police. Now—'

There was a click and the line went dead. Kate slammed the phone down, her anger still at boiling point. She knew she shouldn't have lost her temper – she'd been venting her frustration over Andrew. All the same, she'd got to the point where she had to report the calls to AeGen, she should have done it some time ago.

When the phone rang again, immediately, she picked it up and barked, 'I *told* you! Bugger off!'

After a beat, an amused voice said, 'Of course I will, if you wish, but I was rather hoping we could discuss your ideas for a community garden.'

'Mrs Arnott! Nicola! God, I'm so sorry. I just had a stupid nuisance call and I thought they were pestering me again.'

'No problem. So long as it's not me you're mad at.'

'Not at all, heavens, sorry.'

'You kindly sent me an email with some ideas for our space.'

'A garden, yes. What do you think?'

'I love it. We all love it.'

'Really? I thought you might have preferred some kind of building.'

'At first we thought so too, but the more we've reflected on your ideas, the better they seem. Now, how do we start? Have you someone in mind for the garden side of

115

things?'

Kate hesitated. Remembering that Ibsen Brown worked for Banksy's mother, Helena, she'd phoned her. The reference had been glowing. 'He's more than just adequate,' Helena had said, 'he's properly trained, he did a college course. His father's a gardener too, of course, over at Forgie House, so he grew up in the business, so to speak.'

On a personal level, Kate found Ibsen to be something of an enigma, but that intrigued her. He clearly didn't care much about his appearance, but there was an innate intelligence in his eyes that she couldn't help finding attractive. His views on wind farms were certainly irritating, but still – if he was as good at gardening as Helena said, then he'd be an excellent person to approach, surely?

'There is someone,' she started, hesitantly, 'but—'

'If you know of anyone who can help us, please talk to them. I'd like to start progressing this. Some of the children are excited already.'

'I will. I promise. I'm glad you like the idea. Truly.'

'Let's stay in touch. And Kate – if those calls are really troubling, do act.'

'I will.'

Nicola's phone call had brought some welcome relief, but Kate still felt as if she had embarked on some kind of game, the rules of which she didn't fully understand. Boxed into corners, she always reverted to type – she became strategic. *Define the problem.* My marriage is growing stale and I suspect that Andrew may be having an affair, plus I feel guilty at letting him down over the Bertolini dinner.

Consider the strategy: Inject loving care, and gather the family round him to remind him of how difficult and traumatic the failure of a marriage is. Eclipse the memory of my failure by initiating something special.

Andrew's fifty-seventh birthday fell this year on a Saturday. Kate, a meticulous planner, had the date firmly in her head and despite all the pressures at work, spent some time considering how to celebrate. Usually they had a meal at home, with Ninian and Harry. This year Jane would be included too, of course. Perhaps, to make up for missing his dinner with the Bertolinis, she should arrange something special, a surprise?

Devise a solution: A festive family dinner.

She tested the solution in her head. It held sound. So, bracing herself, she called Harry.

'Dinner at Martin Wishart's in Leith? My treat? What do you think?'

Martin Wishart's restaurant was Michelin-starred and luxurious. The service was as meticulous as the cooking, the tablecloths starched and whiter than porcelain. It was a place to be pampered and Harry's response was predictable.

'Your treat? How could we say no? What does Ninian think?'

'I haven't sounded him out yet, but he's at an age where he's beginning to be willing to be seduced by good food. I imagine he'd go for it.'

'Excellent.'

She was pleased that Harry approved. 'I'd like to surprise your father.'

'No problem. The secret's safe with me.'

Ninian, though, was not as enthusiastic as she had anticipated.

'Why're you treating *Dad*? He doesn't deserve it.'

'Ninian! Why ever not?'

'Haven't you noticed, Mum?'

'Noticed what?'

'Duh! Why's Dad out all the time?'

'He has meetings. He's researching a new book.'

Ninian threw her a look of utter contempt and headed

117

for the stairs. 'Right.'

'Ninian? Will you come?'

There was no reply, only the pounding of boots on the stairs.

She pressed her fingers against her temples, where the pounding was echoed in the makings of a monumental headache.

Chapter Thirteen

'You haven't got fixings for the cot in your van,' Cassie told Ibsen, 'and to be honest, I think the thing's so rusty nothing would hold anyway. So you've got two choices. Either you strap her in front of you in the baby carrier, or you put her in the pram.'

'How long did you say you were going to be?' Ibsen eyed Daisy Rose apprehensively.

Daisy Rose blinked and blew him a bubble. She grabbed hold of one toe and pulled it to her mouth.

'Here, baby.' Cassie deftly unfurled her and slipped on a babygro. 'It's just a check up at the hospital, I won't be long, but Mum's getting her hair done and I didn't want to ask her to change it, she's done so much for me recently. As for Dad—' she leaned towards Ibsen, '—well, bless him, I wouldn't want to leave her with Dad, he'd probably forget she was there.'

Ibsen could feel his shoulders rising. It was touching that Cassie trusted *him* with Daisy, after what happened to Violet, but it was an enormous responsibility.

'You'll be fine, Ibs.' Cassie put her arm round his shoulders and gave him a quick squeeze. 'Just because … you know … it's not going to happen again.'

He knew she was right, but it was going to take some courage.

'What's it to be? Sling or pram?'

'Pram. I have to get some work done. You did say she'll sleep?'

'Like a baby,' Cassie laughed. 'Right. Pram it is.'

So now Ibsen found himself striding along Forgie Main

119

Street pushing Daisy Rose in front of him. He prayed Melanie wasn't around to see him because heaven knows what ideas that would trigger. His head was down and his shoulders were hunched forward because the handle of the pram was too low and besides, he was feeling extremely self-conscious. He just hoped Frank was going to be understanding.

It was ten weeks since little Daisy shot into this world in defiance of everyone's diary and now here he was, in sole charge of her, his heart bursting with love and his brain scrambled by panic. What if she needed changing? What if she choked? What if—

He peered into the dimness of the interior to check that she was still breathing. He'd looked at her a dozen times already, because he needed to know she was all right. He was becoming obsessive about it, which was ridiculous but maybe understandable. Daisy Rose blinked at him from under a slightly crooked lace bonnet, her eyes already turning intense blue just like Ibsen's, and Cassie's, and Tam's. A slow smile spread over her face.

'Don't you laugh at me, you little monkey,' he muttered, but couldn't resist grinning stupidly back at her. He was in love. Daisy Rose had captured his heart in a way no woman had ever quite managed.

Beside him, a car screeched to a halt. Wellington jumped sideways in alarm and the pram nearly jolted out of his grasp. He swung round. The engine died to silence and Kate Courtenay climbed out of the car. Ibsen's face tightened. First she wanted to smother the countryside with wind turbines and now she was trying to kill him, his niece, and his dog. He hadn't forgotten their encounter on Summerfield Law, but he hadn't understood what happened that day either. Whatever way you looked at it, though, she made him feel uncomfortable.

Kate hopped round to the pavement. 'Hi! Sorry about the sudden stop, the pram was unexpected, I didn't recognise you until I spotted Wellington. I've been wanting to talk to you. I didn't know how to get hold of you.'

'I don't have time for an argument about wind farms today.' He was curt, nodding at the pram.

'Yours?' She touched the handle of the pram inquiringly. 'May I?'

She pushed a tentative finger inside the pram and moved the cotton gently aside. Daisy gazed back at her with solemn blue eyes, then she opened her tiny mouth opened and executed a charming yawn. 'Oh, she's so beautiful!' Kate exclaimed, with such heartfelt appreciation that Ibsen began to thaw.

'She's not long out of hospital, we had a real scare with her.'

'Is she all right?'

'So far as we know, yes.'

'Are you taking her to work?'

'I had to, Cassie's off to the doctor's. If you want the truth,' he confessed, 'I'm trying not to panic about all the instructions I've been given. There's a spare nappy in the bag. If she cries, just jiggle her about a bit. If she seems thirsty, there's a bottle of water. Personally, I'm happier with dahlias.'

'The instructions sound about right.'

'She's not a packet of seeds, I'm told. Apparently she's not to be planted by the feet and covered in soil. I'm worried I might get confused.' He grinned at her, his earlier apprehension forgotten. 'What brings you here, Pocket Rocket?'

'Is that a reference to my size? Because if so, I have to tell you I find it—'

'Just a little joke. It was a tribute to your obvious energy.'

'I've got the energy, you've got the tool kit handy on your head.'

121

He lifted a hand up to his ponytail and touched string. His grin widened. 'First thing to come to hand this morning.'

'Vanity isn't one of your vices, then?'

'Dangerous ground. If you want to talk about my vices, I've got others I can describe to you.'

'Oh please. I'll pass.' She was laughing.

He said, 'You look nice when you're not being pompous.'

Kate looked startled. 'Thank you. I think.'

Wellington, tired of being ignored, pushed his nose into her hand and she bent to stroke him. 'Hello, Wellington. Don't you look gorgeous in this sunshine? Your coat's gleaming. You're a lovely boy.' Wellington's tail redoubled its wag. She straightened up, but kept stroking Wellington's insistent head. 'Listen, I wanted to talk to you. I've had an idea.'

Ibsen raised one eyebrow. 'Another wind farm?'

'One is enough for round here, I'm sure you'll agree. No. A garden.'

That *did* surprise him. 'What, round the bottom of the turbines? Forget-me-nots, perhaps?'

She ignored the sarcasm. 'In Summerfield, next to the primary school.'

Surprise jolted him out of defensiveness. 'That bit of waste land? I thought it belonged to the council?'

'It does in a manner of speaking. Actually, the land is part of the ground that the school is built on. It never got developed, just got overlooked somehow.'

'Why do you want to make it into a garden?'

'Everyone can get involved, see?' Her hands were moving expressively. He watched them, half mesmerised. She really could be engaging when she got caught up by her enthusiasms. 'The kids can be included in the decision making, it'll help parents and grandparents do things with their children, it can be a beautiful place, for sitting, and

122

listening and learning. Getting to know where food comes from. I've got lots of ideas.'

'Right.' He planted his feet squarely on the pavement and crossed his arms. 'And you mention it to me because—?'

'I'd like you to be on the committee.'

Ibsen threw back his head and laughed out loud. 'Committee? Me? You've got me all wrong, Mrs Courtenay—'

'Kate. Remember? Spiky and short.'

'I'm no committee man.' His ponytail swayed as he shook his head. 'I hate meetings. It's all I can do to go to the Skittles Club meeting once a year down at The Crossed Keys.'

'You were at the Community Council meeting.'

'I wanted to hear what possible justification your lot could give for the bloody ugly mess you're going to make of the countryside round here.'

'Don't swear,' Kate said, then looked up at him swiftly from under her lashes. God, she had terrific eyes. 'Sorry. Habit. I've got a teenage son. Anyway, it's not about the committee, I'm not explaining this well. Of course, there will be decisions to make, but what I really want is for you to head up the volunteers and help with designing the garden. Getting it up and running. There's going to be a lot of work.'

'*You* want me? Dare I ask – what has the waste land at Summerfield Primary got to do with you?'

'If the school likes the idea, and I think they do, the first thing will be to get some money in place. And once it gets going, the Summerfield Wind Farm Community Fund will be able to help.'

He could feel his face tighten.

'Assuming the wind farm is given the go-ahead, of course,' she qualified, seeing his expression. 'But in any case, the garden is still a great idea. If the money doesn't

123

come from the Fund, then we'll have to raise it another way, because it *is* a fantastic project, don't you think?'

'I think you're being manipulative, Kate.'

'No! I asked you because I knew you'd be good. I just—'

There was a whimper from the pram. 'I've got to go. Madam needs attention.'

'Think about it?'

'Maybe. Here, Wellington.' He turned away and started to walk. The dog gave Kate one backwards glance as he followed obediently.

'How can I contact you?' she called after him.

'I'll be in The Crossed Keys in Summerfield on Friday night.'

'And you'll give me an answer then?'

'You'll have to come and see, won't you?' he said over his shoulder.

'Okay! I will,' she called after him. 'And I'll bring a ribbon for your hair.'

She wasn't lacking in spirit, he had to give her that. Maybe it was just what he needed – a shot of pure adrenalin to jolt his heart into beating with excitement.

Besides, Wellington liked her.

Tam and Betty's modest kitchen was the hub of family life. Ibsen grew up in this cottage. He learned to make scones and pies here with his mother, and spent hours dropping batter off the end of a spoon onto the hot girdle, then flipping the small Scotch pancakes over when bubbles rose to the surface. He remembered running in, aged five, covered in mud but triumphant with the first carrots of the season ready for scrubbing and chopping. Once, he'd covered the entire table with strawberries and counted them – one hundred and sixty four. On winter evenings, when supper was over, homework finished and the chores done, they'd all gathered here to play ludo, or

Monopoly or happy families. And here, with the smell of Betty's rhubarb crumble still in the air, they'd argue over football, or the best way to deal with the economy, or the state of farming. And it was here that he fell apart after Violet died, and where he was slowly glued back together again, the cracks and breaks in his soul disguised just as his mother would conceal the flaws in a cake with butter icing.

Tam poured two beers and sat at the kitchen table with Ibsen while Betty, happy in her domain, fussed around them preparing supper. Wellington lay in the dog bed that was kept there for him and snuffled gently.

'Everything all right with Daisy Rose today then?' Betty asked, knowing the answer.

'You mean, did I cope? Yes, I did. I thought I might have to tie the nappy on with string, but I just about managed.'

Betty laughed. 'It's great to see Cass so happy, isn't it?'

'Yes.'

He didn't mean it to sound curt, but his mother picked up on his tone at once. 'Oh lovey, I didn't mean ... I know it must be hard for you.'

'Not really. It's a long time ago, Ma.'

He had to lie to her because otherwise she'd never stop fussing. Best to change the subject. 'Frank Griffiths was on about this wind farm again today, Pa. Says they're a waste of space, these companies just build them because the government's giving out big subsidies.'

'Is that right?'

'Here you go,' Betty interrupted, setting down steaming plates of shepherd's pie and veg. Betty Brown's shepherd's pie was the best in Summerfield or anywhere for miles around, so silence fell for some minutes as they all tucked in.

'And they kill birds,' Ibsen added eventually, laying down his fork to draw breath.

'And where does he get all his facts from?' Tam Brown was a stockier, more weather-beaten version of his son. He'd left school at fifteen to learn his gardening at his own father's knee, but he was a keen reader and had a questing intelligence.

Ibsen shrugged. 'I didn't ask, but he seemed to know what he was talking about.'

'Have you checked it out?'

'Give me a break, Pa, I only just got back.'

Betty said, 'Tam, you know why Summerfield's so important to the boy.'

Tam looked at Ibsen levelly. 'I know. But the wee lass isn't there any more, she's gone back to the earth long since, and the wind farm's a thing for the future.'

'We don't have to let it happen,' Ibsen said, his voice harsh.

'If you're going to be one of the protesters, son, I should warn you I'll be on the other side.'

'You're kidding!'

'From where I sit they're good on a lot of levels. Renewable means just that, remember. There's always more where it comes from.'

'But—'

'The Forgie lot won't like it, I can see that. They'll think it'll bring down their property prices, I dare say. But look at it this way, there'll be a lot of jobs. Maybe not for the posh folk so much, but for people like Davey Fegan, down the pub, the construction workers. There'll be lots of folk needing to stay locally while it's being built. The caff'll be hard pressed to make enough rolls in the mornings and the pub'll have to get in a lot more beer.'

'And what about the damage they do to the environment? Killing birds. Noise. Ugliness. And for what? Not a lot, according to Frank. And don't forget, we'll be able to see them from here.'

'That's the worst argument I've heard yet.'

'Now now, you two.' Betty got up to clear away the plates. 'I won't have arguing round the table.'

'There'll be a lot more arguing before this wind farm thing's settled, I suspect,' Tam said dryly. 'And not just round this table either.'

'The woman in charge of the thing, Kate Courtenay—'

'A *woman* in charge?'

'Five foot three of chutzpah, thinks she knows everything.'

'If she's in charge, I daresay she does know a great deal.'

Attraction was one thing, opposition to the wind farm quite another. 'She knows what she wants to know and conveniently sets aside the things that don't fit with her grand plan.'

'Or maybe you're just not listening.'

'You're an obstinate old bugger, aren't you?'

'And you need to face facts.'

'Stop it you two.' Betty intervened. A lifetime of living with these males had forced her into the role of peacemaker, which she undertook with gusto. 'Time out.'

There was silence. Tam reached into his pocket and pulled out a pipe and a tin of tobacco. He opened the tin, pulled out a reamer and cleaned the bowl of the pipe, then packed it with fresh tobacco and tamped it down. Ibsen watched the ritual, his growing agitation calmed by the familiarity of it.

He said, 'Anyway, I was about to tell you, this woman, Kate – she's asked me to help out with a community garden they're planning, on that old bit of waste land next the school.'

Tam grunted. 'Wondered when someone would finally think about something like that. You'll do it?'

'I dunno. It'd be like sleeping with the enemy—' Ibsen broke off, startled by the train of thought the stock phrase set in motion.

127

'John Stuart Mill,' Tam said.

'What?'

'Father of Utilitarianism. If it promotes happiness and reduces suffering, then it's for the greater good. Do it.'

Ibsen rolled his eyes to the ceiling and shook his head at his mother. 'Trust you to turn a simple decision into a philosophical argument.'

'You've got it wrong. The philosophical argument informs the decision.'

Wellington gave a low growl and twitched. 'Chasing rabbits again,' Ibsen grinned.

'The garden?' said Tam.

'Jesus, Pa, if it stops you nagging I'll do it,' Ibsen groaned. 'Anything for a quiet life.'

But he had a feeling that if he took on the project, his life would be anything but quiet

Chapter Fourteen

Andrew ladled spaghetti into bowls and handed them to Ninian and Kate.

'Thanks.' Kate slopped the pasta round her bowl without interest. 'Andrew—'

'Yes?'

'I thought I'd take you for a drink before supper on Saturday, maybe somewhere in town for a change? Malmaison? If it's nice we can sit outside. Harry and Jane can join us, then we can all come back here to eat.'

'I'm going to be in Elgin.'

'In *Elgin*? On your birthday?' Elgin was in the north of Scotland, a hundred and forty miles from Forgie.

'I've made an arrangement to see the abbot at Pluscarden Abbey.'

'You've had the call? Surely the visit could wait a few days.'

'It's all arranged,' Andrew said with finality.

Ninian stared at his father, then at his mother, then mumbled, 'Oh fuck,' but as neither of his parents told him off, he blew out his cheeks, then carried on shovelling spaghetti into his mouth. Growth requires nourishment.

'But we always have a birthday dinner.' Birthdays were important to Kate. Andrew spent his first birthday after they'd met with his family and her memories of loneliness and anxiety still lingered.

'Sorry.'

'Brilliant,' Ninian muttered. 'Just fucking brilliant.'

'Don't swear, Ninian. When were you planning on going?'

129

'In the morning.'

'Just for the day?'

'A couple of days.'

Kate felt unease well in her stomach and pool there. This was unlike Andrew. Research, yes, but to be away on such a special day? Family had always been important to him. There *was* something going on, there had to be. 'Well at least shift it, Andrew, so that you're back by the evening. Your family wants to see you. Dinner's important.'

'*My* dinner was important.'

'Oh for Christ's sake.' She spat it out between gritted teeth. Ninian tossed his fork into an empty bowl, then stood up and walked out. 'You're punishing me – all of us – because I had to go out that night?'

Andrew met her stare defiantly, his jaw set and hard. Then his eyes flickered and he dropped his gaze. 'If it means so much to you, Kate, I'll try to go the day before and make sure I'm back in time for dinner. All right?'

It was a victory, but it didn't feel much like one.

Kate hadn't forgotten about meeting Ibsen Brown and, as Andrew was away, an evening at The Crossed Keys would fit in very nicely. She scanned her wardrobe. What was appropriate? She had never been in the pub in Summerfield. She settled on skinny jeans and heels, teamed with a crisp white shirt and a vintage silk crepe scarf festooned with a riot of pansies. Casual but comfortable, nothing too expensive, flowers for a gardener. Before she left, she tried Andrew's mobile.

'*Andrew Courtenay, sorry I'm unavailable, please leave a message.*'

He would have it switched off, of course, he was in an Abbey. There was probably a rule of silence or something. She imagined stillness and the sun slanting through stained glass windows onto old stone, and Gregorian chanting. A 'no mobile phone' rule made sense, but she left a message anyway. Hopefully he'd pick it up at some point.

'Hi it's me. Just wanted to know you're safe. Call me when you can.' After a second she added, 'Love you.'

There'd been another time when he'd been unable to call her: when he'd still been with Val. Then there'd been months of furtive conversations during manufactured tasks – 'I'm putting the bins out...' or 'I've just dashed out to get some milk...'. There'd been rushed arrangements, frantic declarations of love, assurances that it would all be sorted soon. Kate had hated that period. Duplicity was not in her nature. That first birthday, she'd still been trying to come to terms with what had happened, but not being with Andrew was not an option. It wasn't just lust – though she'd never experienced such overwhelming desire. He was disarmingly romantic. In those early weeks, he'd sent flowers every day, so that her flat was filled with the heavy scent of lilies and roses. He was staunch through the nightmare of her boyfriend's acrimonious departure, when, almost constantly in tears, she'd felt herself drowning in guilt.

She remembered saying to Andrew, 'We should celebrate your birthday,' and the shadow that had crossed his eyes. Birthday meant family, which meant that Andrew would be celebrating with them and she'd be here, alone.

'I want to be with you always,' Andrew had assured her, 'I just need to find the right moment to tell Val.'

'Oh.'

I need the right moment to tell Val. Could she believe him? Charlotte, surprisingly judgmental about her affair with a married man, told Kate in no uncertain terms that he was just toying with her.

'Men like that never leave their wives, whatever they say,' she told Kate brutally. 'Don't waste your life on him, Kate.'

'Men like what?' she said, surprised by Charlotte's

vehemence.

'He's just a womaniser, believe me.'

She didn't believe Charlotte, of course. And she did see Andrew on his birthday. He'd found time, an hour snatched on some flimsy excuse, to come round to the flat and she'd fed him on fruit and cheese and cake and they'd made love. She bought champagne – not Cava, she'd splashed out, even though she wasn't earning much – but found when he poured her a glass that she couldn't drink it.

'Val was like that when she got pregnant,' Andrew had remarked casually, and they'd looked at each other, both suddenly horrified by the possibility, for different reasons.

Andrew had been forty-one. She'd been twenty-two. And yes, she had been pregnant.

In some situations, Kate was fearless. She didn't mind dealing with spiders or mice. She could climb an eighty-metre high wind turbine without feeling giddy. She could face an angry group of protesters and challenge prejudice with explanation. For some reason, though, as she strode to the front door of The Crossed Keys, she was forced to admit to herself that she was edgy about seeing Ibsen Brown again. He was so damned attractive.

Silly. He's married, and a father.

The pub was an old one and sat in the middle of an array of miserable-looking Council-built houses. Many had front gardens filled with rubbish or paved over, others had boarded-up windows. There was graffiti on some walls and an array of satellite dishes. The contrast with Forgie could hardly have been greater. Still, there was no pub in Forgie. At least Summerfield had a lively hub.

She put her shoulders back and her chin up, and pushed the door open.

There was upholstered seating round the edge of the room, with low bar stools scattered by dark-stained tables.

132

The bar itself gleamed. The brass rail running round it was supported by a dozen glorious brass elephant heads, their trunks curled to form the ring that held the rail. Curious, she forgot her nervousness and crossed the threshold to look.

'Hi, Kate.'

'Hi.' Ibsen's smile blew away her unexpected shyness. It was the first time she'd seen him wearing a shirt, rather than a tee shirt. It was pale lapis, exactly the colour of his eyes, and the sleeves were rolled up to his elbows, showing tattoos. 'Poppy' and 'Hebe'. Old girlfriends? His mother and grandmother? Or maybe he just liked flowers.

'What's yours?'

He was waving a wad of notes and looking at her inquiringly.

'I'd love a gin and tonic, but I should be—'

'My treat. Here—'

He pulled a high bar stool out for her and she clambered onto it, feeling precarious.

'Nora!'

The Keys' barmaid had hair the exact colour of the elephant brasses. She turned and smiled. Her lips, carelessly splashed with scarlet, parted to reveal a tooth smeared in matching red.

'C'me here, Nora darling.' Ibsen beckoned the barmaid towards him, then levered himself across the bar on strongly muscled arms. He reached out his right hand and used his finger to wipe the lipstick smudge off her tooth. It was an oddly tender gesture for such an obviously strong man. 'There. Beautiful again,' he said, and kissed her cheek with a luscious and noisy smack of his lips, which were full, and restlessly mobile, and arched like angel's wings.

Nora fluttered a hand. 'Get away with you, Ibsen Brown,' she said, blushing.

'The lady would like a gin and tonic. And a coke for

133

me, soon as you like.'

'Coming right up.'

She said, making conversation, 'Where's Wellington?'

'My parents have got him this evening.'

'As well as the baby?'

The barmaid set down the drinks. 'Ibsen's been a rock for that sister of his.'

'I'm sorry?'

'Cassie. Ibsen's sister.'

'I don't—'

'Cassie Grant,' Nora explained patiently. 'She couldn't have done without Ibsen when her old man was away on the rigs. Not after getting pre eclampsia and being rushed in, and the baby being so poorly.'

Comprehension dawned. She swung round to Ibsen. 'Oh! The baby isn't yours?'

He'd clearly been bottling up his amusement. His smile erupted into a belly laugh. 'I was just lending a hand.'

'Oh. I see.'

'Cassie had to go see the quack. The best thing about being an uncle is you can hand the infant back.'

'Yes. I guess you're right.'

'Don't you take any notice of him,' Nora said. 'Ibsen's crazy about little Daisy Rose. Can't stay away from her.'

'Thank you, Nora,' he said sternly. 'Davey Fegan wants a pint.' He waved along the bar to where a puffy-faced man in jeans and a hooded sweatshirt was brandishing a note and trying to catch Nora's attention. 'She thinks I'm a softie,' he said to Kate.

'Well? Are you?'

'Do you think I am?'

She thought of the meeting in the village hall. 'I don't think... Hmm. Not always, certainly.'

'Hey Ibsen.' The man he'd called Davey passed by, two foaming pints clutched in large fists. 'Melanie'll kill you.'

'I'll survive,' Ibsen said cheerfully.

Kate raised an eyebrow.

'Melanie McGillivray. The girl you met on the Summerfield Law. I expect she'll drop by later.'

'With a gun?'

'Looks can kill. Davey thinks she'll be jealous.'

'Of *me?*'

The twinkle in his eyes turned into something altogether more intense. 'Why not?' he said softly.

She jerked away, flushing. 'I should go,' she heard herself saying. Go? Go why? Because he was teasing her and she was rather enjoying it? Or because he had got a girlfriend with deadly eyes? Or – the thought did flit across Kate's mind – because *she* was married and had a husband, who was currently in an Abbey?

'Go? You've just come.'

'I—' This was ridiculous. She'd come for an answer about the garden and she was going to make sure she got it. 'About the garden—'

'Ah yes.' He picked up his glass and took a long draught of the dark brown liquid. 'The land by the Primary School.'

'Have you given it any thought?'

'I seem to remember saying I'd give you an answer tonight.'

'Well?'

Kate tried to soften her impatience with a smile. Then she worried that the effect was too encouraging – on a personal level – so she tucked away the smile and tried to soften her expression to one of quiet expectancy. This was ridiculous. When had she last felt so self-conscious?

'Is there anything else you'd like to know? I mean, have you made a decision or do you need more information?'

Ibsen looked thoughtful. He scratched his hair. She remembered her comment about a ribbon and realised she

135

hadn't brought one as she'd threatened. He turned his face to the bar for a second and she saw a dull gleam at the back of his head.

'Wait.'

She reached out and grasped his arm, then turned his head, firmly, further away from her so that she could see his ponytail properly. What was securing his hair? It was black and satiny, and wrapped round and round, and it was knotted, not tied in a bow – but it was, very distinctly, a ribbon. She laughed out loud. 'I don't believe it!'

His lips were twitching. 'I couldn't trust you not to bring pink. Or something sparkly.'

She still had her fingers on his hair when a voice said, 'And a very good evening to you, too.'

She dropped her hand. Melanie was standing behind Ibsen, glaring at her. Her auburn hair was gleaming and thick and a miniscule dress in electric blue slithered across her hips, revealing a sensational figure – but her heavy eyebrows were knotted and the glare of the emerald green eyes was drilling into Kate's skull.

'And hi to you too, Mel.' The amused look on Ibsen's face hadn't changed, but something in his eyes had. The twinkle had gone.

Melanie slid an arm round Ibsen's waist possessively then deliberately turned her back on Kate so that she almost obscured Ibsen. 'Mine's a peach schnapps and orange juice, Ibs, ta.'

He moved her gently to one side, but gestured to Nora and ordered the drink. 'And another gin and tonic for Kate please, Nora.'

'Is *she* staying?' The sulky voice rose in disbelief.

Kate slipped off the bar stool and reached for her handbag. There was absolutely no reason why she should stay here and suffer this kind of rudeness. 'I see you're busy, Ibsen. We can discuss the garden another time.'

Ibsen said levelly, 'No need. Mel, here's your drink, be

136

a doll and go talk to Sonja for ten minutes, okay? I'm talking business.'

Kate had entered foreign territory in more ways than one. First, she was in Summerfield, second, she was in The Crossed Keys, and third, she was alone in a strange pub. She had no wish to add to all this by entering into some weird contest, with unclear rules, over Ibsen Brown. For a few seconds she hesitated, while Melanie scowled at her. Then there was a toss of red hair and a glare – *if looks could kill* – and she shrugged and moved off, clutching her drink.

'You should have told me. I don't mean to spoil anyone's evening.'

'Mel likes to be the centre of attention.'

Kate grasped a brass elephant head and levered herself back onto the stool with some reluctance. 'If you're sure. I won't stay long anyway. I promised I'd do something about this garden, that's all.'

Ibsen's glass was empty and she realised he hadn't order a refill for himself. 'Can I get you another?'

'No thanks.' He pushed the glass away. 'Thanks anyway. So. Tell me more.'

'It doesn't just need clearing, it needs a lot of planning and organising too. It needs expertise.' She outlined her thoughts.

'Ambitious.'

'Yes, but something great, at the heart of this community.' She looked squarely at him and issued a direct challenge. 'Are you up for it? Or is it too difficult a project for you?'

It was a trick question, of course. She expected either a speedy denial (and therefore, by implication, acceptance of the role), or a simple refusal to rise to the bait ('Thanks for thinking of me, but I really don't have time').

Ibsen saw through it immediately. He laughed. 'You're being manipulative again.'

137

'How?'

'I suspect you're trying to buy off my opposition to the wind farm. It won't work. I'll always hate that.'

'You're wrong. Ibsen, I know some people will always hate wind farms and I'm sorry you're one of them. I happen to believe in them myself, but surely we can accept we're on different sides over that, but still work together on the garden? That's all I'm asking.'

'You don't expect me to stop campaigning against the Summerfield project?'

She shook her head. 'Only if I can find a way of persuading you otherwise. But this project needs you. You have expertise and I suspect you'd work well with young people and volunteers.'

'You don't know me very well. I can get very irritated with idiots and I suspect managing volunteers would require a lot of patience. I might seem sociable, but at heart, I'm quite a solitary person.'

That came as a surprise – she hadn't seen him that way. 'You don't have to be there all the time. There'll be other helpers. At least say you'll do the overall planning.'

Melanie appeared, her glass empty. Ten minutes were up and her reappearance was prompt. She'd been timing it.

'I thought this evening was about me,' she said truculently. 'Not her.'

'Be with you in a few minutes, love.' He turned back to Kate. 'It sounds like a lot of work. There's no cash involved, I take it.'

'All voluntary – but I'm sure you'll find it'll be very rewarding.'

'Christ, Ibsen,' Melanie interrupted, 'What's this all about? You've got enough work without doin' more for free.'

He put an arm round her waist and pulled her close, which shut her up for a moment. Ibsen's blue eyes met Kate's black ones. He said, 'You're very persuasive.'

138

This time Kate did slip off her stool with finality. 'That's part of my job. I take it that's an agreement. Thank you Ibsen. You won't regret it.'

She held out her hand to shake farewell but he released Melanie and took her by each shoulder, kissing first one cheek, then the other. All the breath seemed to leave Kate's body.

'It's on one condition,' Ibsen said, grinning.

'Yes?' she gasped, trying to breathe again.

'That you are one of the volunteers.'

'Gardening? Me?'

The amused glint was back in his eye.

'It's a non-negotiable condition.'

'Well, what can I say then? Thanks for the drink. Bye Melanie, nice meeting you.'

Seeing that she was finally leaving, Melanie allowed herself to relax.

She had a pretty face when she smiled.

Chapter Fifteen

Kate and Ninian arrived at the Malmaison Hotel at exactly the same moment as Harry and Jane. It was an evening of rare beauty. There was no breeze to ruffle the surface of the Water of Leith, which flowed past the hotel into the nearby docks, and the sun was still high enough in the sky to spread a golden glow over the steel tables set outside.

'This is lucky!' Kate called, smiling.

Harry was in an expansive mood. 'There's a table, look, in the sun. Let's have champagne, will we? On me.'

He was thirty-eight: still a year older than Kate. For years, though, she had thought of him as middle aged, possibly because there had always been something a bit pompous about him. Jane had changed everything – he looked younger these days, more relaxed, much happier. She had a sureness of touch that Kate couldn't help but admire. She took trouble with her appearance, but the results were always pleasingly understated. She thought of Melanie, Ibsen Brown's girlfriend, who was equally pretty, maybe more striking. Jane, wearing a graceful flowing silk crepe dress in tones of gray and dark purple, looked subtle and sophisticated. Mel's dress had clearly been chosen to emphasise her best features – long legs and a great figure – but in revealing them too much, all sense of mystery had been lost. Jane was like a gift that was intended to be carefully unwrapped, but in private, while Melanie's message smacked of desperation. In a flash of insight, Kate understood – Melanie feared Ibsen wouldn't notice her. Her lips tightened. Poor girl.

Ninian said, 'Shouldn't Dad be here by now?'

141

Kate checked her watch. They'd agreed seven o'clock but already it was a quarter past and the table was booked for seven thirty. 'He must have been held up somewhere. I'll call him.'

She dialled his mobile, but it was switched off. 'Tch! He must be driving.'

'What are we going to do, Mum? Told you this was a crap idea.'

'It's not a crap idea, Ninian.' Kate had an unexpected ally in Harry, who turned to Jane. 'We're looking forward to it, aren't we, darling?'

'Maybe he'll just head home, knowing he's late,' Ninian contributed. 'Then we'll be stuck here, and he'll be stuck at home, alone.'

'Oh surely he won't?' The possibility hadn't occurred to Kate, but as she spoke, her mobile rang. 'It's Dad,' she said, relieved. 'Hello? Where are you? ... No – no, don't do that. ... Well because—' she hesitated, looked round the silent faces turned in her direction, and grimaced. She'd have to come clean. 'We're all here. ... Why? Because I'd planned a surprise. I've booked a table for us all, we're not eating at home.'

She covered the phone with her hand and hissed, 'He's heading for home.'

'Think we got that, Mum,' Ninian growled.

'Well, you'll just have to turn around and come back here. ... As soon as you can. How long will you be?' She covered the phone again and whispered, 'He's going to be another half hour. What'll I do?'

Harry said, 'Just tell him we'll see him at Martin Wishart's.'

She made an exasperated face, but bowed to the inevitable. 'We're eating at Martin Wishart's. We'll just head there now and get settled. Join us just as soon as you can, love. Yes. Yes. Okay. Bye.'

'Some surprise.'

'Stop moaning, Ninian,' Harry said, 'These things happen. Let's go. Dad'll be with us by the time we've got our first drink lined up.'

Martin Wishart's was a five-minute walk from the Malmaison. This part of town was filled with graphic design firms and television production companies, event management outfits and marketing consultancies – a generally young working population. Over the past decade business had responded to demand and it had become trendy, with good restaurants and popular wine bars. Martin Wishart's, where they were headed, was one of Edinburgh's Michelin-starred establishments.

Kate, her senses sharpened by anxiety, saw Harry expand as he stepped in the door. She smiled, recognising the reason. The place reflected his image of himself – comfortably off and absolutely at home in such surroundings. Ninian's shoulders, she noted with apprehension, were lifted and his head was down. The old self-consciousness was back. This restaurant was too formal, too quiet, too adult for Ninian. She should have considered that before booking – perhaps if he'd talked to her instead of ducking the issue, they might have settled on a compromise location. Impossible to please all her family, she should just be glad he'd come. Hopefully, he'd be happy when the food arrived.

'Well. Here we are,' she said with forced brightness as the waiter took her jacket and pulled out a chair. She sank into it. From here she could see the road outside. Harry and Jane slid round the far side, while Ninian slithered down beside her, leaving a space for Andrew at the head of the table.

'We've set a date for the wedding,' Harry said, picking up the menu.

'Really? Fantastic. When is it to be?'

It was Jane's moment and she stepped happily into the

light. 'Next April. We've booked St Andrew's in Hailesbank and the reception at Fleming House. They've got a fabulous ballroom there, Sir Andrew showed us round, they've been upgrading the—'

Kate smiled and nodded and was genuinely interested, but at the same time she was wondering how long Andrew would be and whether this dinner had been a good idea at all or not. Ninian was fidgeting with the menu and his expression made his view of the forthcoming wedding absolutely clear. A car drew up on the far side of the road. Andrew's, surely? She saw his profile clearly as he parked, neatly, then turned off the ignition. She was about to say, 'He's here!' but closed her mouth, puzzled. Why wasn't he getting out?

There was another figure in the car. She glimpsed pink and purple, a long white neck and a pale profile. Kate's hand flew up to her chest and she forgot that breathing was essential to existence. Andrew leaned away from her. It looked as if he was kissing the woman, who climbed out, flagged a taxi, hopped in and disappeared before Kate could properly identify her. Andrew emerged, clicked his key fob and she saw the sidelights on his car flash orange as the car locked. He stood for a minute, looking up at the sign above the restaurant as though to check he was in the right place, then walked briskly towards the door.

Kate swallowed.

She couldn't be certain, but she was pretty sure that the woman had been Jane's young cousin, Sophie MacAteer.

Ninian had seen it too. He turned his head and looked at her, his expression a complex mixture of panic, disgust, alarm and hatred. Quickly, Kate got a grip of her own feelings. She was not going to let this evening be spoilt by this. Her worst nightmare might be coming true, but her strategy was in place. *Keep the family together, remind him of what he has to lose.* Whatever happened because of this, it had to be later, and in private.

'It's not what you think, Ninian,' she said softly, briskly dismissive of the hurt in her heart. 'Go and meet Dad, please, show him where we're sitting. '

For a few seconds Ninian held her gaze, his dark eyes, so like Andrew's own, a blaze of fury. Despite her best efforts, her mouth trembled and for a horrified moment she thought she might cry. Just as she was about to plead with him, Ninian pushed back his chair. 'I'll fetch him,' he said, his voice raw.

Kate's instinct was to sink her head in her hands, but she had to hold it high, put a smile on her face, pretend that everything was fine. The evidence suggested that Andrew had betrayed her, and in the most outrageous way possible, but this was not the place for a showdown. Her mouth felt dry and she tried to swallow. A muscle in her cheek vibrated and she put a hand up to cover the telltale tic.

'Surprise!' Jane called cheerfully as Andrew strode towards them. 'Not. Anyway, happy birthday, Andrew.'

'Hello everyone, so sorry I'm late. Traffic. I thought I'd head straight for home, but it seems I was outmanoeuvered.' He said it with a smile so relaxed that Kate wondered if he had been practising it. In the car, perhaps. With Sophie? *Is this right? A little wider?* Did she say, *Think of me when you smile.* Or perhaps he didn't need to be told to do that. She looked at the smile again. Was it the smile of a cat with a bowl of cream? She imagined him lapping and licking and her growing tension triggered a surge of nausea. She inhaled sharply. She had to control her fears.

'Hi Dad. Happy Birthday.'

The greetings were effusive, gifts were exchanged, champagne was sipped, toasts made. To all outward appearances, Kate was as bright as anyone. Only Ninian was sombre and uncommunicative, but whatever he was thinking or feeling, it didn't seem to affect his appetite.

145

Kate's own hunger, by contrast, had disappeared almost completely. She toyed with the delicious food, but drank more than normal. She asked herself a hundred different questions in an effort to circumvent the one, inevitable conclusion. Why had Sophie been in the car with him? Surely he hadn't taken her to Pluscarden Abbey? It was unthinkable. Had he even gone to the Abbey? Had his phone been switched off because he was in bed with *her* in some hotel room? Had he – appalling thought – *meant* her to see Sophie? Why else drop her off right in front of the restaurant? If he had meant her to see the girl, what was his intention?

So many unanswered questions. So many questions Andrew would have to answer – but later.

Ninian was silent in the car home – they were all silent – but as soon as they get through the door, he said '*Mum,*' in a low, urgent voice.

Andrew was putting the car in the garage and they had perhaps thirty seconds. She laid a hand on his arm. 'I'll deal with this, Ninian. It's all right.'

'But there's something you need to know.'

'There's nothing to worry about. Go to bed. We'll talk tomorrow.'

'I saw—'

'Ninian, I will talk to your father.'

He swung round and glared angrily at her. 'No. Listen. I saw them snogging.'

'What?'

'Dad and Sophie. At Harry's engagement party. Why do you think I threw up?'

'Too much drink,' Kate said, but her eyes were wide with shock.

'Give me a break. And after the book launch, he went to dinner with her. Alone.'

Andrew was inside the front door now. He was locking

it. In a second he would be in the kitchen. 'Go to bed,' Kate said quickly. 'Everything will be all right, I promise.'

It was not fair. Whatever Andrew was up to, it should not impact on Ninian. The anger Kate had been struggling to control all evening was so near the surface that she was frightened. To hide it, she reached forward and hugged her son. For a second there was resistance, then he hugged her back and she sensed his need for reassurance. When he shot out of the door, he narrowly avoided Andrew, who was coming in.

'Whoa there! What's the hurry?'

Ninian mumbled something unintelligible and raced up the stairs. Kate heard his door slam shut. She closed the kitchen door, then braced herself against its cool surface and turned to face her husband. She noticed little change from the Andrew he'd been when they'd met. A few gray hairs, some more lines on his face, but he still wore his quiet assuredness like a velvet jacket, softly. He still had – she supposed – the sensitivity and awareness that made him such a good writer. Why, then, was he being so profoundly insensitive to *her* feelings? And to their son's?

'What's up with Ninian?'

'I think you know.'

'Know? Know what?'

'Ninian is convinced you're having an affair with Sophie MacAteer.'

'Soph— who? Oh, you mean that cousin of Jane's? The musician?' His tone was offhand, as though Sophie was of no consequence at all – but then, why pretend he didn't know who she meant?

'Come on, Andrew. I'd appreciate it if you would tell me what in hell's name you were playing at.'

He looked startled at the barely-controlled acrimony in her tone. 'I'm sorry I was late, Kate. If you'd told me your plans in the first place, it would have been easier.'

His strategy infuriated her. 'Oh no, don't you turn your

failings back on me.'

'I made a huge effort to change my arrangements and get back as you'd requested.'

'You didn't need to go to Pluscarden on your birthday at all! You could easily have put it off for a week. Or wouldn't that have fitted in with Sophie's plans?'

'Sophie? What is all this about Sophie, for goodness' sake? What has Ninian been saying?'

'He saw you snogging at Harry's party.'

Andrew laughed, the sound so natural it was hard to believe he was play-acting. 'Ninian's like me, darling. He has a vivid imagination.'

'He was so shocked he threw up.' The scene came flooding back to her. She'd been so concerned with dealing with the Abercrombie Club's plush carpet, and so embarrassed about her young son's state of inebriation, that she'd forgotten what had happened next. Now, though, she saw it all again with perfect clarity. 'You were out on the balcony,' she said accusingly. 'You and Sophie. You came rushing in when he was sick. I remember now.'

'I'd been talking to her on the balcony, yes,' Andrew said defensively.

'So Ninian's not lying.'

'I was *talking* to her, that's all.'

'Ninian said you were kissing her.'

'I might,' he said, 'have given her a cuddle and a peck on the cheek. Her boyfriend had just left her and she was in floods of tears.'

'We're getting nearer the truth, I think.' Kate abandoned the security of the door and marched right across to where Andrew was standing. Her hands were on her hips and her head tilted up towards his, fury taking over from hurt.

'He's imagining things.'

'Really? What about tonight? I *saw* her. She was in the car with you.' Kate realised her impression had been right.

148

'Don't tell me I'm imagining things too. What the hell was that about? Taking your mistress away with you is bad enough, but flaunting her in front of me is just—' she stopped abruptly, unable to find a word that adequately conveyed the depth of her anger.

'Mistress? What on earth...?' He turned towards the back door. 'If you're going to be like this, I'm going to go out for a walk.'

'Oh no you don't.' Kate marched across the kitchen and stood between him and the door. 'I know you hate rows, Andrew, but you can't run away from this. I need answers. Actually, I *deserve* answers, don't you think? Why are you doing this to me? Don't you care about me any more?' Her look was steady, but inside she was a cauldron of raw emotion. Their relationship seemed to be balanced on the edge of a blade, so finely that one small nick might cause fatal bleeding. 'Have you stopped to think, for one minute, what your behaviour is going to do to our marriage?'

Andrew's expression changed from shadowed secrecy to defiance. 'Of course I care, Kate. But do you? You're never around. There's always something, isn't there? Some project at work that keeps you there all the hours or some emergency that we have to work around. You cancel our holidays, you let me down with my guests—'

'*Jesus*, Andrew, not that again! That's so unfair! I will absolutely not let you use that dinner as an excuse for you to go off and screw Sophie – because that's what I imagine this is all about. Isn't it? You have no excuse, Andrew, none at all, for betraying our marriage vows – for upsetting your *son*, for Christ's sake!'

'Sophie loves me,' he said, softly.

That stopped Kate short.

'And I love her,' he added, his chin jutting forwards.

The bubbling in her gut was not just the rich food she'd eaten this evening. The thought of Andrew's hands

149

caressing another woman's body was hideous. She imagined him winding his legs round young, white limbs and the nausea intensified – but all the same, this was not a game she intended to lose. She swallowed hard, fighting for self control.

'I don't believe you.' She stared at him as levelly as she could, forcing him to hold her gaze. 'You're playing out some middle-aged fantasy. Life isn't like that. Life isn't simple, or easy, or filled with lovey-dovey, commitment-free adoration, however pleasant that may seem.'

She gripped the back of a chair, the wood hard and rough under her fingers. 'It's about earning a living, about compromise, about taking the hard decisions that have to be taken every day about what priorities are and what has to be put second so that bills can be paid and children reared. And it's about thinking about someone else's needs as well as your own.'

'Don't preach at me, Kate. You haven't earned the right.'

'*Preach?*'

'And don't talk to me about children. I believe I know more about child rearing than you do.'

'*Fuck* that, Andrew! If you let your vanity ruin our marriage, I think a whole lot of school runs will be cancelled out, don't you? Have you thought about what you're doing to Ninian? He *saw* her tonight.'

Andrew pursed his lips. 'Oh.'

'Yes, oh. You need to talk to him. You need to give him some reassurance that the life he knows, the family he knows, is safe and sound and is not going to collapse around him. He's a teenager, for heaven's sake. He's probably at the most difficult, vulnerable age he can be. He needs a father, Andrew. He needs a role model, not some self-centred, deluded, narcissistic, cradle-snatching egomaniac who's off screwing some teenager—'

150

'Sophie is twenty eight.'

'And you're fifty-seven, for Christ's sake. Look at yourself!' She reached out and grabbed his arms. 'This has to stop, Andrew. Think about it. Please. Whatever you think has gone wrong between us, let's talk about it. We can work it out. Don't fall for whatever line it is Sophie is feeding you, because your family deserves better than that. Your first family and your second family.'

She could see his eyes flicker, then he looked down. She changed her line of attack to press home the advantage. '*I* love you, Andrew. I've loved you from the moment we met, in that café, remember?' Her smile was shaky, but she persevered. 'You changed my life. I was a young graduate, then suddenly, you were there and I became a stepmother and a mother and I had to deal with all that. But through it all, I have loved you, always loved you, more than anything in this world.'

He dragged one arm out of her grasp and wiped a hand tiredly across his face. 'Oh,' he said tiredly, 'Love —' as if thinking about the word exhausted him.

'Stop seeing her, Andrew. Please. Don't put Harry through the upheaval, *again*, that they went though after we met. And talk to Ninian. He needs reassurance.'

There was a pause. Her instinct was to fill it with words, but she had pleaded her cause, and played the family card, so she forced herself to let the silence lie.

He looked at her. His eyes were troubled, but he said, 'All right, Kate. You win.'

'You'll tell her you won't see her again?'

'I'll tell her.'

The relief was so intense that Kate had to sink onto a chair. 'Thank you, Andrew,' she said quietly. 'Thank you.'

In bed they hugged each other intensely, as though closeness could mend cracks. But they didn't make love.

151

Chapter Sixteen

By the beginning of July, the Met mast results were in and looked favourable. With the planning application about to be lodged, it was time to start the communication with locals rolling, and the first local exhibition about the Summerfield wind farm was in Forgie village hall.

'I'd rather it was in Hailesbank, ' Kate said to Gail, who was in charge of organising the schedule. 'Or even Summerfield, come to that.'

Gail, who was the most experienced person in Kate's team, was apologetic. 'It just wasn't possible, Kate, sorry. The hall in Hailesbank is booked out with all sorts of things for the next few weekends and there's a Summer Fair in Summerfield school, followed by a Scout Jumble Sale and a—'

'Okay, I get the picture. So we have to cut our teeth on Forgie, the hardest nut to crack. Or is that a mixed metaphor?'

Gail smiled. 'So long as we don't break our teeth I guess it'll be okay. Be positive, Kate, look at it this way – we get Forgie over with.'

'Hm. I'm not sure we're ever going to win Forgie over to the wind farm, but I guess it'll do us no harm to discover the worst about what we're up against. So – who's going to be on duty, will we have all the displays we need, and what do you need me to do?'

It was a week after Kate's run-in with Andrew and she was still feeling raw. True to his promise, Andrew had had a talk with Ninian, and reported back that he seemed reassured. She didn't believe that reassurance would come so easily. Ninian now spent most of the time in his bedroom, with the sound turned up high on his iPod speakers, or playing some game with his friends Banksy and Cuzz. Cuzzer was round at the house almost every day, a new trend that Kate found worrying. She was uneasy about her son's friendship with Steve Cousins and couldn't work out why Andrew wasn't.

Gail said, 'You don't need to come, Kate. I know it's difficult for you, living in the village.'

'Nice someone appreciates that. But I'll be fine. Mark put me in charge because he thought I'd have some influence locally.' She pulled a wry face – woman-to-woman, confidential. 'Of course I'll be there.'

She felt as though she was on trial, at home and at work. She thought of Andrew – *You're never here* – and, Jack snapping at her heels and desperate for her to trip up. She couldn't afford to make a slip in either place and she was beginning to feel the pressure.

'Great. That's good. I'm sure you will make a difference, you were terrific at the Community Council meeting. But we can get the exhibition up, just drop by whenever you want to.'

When reliable, hard-working Gail said, 'We'll get the exhibition up,' Kate knew she'd do exactly that, so by the time she got there on Saturday, still drained from the previous week's drama with Andrew, work was well under way.

'Is there an extension lead, anyone? This telly needs to be in this corner.'

'Can we get a small table from somewhere? I'd like to stack these leaflets on it.'

'Where's the best place for these pop-up banners?'

She stood in the centre of it all, happy to let Gail field the queries. It was nice not to be where the buck stopped, for once. Someone was missing though. She caught Gail as she strode past clutching a box full of leaflets. 'Where's

154

Jack? I thought he was coming today.'

'He's picking up the blueprints. He should be— ah, look, he's here.'

Right on cue, Jack Bailey strolled in. He couldn't have known Kate was there already, but he still had that slight air of arrogance that got under her skin. He stopped dead when he saw her, then smiled. Kate didn't much like that smile. She said, 'Hello, Jack. You've got the plans, I see.'

'Right here.'

'There's some Blu Tack on the table there, do you want to start getting them up on that wall?'

With everyone else buzzing around like bluebottles, Jack Bailey was as laid back as if he was about to sit down with a coffee and read the morning papers. 'Sure.'

He did what she asked though. Half an hour later, she checked the hall. 'Looking good. Video showing other wind farms. Pop-ups about AeGen, pop-ups about turbine technology. Fact sheets. Quizzes for the kids. Questionnaires. Outline plans for Summerfield. Great work, team.'

She finished up at the wall where Jack had stuck the plans. The first showed the possible location for twelve turbines. The second blueprint showed possible access routes. These were always a cause for concern because inevitably there was a lot of traffic during construction and people hated the noise and intrusion.

Something on the second plan jumped out at her at once. 'Jack? This isn't right.'

'What's that?'

'The route you've marked in red. This one here.' She stuck her finger on the red line.

Jack didn't miss a beat. 'It's by far the cheapest route.'

'Jack, I explained *exactly* why that route couldn't be used.' Out of the corner of her eye she was aware that the rest of her team had backed away discreetly, anticipating trouble. Jack Bailey's defiance was likely to cause a serious problem and already Kate's mind was leaping ahead to the possible consequences. 'I believe I was absolutely explicit, Jack,' she said, her tone changing from short-tempered to icy. Her regular staff knew her well enough to know this was not a good sign. Did Jack? 'This is not what I expect from members of my team.'

'It's bloody obvious, though, isn't it?' In another place, at another time, she would have dealt with this challenge to her authority peremptorily, but Jack had timed things perfectly because it was ten o'clock and the doors were already opening to admit the public.

'I'll speak to you about this later,' she hissed. 'In the meantime, you will please explain to everyone – and I mean *everyone* – who looks at that map that we will *not* be using that option for the access road.'

A trickle of visitors – easily handled – turned after half an hour into a stream and it became clear that the event was following a typical pattern. A third of people were mildly interested and open to persuasion, a third were reasonably or enthusiastically supportive and a third were completely against all wind farms and absolutely unwilling to examine the evidence. Frank Griffiths, as Kate had anticipated, led the onslaught.

'Good morning, Frank. How are you?'

'Kate, how lovely to see you,' He swept his arm round the exhibition. 'This all looks very professional.'

'Thanks. Would you like me to talk you through it?' Best to lead the bull by the horns, so to speak.

'Why not?'

For the next fifteen minutes, she watched video clips with him and balanced his comments with proven facts, again fielded his questions about noise and flicker, discussed lifetime costs and the carbon footprint of the manufacturing process, and the general question of unsightliness.

'You won't see them from Forgie,' she stressed, as she

had so often before.

'But you will from Summerfield. They'll rear up right behind Forgie House.'

'Not really, not even there. They'll be far enough back on the hill to be barely noticeable.'

'The drawings we've had done show quite the opposite.'

'Well I would have to query the perspectives and sizes your artist has been working to. In fact, you'll only see the top of the blades and once the re-landscaping has been done and the trees mature, I don't think that even they will be noticeable.'

'Our artist—'

Kate interrupted politely. 'If it helps, I could fix up a meeting with our technicians and landscapers. I'm sure we could reassure you.'

'Well, the Community Council would appreciate that.'

Was this the moment to bring up the matter of the silent phone calls?

Gail touched her arm.

'Sorry to interrupt, but there's someone here from *The Stoneyford Echo*. Could you maybe manage a few words?'

In the absence of a press officer, it was Kate's job to field media queries. Frank said obligingly, 'You go. I'll just finish looking round myself.'

'Fine. Thank you. Do come and find me afterwards if you have any more questions, won't you?'

She was finishing what felt like a good interview with an intelligent young reporter, when she heard angry voices from the far side of the hall. Frank was gesticulating at Jack Bailey and jabbing a furious finger at the plans. Her heart sank. The idiot had obviously ignored her orders. 'Excuse me a moment, will you?'

It was fifteen steps across the room and as she took the last few Frank's voice rose clearly above the hubbub. 'This road goes right through Bonny Brae Woods!'

'It is only one of the possible access roads,' she heard Jack saying, smoothly.

'Bonny Brae Woods is one of the few remnants of our ancient oak forest left! This can't possibly be allowed—'

She intervened in a calm voice. 'Actually, that route is shown there in error. There is no intention of putting the road through the Woods. We just didn't have time to get the plans reprinted.'

He swivelled round to face her. 'It's there because it's been thought about. I know how you lot operate. It's all smoke and mirrors. Let me tell you, Kate, this will—'

'I promise you, this is an error.'

Frank was not for calming. Kate guessed that he'd seen little to object to in the rest of the exhibition, so he was picking on this. Out of the corner of her eye, she saw that the reporter was still scribbling and she diverted her attention. 'This route is not on our agenda,' she said, as equably as she could. 'I would like you to make that clear in your article.'

'Oh, sure.'

Apprehension gripped Kate's chest, but there was little more she could say. She'd have to call AeGen's Press Manager to explain what had happened and hope that a direct plea to the editor would sort things out.

As soon as Frank and the reporter had gone, she turned to Jack. 'Take that plan down.'

'I did tell him—'

'Jack, you told him it was one of the possible access routes. I heard you myself. That was in direct contravention to my orders. I hate to think what damage this might have done. Take it down. Now.' She kept her voice low, because the hall was still full of visitors, but her glare could have felled an ox at thirty paces. 'You'll have to talk through access roads with anyone who specifically asks about them, and you will make it absolutely clear, but only if anyone asks, that there is no intention of going anywhere near Bonny Brae Woods. Understood?'

He shrugged in grudging acceptance and by the time she had crossed the hall to greet some of the Hailesbank Community Council members, who were just arriving, he had removed the plan.

The Stoneyford Echo came out on a Wednesday. This was Saturday. She had three days' grace.

Sunday was a day they usually tried to keep for family. Generally speaking, Kate liked Sundays. It was a day of rest, a day for reading the papers, eating together, relaxing. This Sunday, though, something else was on the agenda.

'I take it you are remembering that it's Forgie House Open Day today,' Andrew said. 'I promised the Nesbitts we'd go.'

He'd just emerged from the shower, pink and clean, his hair ruffled and damp. Kate had always been tempted to gather him close when he was like this – the softness of his newly washed skin turned her on. What once seemed so natural, though, had now become self-conscious and forced. By her reckoning they'd had sex just twice in recent weeks, and both times had been a fumble in the dark, not the kind of delighted romp that had always characterised their lovemaking.

She was still in bed, reading – but a thriller rather than papers from work, because she'd decided not to bring work to bed any more. 'I had remembered. Nice day for it. What time do you want to go?'

'About eleven?'

'Fine. I'll just finish this chapter then go and shower.'

There was a strain between them that had never been there before and she hated it. Andrew wasn't aggressive, nor overly loving, he wasn't even indifferent. He was obviously trying to be natural – but that was the problem. *He was having to try.* She bit her lip and turned a page, then glanced across to where Andrew was pulling on his

159

trousers, an action she'd seen several hundreds of times before. It was a mundane, everyday act, but she felt faintly embarrassed. The comfortable closeness they'd had for years was being nibbled away by the spectre of suspicion that now sat blackly on her shoulder. This was *Andrew*, for heaven's sake. She was irritated at herself for feeling uncomfortable, then she got mad that he'd been selfish enough to create this situation. Reading became impossible. She flung back the duvet and squirmed out of bed.

'Actually, I'll go now.'

'I'll have breakfast ready by the time you're dressed.'

'Thanks.' She said the word stiffly. How could this be happening?

Perhaps their life had become dull. Perhaps as Andrew seemed to imply, it was *her* fault for having a career instead of devoting all her attention to him. It was true that she was often out long hours. Perhaps she had been guilty of neglecting him. He had clearly found Sophie's obvious adoration flattering – but *love?* He couldn't be serious, could he?

Forgie House sat half way between Forgie village and the Summerfield council estate. When it was built, the intention of its wealthy owner was clearly to proclaim his superior wealth to his country neighbours in Forgie. To smooth his path to comfort, he was conveniently able to draw on a pool of cheap labour from the inhabitants of the small settlement of Summerfield for the many services such a grand mansion requires in order to function. Nowadays the estate was looked after by a Trust, and let for a reasonable sum on certain conditions about upkeep and maintenance. One condition was that the gardens should be open to the public on an annual Open Garden Day.

They were hardly in the gate when— 'Mr Courtenay!

160

So pleased you could come.'

The greeting was for Andrew, Kate might as well not have existed. She didn't mind. Andrew had a wide fan base and was looked on as a real celebrity locally, whereas – at least until the Summerfield wind farm project had been set in motion – Kate had slipped quietly under the radar.

He was led off to admire the walled vegetable garden. Kate didn't protest and Andrew didn't apologise. She wandered into the café that had been set up in a small marquee and found Nicola Arnott was filling coffee pots from a large urn. Kate wove her way through the crowded marquee towards her.

'Hi, Kate!'

'You're busy.'

'All in a good cause. Coffee? Two pounds to charity.'

'Sold to the woman in the blue scarf.'

'Try some carrot cake. Drink and a cake for three pounds. Betty made it.' She waved an arm in the direction of a small, wiry woman who was setting out two more delicious-looking cakes on raised cake stands. They were improbably deep and bulging with cream and fruit. 'She cooks for the Nesbitts and she lives in Holly Cottage, on the estate.'

'How can I say no?'

'Quite right, she's a brilliant cook. Her husband, Tam, is the gardener here.' She poured Kate a coffee and put a generous slab of cake on a plate. 'And guess what? Their son is Ibsen Brown, the man you recommended for the community garden project.'

'Really? Have you met him?'

Nicola was enthusiastic. 'Oh yes, and thanks for the tip. He's going to come in next week and we'll start talking over the plans. Listen, I'd better get on with serving. Pay at the till there.' She waved towards the far end of the trestle table. Everything seemed to be well planned.

161

'Sure. Catch you later.'

Kate finished her coffee and wandered outside. May Nesbitt, the current tenant of Forgie House, was hurrying up the grass, her arms laden with soft toys. A giraffe of unlikely proportions fell out of her embrace as she saw Kate and she stopped, abruptly. Kate bent and picked it up.

'Thanks, they're for one of the stalls,' May said, her normally friendly expression slithering into guardedness as she realised who it was.

Kate knew what was coming. It was a pattern of conversation she was finding increasingly familiar and which no doubt would grow worse as the Summerfield project progressed.

'I have to tell you, Kate, Jerry and I are dead against this wind farm.'

'I'm sorry.'

'It'll be right behind us—' she swept one arm in the direction of the hill, dropping an elephant, a tiger and three rabbits in the movement, '—and we won't be able to sleep at night. It'll have to be stopped, you know.'

Please, not now. Kate tucked the toys back into May's arms and smiled sweetly. 'We'll talk about it some other time, shall we? You must be incredibly busy today.'

May looked grateful. 'Yes. Yes that's fine. I *am* busy. I just didn't want you to think that we – anyway—'

'I promise we'll chat soon.'

'Yes. I'm coming!' she called as someone waved at her urgently from the top of the lawn. 'Yes, we'll do that. Thanks.'

She stared after the retreating figure, her earlier mood of optimism waning. She hated the wedge of suspicion and antagonism the project was driving between her and her neighbours. She should have been more forceful with Mark at the beginning, because this had been entirely predictable. Now she couldn't stand down without losing face at AeGen. Irritated, she stood for a moment to take

162

stock. It was a glorious day. The sun was high in the sky, and there wasn't a cloud to be seen. May had reminded her of the relative location of the wind farm to Forgie House – from further down the rolling lawn she'd get a good view of where the turbines would sit. She walked away from all the crowds enjoying the face painting and lucky dips, the craft and produce stalls, and headed towards two small cottages that nestled against the estate wall, a couple of hundred yards away.

Just as she was nearing them, a dog emerged from the gate of a walled garden to the right of the right-hand cottage and bounded up the grass towards her.

'Hello, Wellington!' she bent and patted the Labrador's head as he thrust a delighted nose into her crotch. Damn! This was awkward. This must be where Ibsen lived. Arriving like this made it look as though she'd been coming to seek him out.

There was a whistle from the cottage and Wellington shot off. Too late to turn back. She straightened and smiled.

'Hi, Kate.' He waved, not appearing in the least embarrassed.

His grin could be mocking, or joyous, or gently amused. It drew you in – and after May's thin welcome and days of Andrew's mechanical politeness, it had the virtue of appearing absolutely genuine.

Kate waved back.

It was hard not to notice how powerfully Ibsen was built. Andrew had kept his slimness, but by contrast with Ibsen's compact, muscular power, her husband's leanness seemed more like middle-aged scrawniness. Biceps bulged from below the sleeves of Ibsen's tee shirt, which today featured a computer power switch symbol and the words 'TURN ME ON'. She smiled because she couldn't help it. Ibsen's sexual attractiveness was quite powerful enough, he had no need to make suggestive comments – one of

163

these days, he might just get what he asked for.

'Melanie bought me it,' he said, noticing the direction of her gaze.

'Did she buy a "his and hers" set?'

'Christ no, she needs no encouragement.' His grin was shameless. 'Now you're down this end of the estate, would you like to see my garden?'

'Sure.'

He touched her elbow and guided her down the hill towards his cottage. 'I warn you, it's a one-flower patch. I grow dahlias.'

'Okay.' Kate was no gardening expert, but her taste was probably more for the soft blowsiness of roses, with their heady scent and fragile prettiness.

She saw him glance sideways at her, a small smile on his face that she couldn't quite read. She prepared herself for politeness, but when he pushed open the wooden gate into the cottage garden, she stopped dead in her tracks and gasped involuntarily. 'Oh!'

The smile became a full-blown grin. 'What do you think?'

'Wow. Just ... wow.'

Ibsen watched Kate's reaction with a pleasure he hadn't known could be so intense. His garden was a riot of colour. Against the far wall, growing to almost four feet, creamy white flowers caressed the gray stone; in front of them was a band of showy, intense red heads, perhaps two feet tall; closest was a ribbon of delicate lilac, petals that turned to white at the base, each flower head a perfect ball; and in between, every shade from crimson to ginger.

'Do you like them?' he said, almost shyly.

'Like them? Ibsen, I've never *seen* anything like this. It's amazing! And you say they're all dahlias?'

'I like growing dahlias. They're a real challenge because they don't have long roots, so a sudden gust of

164

wind can blow them over – specially in Scotland.'

'It's quite sheltered here though.' Kate gazed round the small garden with its shoulder-high wall.

'Yeah, relatively, but they still need lots of tender loving care.'

She squatted down and gingerly tucked her fingers under a heavy, dense ball of petals. She stroked the flower head. He loved her wonderment, it was almost childlike. 'It's so intricate. Incredibly symmetrical.'

'That one's Barberry Carousel.'

'They have names? Sorry – I guess they must have. What's the red one called?'

'That's Taratahi Ruby.'

'And the huge one at the back? It looks like a waterlily.'

'Spot on. It's a waterlily dahlia called Anna Lindh, after the Swedish politician who was murdered, I think.'

'They're stunning, Ibsen.'

'Thank you. They're my passion.' A telephone somewhere began to ring. Ibsen started fumbling in pockets, while Kate took her bag off her shoulder and delved into it. Ibsen found his mobile first. 'Hi Ma. Sure I'll bring them up. No, don't worry, I'll find someone to help.' He dropped his phone back into his pocket.

Kate was laughing. 'We've got the same ringtone.'

'No, really? Mel hates mine.'

'Andrew hates mine, too.' It wasn't significant, but it amused Ibsen that they shared this taste.

'My mother asked me to bring up some more cakes. Would you mind helping me carry them?'

'Love to.'

'Come on in then. She baked some in my kitchen last night, her kitchen was bursting.' He banged his forehead comically with the heel of his hand. 'Sod it, I should have pretended I'd made them and impressed you.'

'Well, let me tell you, I *would* have been impressed.'

They entered by a side door from the garden, which took them into a small entrance hall. She had the impression of comfortable clutter, of hanging coats and a neat rack of boots. A smell of fresh baking filled the air and Kate sniffed appreciatively. 'Suddenly I'm hungry.'

He bent down and picked up some cake tins and thrust them into her hands. 'Here, grab this. Cup cakes, Ma tells me. We used to call them fairy cakes when I was little. Apparently these are the same thing but bigger and more fattening.'

'That's progress.'

'And this is—' he picked up a large cake covered by tea towel and peered at it, '—carrot cake.' He put it on a tray and added a generously covered chocolate cake, then picked the tray up and levered open the garden door with his foot. 'We can go back out this way.'

The door swung behind them and a figure whirled round at the sound.

'There you are – oh!'

It was Melanie McGillivray, her endless legs encased in skin-tight jeans, one bronzed shoulder emerging from a creamy top, the auburn hair bouncing half way down her back. As soon as she saw Kate she began to hiss, venomously. 'Not *you!*' She spun back to Ibsen and bawled accusingly, 'You *bastard*, Ibsen Brown! You fucking bastard! You won't let *me* into your precious cottage but you let *her* in. You've been screwing her, haven't you? You can't fucking keep your hands off her! I knew it when she came to the pub, you had that look on your face. Well *fuck* you!'

She aimed a furious kick at the nearest dahlias, which collapsed over the path.

'Melanie!' Ibsen dropped the tray he was carrying and two large cakes arced gracelessly onto the ground and lay in a muddy mix of chocolate and butter cream and crumbs. He ignored them. All his attention was on his dahlias.

'Christ! Stop, will you!'

But Melanie was possessed of a demon. 'Sod you, you fucking, fucking bastard!' She jumped into the flowerbed and kicked around some more. Dahlias smashed to the ground and lay destroyed, scarlet petals trailing from shattered heads like beads of blood.

A small crowd gathering at the gate. Perhaps Mel's frenzied yelling had drawn people down here.

'You can't—'

Stamp.

'—fucking—'

Stamp, kick,

'— keep your hands off her—'

Kick.

'—can you? Your sodding fuck-buddy!'

Ibsen caught her at last. He grabbed her from behind and lifted her, still kicking wildly, bodily out of the flowerbed and out of reach of what was left of his precious flowers. He saw Kate with her mouth hanging open, looking at the crowd at the gate.

Her old man – Andrew – was in the front row and he didn't look happy at all.

Chapter Seventeen

Faced with the prospect of losing her husband to a younger rival, all Kate's instincts were to fight. Experience told her, though, that it was a matter of picking the right battle and the right strategy. For now, Andrew was intent on making capital out of Melanie's very public accusations.

As soon as they were home he said, 'Fuck-buddy? I have to say, that's a new one on me.'

'And it's completely untrue.'

'That girl didn't seem to think so.'

'She's bonkers. Completely paranoid. I've barely met Ibsen Brown, let alone slept with him.'

'So you say.'

She stared at him, astonished. 'Surely you don't believe her? You know me better than that.'

'I thought I did.'

'For heaven's sake. My trust in you might be at an all-time low, but you have absolutely no reason not to trust me.'

He turned away, saying nothing.

'Andrew?'

'I'm going out.' He reached for his jacket and picked up his car keys.

She hated how Andrew always ran from rows, so she challenged him. 'We're just back in. Where are you going?'

'Just out.'

'When will you be back?'

'I don't know, Kate. Later.'

'I don't want you seeing *her*. You gave me a promise.'

But he'd gone already. She flew to the front door and watched as he reversed the car and drove off down the drive, fast.

'Come back here!' she shouted after the disappearing car, but of course he couldn't hear her.

When she got back to the kitchen, Ninian had materialised and was raiding the fridge with Cuzzer.

'Hi Mum, was that Dad spraying gravel on the lawn? He went off in a hurry, didn't he?'

'You could say. Hello Stephen.'

'Hi.' Weasel eyes stared at her.

Kate had never understood why Ninian was friendly with this boy – he had no visible likeable attributes. She had an idea that his association with Stephen was a pitch for acceptance. There were other ways of being popular, though, and she wished that she were better at guiding him towards more mature choices.

'My mum says you shouldn't be building this wind farm,' Stephen said, his mouth full of Kate's smoked salmon.

'Is that right?'

'She says wind farms are a manifestation of capitalism gone mad.'

'Really.' She was in no mood to get drawn in to a philosophical discussion of the merits or demerits of wind farms, certainly not with Stephen Cousins.

'She was down at the exhibition yesterday morning. She says you're going to cut down the oak forest at Bonny Brae.'

Kate had been about to leave the boys to it in the kitchen and seek peace in the privacy of her bedroom. Now, though, she did a swift about-turn and eyed him with dismay. 'Where on earth did she hear that?'

'It was on one of the plans.'

Karen Cousins must have spotted the print before Jack had taken it down. Damn and double damn. Kate said firmly, 'You can tell her she's wrong, Stephen. The map had an error. There are no plans to destroy the woods. Okay?'

'If you say so.'

'I do. Ninian, make sure you tidy up after yourselves please.'

Bloody Jack Bailey! This matter of the access road had the makings of a serious problem.

From her bedroom window, Kate could see the walls of the Forgie House estate. She could even – she imagined – just see the roof of Ibsen Brown's cottage through the trees. Was he there now? What was he doing? Had he made it up with Melanie? For a few seconds she found herself wishing that the girl had real grounds for jealousy, then she dismissed the thought. She couldn't deny that she found Ibsen sexy, but this was no time for fantasy. She had to pay all her attention to saving her marriage. Coming to this conclusion, she decided to call Andrew on his mobile and, a little to her surprise, he answered right away. 'Hello Kate.'

'Come home. Please? I promise that girl is completely wrong.'

He laughed. 'Actually, I'll be there in two minutes. Sorry I was cross. I decided to get a take-away. Hope you fancy pizza?'

She was so relieved that he hadn't raced straight off to Sophie that she forgave him immediately. 'Pizza, a glass of wine, and you. What more could a woman want? But there's two hungry boys here, already cleaning the fridge out. How much pizza did you get?'

'Enough.'

She smiled at Ibsen's roof. Poor Ibsen. Poor dahlias.

On Wednesday *The Stoneyford Echo* did carry the story that Kate had been desperate to avoid.

'ACCESS ROUTE TO SUMMERFIELD WIND FARM MAY

171

DESTROY ANCIENT OAK WOOD.'

She tossed the newspaper onto Jack's desk. 'See what you've done?'

He lifted it incuriously. 'Oops.'

'Is that all you can say?'

'It'll blow over.'

'You think?'

'Sure.'

She put two hands on his desk and leaned over it so that her face was just a couple of feet from his. 'It better had, Jack. For your sake.'

There was nothing she could do, but she was worried. She'd had experience of environmentalists before, and there was nothing like trees to get them exercised.

Over the next few days, though, it looked as though Jack might be proved right, because there was no sign of disruption. Kate was still getting silent calls at the house, but she was so used to them now she thought nothing of them. She spotted the iridescent car one day, but after Andrew went out for the newspaper, it disappeared. She'd had no occasion to walk through the village, so she hadn't run into any of the locals she knew were opposed to the wind farm. Everything seemed calm.

There was also a piece of good news. Nicola Arnott had persuaded the Council to send a digger in to turn over the waste ground so that the garden could get under way. After work, she made her way to the school.

Nicola, her face alight with excitement, called to her. 'Hi Kate! Come to help us celebrate? Isn't this fantastic? It's starting to happen. And look at the crowd!'

'There's a great buzz.'

Kate was every bit as excited as the head teacher. Together they watched and cheered as the digger dipped into the mess of grass and soil.

Nicola said, 'We had to spend all week clearing out the rubbish. It was such a tip, Kate, you've no idea. We couldn't let the children help, it was too dangerous. It wasn't just broken bottles, there were loads of discarded needles and old condoms.'

'Oh, yuk.'

'Quite. Anyway, Ibsen was terrific, he—'

'Ibsen Brown? Is he here?'

'Somewhere.'

Kate peered round the crowd. The digger was working with astonishing speed. Already half the patch had been turned over. Kate watched, riveted, as scrub and wasteland became dark chunks of soil. There was something pleasingly primeval about that virgin clay. It held the secrets of life in its rich loam. It was moist and fecund, its nutrients probably enhanced by lack of cultivation over the years rather than spoiled by surface rubbish. By next spring, it would nourish flowers of multi-coloured splendour, vegetables that could feed the entire school, and perhaps some fruit trees and bushes as well.

Kate thought of Ibsen's dahlias, lying flattened and dying. He had spent most of his spare time in his garden last autumn, he'd told her, preparing the soil, digging in compost, peat moss, sand and rotted manure. In the spring, he'd dug it all over again. Only now, watching the digger, did she appreciate how much work it must have been – and everything he had worked for had been destroyed in a moment of mad jealousy.

'There's Ibsen now.' Nicola nudged her and pointed.

Kate spotted him at the far side of the waste ground, talking to a man who must surely have been his father. The hair was white and thick, the face was tanned and crisscrossed with lines that read like the book of a life, but the eyes were unmistakeably Ibsen's, that unforgettable shade of bluebells in the woods.

'See you in a bit.'

The crowd was thick and for a few minutes Kate lost the two of them. She saw their hands first, placed

173

comfortably side by side on the back wall as they watched the digger working. She was used to Andrew's hands, which were slim and elegant, with long, tapering fingers that could pick out the keys on a computer with speed and surprising accuracy. These hands might find such actions difficult. They were all squarish, with short, slightly spatulate fingers. Ibsen's father's were weather-beaten and tanned, gnarled with age and long exposure to the elements. Ibsen's would go the same way. She remembered how he had caressed the dying dahlias with such extraordinary tenderness and something tugged inside her.

'Hello, Kate.' He lifted one hand off the wall and gestured her in beside him. 'Have you met my father, Tam?'

'Delighted to meet you.' She took Tam's proffered hand. It felt warm and worn, as though it had been burnished with decades of hard work, and his smile was as welcoming as a warm bath on a cold winter's night. She turned to Ibsen. 'Dare I ask how your mother managed without two scrumptious cakes?'

'Ah. There was a little trouble,' Ibsen said gravely.

'You mean, when she saw two plates full of crumbs she went ballistic,' Tam said.

'I did offer to nip down to the supermarket for a couple more, but my offer wasn't well received.'

'Aye. Well. The crumbs were bad enough but winding her up like that was not nice.' Tam was laughing. His eyes were more like Ibsen's than should have been possible – brimming with mischief, but with undertones of surprising wisdom.

Ibsen grinned. 'But it is fun, she rises to the bait every time.'

'Tch.' Kate tutted severely. 'Ibsen, you're a bad boy.'

'I can be.'

She wished she hadn't said it because the look he gave

174

her was impossible. She changed the subject hastily. 'What do you think?' She waved at the digger, which was now finishing its job.

'It's a start. There'll be a mass to do, though. Can you come down tomorrow?'

'I'll be at work.'

'Seven o'clock. You can eat first, give yourself some strength. You'll need it.'

'I'm not sure—'

'It's a non-negotiable condition, remember?'

Kate wrinkled her nose at him. She had a feeling Ibsen Brown was going to take some delight in testing her fitness and resolve. For her part, she was going to enjoy showing him that she was not the weak little woman he perhaps imagined her to be.

'Okay,' she agreed, 'tomorrow.'

She was humming to herself as she unlocked the front door at Willow Corner. Andrew had committed to their marriage and she was confident that they could mend things between them, the garden had been started, and she was rather looking forward to showing Ibsen what she was made of.

'Hello?'

There was no reply. She was a little puzzled, because she'd expected both Andrew and Ninian to be at home.

'Anyone in?' she called again, picking up the mail from the doormat and tossing it onto the hall table.

When there was still no answer and she had established that Ninian was neither plugged into earphones in his room nor asleep, she went into the study as a last resort. Sometimes Andrew became so deeply immersed in his work that he was able to block out the twenty-first century absolutely and completely.

He wasn't there. No-one was there. But on the floor, in a crumpled heap, was what appeared to be pages from his manuscript. She crouched down and picked up a few sheets of paper, then smoothed them out.

'*Martyne could not stop looking at the woman,*' she read. '*She was more like a girl, with skin as soft and smooth as a newborn babe's and eyes that stared at him, unwinking, as though they knew everything, and nothing.*'

It was clearly a draft, and as she didn't recognise the lines, she guessed that they must be from Andrew's new novel. Usually, she didn't read his work until it was nearly ready to send to his editor, though she knew that Andrew sometimes shared his drafts with Ninian. Why was this on the floor? Whatever faults Andrew had, untidiness was not one of them. She had never seen him toss papers down like this, especially pages from his manuscript, which he protected carefully so that his new novels bounced onto the market with enough anticipation to make them fly off the shelves.

'*He reached out one hand, tentatively, as if afraid of what she might do to him. But she was compelling. She was like a spider, drawing flies into her web for her pleasure. Martyne knew this, but he was unable to hold back. He thought of Ellyn – sensible Ellyn with her no-nonsense remedies and her way of speaking her mind so that you knew what she thought. With Ethelinda – the word meant "noble snake" – you could never know what she was thinking. That, of course, was part of her attraction.*'

Kate frowned. Martyne Noreis having an affair? It seemed so unlikely, so completely out of character, that the words jarred. She smoothed out another piece of paper and read on.

'*She caught his hand just as the fingers touched her cheek, and held it there. He could feel the warmth of her touch and it burned like a fire that spread all the way up his arm and down into his belly. He must have her – this girl, with her unreadable eyes and hair like the mantle of the night and lips made for love. Slowly, he trailed his* hand down her face to her neck. He caressed the long smoothness of it, felt the bones of her back against the palm of his hand to where they disappeared under her robe. Her eyes, all the while, never left his face, but her hands went to the cord the secured her gown above her breasts, and slowly, deliberately, she pulled at one end so that her bodice fell loose.'

Kate dropped the papers onto the floor, where they lay shivering in a faint draught from under the door.

These pages were not here because Mrs Gillies had inadvertently dropped them out of the wastebasket while she was cleaning. The housekeeper had many faults but sloppiness was not in her make-up. Andrew would never have been so careless with his work. There was only one reason for these crumpled balls of paper. Ninian had read this – and he must have read into it exactly the same as she had.

No character, for Andrew, was ever wasted.

If Martyne Noreis was having an affair with Ethelinda, while the fabulous Ellyn was at home, waiting for him, trusting him, it was because Andrew was drawing on experience in his own life.

She was in unknown territory, without a compass.

Ninian texted her. <At Cuzz for supper. Back later.>

That was all right, except how was she going to ask him about whether he had read the manuscript? If she and Andrew were to separate, what would happen to him? Kate couldn't bear to think about it.

She took the smoothed-out sheets of paper and dropped them onto the kitchen table. Mrs Gillies had placed a vase of flowers from the garden in the centre. It was a riot of colour – coral pink gladioli, purple ball-headed allium, orange cosmos, deep burgundy and pink stargazer lilies and white lisianthus – and any other day it would have brought a smile to her lips. She lifted it an inch and slipped the sheets under it. When Andrew came in, she would ask him about his strange storyline.

She called him.

On the far side of the kitchen, his mobile startled her by ringing. Wherever he'd gone, he'd forgotten to take it. She crossed the room and picked it up. A 'New Message' sign was flashing and she clicked it in case it gave her a clue as to his whereabouts.

<Hi Squishy, RU still coming? Im waiting. Let me no if ur gonna be late. Cant wait. Sxxxxxxx>

She almost dropped the phone. She didn't hear the door open, but right behind her Andrew said, 'Hi darling, you're back!' and bent to kiss her neck.

She'd heard the expression 'I almost jumped out of my skin', but had never understood its exactness as a description until now. She whirled round. 'Jesus Christ!'

'What?' He was looking at her, amused, and so damned *normal* that she found it hard to believe anything had changed between them. 'Sorry, love, I didn't mean to give you a fright.'

She was shaking from head to toe. She thrust the phone at him, barely able to speak. 'What's this?'

He looked at it incuriously. 'My phone? Did I leave it here?'

'If you hadn't noticed, I guess you managed to meet up with her despite being late.'

'Kate, what are you talking about?'

'She sent you a text.' She located it. 'Hi Squishy. *Squishy?* She really calls you Squishy? Are you still coming? I'm waiting.'

A hand came out and he took the phone gently out of her trembling grasp. 'Let's see. Yes,' he went on calmly, 'that looks like Sophie.' He dropped the phone into his pocket. 'I had to see her, Kate, but it's not what you think. She was devastated because I'd told her we had to stop meeting—'

'So *Squishy* went to see her? Makes sense,' she said

sarcastically.

'Just to explain again, Kate. She can't seem to understand what I'm telling her.'

'Her expectations seem quite explicit.'

'Her expectations are quite wrong.' He pulled her to him. 'You're in a real state, love, aren't you? There's no need.'

It would be so easy to accept what he was telling her. It would be wonderful to think that the whole Sophie episode was over – but it clearly wasn't. Whatever the reason he was seeing her, the fact remained that he *was* still seeing her. She pulled away.

'I think Ninian's been reading your manuscript.'

'Oh?'

'I found some pages crumpled up on the floor in your study.' She marched across to the table and jerked the papers out from under the vase. It gave a little judder and a few fragile petals drifted down onto the scrubbed pine. 'Martyne Noreis in love with some enchantress? Your story reflecting fact?'

He took the printout. 'It's a novel, Kate. That's all.'

'A novel.'

'A work of fiction.' He enunciated the words slowly and with heavy emphasis, as if explaining to a child with learning difficulties.

'All fiction draws from experience.'

'No. All fiction draws from imagination.'

'Ninian read this and he's fled to Stephen's house.'

'What do you mean, fled?'

'He wasn't here when I got in. There was just this crumpled paper and then I got a text saying he's having supper at Stephen's. He *knows*, Andrew, and it's killing him.'

'Heavens above, Kate – your son reads some of my made-up story and goes to have tea with his friend and you're making it into a major crisis? What's got into you?

179

Calm down.'

Put like that, her interpretation of everything did seem exaggerated. Andrew's whole attitude was relaxed, almost offhand. Sophie couldn't matter much to him, surely, or he'd be more keyed up. She said in a small voice, 'It really is over with Sophie?'

'It really is over.'

'You won't see her again?'

'I'm doing my very best to settle the situation down as smoothly as I can.'

'Promise?'

'I promise. Now, if we can stop this ridiculous conversation, do you think we might manage to find something to eat? I'm really rather hungry.'

She looked at him shamefacedly. 'Sorry. Panic, I guess.'

'Okay. How do you fancy an omelette?'

So, with a mundanity, the episode was closed.

Chapter Eighteen

Kate started helping out in the community garden on a regular basis. It was dull, heavy work but she began to like the unthinkingness of it. After a day at AeGen, her head filled with figures and contracts, environmental reports, soil tests, wind measurements, consultant reports and deadlines, nothing seemed so appealing as the idea of picking up a spade and turning over soil. She found the primitive connection with the land thoroughly – and unexpectedly – restorative.

Even more to her surprise, she discovered that her initial reservations about Ibsen Brown were changing into genuine admiration. For a start, he was in the community garden most evenings too – and, unlike her, he must have been labouring hard all day already.

She got to know many of the volunteers. One evening as she struggled to sift stones from the heavy soil she asked a hard-faced woman with nicotine-stained fingers, 'What started you coming down here, Maisie?'

'That Ibsen Brown,' Maisie said, stabbing her fork into the ground and reaching into her pocket for a cigarette. 'He's got a mighty persuasive tongue on him.' Her grin revealed nicotine-stained teeth, but had genuine warmth. 'It's good, though, int it? Gets you oot.'

'Aye,' said the woman on the other side of her, 'Tho' you'd tak ony excuse tae get awa' frae that man o' yours.'

Everyone laughed. An atmosphere was developing here that was unlike anything Kate had come across before. This was a warm-hearted, funny, and genuine community, in which she sensed none of the subtle complexities and underhand scheming she knew abounded in Forgie. People here knew who she was, and of her connection with the wind farm, but they accepted her without comment. Most evenings there were anything from three to ten people at the site, digging, chatting, joking and teasing each other with an easy camaraderie.

'Hard work, though,' a young woman called Jodie grumbled, examining a blister on her hand.

'Aye. He has tae crack the whip sometimes.'

'You wish, Maisie,' cackled someone else. 'Dream on.'

'Fifty Shades of Brown,' came a shout, and there was more laughter.

Kate grinned as she bent again to her task. The mood was certainly very different to her office, where everyone was driven because deadlines pressed. There, all was reaction rather than action. The stress levels were high and most people dealt with them by plundering their reserves of energy until they were utterly depleted. Small successes buoyed them up enough to carry on, errors and failures dragged them down. She was beginning to discover that gardening was not like that at all. It was impossible to hurry nature and preparation was everything – though that, at least, she understood.

A couple of weeks after the debacle at Forgie House, she found herself alone with Ibsen for the first time. It was a windy evening, and decidedly cold, which might have been the reason no-one else had shown up. When she arrived at the garden, her geometric black and ivory Missoni wool scarf wound round and round her neck to combat the chill, he was already sturdily there, a man who inhabited his environment as naturally as breathing. She stood at the gap in the wall for a moment and watched him, with secret pleasure. Despite the cold, he'd taken off his jacket and was wearing another of his seemingly inexhaustible wardrobe of comic tee shirts. She squinted across the space between them and made out a yellow recycling symbol with the words 'YOU CAN USE ME AGAIN

AND AGAIN'. Another of Melanie's gifts, perhaps?

Perhaps he sensed her presence, because he lifted his head and smiled.

Ibsen wiped the sweat off his forehead with the back of one hand, not caring if he left grimy streaks. He'd been completely lost in the rhythm of digging – in, twist, out, in, twist, out – so that Kate's arrival threw him.

She looked so small. It was the first thing he noticed about her. It was always the first thing he noticed. It made him feel protective. How could she do that job she did? A small woman building very big things. It was sexy, in its own way.

And she had guts. It needed courage to put yourself in the middle of a situation that drew out such bile.

'Evening, Kate.'

She looked forlorn, standing there all alone. Christ, he wasn't exactly making her life easy, was he? But he had to be honest. He hated wind farms, and he always would.

'Hi.'

She did sound low.

He threw his fork into the soil, hard, so that it stood erect, and crossed the few yards to where she was standing and swivelled round. 'Put your hand in my back pocket. My hands are filthy already, I don't want to mess up the paper.'

'Or you just fancy someone feeling you up.'

'Want to see what's in there or not? Your choice.'

'What will Melanie say if she sees me with my hand down your back pocket?'

It was the first time either of them had uttered Melanie's name since Dahlia Destruction Day.

'Oh come on, Kate,' he said, keeping his voice light, 'you know the answer to that.'

'Do I?'

'You don't imagine I'd still be seeing her, do you?' He

183

was still holding his hands aloft. 'Are you going to get that paper out of my pocket or what?'

She plunged her hand into the denim and he heard the crinkle of crisp paper. She said, 'I'm guessing dahlia-kicking might be a relationship-breaker. What's this?'

'Unfold it and see.'

'Wow.'

'What do you think?' He felt suddenly shy, and realised that her opinion mattered to him.

'It's beautiful.'

He picked up his waterproof jacket and spread it against the wall so that they could sit with their backs to the stone, out of the wind. 'I had a feeling folk might be getting a bit pissed off with digging. We need to look ahead to what we're doing it all *for*, don't you think? So I put this together. Course it's not final, it's only up for discussion. Thought the Committee might look at it first, then once it's updated, maybe they can find a notice board to stick it up on.'

He'd done the plan in watercolour, with detail added in fine pen.

'Where did you learn to do this?'

'At college. We were always having to present ideas and designs and we all developed different ways of doing it. I found this easiest.'

'Hardly easy.'

He'd sketched in a wrought-iron gate between the garden and the school playground, with another at the other end where the path from the road ended. This was currently walled up but opening it would be straightforward. In the north-east corner he'd drawn four trees with a tent-like covering slung between them.

'What's that?'

'I thought rather than applying for planning permission for a small building, we might just have a stout canvas covering there. It could be a teaching space, or a picnic spot, or a music area, anything really. It could be a proper building, if there's enough money and people want to wait for planning.'

'It would take years to grow trees big enough to support it, wouldn't it?'

'If there's enough cash, you can buy big trees.'

'It's just a question of cash?'

'Everything's about money, isn't it?'

'Even trees?'

'Especially trees.'

She pointed to another section of the drawing. 'And is this a maze?'

'Probably just low box hedges, or stones, or maybe a one-foot high willow fence. We could get people weaving. Anyway, we don't want to lose children – or have them playing kiss chase out of sight of the teachers.'

'Now there's the voice of experience.'

He laughed. 'And this—' he pointed at a substantial area in the corner, '—would be the allotment area, fruit bushes and veg. Over here, maybe a pond. We could bring in frogs.'

He'd spent ages thinking the design out, varying it for interest, crisscrossing the patch with paths so that you could make a dozen different choices to reach any one spot. You could get lost, if you wanted, but of course, you would never be lost.

'What's this?' She peered at the southeast corner, where a series of blue and pink spots had been painted.

'A friendship garden.' He smiled at her quizzical look. 'Tree stumps, sawn flat to make stepping-stones. You take your friend's hand, boy on blue, girl on pink – or the other way round if you like,' he added hastily, seeing the look on Kate's face, 'or you could make them green and red, whatever. Anyway, you stay on the colour you started on. The idea is to work your way round the stepping stones without letting go of your friend's hand. Sometimes you'll

185

have to stretch as far as you can because the blue stone might be three yards from the pink. Sometimes blue and pink will be on the same spot, half and half, with the next stone the other way round, so you have to snuggle up really close or wind yourselves round each other to find a way past. You have to work at it a bit, it won't be easy. It's a game.'

'And a metaphor.'

'Take it any way you like.'

'I like.' Kate stretched up and kissed his cheek, then sat back immediately, as if shocked by her own temerity. 'You're right – people need a vision or they'll lose interest, but not everyone would have been wise enough to understand that.'

He wanted to take her face between his hands and kiss her lips till they frayed. Kate Courtenay was fast becoming a temptation that was difficult to resist.

Kate began to suspect that Andrew was still seeing Sophie, but decided not to spark another confrontation. Such clashes always ended in fervent denials and made her feel as though she was the one in the wrong. It seemed easier to ignore it and pretend, though discomfort about Andrew's ever more frequent absences was swelling inside her. She couldn't bear to think of Andrew's hands on Sophie's alabaster skin, of words of endearment passing between them like gift-wrapped parcels.

When she came home from work one day, she discovered that Andrew was out – again. Ninian was out too. His mobile was off and she had no idea where he was, either with Banksy or Cuzz, at a guess. She hoped it was Banksy, and she hoped he wouldn't be too late home because she never slept properly until she heard his key in the lock and the front door opening and closing. She eyed the papers in her briefcase, but she'd had enough of work. She needed air. Clean air and bracing exercise. She needed

– if she had a shred of honesty – to see Ibsen.

By the time she got down to the garden, it was late. It was almost October, and the days were much shorter now. In another couple of weeks, the clocks would go back and the evening would start to get really dark. For a moment she thought there was no-one in the garden, but then she caught sight of Ibsen in the corner, packing up his tools.

'Hello.'

'Hi.'

'It's getting dark.'

'Yes. Sorry I'm late.'

'No worries. There were a few folk here.' He surveyed the land. 'Almost finished.'

'Yes.'

'Fundraising's going to start soon.'

'That's good. There'll be money, you know, if—'

'Don't say it. Don't mention the words "wind" or "farm".'

'No. Sorry.'

'There are too many minuses, Kate.'

She couldn't just ignore it, not because it was her job, but because she felt passionately about turbines too – she just happened to have the opposite view to Ibsen's. Yet there was no point in arguing because his views were entrenched. Might there be any other way of winning him over?

Don't tell him, something in her head said, *show him.*

She glanced at her watch. It was only eight o'clock. Ninian was unlikely to be back for hours, ditto Andrew, and anyway, she was angry with both of them and tired of being left alone in Willow Corner.

'Are you in a hurry?'

'Not really. Why?'

'Fancy a spin?'

'Where to? My van's shockingly dirty.'

'I have mine.'

187

He shrugged on a sweatshirt. Kate could smell the evening air on him like the sweet breath of freshly-cut grass and shivered.

'Well, I'm willing to risk it. Where d'you want to go?'

The mischievous grin was Ibsen's trademark, but this time Kate got to do it first. As he climbed in, she flashed him her best smile and said, 'Wait and see.'

She turned the car towards Gifford and smirked into the darkness. She liked being in control – and especially, for once, in control of Ibsen Brown.

She threw the car along winding country roads in the gathering gloom and they reached the site in twenty minutes. The entrance was secured with a coded lock and the codes were changed weekly, but they were the same on all AeGen gates. She had to stop to open up. When the headlights illuminated the large board, 'Dun Muir Wind Farm', Ibsen groaned.

'Good God, woman.'

'I thought I'd show you something magical.'

'You're kidding.'

'You could look on it as an educational visit, if you like.'

'You're dragging me up to some wind turbines in the middle of the night and you think you're going to change my mind.'

'Perhaps, though it's hardly the middle of the night.'

'Hah!'

She'd made a series of rapid calculations in her head before she'd made the suggestion in the first place. It was dark, but the sky was completely clear. Soon it would be filled with stars and she knew that the moon would be large. There was something that happens around wind turbines in these conditions – to her biased eye, anyway. She set the car up the hill, slotted it into first and took the slope gently.

'Just open your mind, Ibsen. That's all I ask.' She

glanced at his profile but in the dim light from the beam of the headlamps it was unreadable.

From this side, the turbines were invisible, but when they crested the hill a few jerky minutes later, she knew they would spring into full view. At exactly the wrong moment, though, a cloud passed across the moon and they couldn't see anything. This wasn't the spot Kate had had in mind, so she didn't panic, she merely turned left and up another hill, where they wound up a small sidetrack.

The Dun Muir wind farm was only five years old, so the technology was modern, but because of the nature of the terrain, the landscaping already looked quite mature. The land itself was undulating, so although there were thirty-eight turbines, it was impossible to see all of them from any one spot.

'Here.'

She cut the engine and sat for a second, tense with anxiety. She desperately wanted Ibsen to see this through her eyes, as she had seen his cottage garden before Melanie's tantrum.

A blade of a wind turbine, as beautiful and symmetrical as a petal on a dahlia. Her wind-flower.

She opened the door. 'Come on.'

They walked ten yards to the brow of the hill and just as they reached it, the cloud moved away and the moon shone silver. Below them, as far as they could see, a small army of turbines arced skywards. Some of the blades were rotating slowly, others stood still. They were miles from any road, there were no houses or farms on this wild bit of moorland. The silence was absolute.

She pursed her lips together and found she was trembling. *Speak*, she willed him. *Say something. Anything.*

'It's really quiet.'

Her heart lifted. 'Yes.'

'I thought they were noisy.'

She tried not to smile, or to lead his thoughts.

'They must get much noisier when they're really turning.'

'New turbines are both effective and quiet. Anyway—' She swept an expansive arm from left to right across the landscape, '—there's no-one to hear.'

They stood in silence. Something flew across the moon. A buzzard, out hunting. She touched Ibsen's arm and whispered, 'Look.'

He'd already seen it. They watched in silence as it hovered in the indigo sky to locate its prey, then plummeted, like a stone, towards its kill. As it rose, she could see the shape of some small creature in its beak. Nature is cruel.

'Christ.' It was barely a whisper. 'Look there.'

She felt his arms come around her as he turned her thirty degrees to where a ghostly white shape was swooping across the dark heather. 'What is it?'

'A barn owl.'

The bird passed like a phantom, soundless, mysterious, and eerily beautiful, but Ibsen still held her tight. She could feel the warmth of his body seeping into hers and was grateful for it because the night had grown chilly. She scanned the landscape in front of them. Where the last fold of rock gave way to an infinity beyond, there was a small ruin, the remains of an ancient watchtower, its crumbled masonry like jagged teeth against the sky. The sky was darker now, and the moon brighter. Its clear, luminous light picked out the dull gray of the turbine towers and the elegant sweep of the blades so that they gleamed and shone. They stood like sentinels guarding this lonely landscape.

'Still, Kate, they're not natural, are they?'

'Natural? No.' She pointed at the ruin. 'Nor is that. It was built to safeguard this land when it was under threat from raiders. These turbines have been built because our world is under threat from carbon emissions.'

'I can't win, can I?'

She snuggled back against his warmth. 'I hate fights,' she said. 'I just want to do my job. Sadly, it seems I have battles every day. Did you know that someone has been calling me at home, all the time. A heavy breather.'

'Really? Don't you find that threatening?'

'You have no idea. I've been prodded in the chest, spat at—'

'*Spat* at?'

'Not in Forgie, not this time, but yes, there has been aggressive behaviour. Someone sits outside the house in a car. They're watching me.'

'I hope you don't think I – Kate, I'm opposed to Summerfield Wind Farm, but I would never—'

'I know.' He'd eased back from her and she hated the space between them. 'Listen, I have a rug in the car. Shall we sit for a little?'

They found a spot under a tree and spread the rug. The grass was springy and soft below their feet. She could feel the bark of the tree rough against her back and hear the gentle rustle of its leaves above their heads.

They sat in silence until Ibsen hooked an arm round her and tucked her in close. 'Cold?'

'Not now.'

'It's—' She could feel him hesitate, '—better than I thought.'

'When Melanie trashed your dahlias,' she said tentatively, 'how did you feel?'

'Do you need to ask?'

'When people tell me they hate my turbines—' She let it hang. The silence was profound. Nothing stirred except the leaves above their heads, gently moving.

At last Ibsen said, 'Is that really how you feel about them, Kate?'

She nodded. A hand curled round her cheek and gently

191

turned her head towards his. In the darkness, his eyes were no longer blue, but inky. His lips came down on hers, so softly that she thought at first that she had imagined the touch. Then she felt his breath, warm, on her face, and all thoughts of propriety were swept away in the need to touch him, to join her mouth to his, to feel the urgency of his desire fuse to hers in an incandescent blaze.

'I want you, Kate.' The confession was barely more than a breath. 'I've wanted you for ages.'

It seemed a very long time since someone had truly desired her. Years of child rearing and homemaking and career building had bundled ardour into a damp wad and tied it with a yarn made of habit. Even so, a deeply ingrained sense of loyalty and her marriage vows should stop this. Andrew's face insinuated itself into her desire, a reminder and a remonstrance. She had never strayed before. She had never even questioned her love, in her mind it had remained as strong and as steadfast as the day she had fallen in love with him. But now all the anger that had been smouldering inside her ever since Ninian had burst out with his accusation reached the end of the slow fuse and ignited. *I have the right to do this,* she argued silently in her head, *he has given me the right.*

'Kate.' It was a whisper. 'Are you sure you're okay with this?'

She loved him for asking, she loved that he had the self-control to think of her at that moment. 'I want you too, Ibsen Brown.' It was impossible not to thrill to the urgency of his desire and set it in the scale against the slick, unemotional action that her lovemaking with Andrew had become.

In the still of the night, their panting was the only sound, and when they climaxed, together, it felt as though they were joined to the universe.

'You know I'm divorced,' Ibsen said.

They were huddled together, wrapped in the big rug. Kate felt suffused with warmth and peace, so his words spun out of the dark like an arrow, right into the soft part of her head.

'I didn't know.'

He hunched closer and rested his chin on the top of her head. 'Lynn was a teacher – at Summerfield Primary, as it happens. She was a pretty girl and I'd have done anything for her.'

'How long were you married? What happened?'

For a few minutes he didn't reply and the night seemed more silent than ever. Kate waited as patiently as she could.

'We had a baby. Violet. She died.'

'Oh, Ibsen. How?' Kate tried to turn so that she could look at his face, but he kept his arms like a vice around her, keeping his expression private.

'I went in to get her one morning, and she was dead. There in the cot, looking so sweet and so—' His voice caught and he stopped speaking. Kate clung to his hands. '—so perfect. But she'd stopped breathing.'

'What was wrong?'

She felt him shrug. 'They couldn't find any reason. We'd done everything right. Neither of us smoked or took drugs. She wasn't too hot, she was on her back. We don't know.'

'I can't think of anything more terrible.'

'No.'

Somewhere below them, a deer crashed out of the woods and bounded across the heather and out of sight.

'I don't talk about it. I just wanted you to know.'

She said, 'And Lynn?'

'We staggered on for a couple of years, but being together was too painful and in the end we decided we'd be better apart.'

'Do you still see her?'

193

'Sometimes.'

'I can't imagine what you've gone through.'

'It hasn't made me a better person. I wish it had. I'd like to have another serious relationship but I can't face what it might lead to.' He gave a self-deprecating snort. 'I'm a shit, really. I do tell them, no strings, no commitment, but they all think they can change me.'

Kate shifted away. She said, 'It's all right, Ibsen, you have nothing to fear from me.'

'I didn't mean— God, Kate, not you! I didn't tell you this because— Christ! I've never told anyone before.'

But the spell had been broken. Whatever form of lust had overtaken them under the trees and lifted them to the stars, it had been dumped back on earth with a thud. They drove back to Summerfield in silence.

Chapter Nineteen

Andrew was still asleep when Lisa Tranter called a week or so later, his graying hair visible above the duvet, his skin more aged than she had realised. Now she compared everything about her husband and her guilty secret, at least subconsciously. Ibsen was broader shouldered and more powerful. Andrew's hands were slender and graceful, but showed signs of liver spots. Ibsen's skin glowed with outdoor energy, Andrew's had an indoor pallor. She was not used to viewing her husband in this way and it was not wise. It diminished him and made her uncomfortable.

'Lisa?' Kate snatched the mobile before it could waken Andrew. 'Is something up?'

'You could say. I just drove along that road through Bonny Brae Woods.'

Kate knew what she was going to say before she even said it. 'Don't tell me.'

'They're setting up a protest camp there.'

'I *knew* it. I *told* Jack!'

'There's a couple of guys slinging ropes up the trees, I think they're going to hoist some kind of shelter up in the branches. There's tents going up too. It looks serious, Kate.'

'It is serious.'

'But that isn't all. I'm sorry.'

'What? There's worse?'

'Kate, I'm sure I saw your son there.'

'Ninian?'

'Yes.'

'But he's here. In bed.'

195

'Oh, that's all right then.' Lisa sounded thankful. 'Must be someone else. What do we do about the camp?'

'I'll get in to work, then we can decide. I'll be in shortly. I'll just nip up and take a look for myself. Thanks for phoning.'

'Okay. See you soon, then.'

Kate glanced at her watch. It was exactly eight o'clock.

She checked on Ninian. The death notice was still on the door. She grimaced at it and knocked, but there was no response, not even the anticipated growl. She knocked again. Silence.

'Ninian?' She opened the door and poked her head round it. The floor was the familiar obstacle course of discarded clothing, dropped biscuit wrappers and abandoned shoes, but the room felt uninhabited. There was no warmth, no slight odour of ready-to-be-showered body, no quiet snuffling. The bed was flat – there was no familiar Ninian hump under the duvet either.

She didn't stop to think, she was white-hot with anger. Ninian must have sneaked off after they were asleep. If her son wanted to punish her for all the days she'd come home late, all the weekends she had worked instead of watching him play football for the school, all the times she'd sent him down to Devon instead of going on holiday with him, he had certainly calculated the most effective way to do it. The eco protest camp at Bonny Brae was going to damage her reputation at AeGen: her son participating in the protest made matters even worse.

Bonny Brae Woods was bisected by a single-track road. The larger part of the wood comprised several acres of mixed deciduous forest, the smaller was little more than a couple of dozen trees. A burn tumbled through the woods, just a trickle in high summer, a torrent after heavy rain or snow melt. Mosses and ferns thrived in the moist spray on its banks and there was a network of paths in and around the trees that offered pretty walks. In the spring, snowdrops heralded the season of growth. Later, the woods were a carpet of bluebells. Now, though, autumn was nearing, and the forest would be thick with velvety carpet moss, mushrooms like golden chanterelles or tawny milk-caps, and pretty lady ferns. Dog-lovers adored Bonny Brae Woods. Human lovers liked them too, because of the secluded glades and private clearings.

Kate had always known that hell would be unleashed if AeGen tried to fell any of the trees and if they used this route for access they'd have to double its width. Construction traffic was heavy enough, but they'd have to bring the huge turbine towers and blades this way too. Frank would find it unthinkable. Karen Cousins would certainly be up in arms. Kate could picture the scene already.

She rounded the bend in the road and for a moment it felt as though she'd stumbled into a film set. A tentative sun was just emerging from behind the hill to commence its work of burning off the early morning mist. Trees loomed spookily out of the swirling vapour and she could just make out the shapes of figures scurrying through the haze.

'What the—?' She lurched to a stop as a black Labrador dashed out in front of her car so that she was forced to pull it onto the grassy shoulder. She jumped out, shaken by the near miss, and called angrily at whoever might be listening behind the vapour screen, 'Can't you control your dog?'

The operation had clearly been meticulously planned. Overnight, this peaceful spot had been transformed into something resembling an army base. Dozens of people, mostly dressed in combat gear, swarmed around busily. Some were pitching tents, others lashing ropes around trees to secure platforms and shelters higher in the branches. Women passed provisions along a line from a beaten-up old Land Rover to what seemed to be a kitchen

197

tent. Three men, one shaven-headed and two with lank, shoulder-length hair, clustered together smoking and gesticulating. The Labrador she'd almost clipped trotted up unconcerned and dropped at their feet. A few yards further on, two Alsatians struck up an argument and started to circle round and bark at each other. Two youths braved the cold bare-chested, protected only by an astonishing tangle of tattoos. They were wiring crudely painted signs to some of the trees:

SAVE BONNY BRAE WOODS

NO TO SUMMERFIELD WIND FARM

TREES ARE SACRED

She couldn't see Ninian. She drew a deep breath. However angry she was, nothing would be served by losing her temper at this point. She marched up to the group of men who were smoking and said cheerfully, 'Good morning! I see you've been busy.'

One of them responded to her smile. 'Morning missus. Come to join us?'

Before she could reply, the shaven-headed one glowered at her, 'Jesus, Mickey, look at her, does she look like one of us?'

'I'm interested in what you're doing here.'

'You a cop?' The third peered at her suspiciously.

'I'm not a cop.'

'So if you're not a cop and you're not here for the cause, what in the name are you doing snooping—'

'It's all right, Seth.' Frank Griffiths emerged from the mist. 'Morning Kate. I didn't expect you quite yet.'

'I suppose not. It would have been courteous to have talked to me though, before setting all this in motion.' She waved her hand at the activity.

'Not my doing, actually. I only found out myself yesterday.'

'Oh, really?' She found this hard to believe.

Frank took her elbow and eased her away from the

198

circle of men. 'You'd be best clearing off, Kate, to be honest. Some of these guys mean business.'

'By "business" you're implying—?'

'Kate, you know I'm opposed to this wind farm, but this isn't my scene. I find it a little alarming, in fact.'

'What I don't understand,' she said, planting her feet squarely on the turf and her hands on her hips, 'is why they're here at all. The road isn't going to come this way. I made that abundantly clear to you.'

'The newspaper said—'

'Frank, you were there. I briefed the reporter very clearly. Her report was pure mischief-making.'

'I did suggest that, but this lot is convinced that there's no smoke without fire, so to speak. And anyway,' he paused, then said with an apologetic smile, 'it *is* good publicity for our campaign, Kate. It's regrettable that you're in the sniping sights, but there you go.'

She looked around. 'Are you going to be staying here?'

'At my age? I need to be in a warm bed at night. But I'll be spending quite a lot of time here, yes. No-one wants these trees cut down.'

'Including AeGen,' she reminded him.

The gloom brightened suddenly. A shaft of sunlight had found a hole in the blanket of mist and was spotlighting a mossy green clearing beside the main encampment. The tiny rise in temperature brought with it a whiff of dank autumn, earthy and musty. Two men, deep in conversation, wandered out of the trees and into her consciousness. Men? One man, rather, and a boy. *Her son*, his sandy hair familiarly tousled and his gangly limbs clad in joggers and a hooded sports top,

'Ninian!' she shouted, moving towards him, fast.

He glanced up, startled. Even at this distance, she could see the look of guilt that flashed across his face before his chin set defiantly.

Then she saw who he was with. Ibsen.

She stopped dead, assaulted by the memory of soft lips and strong arms and overpowering desire.

'Don't jump to conclusions,' he said, clearly reading her face.

'What is it then?' The anger she'd felt when she'd realised that Ninian had gone to the protest surged back. 'What is it, Ibsen? A tribute to my beliefs and expertise?'

'Mum—'

'As for you—' she rounded on Ninian, 'this is completely out of order. For a start, you should be in school. And besides, it's not only inappropriate and unnecessary, it's just bloody *stupid*. You're being stupid! Can't you see?' She waved a furious arm at the encampment, 'You're all idiots! Misinformed, misguided, gullible, bigoted, sodding delinquents!'

Diplomacy and negotiation flew to the skies and beyond reach. She was doubly betrayed, by Ibsen and by Ninian, and she didn't know which disloyalty hurt her more.

'Kate—'

'Mum—'

'Hey, missus!'

Suddenly she was in the middle of a mêlée. Everyone was shouting, arms were grabbing at her, something tripped her up and she sprawled to the ground. She grazed her face on the root of a tree and could feel blood on her forehead, warm and sticky. Her anger turned to alarm as the brawl above her turned into a full-scale skirmish.

'This way!' Strong arms hauled her to her feet and she half stumbled, was half carried out of the scrap and into the cover of the mist. 'You're a fucking idiot, Kate, do you know that?' Ibsen hissed at her, his normal amusement replaced by exasperation.

She tried to shake herself free. 'I didn't—'

'You didn't think, you fool, you jumped to conclusions and now look what you've—'

'Don't you *dare* criticise me! I had every right to say what I did, this protest is entirely unwarranted and—'

'And now it will be on the front page of every newspaper in Scotland.'

She stopped dead and stared at Ibsen. 'What?'

'You don't think this won't get reported, do you? Kate, can't you see that this is meat and drink to these people? As soon as they know who you are, which will take approximately ten seconds because Karen Cousins and Stephen are both here, they'll be onto the press. I wouldn't be surprised if some bright spark didn't film the whole thing on a mobile.'

'Oh my God,' she whispered, appalled. Her head was throbbing and she put a hand up to her face and looked at the mess on her fingers.

'Go home, Kate. Clean up. Stop worrying about Ninian, or at least, find another way of persuading him this is a bad idea.'

Someone had realised that the cause of the punch-up was no longer at the scene and they could hear shouts through the mist, coming closer.

'Where's the bitch?'

'Corporate fucking greed—'

'Snooping around—'

'Let's get her!'

'Go!' Ibsen bundled her into her car and she skidded away, wheels spinning on the grass, just as the pack burst out of the wood and into view.

She was trembling from head to toe and it was all she could do to keep the car on the road. There was obviously no way she could turn and go the direct route back to Willow Corner, so she drove the five miles through Hailesbank and back along the coast road.

It seemed like an eternity, but in fact she'd been away less than an hour. By the time she got home, Andrew was enjoying a leisurely coffee in the kitchen with the morning

201

paper for company. She stood shakily in the doorway and could see that he had filled in about half the crossword. It felt like a parallel universe.

'Back already?' he said, without looking up. 'Wish my working days were as short as that.'

She ignored the sarcasm. 'Seen Ninian this morning?'

'Nope.'

'Still in bed, is he?'

'Yup.'

'You sure about that?'

He looked up and Kate experienced a brief moment of pleasure at the expression on his face as the sight of her bruised and bleeding face registered. Andrew had taunted her with her alleged failures of motherhood too often recently. On this occasion, he was not even aware of his son's whereabouts, whereas she had been hurt in an attempt to rescue him from the clutches of maniacs.

'Kate?' There was a harsh scraping noise as he shoved back his chair and half stood, gawping. 'Are you all right?'

The pleasure was over. Her legs felt desperately weak and she thought for a moment that she was going to faint. Andrew caught her and pulled out a chair. 'Sit down. Put your head between your knees.'

Through the swaying half-darkness, she was dimly aware that she rather liked his concern. Recently, her feelings had been of little interest to Andrew Courtenay.

'Here. Drink this.'

A glass of water was held to her lips and she raised her head a fraction and sipped it cautiously. Her hands were trembling with delayed shock.

'What happened?' Andrew perched on a chair in front of her and she allowed him to capture her hands in his. 'You're shaking.'

'There's a protest up at the Woods. Ninian's there.'

'*What?*'

'I think he's been egged on by Karen Cousins and

Stephen.' She couldn't bring herself to mention Ibsen.

'What kind of protest?'

'Oh, full-scale. Tree houses, rope webs, an encampment, banners and slogans, eco warriors, the lot.'

'What the hell does Ninian think he's playing at? What about school?'

Kate took a deep breath to steady herself because the room was still spinning. 'I'm afraid I rather lost the rag.' *Goaded by Ibsen's presence*, the whisper in her head reminded her. 'I shouted at him, then some men got a bit aggressive and I fell.' She freed a hand and touched her forehead gingerly. 'There was a real punch-up, I think they're spoiling for some kind of fight. I was lucky to get away.'

'But he's still there?'

'Yes.' She was deeply exhausted. All her energy had been sapped by the drain of adrenalin from her system.

'Right.' He stood up purposefully.

'What are you going to do?'

'Go and get him, of course.'

'You can't, it's too dangerous. As soon as they know who you are— It's no time for heroism. Don't go, not yet anyway. He won't come to any harm there. Let's just think about this.' When he hesitated, she said, 'Will you clean up my face? Please?'

He dabbed on antiseptic, peering short-sightedly through his half-frame glasses. The tenderness of his ministrations touched her. Could they recover their old closeness? She caught his wrist and looked at him, hoping that a corner might be turned. 'Andrew?'

She thought for a moment he might kiss her, but he drew away, stiffly. 'There. Done. You go and shower. I'll make fresh coffee.'

An opportunity had slipped away.

Whoever built Willow Corner had an eye for location. It

was one of the first houses to be built in Forgie, it sat high on the hill so the views, particularly from the upper floor windows, rolled out for ever – south towards the Borders, north across the Forth to Fife, west to Edinburgh. Kate loved Willow Corner, but what she liked most was the way it inhabited the space in which it sat. A small burn ran across the northern reaches of the garden, then disappeared through a narrow culvert under the high stone boundary wall. A hundred yards further on, the little stream swelled in importance by flowing in the River Hailes, on its way to the sea. It was this stream – Forgie Burn – that nourished the willow trees after which the house had been named.

There were two willows – *Salix alba 'tristis'* – literally, 'sad white willow'. She'd never thought of them as sad. She considered them beautiful. Ibsen, who knew every tree in the neighbourhood, once told her that willows were short-lived – by which, apparently, he meant around fifty years.

'One of your trees must be a lot older than that, maybe eighty years,' he'd informed her as they chatted over spades and forks down at the community garden, 'It'll need to be replanted some time, maybe even soon.'

The thought dismayed her, because the willows defined the house, but she could see what he meant. One tree drooped and spread magnificently, the older one was threadbare and shabby.

Sad white willows. After she'd showered, she walked down to the trees with a mug of coffee in her hand. The sun was bright now and there was a spot between the two trees that she really loved. Years ago, some previous owner had thrown together a seat here, rough-hewn but so perfectly suited to its environment that you almost didn't notice it. The bench took advantage of a rise in the contours of the bank so that, even seated, it was just possible to glimpse the sea over the wall. But it was the view the other way that Kate liked best, back to the house.

From here, its angles and corners jutted out with the confident assertion of ownership. This is our space, this is our land, they said, you are merely our caretaker.

A car turned into the drive and began a spluttering, crunching kind of progress up the gravel. She turned at the sound of the cough, and saw Ibsen's rusting black estate car come to an apologetic halt by the front door.

Chapter Twenty

Ibsen had anticipated some kind of confrontation with Kate, he just hadn't expected it would come so soon. Mind you, he should have known as soon as Ninian Courtenay rolled up with his pal Cuzzer, that there would be trouble.

Kids. Thought it would be cool to be in a protest.

'Shouldn't you two be at school?' he asked as they appeared at daybreak with backpacks and sleeping bags, yawning.

'Chill, Ibsen,' said Cuzzer's mother, Karen, the hippy-type Ibsen had seen at the meeting in Frank Griffiths's house. 'This will be an education for them. There aren't many chances round here to get involved in something like this.'

Thanks goodness, Ibsen thought, swinging away.

Then Kate had appeared, swinging metaphorical nunchaku left, right and every which way and getting everyone inflamed.

He had to admire her – five foot three of utter fearlessness and complete conviction – but when she'd tripped and fallen, he'd experienced a surge of adrenalin like he hadn't known for years.

Protect her!

Save her!

Get her out of here safely!

Who did he think he was? Tarzan?

Once she'd gone, he was able to reflect on matters more objectively. Kate was a wind farm engineer. He hated wind farms. All other things being equal, this shouldn't keep them apart, but of course, things were not equal because Kate was a married woman. The attraction between them was undeniable, but what happened the other night on the moor was a one-off, she'd made that very plain.

'Is Mum okay?'

Deep in thought, he hadn't seen Ninian slipping away from Cuzzer and his mother. 'Hi. Yes, she's fine. She got away in her car.'

'Cool.'

Ninian did not look like a boy who felt 'cool' about anything. All the bravado he'd displayed when he'd turned up a couple of hours ago had disappeared and he looked deeply uncomfortable. He's only fifteen, Ibsen reminded himself, he's a kid. 'She's worried about you,' he said.

Ninian looked even more ill at ease.

'Tell me,' he said conversationally, 'why you've come to the protest camp.'

'Ah, they're going to cut down the trees.'

'And that's a bad thing?'

'Sure. Once they're gone, they're gone.'

He probed further and discovered that Ninian's convictions were paper thin, no more than bits and pieces of half-understood arguments regurgitated from others, almost certainly Karen Cousins. When pushed, he found them difficult to substantiate.

'It doesn't worry you that you're protesting about something your Mum's doing? That's her job – the job that no doubt keeps you in clothes and video games and pocket money?'

Ninian scowled and pulled his hood more closely round his head. 'You're here. Does it worry you?' he said aggressively.

'Yes, as a matter of fact it does, it worries me a lot. But I'm here for other reasons, that seem to me more important.' They sat for a few minutes in silence, then Ibsen said, 'What would you think about going home? Hey? I could run you back if you like.'

At the far side of the glade, they could just see Stephen, skinny as a lizard and just as nimble, scaling a tree and whooping.

'I guess,' Ninian said at last.

'There's your Mum, down by the willow tree,' Ibsen said as he turned his old van up the drive at Willow Corner.

Kate had turned at the sound, stood up and started to walk towards them. When she spotted Ninian in the passenger seat, her mouth dropped open in astonishment.

Ibsen killed the engine and wound down the window, while Ninian creaked open the door and stepped out.

'Hi Mum,' he said, tugging open the rear door and pulling out his backpack.

'Hi!' Kate's greeting came out as a squeak.

Ninian slipped into the house without hug or apology. *Adolescents,* Ibsen thought, amused.

Kate's expression was opaque. Was she mad at him for being at the camp, or did she still desire him as she undoubtedly had the other night?

'He wanted to come,' Ibsen said neutrally. 'I think he was concerned for you.'

Her eyes widened but she said nothing.

'And I think, because of the punch-up, he saw that the peaceful protest camp wasn't perhaps quite so peaceful after all.'

'Evidently,' Kate said, her hand going subconsciously to her forehead.

'Are you all right? It doesn't look too bad.'

'Andrew cleaned it up for me. I'm all right. Just tell me—'

'You're going to ask why I was there.'

'Why were you there?'

'I wanted to see what they were doing. And I wanted to show some support for the Woods.'

'I told you that road was never seriously considered for

209

the access route.'

'It's not the story that's going round.'

'Ibsen, can't you—'

'Hi there,' Andrew said from behind her, 'I take it we have you to thank for bringing our son back?'

She swivelled round.

'I just gave him a lift,' Ibsen said, relaxed.

'Well, thanks.' Andrew curled an arm round Kate and he could see surprise in her eyes. He had no real idea of what their marriage was like and he wasn't sure he wanted to find out.

'You're very welcome.' He wound the window up, turned the car briskly, and drove off.

Some instinct made him distrust Andrew Courtenay, though what it was he didn't like he really couldn't say.

Life is a series of goals, targets and building blocks. Sitting, feeding, talking. First steps, walking, running. Nursery, school, maybe university. Graduation from the top, new start each time at the bottom. Career-driven professionals take it for granted that the natural way is to keep on rising. It was certainly an assumption that Kate had made. In the biggest post-graduate college of all – life – she had gone from promotion to promotion and been handed bigger and more challenging projects year on year, and she had every expectation of continuing to rise.

She dropped Ninian off at the school gates and drove on to work.

'Kate? In here a minute please.' Mark Matthews beckoned her into his office and closed the door. He pointed at her forehead. 'Are you all right?'

'Fine. Sorry I'm late. I went up to take a look at this protest camp in Bonny Brae Woods.'

'I know.'

'You know?'

'We've had a complaint. One of the protestors, a

woman called Karen Cousins. She says you were very aggressive.'

'That's not true! I was annoyed with my son—'

'Your son? He was there?'

Kate bit her lip. She hadn't intended to tell Mark that Ninian had joined the camp. 'It's all right. He's back home now.'

'It's hardly all right. This woman tells us she's going to speak to the press.'

For the second time that day, Kate's legs refused to hold her vertical. She sank onto a chair. 'Oh.'

'I need hardly tell you, Kate, that aggression in these circumstances is not something we expect of our senior managers.'

'No. Absolutely not. I was only angry with Ninian.'

'But that's not how it came across.'

'Don't you see, Mark? These people are twisting the facts. That's what they do. That's the very basis of their whole approach.'

'I know, but I need to give you a warning. Control your temper, Kate, no matter what the provocation.'

She stood up. 'I will. I promise.'

'Right.'

She thought that was it. She called a meeting of the team and they spent much of the morning discussing their strategy for dealing with the eco camp and its band of so-called warriors.

At one o'clock, a shout came from Mark's office. 'Kate! In here. *Now.*'

Alarmed, she hurried across to his office. A small television in the corner was switched on and a reporter was saying, '—and meanwhile, in Scotland, protestors at a camp set up to protest against planned destruction of an ancient oak wood by wind farm developers have been involved in a scuffle with a representative of the company concerned, AeGen.'

She gaped at the screen, horrified. But what came next was worse, far worse. A slightly blurry image of a small, wildly gesticulating woman – *her* – shouting and screaming.

'—this is completely out of order. It's not only inappropriate and unnecessary, it's just bloody *stupid*. You're being stupid! Can't you see? You're all idiots! Misinformed, misguided, gullible, bigoted, sodding delinquents!'

'A spokeswoman for AeGen refused to comment. This is —'

Mark flicked the television off and looked at her.

'They've taken it out of context, Mark, don't you see?' she stuttered, appalled. 'I was talking to—'

'To your son. You said. But it doesn't make the slightest difference, Kate. This is what the world sees.'

'I gave instruction that the access road—'

'We're not talking about who did or didn't do something, Kate. We're talking about your behaviour, in public, in the media. Get your handbag, Kate. Leave everything else on your desk. I'll take you to the front door, there's no need for me to call security, but I'm going to have to suspend you while we consider what action to take.'

Kate lifted her chin, shocked. There was nothing she could do, but the facts were all on her side. It would all be sorted and she'd soon be back at her desk.

She could feel a dozen pairs of eyes staring at her back as she walked the long walk through the open plan office. Lisa, Gail, Jack – each would have a different expression, each would hide a different sentiment, but each one of them would be sending up a small prayer of thanks that they were not in her shoes.

Andrew was less than sympathetic. 'I don't know what you thought you were doing, Kate, racing off down there without even waking me to discuss it.'

'Call it a moment of impulsiveness.'

'Or foolhardiness.'

She sighed. Andrew was infuriatingly right.

'So what's going to happen?'

'I don't know. They've suspended me. Until they make a decision, there's nothing I can do.'

'Are they paying you?'

She stared at Andrew. He wasn't normally mercenary. 'Full pay. For the moment. Anyway, it's immaterial. It'll all be sorted out in a few days.'

'That's something, I suppose. So what'll you do?'

'Do? As in fight back?'

'As in from getting up in the morning to going to bed at night.'

This was a new thought to Kate. For the first time since the summer she'd spent hiking round Europe before going to university, she was going to have time on her hands. She looked around distractedly.

'I'll paint the kitchen.'

'What?'

'It's looking shabby. I hadn't noticed. I'll paint it.'

'You've never painted anything in your life.'

'So? It can't be difficult.' She touched a patch on the wall by the back door where years of bodies brushing past had left a grubby gray mark. 'See what I mean? And here?' She indicated black streaks at the base of the door. She had a habit of coming in with shopping and kicking the door shut behind her.

'We can get a decorator in if it disturbs you.'

'No, I can do it. I'll start tomorrow.'

'I hope it's not going to interfere with my writing.' Andrew was scowling. He wasn't given to sulking so it was not an expression she saw much, but it underscored the resemblance to Ninian so thoroughly that she couldn't help laughing.

213

'What's so funny?'

She reached a finger up and smoothed away the vertical line between his brows. 'You. Ninian. The pair of you. I suppose Ninian can blame his moods on hormones, but you don't have any such excuse. I won't get in your way, Andrew, I promise you. And don't you think I'm the one who has the right to scowl, not you?'

'Will you look for another job?'

'No, why should I? I have every intention of getting my own job back.' She couldn't believe that this morning's suspension was anything other than a formality, a show for the rest of the world that some action had been taken. She would get a formal warning, that was all. 'By Monday I'll be back at AeGen. In the meantime, we'll have a freshly decorated kitchen.'

A little to her surprise, Harry and Jane appeared after supper. Harry didn't call often, and certainly not uninvited. He was a man for formalities, for dates and diaries and arrangements. Perhaps Jane's influence was more extensive than she had imagined and some spontaneity was being injected into her plodding stepson.

Andrew thumped Harry on the shoulder. 'Hello, Harry. To what do we owe the pleasure?'

She kissed Harry's cheek and embraced Jane. 'Hi! Come in!'

They sat in the living room, which felt cold and unused. It was a summer room, with its cool blue decor and draughts they had never been quite able to eradicate. She ignited the gas flame fire, switched on small lamps and drew the heavy curtains so that the room began to be more welcoming.

'Glass of wine? Coffee?'

'Nothing, thank you, Kate. We've just finished eating.'

She sat down, disappointed. A show of hospitality would have kept her busy and useful – and established her position as mistress of the house. Ridiculous, of course, that she needed to feel that, after all these years as Andrew's wife.

There was some idle chat – 'How's work?' – 'How are the wedding plans coming on?' – and after half an hour Kate began to wonder what the visit was about. Perhaps they needed a loan, but were loath to ask. Weddings weren't cheap. Kate wondered if she should offer. It wasn't, perhaps, the best time, in the light of today's events.

Harry said, 'We had a visitor yesterday.'

'Oh?'

'Yes.' He glanced at Jane, as if for encouragement, then ploughed on determinedly. 'Jane's cousin Sophie came round.'

If the atmosphere in the room had been chilly before, it certainly dropped another few degrees now. Kate hardly dared to look at Andrew's face and she knew her own was paralysed.

'She was in a terrible state. We're quite worried about her. Her last relationship broke down quite acrimoniously and she rather fell apart.'

Kate and Andrew stared at him. Kate had a deep sense of dread, and heaven knows what Andrew was thinking. She didn't dare look at him.

Harry turned to his father. 'She claimed that you and she are having some kind of affair.'

Harry the Confronter. Where Andrew, wimpishly, turned from altercation, Harry challenged what he feared, even if it required a descent into rudeness.

'Of course,' Harry said into the silence that greeted his last remark, 'she has always been something of a fantasist, so we were quite sure she was lying.'

He snickered. Was he expecting denial, Kate wondered? Were they looking forward to a dissection of young Sophie's wild imaginings? Or even, maybe, half-

215

hoping to discover that his stepmother was about to be ousted from his father's bed, in some kind of just retribution for her behaviour half a lifetime ago?

'And you thought,' Andrew said quietly, 'you'd just come and find out, the pair of you.'

Harry blanched. 'I – we – thought—'

'If you were sure she was lying, why have you come to ask me if it's true?'

Kate almost admired Andrew at that moment because it was none of Harry's business one way or the other. His next words, though, exploded her budding esteem.

'Yes, I'm having an affair with her. We've been shagging each other day and night for weeks. What do you intend to do about it?'

Harry's jaw dropped open. Jane, normally so effervescent and smiling, looked thunderstruck. Kate's eyes grew round as she stared at her husband, unsure how to take his words.

Andrew laughed. 'See what I mean? If I am sleeping with Sophie, Harry, that's my affair. If I'm not, the subject is irrelevant.'

He sat back with a bland smile and crossed his arms.

Jane said, 'But Sophie is my cousin, and I was concerned. She seemed so wound up. And she's terribly young. I mean, half your age— If you are ... if you were... I felt I should...'

Kate had always thought Andrew adored Jane, so she was shocked by the savagery with which he rounded on her now. 'You should what, Jane? Take her in hand? Protect her from the preying older man? Reprimand me? What?'

Jane shrank back in her chair. 'Yes ... no ... I'm sorry, I— I see now that... Harry, we should never have come.'

Andrew said, more quietly, 'You are always welcome here Jane, you and Harry. But you're right in one thing, you were not well-advised to raise this question.'

'*Wrong.*'

The voice came from the doorway and four heads swivelled as one, to see Ninian standing there, his face contorted.

'You're wrong, Dad. It was absolutely fucking right to raise this question. Someone had to. Someone had to challenge you.'

Andrew started to get up. 'Nin—'

'*Don't start.*' He spat the words with venom. 'Don't start trying to make excuses, Dad, or pretend. Don't *lie*.' He imitated his father's voice, reading. ' "*He must have her – this girl, with her unreadable eyes and hair like the mantle of the night and lips made for love.*" '

Kate stared at him, appalled. Andrew's manuscript! He *had* seen it. Not only had he seen it, he had *memorised* it. Harry and Jane looked mystified. Kate looked from Ninian to Andrew, then from Andrew to Ninian.

Andrew smiled. 'Ah. You read my draft.'

'I always read your fucking drafts.'

'Don't swear,' Kate muttered automatically, but no-one took any notice.

'It's a story, Ninian.'

'*Dad!*' Ninian's fist thumped into the doorpost. It must have hurt. She could see him wince, but he ploughed on, furious. 'Don't give me that story thing. You always fucking hide behind it. It's such a great cover, isn't it, for absolutely everything. "It's just a story." '

Andrew was about to say something, but Ninian cut in over him. 'And the silent calls are part of the story too, are they?'

Andrew said, 'What are you talking about?' just as Kate said, 'Silent calls?'

'It's *her*, isn't it? Wanting to talk to you.'

Kate said, puzzled, 'I thought it was Frank Griffiths.'

Ninian gave a dry, sarcastic laugh. 'You're so naive, Mum.'

217

Her head was whirling. 'Am I? I certainly thought it was some wind farm protestor, trying to upset me.'

'Didn't you realise? The calls only ever come when Dad's not around? She phones him all the time, she speaks to him whenever she can. Haven't you heard him breaking off conversations when you come in the room? Stopping suddenly when you come in the front door? Looking fucking *guilty?*'

Kate's mouth fell open, but the moment Ninian said the words, everything fell into place.

'And the funny-coloured car outside? Sophie, waiting to see if Dad's around and can come out to play.'

'No!'

'Haven't you seen her, Mum?'

'No. Whenever I opened the front door, the car drove off. I thought they were spying on me.'

'*She* was spying on you. She's such a fucking attention-seeker. She wants Dad all the time.' He turned savagely on Harry. 'Maneater MacAteer was telling you the truth, Harry. For bloody once. Didn't you realise? Remember what I told you at the engagement party? That I saw Dad snogging someone? Well, no prizes for guessing who it was he was snogging.'

He swung wildly away from them all and slammed the living room door behind him. Kate could hear him pounding up the stairs and the muffled sound of his bedroom door slamming.

She'd spent half a lifetime trying to appease and please Harry, overcompensating for her nervousness around him by a politeness that probably verged on smarmy, but now she rounded on him with a ferociousness she didn't know she had in her. 'See what you've done?'

Harry stood up, his face set and strained. 'We didn't mean to stir things. We thought it was funny, actually. We thought it was all some wishful invention of Sophie's.'

Kate didn't believe him. He'd had every intention of

stirring things up, he just hadn't anticipated having quite such a cataclysmic effect.

'Ninian,' she hissed, 'is a teenager. He deserves a stable home and a loving family around him. He does not need to overhear a conversation like this.'

'Oh,' Harry said. 'Like I had a stable home, you mean?'

'Oh Christ,' Andrew said wearily as Kate's hands flew to her mouth. 'Harry, I think you'd better go, don't you?'

Harry looked mortified, Jane stricken, Andrew exhausted. Kate, watching Harry and Jane leave, felt flayed. It was, without a doubt, the worst day of her life.

Chapter Twenty-One

Kate dreamed that night of ash-coloured paint and of her mother, with her disapproving face on, saying, 'Too *gray*, darling, too gray,' and she didn't know whether she meant the paint or Andrew. It was chosen for the kitchen, she supposed, but why had she selected the colour of turbines? Ninian was there too, calling to her, begging her to do something, and she knew he was unhappy and in need, but what he wanted her to do she had no idea. She was covered in the paint, rolling in it, and it was warm and sticky and glorious, then she realised it was not paint at all, but a blanket made of stars. Its light shimmered and glowed and bathed her in its beauty, and she felt alluring and powerful. Her face was being stroked, so lightly that she thought the feathers of an owl had skimmed her cheeks, but it was not an owl, it was Ibsen's pony tail, and the realisation of that woke her, guiltily, to the cold comfort of her own bedroom, and Andrew, deep in sleep, curled beside her as untroubled as a child.

For some time she tossed and turned, picking apart the seams of her dream and clutching, like a comfort blanket in her memory, the pieces that had pleased her. But in the end, the gray dominated: gray turbines, whirling out of her reach and her control; gray hair – Andrew's – like a reproach to her broken vows; the dismal gray days of a future that stretched in front of her without apparent end. At last, as the cold light of dawn showed itself as a slit of silver at the side of the curtains, she slotted her body, spoonlike, behind Andrew, her knees angled in behind his knees, her stomach against the smooth, warm curve of his

221

bottom, her cheek nestling against the sharp angles of his shoulder blades, and fell asleep.

It was unlike her to sleep late. She was used to rising with the dawn. Perhaps it was because this morning there was nowhere to go – or, more likely, because her night had been so disturbed – but she woke with a start to a tentative rapping on the door and the sound of Mrs Gillies's voice calling, 'Hello? Andrew?'

Confused and disorientated, she shot a glance at Andrew, who was beginning to stir at the noise.

'What is it?' she called, slipping out of bed and throwing her dressing gown round herself.

When she pulled open the door, Mrs Gillies took a quick step back, startled. 'Oh, Kate! You're here.'

'What's wrong?'

'I just wondered – I didn't know you were here – sorry, I thought Andrew might be – it's Ninian.' The words tumbled out of her like drips from a leaking tap, faster and faster, splishing and splashing with increasing incoherence.

Kate said firmly, 'Mrs Gillies, you're not making any sense. Will you please take a deep breath and tell me what you're so concerned about.'

One of the woman's large hands was planted firmly on her chest, so that it moved up and down in syncopation with her rapid breathing. Kate stared at the movement, half hypnotised. 'It's Ninian,' she said. 'He's not there.'

Not again, was her first thought. She sighed. 'He'll be at the eco camp up the road,' she said through a yawn. 'Don't worry about it, I'll check it out.'

'If you're sure.'

'Listen, Mrs Gillies, Ninian is my son and my responsibility,' she said, irritable with tiredness.

Mrs Gillies retreated downstairs, sulking.

When she turned back into the room, Andrew was

222

heading for a shower. 'What's up?'

'Ninian's not in his room.'

'Little bugger,' he said unfeelingly.

The scene from last night replayed itself in her head. *The Maneater was telling you the truth, Harry. For bloody once.* What had Harry really thought he was doing, for heaven's sake? Why confront Andrew and her together? If he'd had concerns, why not have a quiet word with his father? In the light of morning, some of the fears and nightmares of the night before seemed diminished, others magnified. She could examine them more rationally, but looked at with an application of common sense, they seemed on the whole more justified rather than less.

Didn't you realise? The calls only ever come when Dad's not around? Haven't you heard him breaking off conversations when you come in the room? ... Looking fucking guilty?

'You're still seeing her, aren't you?'

He was tying the belt on his dressing gown, but at her words he stopped, looking like a small boy caught with his hands in the cookie jar. 'I promised I would tell her, and I did.'

It was the classic Andrew sidestep. 'But she didn't accept that? Or, she couldn't? Oh Andrew. What have you got yourself into?'

She saw his face tighten, then he swung away. 'I'm going for a shower.'

'What about Ninian? What about your son?'

'Have you checked your phone?'

'Have you checked yours?'

Like synchronised swimmers, perfect mirror images of each other, they each reached out a hand to their bedside tables, picked up their mobile phones, checked for messages, replaced the phone with a blank face, shook their heads.

'Nothing on mine.'

223

'Or mine.'

'He'll be at that eco camp again.'

'Will you go and look? I can't.'

'Why don't you start by calling round some of his friends? Banksy and Cuzz, for a start. He's probably just gone off in a sulk.'

'I'll phone Helena Banks, but you'll have to deal with Karen Cousins. If you can reach her. I'm sure it was Karen who encouraged Ninian to go down there. She won't talk to me, no chance.'

He sighed. 'Let's not panic. Ninian'll be holed up somewhere, making a point. I'm going to shower and dress. I'll start phoning once I've got a coffee in my hand.'

Kate didn't argue, she was inclined to agree with him. She thought it was very likely that Ninian was punishing them, though while Andrew was in the shower, her dream came back to her, and she started to fret. *He wants me to do something, but I don't know what.*

Kate had only met Helena Banks briefly, but she admired her straightforward, no-nonsense approach to life and to child rearing. 'I'm so sorry to call so early, I just wondered if by any chance Ninian spent the night with you last night?' She gave a small, embarrassed laugh. 'He's been a bit—' she searched for a neutral word that might give some indication of Ninian's recent behaviour, '— erratic, recently. Teenage boys.'

'From cuddle to cold shoulder overnight. I know.'

There was a small measure of relief in knowing Helena understood – that she wasn't the only parent whose son had transmogrified from dear and dependent to grumpy and testing.

'—But I'm sorry, he wasn't here. Just a moment.'

She must have covered the receiver because Kate heard a muffled exchange with someone in the background, and then she was back on the line. 'Elliott says he hasn't seen him for a few days. I'm sorry.'

'He hasn't been in school?'

'As I say, Elliott hasn't seen him. Maybe they've had different classes?'

'Maybe.' Now she wanted to get off the line, fast. She hated that Helena Banks knew that she had so little control over her son that she couldn't even keep him in his own bed at night. 'Not to worry, I must have misunderstood what he told me. Thank you.'

'Kate—'

'Yes?'

'I know you're a busy, working woman, but it would be nice to have coffee sometime?'

'I'd like that.' She put the phone down and stared at it. It *would* be nice. When had she last made a new friend? When did she last meet someone, other than Charlotte, for coffee, to go shopping, to have a girlie night out? Work and family monopolised her life and perhaps she had neglected other parts of it.

'Not there?'

Andrew had fortified himself with a coffee and was hovering, hopefully, by her side. He didn't want to call Karen Cousins, she could tell, and she couldn't blame him – but it was not a call she could make. She handed him the phone. 'Nope. Your turn.'

He took it reluctantly. 'I could just go up to the camp.'

'If you prefer.'

She could see him glancing at her forehead, where yesterday's graze had hardened and darkened and the shadows of a bruise threatened to invade her eye socket. He dialled. She left him to it – she had no wish to eavesdrop on Karen Cousins' peculiar brand of invective.

In the kitchen, Mrs Gillies was swabbing the floor vigorously with a wet mop. 'He never goes out without eating. If he's not in his bed, there's cereal everywhere and a bowl swimming with milk. That's how I knew something was wrong. There was nothing there.'

'Mrs Gillies—'

'He needs a bit of loving care, that one. You can see it, poor lad. He's—'

'Mrs Gillies,' she said, more firmly, 'Ninian has plenty of loving care, as you put it. He's simply a teenage boy, testing where the boundaries of acceptable behaviour lie. Now—'

'Father stuck in that room all the time, or off out heaven knows where, mother out at work—' she grumbled more to herself than to me, all the time dab, dab, dabbing at the floor.

'*Mrs Gillies.*' This time she used her most authoritative voice and Mrs Gillies stopped and glared at her rebelliously. 'Thank you for pointing out Ninian's absence. Now, I think the floor is pretty much spotless, don't you? It's time that the dining room had a good spring clean, I noticed the brass fender was distinctly tarnished, and I'm not sure when the silver in the cabinet was last polished.'

Jean Gillies bristled at Kate's criticism of her housekeeping, her faded brown bun wobbling ominously, but her righteous indignation was easier to manage than her possessive attitude towards Ninian. Kate sent her scuttling out of the kitchen, clutching a basket full of polishes and dusters, tut tutting under her breath, just as Andrew appeared in the doorway. She stopped abruptly.

'The silver, Mrs Gillies.'

Mrs Gillies trudged off again, reluctance in every step. When she was out of earshot, Kate said, 'Well?'

'That Karen Cousins is some woman, isn't she? I got a complete lecture on the nature and repugnancy of capitalism.'

'Yes, I expect you did. Is Ninian there?'

'Actually, no.'

'*No?*'

'Apparently he was there around eleven o'clock last

226

night—'

After the row with Harry.

'—but he and Stephen wandered off together and didn't come back.'

'Wandered off? At that time of night?'

'Apparently.'

'Didn't she care?'

'She seemed quite relaxed.'

'Isn't she worried about Stephen?'

'Oh, he's back there, sleeping.'

'*What?* And Ninian's not?'

'Nope.'

'Didn't she wake him to ask him where Ninian is?'

Andrew laughed mirthlessly. 'Apparently even suggesting such a thing was gross selfishness on my part. Her boy needs his sleep – though not, apparently, an education.'

'We'd better get round there.'

'Hang on a minute – what about phoning the school? Just in case he's actually gone in to classes.'

Ninian was not at school. According to them, he had not registered there for a few days and his guidance teacher had a note to call us to discuss his repeated absences.

Kate looked at Andrew with mounting alarm. 'I dropped him at the gates yesterday, on my way to work.'

'He can't have gone in.'

'But why not?'

Andrew stared at her, his feelings of helplessness plain on his face. Kate loved her son, but Andrew, she forced herself to remember, had spent more time with him – and whatever faults Andrew might have she could not criticise him for being a bad father. She reached out a hand. For a second, she thought he was not going to take it, then he raised his slowly, and twined his fingers through hers. They were joined, for now at least, in their concern.

The familiar coughing of an aging engine overrode the moment. Kate raised her head. Ibsen? Here? Again?

'Sounds like the gardener chap.'

'The gardener chap has a name,' she said, irritated by his condescension. 'Ibsen Brown.'

'What kind of name is that, for heaven's sake?'

Despite everything, she couldn't repress a small smile. 'Different,' she conceded.

'What's he doing here, anyway?'

They didn't need to ask. There was a startled squawk from Mrs Gillies and Ninian appeared. Relief was swiftly followed by anger.

'Where the hell have you been? Don't you know how worried we've been? We were just on the point of calling the police.'

Kate took in his pinched, gray face and hollow cheeks and gasped. There were dark rings under his eyes and his hair looked matted and dirty. 'Ninian?'

He avoided her gaze and pushed past her. 'Going for a shower,' he mumbled.

He disappeared upstairs, leaving four adults gazing up at his muddy heels.

Ibsen, hovering at the front door, said, 'I should explain.'

All Kate's anger turned on Ibsen. She said, 'Yes, I think you should.'

Andrew said, 'Can we offer you a coffee?'

'He doesn't need a coffee.'

Andrew was clearly taken aback. 'I think it's the least we can do, don't you?'

Kate was horribly conscious of Ibsen's proximity. This was the man she had made love to, wrapped in her blanket of stars. His presence in her house was a living reproach to her infidelity and she wasn't sure she could hide the way she responded to him. She avoided his eyes. She avoided Andrew's eyes.

'Okay,' she said gruffly, 'come in.'

'I was on my way home from the skittles at the pub last night,' Ibsen said, 'when something made me stop at the community garden. I had a sneaking suspicion that the volunteers who were there last night might not have locked away their tools properly in the hut. It was a still night, and as soon as I got out of my car, I smelt skunk.'

'Skunk?'

'Cannabis. Marihuana. Pot. Skunk.'

'Coming from the garden?'

'That's right.'

'Not Ninian?'

'Ninian and that friend of his, Cuzz. They were sitting on the ground with their backs to the wall, so far gone they didn't even notice me.'

'Ninian was smoking *cannabis*?'

'A rather stronger version of cannabis, yes.'

Every mother's worst fear is that her child might become addicted to drugs. In the Courtenay household they had always talked openly about such things and Ninian knew her views.

'Oh, God.' She sunk her head into her hands and thought about it.

Andrew said, 'What happened?'

'Cuzz, I suspect, has been using the drug for some time. He just swore at me, then got up and sauntered off. Ninian was in no state to join him, I'm afraid. Ninian was having a bad trip.'

'This was last night? Why didn't you call us?'

'I did call. I left a message on your mobile.'

'No you didn't. I checked my mobile. There were no messages.'

'I promise you, I did. When I didn't get an answer, I sat with him for some time, then managed to get him into my car. I was going to bring him here, but he'd come down enough to beg me not to.' The hyacinth eyes were more

229

intense than ever. 'I'm sorry.'

'What are you sorry for? For not bringing him here? For knowing that Ninian didn't want to come here?'

Ibsen ignored her questions. 'I took him home. It seemed the best thing to do. I sat up with him most of the night. He was having a bad downer. If it's any consolation, I suspect this was a first time for Ninian – certainly the first time with a strain of cannabis as strong as skunk.'

'You took the responsibility of sitting with my son through that and didn't even let us know?' Fear was making her infuriated. Fear – and a complicated, multilayered kind of shame.

'The man did his best,' Andrew said, his voice conciliatory.

Her husband was defending her lover. It was too much. 'I want you to go,' she said to Ibsen.

He stood. 'My pleasure.'

As soon as she heard the bitterness in his voice, she regretted her words, but by then it was too late.

Chapter Twenty-Two

If Violet had lived she'd be five years old. Five and a half. She'd be a pupil at Summerfield Primary School, one of the little girls skipping through his maze or holding hands with some new best friend on his friendship path.

There were times, working at the garden, that Ibsen found these thoughts almost too much to bear. Still, at least he didn't have to face the challenges of parenthood that Kate and her husband were facing, maybe that was some consolation.

He dug his spade into the ground with such force that it took considerable effort to pull it out again. That argument was such rubbish. He'd give anything to have the challenges of parenthood ahead of him, and he knew it.

'Hi, Ibs.'

He looked up, startled. It was windy and wet and he hadn't expected any of the volunteers would join him. It wasn't a volunteer, though – it was Melanie McGillivray her auburn hair half hidden under a hood, her nose pink with the cold.

'Melanie.' He straightened up. 'What are you doing here?'

'Thought I'd see what you're up to. Everyone's talking about the garden.'

'You haven't picked the best of days to visit.'

She shrugged. 'I had some free time.'

He'd only seen Melanie once since the episode of the dahlias, and that had not been a comfortable meeting. He stared at her, his eyes narrowed. She was up to something. She had to be. Melanie and an interest in gardens didn't

231

mix.

'I'm sorry, you know. About the flowers.'

'You said.'

'No, but I mean it.'

He said nothing. After a minute, she tried again. 'How's the baby? Cassie's little girl?'

'She's fine.'

'Good.'

'You got time for a drink?'

'I thought you wanted to see the garden.' This was mischievous, but the devil in him couldn't resist.

'Oh well, yeah, sure. Or you could tell me about it in the pub.'

Ibsen grinned. 'Never change, eh Mel?' He looked around. There wasn't much more he could do here today anyway. 'Give me a minute, then, till I get the tools locked away.'

Nothing had changed in The Crossed Keys, except that he hadn't been in here with Mel in three months. When they walked through the door together, Davey Fegan turned and gawped. His mouth opened to shout something, but at Ibsen's glare he clearly thought better of it, and shut his mouth again.

'Peach schnapps and orange, Nora, and a coke.'

They settled in a quiet corner.

'So,' Ibsen said after Nora had brought the drinks over, 'What is it you really want, Mel?'

'You don't miss nothing, do you?' She slid along the bench as close as she could to him. 'I thought we might get together again, Ibs. You and me.'

'You did?'

'We were good.' She fluttered her lashes at him. 'Remember? Curled round each other in that bed of yours? Best sex I ever had. You too, you told me.'

A man's cock, Ibsen thought with wry amusement, is sometimes *not* his best friend. Memories of nights spent

232

with Mel gave him an instant erection. He crossed his legs and shifted away from her. 'That was then, Mel.'

She moved closer again. 'Come on, Ibs, You know you want to. And don't tell me there's someone else, 'cos I know there's not.'

'Really? How?'

'Not difficult to find things out around here.'

It was true. Summerfield was a small community. Ibsen was profoundly thankful that Mel and her spies hadn't happened to glimpse him driving up to the moor with Kate Courtenay that night, because no doubt the fires of rumour would have spread in an instant.

'Hmm.'

'So how about it? You and me?'

He shook his head. 'Sorry.'

'You said you'd forgiven me,' she wheedled.

Maybe he had said that, but only to get her off his back because destroying his dahlia garden was something he'd never forget. He said, 'I'm moving away.'

She sat back, gaping. 'Moving? Where to? What'll your folks say?'

Ibsen had no idea where the words had come from, they'd just emerged from his mouth. He improvised rapidly. 'I've applied for a job down south. Northamptonshire.'

He'd *seen* a job advertised in one of the trade magazines. It looked interesting – head of a sub-team at a large estate, much more the kind of thing he'd trained for than the jobbing gardening he was doing right now.

Mel shut her mouth. It sagged open again. 'But you've always lived in Summerfield. You can't go!'

'Maybe you've just given me the best reason of them all. I need a change, Mel. And a challenge.'

She used the biggest weapon she could think of. 'What about Daisy Rose?'

Ibsen's hand clenched round his glass. She thought she

233

was being clever, but she'd picked the wrong line of attack. He would not be blackmailed. He finished his coke.

'Nice seeing you again, Mel. All the best.'

He stood up.

'That's it? You're going? Just like that?'

'Well, not tomorrow,' he admitted. 'But I'm moving on, that's for certain.' *Moving on from you, if nothing else.*

'You'll never get a better lay,' she shouted after him as he strode across the pub.

By the bar, Davey Fegan snorted with laughter, but Ibsen didn't care. He was thinking of Kate Courtenay. Now *that* had been precious.

Trouble was, he couldn't get rid of the memories of Kate. He'd felt such closeness, up there on the moor. She'd been smart, taking him up there to show him the wind farm rather than just talking about it.

The damned Summerfield project was driving a wedge through the whole community. Ian and Cassie were against, because Ian, as an oil worker, couldn't see past oil as the answer to the energy problem. His Pa was all in favour, because he liked the idea of energy that came from nowhere and worked on nothing more than a puff of air. A lot of Summerfield folk wanted it, because all they could see were pound signs. There'd be work for quite a few of them and more money rolling in than they could spend on local projects once the AeGen sweeteners – *blood money* as Frank called it – came into play. Frank and quite a lot of the Forgie crowd hated the whole thing. The Cousins woman was a professed environmentalist who didn't want the scenery spoiled, though there were other people who called themselves environmentalists who said renewable energy was the only way to protect the planet.

'You've kept very quiet about it all, Ma,' he said to Betty, as he was putting up some shelves in his parents' kitchen.

Betty waited till he'd drilled the holes for the rawlplugs. 'I think I'm with your father,' she said carefully, when Ibsen glanced over at her, four screws held between his lips ready for screwing the shelf into place. 'I like them. I find them peaceful.'

Ibsen's eyebrows rose, but he wasn't in a position to speak. He turned his attention to the shelf.

Betty said, 'They're hypnotic and quite graceful. But I understand how you feel, son – you know, 'cos we said goodbye to Violet up there. I know what that means to you.'

He finished the last screw and stood back to survey his work. The shelves would accommodate Betty's saucepans so that she'd be able to get them up out of her way – she'd been tripping over the old stand and moaning about it for years.

'How do they look?'

'Great. Thanks.' She patted the seat next to her at the kitchen table. 'Sit down, love.'

Ibsen tested the shelves by wiggling them sharply. They were rock-steady. 'They'll do. Want me to put the pans up for you?'

'No, I'll clean them first. I want you to sit down.'

He sat.

'I don't like you getting involved with that crowd up at the protest.'

'Ma, I—'

'Violet's gone, love. She'll never be gone from our memories, or our hearts, but she's gone. Whatever you think about wind farms, you mustn't take up a position on Summerfield because of that.'

'I don't—'

'I don't like it. Lot of unwashed thugs, moving around the country making a nuisance of themselves. They're protesters all right, but it's just a game for them. They're professionals, not locals.'

Ibsen opened his mouth to say something, but Betty interrupted.

'Now, I don't want to hear another word.'

Ibsen closed his mouth. When his mother took that tone, there was nothing more to be said. If he were to get involved, it would have to be with great care.

'You needn't worry,' Ninian said to Kate, 'that I'll do it again. It was rank.'

They were sitting on the bench under the willows, sharing a rare moment of quiet. When Ninian had been little – a rumpled, energetic, bright-eyed four-year-old – they used to come down here to weave daisies into chains and makes wishes on the puff of a dandelion head.

'Do you remember asking not to be brought home?' She had to know, because this sliver of information had needled into her flesh and was festering there.

There was a shrug. 'Sort of.'

She bit her lip. The little boy who blew wishes on dandelion seeds would have wriggled onto her lap in times of distress, and burrowed his head into her chest for comfort. 'Can you explain why?'

'Mu-um.'

'You think we would have been cross?'

'Well? Wouldn't you?'

Of course they would have been angry, and worried and – probably – unsure how best to handle it. She had never been into the drugs scene, she'd been too busy being Miss Smart-Ass, the top-of-the-class engineer. As for Andrew, Kate thought that the summit of his experience was the rat-end of the odd toke at arty parties in the eighties.

'Ibsen was so cool.'

'Really?'

'He sat with me all night. I don't think I was pretty.'

'He should have phoned me.'

236

'I'm sure he did.' Ninian screwed up his face in concentration and again she saw again the small boy, this time doing his sums, crayoning a drawing from a colouring book, building houses of cards. She wanted to fold him in her arms and roll back the years so that she could play her part in his life differently. 'Sure as I can be.'

'There was no message, Ninian.'

The events of those few days were etched in her memory. Lisa's call, her visit to the protest camp and her impassioned outburst, triggered by worry over Ninian and – here her mind halted in its tracks and challenged her to acknowledge the truth – all right, she conceded, by her hurt at discovering Ibsen among the protestors. Then there had been her suspension and rapid departure from AeGen's forest-green offices.

Her suspension!

Her eyes widened and she thumped her hand on her thigh. 'Oh, Christ!'

'Don't swear, Mum.'

'My phone. I gave him my business card, so he'd have called my work mobile.'

'So?'

'I don't have it any longer. It's in the office.'

Ninian looked at her as though something had just registered in his brain. 'Why aren't you there, anyway?'

'They suspended me.'

'What?'

'Suspended. You know, as in told me to go home and not come in to work.'

'Wicked.'

'You don't get it, Ninian. I'm in disgrace.'

'What about?'

'For shouting at you up at the camp. Someone filmed it and it got on the news.'

'So?'

'They believe I've brought the company's reputation into disrepute. It doesn't look good.'

'That's pants.' As the news sank in, he said, 'Bloody hell. Was that because of me?'

'I lost my temper, Ninian. I shouldn't have done that.'

'But you were cross because I'd gone up there. Shit.' He ran his hand through already messy hair. 'I didn't mean you to get screwed, Mum. I was just— Cuzz's Mum said— and I was pissed off. About everything, I guess.'

'I know.'

'Will it be all right? At work?'

'I don't know. Hopefully.'

They both fell silent. A neighbour somewhere was cutting the grass and far, far above them, an aeroplane left its vapour trail in a clear blue sky. A bird trilled from a bush near the garden wall. The small sounds of everyday life.

Ninian said, 'Sorry, Mum.'

The words were sweeter to Kate than any birdsong. 'Never mind.' She studied him. He was taller than her by a good ten inches these days, and strong enough already to pick her up easily. But in all the realities that mattered, he was a child – *her* child – and she had failed him in so many ways. 'I should say sorry to you too, Ninian.'

'What for?'

'Everything.' She tried to be more specific. 'For not being here for you when you needed me. For working when I could have been a better mother. For not realising how hurt you were feeling. For—'

He laughed. It was the first time she'd seen him laugh properly in an age, but now it was her turn to be puzzled. 'What?'

'That's not lots of things, Mum, that's one thing.'

'Well then.'

He looked at her, his chestnut eyes so like Andrew's. 'You should apologise to Ibsen, you know. He's an okay

238

bloke. He looked after me.'

'I'm glad he did.'

Truth be told, she longed to apologise to Ibsen. She longed to speak to Ibsen, full stop. More than that – she wanted to be in those arms, wrapped up close to the shirt that read 'YOU CAN USE ME AGAIN AND AGAIN', and doing just that. But Ibsen Brown wasn't into relationships, he had a serious commitment problem, and for very good reason.

Whatever spark there was between them, it was no more than a sexual frisson. And nice as it had been, the man had made it very clear that it was not something he wanted to repeat. Full stop.

Chapter Twenty-Three

It was a time of struggles. If the first struggle was the important matter of parenting, the second was the altogether trivial mini-war between herself and paint, which nonetheless took on monumental proportions. Kate had thought that painting the kitchen would be an easy, perhaps even a calming, activity, but she could not have been more wrong.

First of all, the paint she chose was described as 'butter'. It looked nice and creamy in the illustration. The kitchen shown in the paint chart gleamed softly. It was fresh and inviting, like a cold glass of milk on a hot summer's day. When she got it home, however, she discovered a sickly yellow in the can.

'What's that?' Andrew asked, horrified.

'Butter, it's called. Look.' She shoved the paint brochure in front of him. He glanced at the picture.

'That's not the same colour.'

'It's supposed to be.'

He put on his glasses and inspected the illustration. 'The paint here is called Buttermilk,' he announced, 'with the wall behind the shelving picked out in Butter.'

Kate groaned. 'Oh, God. I must have read it wrong.'

'Take it back.'

She put the lid on the can and pressed it down by dint of leaping onto the tin and stamping around the edge. 'Tomorrow,' she said dispiritedly. Her enthusiasm for painting the kitchen was rapidly receding, but in the light of Andrew's scepticism at her abilities, she felt she had no choice but to plug on.

The way things were going with Andrew was, of course, her third struggle. She'd been right in her suspicion that he was still seeing Sophie MacAteer.

'She's very persistent,' he said, by way of excuse.

'I'm very persistent,' she countered, 'and I have prior claim.'

Andrew seemed flattered to be battled over and, given the general comfortableness of life at Willow Corner and the fact that he loved the house almost as much as she did, Kate suspected he might have tried to conceal the Sophie affair until – possibly – it fizzled out. His problem was that now she was at home, rather than out all day, concealing telephone conversations with the Maneater and slipping out to see her had become so difficult as to be nigh on impossible. He knew Kate wouldn't tolerate it and Sophie didn't seem about to let go either.

Kate despised snooping. They had always respected each other's space, or at least she had thought that was one of the founding principles of their relationship until she realised that she'd never had anything to hide. Now, when Andrew slipped out to the village for the papers, or down to the pub for a drink with Mike Proctor or other friends, she was onto his computer like a shot, to check his emails and to read the latest episode of *Martyne Noreis and the Witch of Lothian*.

'Ellyn had discovered the truth about Martyne's absences. He knew it first from the change in the fare put before him at night. "Plain gruel? No meat?" he asked, puzzled.

' "Only honest men eat meat," Ellyn answered cryptically, her blonde plaits swinging ferociously as she added a quarter of cabbage to his bowl. The statement was so patently untrue that he was forced to consider its underlying meaning.

'Later, when he tried to bed her, she rolled away from him and turned her head to the wall. It was unlike Ellyn,

242

who had always shown ardour. At first he cared little, for Ethelinda was providing him with all his needs, but she was in the next village, and with child, and Ellyn was his wife, and should obey him.'

With child? Kate scanned the paragraph on Andrew's computer again. Ethelinda was pregnant? She checked her watch quickly, and shut down the computer with hands grown suddenly cold. Fifteen years ago, that was what had happened to her, and a marriage had been turned upside down. Was history about to repeat itself?

This furtive searching for information was a peculiar kind of torture. It dripped toxic suggestions into her mind, where they lodged and suppurated and could not be lanced – and besides, her prying lowered her estimation of herself.

She started painting the kitchen. She was covered with Buttermilk from her attempt at rollering the ceiling when Andrew put his head round the door and said, 'I'm off to town.'

She was too proud to beg him not to go. 'Going to see the Bishop?' she asked sarcastically from the top of the ladder, aware that though she might be splattered in paint, this did not make her an oil painting. If she was to compete with Sophie MacAteer, she had to address the matter of the lines at the corner of her eyes and the growing number of gray hairs on her temple.

'I won't be long.'

Long enough for a quick shag, she thought sourly, and remembered all the stolen hours they had spent wound round each other in her tiny student flat before Val had found out about their affair.

Later, when she was showering off the Buttermilk in a sulky rage, she discovered two condoms in Andrew's wash bag and in an uncharacteristic fit of viciousness, cut them in half with her nail scissors and replaced them. There. That would dampen his ardour the next time he saw her.

She glowed with satisfaction for an hour before the crudeness of her action hit home and she repented. The pieces went in the kitchen bin.

She was marching round the house aimlessly and trying to resist the idea of opening a bottle of wine to drink alone when Helena Banks called. 'I hope you don't mind, Kate, but Ninian is here. Elliott has asked if he can stay for supper.'

'No problem,' Kate said, but perhaps something of her mood came over in her voice because Helena said, 'You wouldn't like to join us, would you? You and Andrew? It's nothing special, just lasagne, but there's plenty.'

She visualised a happy family table and her own home felt cold and empty. Andrew hadn't reappeared or called and she baulked at the humiliation of phoning him. She looked around at the dustsheets with their splashes of Buttermilk – her technique wasn't tidy – and wondered if, instead of offering the room a fresh start she was merely obliterating all the moments of happiness and togetherness the space had witnessed.

'That's a really kind invitation,' she said to Helena. 'Actually, Andrew is out this evening, but I'd love to come, if that's all right?'

The girl who answered the door was so absolutely similar in appearance to Elliott Banks that Kate gave an involuntary gasp. 'You must be twins!'

Her hair was exactly the same shade as Elliott's, a deep, dark auburn, though it was long and fell smoothly round her shoulders. Her build was slighter than Elliott's and her features subtly feminine but in all other respects the resemblance was so strong as to be quite unnerving.

She laughed, just as Elliott laughed, easily and openly, so that it was impossible not to be drawn to her. 'I'm Alice,' she said, holding her hand out, 'You must be Kate. Hi.'

'Ninian,' Kate said, 'is a typical boy, I'm afraid. He's not given to elaboration. Ask him how school was and he'll say "Fine". Ask him how his holiday in Devon was and he'll say "Fine". Ask him about his friends and you'll get a grunt. You don't get information, even such basic information as "Elliott has a twin sister". I apologise for not knowing of your existence.'

Alice laughed. 'Come in. And don't apologise. I know what you mean about boys. They just play on the X Box or install themselves, feet up on the sofa, to watch football, don't they?'

'And for hours all you hear is the odd shout of elation or frustration,' Kate agreed. She liked Alice.

'Hello Kate, nice to see you, Alice don't leave Kate standing in the hall, come on in.'

Kate only knew Helena Banks slightly, but seeing her with Alice it was easy to know where the girl got her warmth from. 'This is so kind of you. I'm painting my kitchen, so the invitation is doubly welcome.'

'Oh God, poor you, it's so disruptive, isn't it? But how brave to do it yourself.'

She led her into a sitting room, where a fire burned cheerfully in the grate and Kate had an instant impression of mellowness and warmth. Where Willow Corner was all creams and pastels and neutrals, this room had burnished gold floorboards and a thick oriental rug. Bookshelves lined the walls, heavy curtains were drawn round a large bay window, and not one, but three, large, chenille-covered sofas were ranged round the fire, their plump cushions soft and inviting.

'Oh, this is lovely!' she cried impulsively.

'Haven't you been here before? No, I suppose it was usually Andrew who came to pick Ninian up,' Helena said, tucking a stray wisp of dark auburn hair behind her ear and smiling at Kate's pleasure. 'Wine? Or would you prefer something else?'

'A small glass of wine would be lovely. I'm driving though.'

'Red or white?'

'Whatever's open.'

'Pick your sofa and I'll bring it through.'

'I'll get it,' Alice said.

'This wind farm,' Helena said as her daughter disappeared.

Kate's heart sank. For a few minutes she'd been able to forget Summerfield, and AeGen, and the unhappy and aggressive residents of Forgie, and now it was all about to start again.

'I just thought you should know that we're all very supportive.'

Kate burst into tears.

Helena Banks was that rarest of creatures, a natural empathiser. She leapt up to intercept Alice, who was coming through with the wine – 'That's lovely, darling, perhaps you could find the boys and warn them that supper will be ready in twenty minutes? Thanks, sweetie,' – found tissues, and sat patiently while Kate blew her nose and wiped her eyes and stopped sniffing.

'This is not about the Banks family support of your project, I take it?' she said, smiling so genuinely that Kate had to smile too.

She gave a last sniff and shook her head. 'Actually, I'm not working on the project. I'm not working at all at the moment. AeGen have suspended me.'

And she found herself telling her the whole story, of the pressures she'd been put under by having to run a controversial local project, of Jack Bailey and the way he'd constantly undermined her authority, of how she had cracked when she'd found Ninian at the protest camp, of how she felt attacked and abandoned by people – like Frank Griffiths – who she had known for years and had thought were friends. Another glass or two of wine, and some more time, and she would probably have spilled out everything that was happening with Andrew, and Sophie, and how it was affecting Ninian – though she doubted whether she would have mentioned Ibsen even then. That, in itself, told a story.

'You poor thing. Have you been able to talk to anyone about all this?'

It wasn't until she asked the question that Kate realised that she hadn't spoken to anyone. She shook her head. 'No.'

'So you're at home? Painting the kitchen.'

She laughed and dabbed her eyes. 'That's it in one.'

'What's going to happen?'

'If I knew that I might sleep more easily at night.'

'Will you fight for your job?'

'Oh, yes. Of course.' It had never occurred to her to do anything else.

Helena placed her wine on a small side table, then got down on her knees and poked the fire, sending a flare of sparks up the chimney. She threw on a log, twisted round, eyed Kate with a speculative look and said, 'Maybe you shouldn't.'

A shout came from the hall. 'I'm home!'

'That's Peter.' She hauled herself up from the floor with the aid of the arm of the sofa. 'I'll bring him in.'

Visions of herself as she knew others saw her flashed across Kate's mind. *That's Kate Courtenay. Ambitious. Clever. Driven.* She glanced down at her jeans and sweater and saw the other Kate, in her smart business suit and high heels, a silk scarf the only sop to femininity. *She's hard,* they would say, *but fair. And she's a brilliant engineer.* These judgement defined her. They were, after all, what she had struggled to create over the years. She'd worked hard at submerging the soft, vulnerable, uncertain parts of her character so that she could function at this other level,

247

in this other world. *Maybe you shouldn't.* Helena's words reverberated round her mind. No. Unthinkable to step back now.

'Kate, this is Peter. Peter, meet Kate Courtenay, Ninian's Mum. She's staying for supper.'

Peter Banks worked, Kate knew, as a senior manager in one of the large insurance companies based in Edinburgh. She had expected someone older, more careworn, more corporate, but what she saw was a fresh-faced, smiling, youthful man who had already ripped off his tie and who was busy struggling with the top button of his shirt as if he couldn't get out of his city skin quickly enough. 'Hi Kate. Great to meet you. Can you give me five minutes, Helena, to change?'

'Three.'

'Fine.' He flashed Kate an easy smile and slipped off.

'He's lovely,' she said spontaneously, before wondering whether it was too personal a remark.

'I'm a lucky woman. Why don't you come through?' She stopped at the bottom of the stairs and called up, 'Alice! Elliott! Ninian! Supper's ready.'

They ate in their huge kitchen. Again, it was about as unlike the kitchen at Willow Corner as it was possible to be. Willow Corner was cool and stylish, and Kate had always loved it. But although she regarded her kitchen as the hub of their home, it could not compare with the life-giving joyousness of this room. The floor was stone, all the wood scrubbed pine and two of the walls were rich crimson, the others thick cream. The tiles round the Aga and sink were a wild, multi-coloured jumble. She could not have lived with the effect and it would not have suited her but she fell in love, nevertheless, with its heartwarming exuberance.

Ninian sat opposite her on a stool, Alice on a wobbly old wooden chair next to her. Elliott, his mouth full of garlic bread, said, 'Ninian's in love with Alice.'

'I'm not!' Ninian flared back, but his cheeks flamed.

Alice said serenely, 'Don't be so crass, Ell.'

'He is though. He fancies you something rotten.'

'Even if he does, Elliott, it's unkind of you to tease him in that way,' Helena said, handing Kate a large wooden bowl full of mixed salad leaves. 'There's dressing right in front of you, Kate.'

Ninian's head was down and he was playing with his lasagne. Ninian and a girl? It had to happen some time, and if there was to be a girl, Kate felt that she could not wish for a nicer one. She said, to take the heat off him, 'I'm thinking of taking Ninian to France at half term.'

His head came up. 'Are you?'

'If you want.' She turned to Peter. 'You may not have heard, Peter, but my employers are currently considering my position. I reacted a little too strongly to the eco protest at Bonny Brae Woods for their taste.'

The admission took courage, but she could not hide in her kitchen for ever.

Peter grinned. 'Their loss, Kate.' He shovelled a forkful of lasagne into his mouth and when he'd finished chewing he said, 'Ever thought of setting up as a consultant?'

'Consultant? Me?'

She'd been on a corporate ladder all her working life and it had always been her goal to reach the top. Junior engineer, senior engineer, head of engineering, director – with all the side roles necessary for experience along the way.

'More freedom. And almost certainly more money.'

'I'd never thought about it.'

'Where in France?' Ninian said. 'And would Dad come too?'

Her impulsive effort to take the heat off Ninian and Alice was threatening to take on a new dimension and beginning to look expensive besides. She hadn't considered the practicalities of the suggestion and already she could see difficulties. 'We'll talk about it later, Ninian.'

'When you and Alice get married,' Elliott said, his face a mask of seriousness, 'and I'm best man, I shall reveal all your deadliest secrets.'

'*Elliott!*' Helena protested, laughing.

'Beast!' Alice said, and threw a piece of garlic bread at her brother.

'You're a radge, Banksy,' Ninian said, shoving his tormentor half off his stool.

'Pax!' called Peter and every member of the Banks family instantly stopped what they were doing and raised two fingers in a V peace sign.

'Family tradition,' Helena explained as Kate gawped at them all. 'Necessary to restore order. Now, it *will* be peace or no pudding, okay?'

'What's for pud?' Elliott asked.

'Crumble and ice cream.'

'Okay then.' He made a zipping sign over his mouth, but still could not resist giving Ninian a playful half shove in retaliation.

Kate almost forgot about Andrew. As she and Ninian waved their goodbyes some time later, her mood could hardly have been more in contrast with how she'd been feeling when Helena had called earlier.

It lasted all the way home and until she walked in the front door and saw Andrew's silhouette against the living room window, backlit by the light of the moon through the glass. She knew at once that something was wrong.

Chapter Twenty-Four

'Go to bed,' Kate said quietly to Ninian. 'It was a good evening.'

He stared at her, then at Andrew. He opened his mouth to say something, but she pulled him close, quickly, and hugged him. 'We'll talk tomorrow, Ninian. Go to bed, okay? Love you.'

'You too.'

It was more than he'd given her for many months and it made her emotional again. She managed to smile, though, and turned him towards the stairs. This time, he went up obediently.

She went into the sitting room and closed the door behind her. Down in the garden she could see the willows swaying in the breeze and a gleam, in the bright light of the moon, of the burn as it fell over the stones. Familiar sights in familiar terrain, and yet she knew that the landscape she was entering now was unmapped.

'Andrew?'

He stirred and his head turned towards her. 'Where have you been?'

'With Ninian. We had supper with Peter and Helena Banks. Have you been back long?'

'Some time.'

Kate moved into the room, reluctantly, and sank into the armchair opposite Andrew. The silence was broken only by the faint sounds, overhead, of Ninian dropping shoes and opening drawers, and by the quiet gear change of the fridge in the kitchen as it kicked into a new chill cycle.

She waited silently, not knowing what to say.

'Were we like this, Kate?' he said at last. 'Was it like this for Val?'

She started to shiver, though she still had on her jacket.

'Sophie's compelling, you know. She makes me feel young again.'

He was playing with an ornament he had picked up from the side table next to his chair, the netsuke mouse he'd given Kate way back, before they were married.

Gifts.

Gifts and guilt.

Flowers from a forecourt.

The suffragette brooch, tucked away in a drawer in the bedroom.

Perfume brought back from a promotional tour in America.

A dozen other small gifts, produced randomly, but each time after some absence or other.

Had the netsuke been a guilt gift, even way back then, in the sunrise glory of their romance? Had it been offered by way of atonement? Had all the other little presents? And why had this thought never occurred to her before?

'I don't mean to hurt you, Kate.'

The cruellest thrust of all. *I don't mean to hurt you – but I'm going to.*

'Can we talk about this? Properly, I mean.'

'I thought we were talking properly.'

'I won't let this happen. We have spent fifteen years of our lives building something together. We have a family. We have Ninian.'

'I had Harry.'

'And look what he went through,' she flashed back at him, then bit her lip. She would not stoop to using all the weapons in the armoury. 'Tell me,' she said carefully, 'what Sophie means to you.'

He drew a deep, shuddering breath. 'Innocence.

Vulnerability. Youth. She needs me in all the ways you don't.'

Innocent? Kate almost laughed aloud, but she bit her lip again instead. Pulling the scales away from Andrew's eyes might prove impossible, she had to find other paths to a solution. 'She is half your age, Andrew. She is almost a child still.'

'Do you think I haven't thought about that?'

'When you are eighty years old she will only be the age you are now.'

'She has thought about it too.'

'Will you have children?'

'She would like children.'

Her shivering became almost impossible to control. 'This ever more complicated family of yours, Andrew, how will it work?'

'It will work because I want it to work. It must be made to work.'

'You're so *selfish*!' she cried, wondering how she could not have seen it before.

'And you're so righteous. You've never done anything impulsive or fun in your life.'

Kate's chin came up at the insult. 'Except fall in love with you, you mean? Anyway, you're wrong. I slept with Ibsen Brown.'

An abyss opened at their feet and her words plummeted into it, spoken and therefore irretrievable. She stared at Andrew, her eyes wide with horror at her confession. She had never before understood the word thunderstruck, but his face perfectly expressed it now.

'You ... did ... what?'

There was no going back. 'It just happened. It didn't mean anything.'

'Didn't mean anything? Isn't that rather a cliché?'

It was. And worse, it wasn't even true, because in the indigo world where she and Ibsen had joined themselves, body and soul, it had actually meant a very great deal to her. At the time. This was a reflection she could hardly share with Andrew, though, so she said, 'Andrew, we're not talking about one quick intimacy here, are we? We're talking about something on a different scale altogether, something it might be rather harder to forgive, or forget.'

He was still fiddling with the netsuke and for some reason it was really irritating her.

'Will you put that thing *down*, Andrew. Please.'

He thumped it onto the table with a crash that made her wince. She was fond of that mouse, guilt gift or no, and she would be sorry to see it broken. 'Jesus Christ, Kate, I didn't think you'd do a thing like that.'

'No? It's all right for you to have a full-on affair, but my one brief encounter is to be judged differently?' She was trying not to raise her voice. She didn't want this kind of row with Andrew, and she didn't want Ninian to hear them arguing.

He stood up. 'It shows, doesn't it, that we've come to the end of our road together.'

'No.' She jumped to her feet and glowered up at him. 'It shows we have to address some problems we have between us. That's what we committed to, isn't it? For better and for worse? No-one ever said it would be easy and I'll be the first to admit I should have paid more attention to my marriage, but you're wrong. You're absolutely wrong. Running off to Sophie isn't going to solve the problem you've got.'

'And exactly what problem is that?'

She said wearily, 'There's no such thing as eternal youth. You certainly won't find it by looking for new flesh to caress. Whatever you think you have with Sophie – don't you see? It will still be pots and pans and dirty dishes, and you can add in nappies and broken nights too, if she gets her way? It's not love. It's—'

'Don't try to tell me what it is. You have no idea.'

254

'Oh, I think I do, Andrew. I think I have a very good idea indeed.'

Outside, the wind was getting up and the moon had slid behind a cloud, so that she could barely see Andrew's face at all. All at once, she felt desperately weary, so tired that the bones in her body felt as though they were disintegrating. She had no spirit left to fight.

'Go, then,' she said. 'Go to her if you must. But you must be the one to explain to Ninian.'

A little to her surprise, he baulked at that. It offered them a chink of hope, though she knew it might be only the smallest of respites. Their marriage was caught in a spider's web, trussed up with a thread that was at once strong and extremely fragile. Andrew began to wilt, and spent even longer closeted in his room. She could hear the soft clack clack clack of his keyboard keys followed by pauses so long that she wanted to scream, *Write! Write, damn you!*

There was little else for her to do. She had finished painting the kitchen – and made a good job of it – but she rather regretted redecorating it at all. She missed the scuff mark by the back door and the greasy area above the cooker because these were chapters in their life here.

She longed to go to the community garden, but the digging was finished and the fund-raising team was at work and besides, autumn was turning into winter and now was not the time to do anything in the garden.

She missed Ibsen, but she had no excuse, now, to contact him.

Ninian escaped the house whenever he could and Kate knew that he was spending a great deal of time over at the Banks's. Striking up a relationship with the twin sister of your best friend must pose its own complications, she reflected, but she was pleased for him – and more relieved than she could say that he seemed to have stopped

255

consorting with Stephen Cousins.

One day, Mark Matthews called. 'This is strictly off the record, Kate,' he said, 'but I wanted you to know that I believe we were wrong to put you in charge of the Summerfield project.'

'I see.'

'The senior team believed that it would be a strength, but I recognise now that it put you under intolerable pressures.'

'Yes.'

'And besides—'

'Yes?'

'Jack Bailey has explained about the confusion over the access road. That it was his error, not yours.'

'That's good news.'

'Of course, it still leaves the matter of the incident at the eco protest.'

'Yes. It still leaves that.'

'But there is a growing recognition that you were under undue pressure and that this was the company's fault, not your own.

'I'm grateful to the company.'

'You've probably already heard that there will be a disciplinary hearing? The investigator reckons he'll be finished taking all the evidence in two or three weeks. Sorry it's taking so long - fixing diaries, getting people together, you know what it's like.'

'I know,' said Kate, who had almost forgotten about diary hell.

'I shouldn't be telling you this, but I think things will go in your favour. I expect you'll be reinstated.'

'Who is running the project now?' Kate asked, though she knew the answer already.

'Jack. Don't worry, if the hearing goes in your favour, you'll be put back in charge of Summerfield.'

'I guess if I'm reinstated,' she said with heavy

emphasis, 'that will be my right.'

'Don't be so prickly. I had no alternative other than to suspend you, you know that, but I'm on your side.'

'I know, Mark. I'm grateful.'

Under undue pressure? Whatever pressure she had been under then, she was considerably more weighed down now. Andrew's refusal to talk to Ninian had placed them into stalemate. Harry would be the last person on earth she would take into any kind of confidence, so she had become completely isolated. Willow Corner had become her world.

The evening after Mark called, it occurred to Kate that she had not seen Charlotte for some weeks. In fact, she'd seen more of her when she was a full-time working mother than she did now that she was at home. Why hadn't she called? She picked up the phone.

'Charlotte? It's Kate.'

There was an infinitesimal pause before she said, 'Hi! How are you?'

'Still in disgrace.'

'Poor you. I'm sorry.'

'I thought we could go for a drink.'

'Mike's away at the moment.'

'Then I'll come round there.'

Again there was the tiniest of pauses. 'I'm a little busy, Kate.'

In her state of disconnection, the easiest thing would have been to have put the phone down and pick up another thriller, but Charlotte was her oldest friend, so she persisted. 'What's wrong, Char?'

'Nothing. Why do you ask?'

'You're being very peculiar.'

'Really? Do you think so? I'm just—' She seemed to be floundering. 'It's difficult, Kate,' she came up with eventually. 'With Dad and everything. I need to support him and you're—'

'Suspended,' Kate said dryly.

'—on the other side,' Charlotte ended feebly.

'I can't believe there's anything you can be so busy with that you can't spare time to sort out a problem with an old friend. I'll bring a bottle round and be with you in ten minutes. Okay?'

'Kate, I told you, I'm—'

'Rather busy. Yes, you said.' Kate hated defeat. 'But I miss you, Char, and I know you. Something's wrong and we need to talk about it.'

She heard Charlotte's sigh and was resigned to another knock-back. 'You're right,' Charlotte said surprising her. 'Okay then, come on round.'

'Good.'

Kate dropped the phone back on its cradle and marched to Andrew's study. 'I'm nipping round to see Charlotte,' she said, 'so if you want to talk to Sophie, now would be a good time.'

She couldn't be bothered waiting to unpick his reaction. Ninian was out, Charlotte was in, and she had found a spark of resolve. She needed to know what was bugging Charlotte, because right now she could do with a bit of support and she wasn't getting any. She pulled a bottle of wine out of the fridge and marched out of the kitchen door and down the side path to the gate.

'Have I done something? Is it my fault?' Kate thrust the bottle into Charlotte's hands.

'Oh hell, Kate,' Charlotte grimaced, 'you don't change, do you? You never did know when to call time.'

'Time on what?'

Charlotte went to the cupboard in the kitchen, pulled out two glasses. 'Thanks for the wine. I suppose we'd better go and get comfortable.'

In the front room she flicked a switch and the fire flared into life. She eyed Kate warily. 'So.'

258

Kate said, 'Remember when you burst into my room at uni. It was my very first day. You were a skinny will-o-the-wisp, all cheekbones and flying blonde hair. "I'm Charlotte," you announced, '"and I'm next door."' Kate was looking at the pale gold liquid in her glass, but she was seeing the young Charlotte's greeny-gold eyes. 'Then you said, "I can tell we're going to be friends." Just like that.'

'We've shared a lot of fun, haven't we? Tribulations and tears, too.'

'We got legless together—'

'Shared clothes, even though you're taller than me—'

They both fell silent, remembering. They'd lusted over men, too, and swapped unrepeatable tales of intimacies. For a while Kate had dated Mike Proctor, before they'd parted amicably and Charlotte had swooped on him with glee. 'If you've really finished with him, Katie-K,' she'd said delightedly, 'would you mind if I had a pop? He's so *sweet*.'

'I know you almost as well as I know myself. At least, I thought I did.'

'Don't, Kate—'

'Maybe even better, because right now, I'm not convinced that I know what I want from life at all.'

Charlotte didn't answer. After a few minutes she said, 'So what's new?'

'Oh, you know, still out of work and stuck at home.'

'I'm sorry.'

'Are you?'

'What do you mean? Of course I am.'

'But while I'm suspended I can't work on the wind farm, and that must make you very happy.'

'Oh, Kate. You know it's not as simple as that. I'm boxed in here. Dad's becoming more and more militant – *Dad!*' she gave a rather forced little laugh, 'in combat gear. Can you imagine?' She swilled half her wine at a

259

gulp, then studied the glass.

'You can make your own mind up about things, surely. You're a big girl now.'

'And you know Mike's not in favour of wind farms either.'

'Doesn't stop you talking to your best friend, surely?'

She wouldn't meet Kate's eyes. She crossed her legs, then wriggled and switched them back again, then almost finished the wine in another couple of quick gulps. It takes six cranial nerves to carry out the act of swallowing, and Charlotte's seemed to be working in perfect unison rather than chronological progression, so swiftly did the alcohol slide down her throat.

'There's something else, isn't there?'

'Is there?'

Kate tried another tack. 'Do you remember I talked to you a month or two back about Andrew?'

Charlotte looked even more uncomfortable. 'Still playing away, is he?'

'Is he? You said you wouldn't know if he was. "I'd hardly be likely to know about it if he was screwing the entire Scottish membership of the WRI," if I remember your words correctly.'

'That's true.'

'So what do you mean, is he still playing away?'

Charlotte topped up her wine, splashing a little onto the coffee table, where it spread into a small pool and glistened unnaturally under the light of the lamp behind her head. 'Well,' she said, 'that's Andy, isn't it?'

Kate stared at her, speechless and the silence dragged on into a long, uneasy pause. Eventually she said, 'You make it sound as though he's serially unfaithful.'

'Oh come on, Kate,' Charlotte was suddenly impatient. She sat up with a swift, jerky movement. 'You can't have lived with him all these years and not know that Andy likes his "fans".' She used her fingers to describe sarcastic

260

quotation marks in the air.

Her words barrelled into Kate and knocked all the wind out of her. She fought for breath, shocked beyond comprehension. 'I don't know what you mean.'

'You're not that naive, Kate, are you? Andy's vanity feeds on young flesh.'

'That's *horrible.*'

'But true. Did he resist you?'

'He fell in *love* with me.'

'Never stopped him from testing his pulling power.'

'What?'

'Kate, he has always wanted to feel irresistible. I was jealous, I admit it. You were always so bloody perfect, you got top marks in everything, you were sexy as hell and had bags of personality. I was fed up being second best to you. Even Mike was a hand-me-down, for heaven's sake.'

'I don't understand.'

'I slept with him, you dolt. Your precious Andy, your oh-so-handsome, oh-so-adoring teacher-lover. I went to bed with him while you and Mike were out at some bloody engineering do.'

The breathlessness was back. 'You slept with Andrew? Soon after I met him? I don't believe you.'

'That's why I never told you. I knew you wouldn't. And anyway, what would have been the point?'

Andy. It was a diminutive she'd thought nothing of – but now the familiarity was explained. '*Andy!* You've always been chummy with him, haven't you? Why did I never see it?' She rubbed her temples. They were starting to throb. 'So why tell me now?'

'I never meant to. It was years ago. It just came out. I suppose I was surprised that you didn't realise what Andy was like.'

Best friends are anchors. They listen to problems without making judgements, they want the best for each other, they know the worst things about each other and

261

love their friends anyway. Deep friendships take years to build because they are the sum of ten thousand shared experiences. Years to build, and a moment to shatter.

Charlotte's triumphant little secret. The thought of her friend in bed with the man she loved made her feel sick. She stood up. 'Thank you, Charlotte.'

'What do you mean? What for?' Charlotte stood, wobbled, caught hold of the back of the sofa to steady herself.

'You've opened my eyes. I can't say I like what I see, but I suppose I asked for the truth, and now I've got it.' She turned and marched to the door, Charlotte stumbling and stuttering behind her.

'Kate, wait! Let's talk about this, it was years ago, I didn't mean it. Christ, Mike'll kill me. Oh, *fuck*.'

The expletive was the last thing Kate heard, because she slammed the front door behind her and strode off down the drive, leaving the stone face of The Herons staring emotionlessly after her as she was engulfed by the night.

Chapter Twenty-Five

Kate had assumed that her idyll with Andrew would go on for ever. When you are twenty two and in love, you believe that this state will never change. But nothing stays the same for ever – nothing and nobody. She hadn't understood that, but Andrew should have. Andrew, who had already brought up one child. Andrew, who had watched countless not-quite teenagers come into school as children and emerge, six or seven years later, as young and sometimes frighteningly mature adults. Andrew, who had fallen in love with a teenage Val himself, then out of love again just as easily, when it suited him.

'But it wasn't like that,' he'd told Kate during one of those endless, lazy conversations you have in bed with a new lover, sated with sex and blissfully drowsy with the headiness of proximity. 'It happened slowly, over a long time. It happened, I dare say, because we did both change, Val into a mother and me into—' He paused at that point and spent some blissful moments tracing the contours of Kate's body from her navel to her nipple and up her throat to her lips. He didn't finish the sentence, so she never did hear how he thought *he* had changed. Instead, he returned again to Val. 'I don't know where the exuberant, madcap girl I married went to.'

Maybe he kissed her then and they probably made love once more. She would have been exhilarated with the feeling of power, because she set him alight and she knew it. She hadn't given much thought to Val, though.

She let herself into Willow Corner.

'Ninian called,' Andrew said, emerging from his study. 'He's staying the night at Elliott's.'

She said, 'Good. It will give you time to pack some things and go.'

'I'm sorry?' He stared at her incredulously over his half-moon spectacles.

'It's not too late.' She glanced at the clock in the kitchen. 'It's only nine thirty. Plenty of time to find somewhere to sleep tonight.'

He followed her into the kitchen. 'You can't be serious.'

'Oh, but I am. Deadly serious.'

'I thought we were going to work at our marriage. That's what you said.'

Kate swung round, so abruptly that he almost cannoned into her. 'You slept with Charlotte,' she hissed. 'And that's unforgivable.'

'No I didn't.' The puzzlement on his face seemed absolutely genuine.

'Cast your mind back, Andrew. Sixteen years. One night, a few months before we were married. I'd gone to an Engineering lecture with Mike and—'

'Oh that,' he said dismissively. 'She practically begged me. I'd completely forgotten.'

'It wasn't important.'

'Right.' He tried to take her face between his hands but she shoved him away, so violently that he hit the table and a chair went flying. '*Jesus*, Kate!'

'You slept with my best friend and you didn't think that mattered?' Her voice had risen to a shrewish shriek.

'Not ... no—'

'Have you got any morality at all, Andrew? I've lived with you for all this time and I thought I knew you. How many women, Andrew? How many times have you been unfaithful to me?'

'It's not like that. I don't—'

'Oh, spare me the stories. Time's ticking. Take the big suitcase, then you won't need to come back for a few days.

And that, believe me, is about the only way I can guarantee your safety.'

'Ninian—'

Her anger yielded to anxiety. 'We'll talk to Ninian together and you'll find the words – because you're very good at words, isn't that so? – to help him through this. Until we agree on what and where and how we will do it, however, you won't make any attempt to contact him. Is that understood?'

She glared at Andrew's shocked face and added, more gently, 'I'm not trying to undermine you. I promise I'll never do anything to compromise his view of you, so long as you agree to do the same. Where Ninian is concerned, we are – and always will be – his parents, equally loving, equally fair, equally concerned about what is best for him.'

Andrew said, very quietly, 'Now I'm scared.'

'This is what you wanted. Isn't it?'

'I don't know. I thought I did. I'm not sure.'

'Because I'm the one calling time, not you?'

His eyes flickered away from her and she knew she had hit on the truth. Where women were concerned, Andrew obviously liked to call the shots.

'This is what *she* wants, isn't it?' she said, callously seizing advantage of her insight.

'Yes. It's what Sophie wants.' He sighed heavily.

Her fury returned. 'Go. Just go. I can't bear to talk to you any more tonight.'

She went into the dark living room and tumbled untidily onto a sofa, not bothering to put on any lamps. The room looked ghostly in the shaft of light that beamed through from the kitchen, a cocky intruder from another world. She didn't want light. She wanted to sink silently into the dark oblivion the room seemed to offer. She didn't want to think and above all, she didn't want to feel. Her hand found the netsuke mouse: a treasured gift from Andrew. Charlotte's words scorched her mind as she

265

remembered: he'd given it to her the day after she'd been at that lecture with Mike. The day after, according to Charlotte, he had slept with her best friend.

She dropped the mouse with a clatter. Another sweet memory had been destroyed.

This was what it was like, then, to come to the end of something beautiful and untouchable. This was what it was like to uncover a lie – a whole nest of lies – and realise that your entire life has been a twisted, poisoned scrap right at the heart of it. She had thought that their marriage had been constructed by some divine hand, that meeting Andrew had somehow been *meant*. She'd thought that getting pregnant had been predetermined, that their stars had been charted and their paths had been destined to intertwine – but that was the kind of twaddle only a student fresh out of university could believe. If only she'd talked to Val, instead of pitying her!

'I'm off then.' Andrew clipped on the switch at the door and a cold light flooded the room. Kate blinked, disorientated and confused, and threw her hand up to shield her eyes from the glare. 'I'll call you tomorrow. I don't want this to end like this, Kate.'

'If you must,' she said, hardening her heart at his pathetic look.

'Unless you—'

'Call me tomorrow, if you have to.'

'Yes.' He dropped his head. 'I'll do that. Tell Ninian'

'What?'

'Nothing.'

'Good bye, Andrew.'

She heard him throw something into the car, then his engine started up. She shivered. The sense of power she had experienced, briefly, was gone. The room was cold and shock was setting in.

Kate stirred in the vastness of her double bed, unable to

sleep. How do you accommodate your body to a large double bed when there is no-one to share it with? How do you face the day ahead when it is empty of meaning? How do you reconcile recollections of happy times with the knowledge that even then, even when you were at your happiest, the corrosion had started?

She shivered, unable to get warm. Her bedroom – her favourite room, she had to remind herself – seemed chilled and abandoned. The wardrobe stood open where Andrew had seized clothes, probably at random. She got out of bed and stood, shivering, peering into its dark recesses, trying to work out what he had taken. His dark suit. A couple of pairs of cord trousers. His favourite old threadbare tweed jacket. She pulled out one of the drawers and saw that he had not taken the fabulously soft, richly patterned alpaca sweater she had given him for Christmas a year ago. Its presence seemed like a metaphor: given with love, now rejected. She lifted it up and held it to her cheek. The smell of him was still on the wool and the immediacy of his presence unlocked the tears she had been holding back. She sank to the floor and, cuddling the sweater in her arms, howled for her lost love.

When she could cry no longer, she slipped the sweater over her head and felt its soft warmth envelop her. She crept downstairs quietly, as though she might disturb someone, and filled the kettle. Sleep still seemed beyond her, so she made herself tea and cradled the mug in her hands, then padded around restlessly – but the kitchen floor was cold on her bare feet and the living room still held the dark despair she had nursed there earlier. She could see light spilling out from underneath the door to Andrew's study and a flicker of hope caught in her heart. Could he have returned? Was he in there, writing? Had he come back to fight for her? She pushed open the door – but the room was empty. He had merely left the lamp on his desk burning.

267

She woke the next morning to the sounds of Mrs Gillies clattering dishes in the kitchen. The memory of what had happened the night before flooded back to her. She started to shiver again, though the central heating had kicked in and the bedroom was warm. What had she done? Was it too late to beg Andrew to come back?

The kitchen radio blasted out Chris Evans' breakfast show. Irritated, she leapt out of bed. For years she had tolerated Mrs Gillies changing the station on her kitchen radio from Radio Four to Radio Two, but she wouldn't put up with it any longer. She didn't need Mrs G and she didn't want her around, with her proprietorial manner and annoying assumptions of quasi-ownership. She didn't like the way Jean Gillies implied that she cared about Ninian more than she did. Ninian was her son, and Willow Corner was *her* house – and with Andrew gone she could claim her territory absolutely.

She flung on her jeans and Andrew's alpaca sweater and ran down the stairs. Mrs Gillies's bottom was angled up at her newly repainted kitchen ceiling because she was emptying the dishwasher – Andrew's dirty dishes from the day before – and she couldn't hear anything above the radio. Kate reached across the cream granite worktop and switched it off. The silence was immediate.

'Oh!' Mrs Gillies straightened and whirled round, glowering at Kate as though it was her kitchen and Kate was the intruder. 'I didn't know you were in, Kate.'

'I've been *in*,' Kate said icily, 'every morning for weeks now, as you surely know.'

Mrs Gillies looked away. Her head dropped and she made a play of studying her gold rings, twisting them so that the tiny diamonds showed. Her loyalties, Kate realised now, all lay with Andrew, who she admired, and with Ninian, who she adored.

Too bad.

'Mrs Gillies,' she said, 'how many years have you been

with us?'

'Since just after you came here, Kate.'

'Mrs Courtenay,' she corrected, irked by the familiarity.

'What?'

'My name is Mrs Courtenay. To you.'

'Is everything all right, Kate?'

'No. Everything is not all right.'

She wanted to yell, Alan Sugar-style, 'You're fired!', but she'd been too well drilled about employee rights and employment tribunals and instead she said crisply, 'Mrs Gillies. I'm afraid there's bad news. Mr Courtenay and I are getting divorced and we will be selling Willow Corner, so I'm going to have to dispense with your services. As of now. Of course, I will pay you a month's wages, which I think is the understanding we have, is it not?'

She found her handbag and fumbled in it for her purse. 'Actually, I only have five pounds,' she said, a little deflated, 'so I'll call round to your house later with the cash, if that's all right.'

Kate looked up as Mrs Gillies's mouth rounded into an 'O', a perfect ring in her circle of a face. She realised, too late, that Mrs Gillies's cleaning pals formed a well-entrenched network of gossip and control in the neighbourhood. News of her difficulties would be round Summerfield within hours and probably round Forgie not long thereafter.

Well, so be it.

'If that's all right, Mrs Gillies?'

'Well, I—' The housekeeper sank down heavily on one of the kitchen chairs. 'Is that it then? All these years of service and sacked just like that?'

Kate felt sorry for her before she remembered the dining room she had prepared for Andreas Bertolini and his wife: that hadn't been mere housekeeping, she'd taken over. She recalled her insistence on moving the vase on

269

the mantelpiece in the living room from one end to the middle and the fact that she never put the sofa back quite in the place Kate liked it to be. She remembered the peremptory notes of reprimand and instruction: *We are out of bleach.* The lingering smell of cigarette smoke, which counteracted the freshness of pine cleaner – if she had to smoke, why couldn't she go outside?

'I'm sorry,' she said firmly. 'I won't be able to afford your services any longer. I'll pay you extra for today, but I think it would be best if you just go. Now.'

'But I haven't had my coffee yet.'

Kate thrust the five-pound note into her hands. 'Here. That should be enough for a couple of coffees.'

She watched the housekeeper march down the path with her hat jammed on her head, every step an expression of righteous indignation. She felt victorious, just as she had over Andrew the night before – and, just as quickly, the feeling evaporated and reality set in. Now she'd have to cope with all the cleaning on her own. She'd have to discover all the nasty, dirty places she didn't even know existed and suck out their dark secrets through the nozzle of a vacuum cleaner. Her tale would be all over the neighbourhood before lunch, no doubt with a twist or two that put her in the role of pantomime villainess.

Still, much more worrying than Mrs Gillies's wounded sensibilities was how Ninian would feel about it all.

She need not have worried too much on that count. Mrs Gillies's departure was considerably overshadowed for Ninian by news that his father had left home and that his parents were considering their future together.

'Has he gone to the Maneater?' he asked, his face contorted.

'I'm not sure,' Kate lied. Andrew was the one at fault here and it should be Andrew who explained what had happened and why he had gone. 'We'll talk in a few days, all of us.'

'What is there to talk about?'

'Oh Ninian.' She sank her head into her hands. She wanted to seem strong, but she couldn't manage to hide her hopelessness. The bleakness of her situation became painfully real. She had no husband and potentially no job either. She lifted her head, though, determined that Ninian should have faith in one parent, at least. 'There's so much to think about. Where we will live, where *you* will live, for a start.'

He slammed his fist onto the kitchen table. Two plates, still waiting to be put away, clattered alarmingly. 'How could you do this to me, Mum?'

'We're not going to start blaming anyone. I won't blame your father, he won't blame me, and you won't blame either of us. Shit happens. We will work together to find a civilised way through it.'

She wasn't sure, even as she said it, that she believed it, but she needed to try, for all their sakes.

Ninian's self-regarding outrage crumpled abruptly. 'What's the point of falling in love, then, if it all ends like this?'

His hands were fisted in tight, sour balls. She uncurled them finger by finger, then sandwiched them between her own hands and stroked them softly. This was about Alice Banks as much as his parents.

'She's lovely, Ninian.'

He looked at her, his eyes dull and hopeless.

'Listen to me,' she said, finding the right voice at last. 'You make choices in life, you follow a path, you see where it leads. Sometimes it goes round a blind bend and ends up against a wall. Then you have to retrace your steps and find another route.'

His head had dropped.

'Look at me. Ninian, look at me.' She pumped the words out with urgency. When she had his attention, she

271

grasped his hands more firmly and said, 'It can be hard, of course it can, but there is always the possibility that the new path will be a better one, and of course you will bring to it all the things you have learned on the first path, so you will be stronger and better able to travel along it. That's life.'

His mouth was still slack and his lower lip jutted out like a small boy denied sweeties. 'I don't want you and Dad to get divorced.'

'Let's just take one step at a time. Hey?'

The tension in his shoulders relaxed just a fraction and his hands softened. Kate thought, *I'm getting through to him*, but he jerked his hands away. 'I don't believe this is happening,' he muttered. 'You and Dad—'

Kate didn't quite believe it herself.

It wasn't all gloom. Nicola Arnott dropped by for a coffee and to give Kate an update on the garden.

'The digging's finished, but I guess you know that. We owe you a huge amount, Kate, both for the idea and for setting things in motion. And for persuading Ibsen Brown to get involved.' She smiled across the mug. 'He's quite a character, isn't he? Everyone adores him.'

'Ibsen. Oh yes. Quite a character.' Kate stirred her coffee slowly, watching the treacly liquid swirl and eddy.

'He's done a fantastic plan, you know. We had an open meeting to discuss it. I did email you an invitation but—'

'I'm sorry. Things have been a little strained here,' she muttered. She was only half thinking about what Nicola was saying because the delicate blocks of colour and fine pen work of Ibsen's painting had started to swim in front of her eyes, each stroke the outline of an intricate memory. The paper had still been warm from his body. That was the night they had made love. Two fragile souls seeking solace, perhaps, but it had been a union of sharp delight.

Kate sat bolt upright. The coffee slopped onto the table

as she thudded the mug down, heedless of its fragility or of its contents. Ibsen had allowed her to glimpse his pain. Why had she not understood that that was important?

'Kate? Is everything all right?'

She shook herself. 'Sorry, what? I just thought of something.'

'About the garden?'

Kate could feel her cheeks growing hot. 'No. No, not the garden. A related issue. Listen, I'm sorry, what were you saying?'

Ibsen confided in me. And I turned my back on him.

How could she have been so stupid? Didn't she have an ounce of insight?

'I said, Gail from AeGen came to our meeting to give us advice about what we needed to do about applying for funding. We need to get started now, apparently, because funding kicks in from the day the wind farm comes into operation.'

'If it comes into operation,' she said automatically, her mind still on Ibsen.

'Looks pretty likely, don't you think?'

'I really wouldn't know, I'm not working there at the moment.'

'Neither you are, I keep forgetting. I'm sorry Kate. They don't appreciate how terrific you are.'

Kate's lip curled at the compliment. It was only half a smile. 'Apparently not. They're alleging gross misconduct and they're doing a "full investigation".'

'That's terrible! What are you going to do?'

'I'm hoping they'll reinstate me.'

'That's good.' Nicola must have seen the look on Kate's face because she added, 'Isn't it?'

'Of course it is.'

Andrew called, sounding strained. 'Can we talk?'

'Don't you think the time for talking's over?'

273

'Come on, Kate. For better or worse?'

'What could "better" be?'

'Talking. Trying to understand each other.'

'Where are you, Andrew?'

'That's not important.'

'You're at Sophie's, aren't you?'

His hesitation told her everything she needed to know. She slammed the phone down and went out for a walk.

Chapter Twenty-Six

Wellington hated storms. Lightning made him jittery. This particular storm swept in from the northern Atlantic and past Iceland and Norway, gathering momentum and getting colder all the way. By the time it reached Edinburgh it was three o'clock in the morning. It hit Summerfield half an hour later. Unable to contain his terror any longer, Wellington lifted his head and howled.

Ibsen woke, sweating, from an uneasy dream. It was one he often had – he heard a child crying and was walking down a long, dark corridor towards a crack of light under a door. When he opened the door, the crying stopped. There was a cot – but it was empty.

Damn. He hadn't had the dream in an age.

He rolled onto his side and was about to pull the bedclothes back over himself when he heard the dog.

Howl.

The wind was up. It had found the cracks in the old window frame and was strong enough already to make the flimsy curtains flutter. 'Why don't you get new ones?' Mel used to ask, irritated by his lack of domesticity.

She wasn't around to nag him any more.

Howl.

He sat up, swung his legs over the side of the bed and pulled on a sweater and joggers.

'Okay boy. You're all right.' In the kitchen, he squatted down and gathered Wellington into his arms. The dog was shaking from head to tail. Damn. If he'd known the storm was coming, he could have given him a tranquilliser. Getting anything down him now would be a task and a half. Wellington buried his head as deep as he could in Ibsen's lap, reminding him of how he loved Kate's crotch.

Couldn't blame the dog.

'Okay boy. We'll sit it out together, right?'

He contemplated trying to lift Wellington and carry him through to the bedroom, but the kitchen seemed a better option. He turned on the oven and opened the door, then sat on the floor with a great lump of hairy Labrador in his arms while the lightning flashed above them and the wind seemed to take up the dog's howling.

'Hush, boy. Hush. You're all right.'

After a time, they both slept.

Kate wasn't used to being on her own. She was only just beginning to drop off to sleep when she heard the wind begin to rise. When it started to whistle round the chimneys, whipping twigs and leaves off the trees and slapping them against the windows, she gave up all hope of rest and pulled open the heavy curtains. She saw the lightning first, but the thunder was barely a second behind it. The wind had merely been the herald of a full-scale storm – and Willow Corner was right in its eye.

'Mum!'

She whirled round from the window. Ninian was standing in the doorway, his face white.

'I had a bad dream—'

Ninian hadn't had a nightmare for years. When he was little, there'd been a period when he'd run in to their bedroom with inconvenient frequency, begging to be allowed to share their bed, his small body quivering with some night terror or other. He'd grown out of bad dreams over time, just as he'd grown out of puppy fat and, later, of spots.

'Come here.' She opened her arms and he ran across to her. It seemed strange to be comforting her child again, now that he was almost a grown man, but holding Ninian

276

was comforting. 'It's the storm. It upsets the nervous system. That's all.'

'I know. Sorry.' He pulled away from her, just as a spectacular flash of lighting lit the night sky. 'Wow! That was brilliant!' The thunder was so loud it seemed almost overhead. Ninian, his nightmare forgotten, peered out into the night, his face alight with excitement.

Another flash of lightning lit half of eastern Scotland. Kate's mouth fell open. The power of the storm was terrifying. 'Hope it doesn't do too much damage.'

The rain was battering against the window and the wind hadn't let up.

'Is someone out there with a high-pressure hose?' Ninian asked, more cheerful now. 'By the way, did you know, Mum, that lightning actually goes from the ground to the sky, not the other way around?'

'Really?'

'Yeah. At science, we—'

Ninian's physics lesson was cut short by the next flash of lightning, the most dramatic of all. Electricity mapped the sky with blinding rivers of light that crackled and roared and flared straight to the willow tree down the garden.

'*No!*'

Kate gripped Ninian's arm as the tree appeared to explode. Branches shot into the air and were picked up by the wind and blown in every direction. 'Oh my God! What happened there? I've got to go and look at it!' She turned to the door and started to run.

'No way, Mum.' Ninian caught hold of her arm and pulled her back. 'It's far too dangerous. Don't you see? There might be another strike.'

She watched, appalled, as another flare of lightning sizzled and hissed, then died into the night sky. The storm was moving away, though. The silence before the thunder was longer now and the wind was dying back.

'My willow!'

Ninian put his arms round her – this time, the protector. 'It was getting old anyway, Mum,' he said, as though he was talking about a pet. 'You know it couldn't have lived much longer.'

But Kate was inconsolable. The willows were the sentinels and guardians of her home, and one of them had just been destroyed. Of all the terrible things that had happened to her in past few months, the loss of her tree seemed the hardest to bear. 'It's awful, Ninian, just awful,' she said, over and over again.

In the morning, after Ninian had gone to school, she went out to inspect the damage. It was impossible to believe that the weather could have wrought such carnage. The sky was as blue and clear as a Mediterranean sky in summer and there was not a breath of wind. There was even, for November, a surprising amount of warmth in the sun's rays. Songbirds celebrated with joyous melody. Where had they hidden, last night, to escape the wind's fury?

The ravaged garden had no sweet face to turn to the sky. All around her, the aftermath of the storm was all too evident. Kate scooped up a handful of rose petals and sniffed the devastated flowers sadly. Poor things, they hadn't stood a chance. The rose bush by the study window was all but flattened. Could she save it? She examined the long shoots doubtfully. She'd need to replace the trellis that had supported the climber and tie the whole thing up again. Some growth would have to be pruned away completely, but was that possible without killing the plant? She had no idea how to tackle the job.

The cherry tree in the southern portion of the garden looked just as forlorn. Only a few brave leaves still clung to its branches and one whole branch had snapped off and was hanging by a splinter. The wind must have been whistling round the corner of the house because there was

278

a huge pile of garden debris heaped up against the kitchen door. It had been prevented from whirling any further by the bay window – and it seemed little short of a miracle that none of the windows had been broken.

She left the willow till last. She could hardly bear to inspect it. *Salix alba 'tristis'*. Sad white willow. Today its name was a distressingly apt description. By the stream, the damage was worse than anywhere else. The younger willow looked bedraggled, sadder than ever, but the older tree had been completely destroyed. The trunk had fractured right down the middle. One large branch was lying ten feet away, another half on and half off the garden wall thirty feet further on. Smaller branches and twigs crunched and snapped with every step she took and there were leaves everywhere. Her favourite seat between the two trees had disappeared altogether. She started, half-heartedly, to try to organise the chaos, piling leaves here, twigs there, branches nearer the path. It was thankless work. After half an hour, breathless and increasingly frustrated, she stood back and surveyed her handiwork. She'd accomplished very little. Disheartened, she went back inside. She'd start again after a coffee.

As the kettle boiled, the phone rang.

'Kate Courtenay.'

'Kate, it's Helena Banks.'

'Hi, how are you? How did you fare in the storm?'

'We have a few roof tiles off. How about you?'

'I haven't even looked at the roof yet,' Kate confessed. 'I've been trying to deal with the willow.'

'Problem?'

'The older one was directly hit by lightning. Ninian and I saw it.' She tried to laugh, but the sound that emerged was more like a choked sob. 'It was certainly a spectacular cremation.'

'That bad?'

'It seemed to explode. Literally. There are branches

everywhere.'

'Have you got anyone to help you clear up?'

Andrew would have organised it, Kate thought. She was beginning to realise how much Andrew had assumed responsibility for in the house and garden without her even being aware of it. 'No. Sadly not.'

'Are you going to be in this morning?'

'I wasn't planning on going anywhere.'

'Well listen, I have to go into Edinburgh, but I'll send someone round. Okay?'

'That's really kind of you, Helena, but—'

'No worries. Listen, I must go, but I'll be in touch, I promise you.'

It wasn't until after she'd put the phone down that Kate realised who the 'someone' was likely to be: her gardener. Ibsen Brown.

She ran upstairs. She couldn't see him looking like this, with her ancient Ugg boots and frayed denims. She pulled one item of clothing after another out of the wardrobe, examined it, tossed it on the bed. Nothing seemed right. A skirt was too girly, a dress out of the question. Tailored trousers too much like work wear, a skimpy top too sexy.

Stupid!

She wasn't Melanie and she never planned to be. A scrawl of sadness drew itself in front of her eyes – girls without names or faces, girls who'd been rejected by Ibsen Brown. No. Not for her. And in any case, she was still married and Andrew wanted to talk – and that was something she had to think about, because of Ninian.

Annoyed with herself, she raked through the pile of clothing again and decided on simple slim-fit black jeans and heeled ankle boots, swapping her threadbare old rib-knit sweater for a more stylish long cashmere number in cream, with an asymmetric hem. The left edge dipped half way between her knee and hip, the right edge clipped the very top of her leg. Not too sexy, not too tatty. And because it was cold, she reached for the Missoni black and ivory striped scarf, a winter favourite.

Then she waited.

She tidied away the heap of clothes. She made the bed. She was about to pull out the vacuum cleaner when she realised she might not hear him arrive above its noise, so she found a duster and some polish instead. Wiping the sills and polishing the furniture had an unexpectedly therapeutic effect.

By the time Ibsen appeared an hour and a half later, she had given up altogether and had started to tackle last night's cooking pots. When she heard his asthmatic car, she was up to her elbows in soapy water. She wiped her hands quickly on a towel and wrenched open the front door just as he was raising his hand to ring the bell.

When Helena Banks asked him if he'd go and help Kate Courtenay, Ibsen's first instinct had been to refuse. Then he remembered that Helena was paying him, so refusal would be difficult. After that it dawned on him that in fact there was nothing he'd like more than an excuse to see Kate again – but when he walked up the path and lifted his hand to the doorbell, his stomach was churning.

'Hi!'

She looked sweet enough to eat, all dressed up in some kind of lopsided sweater and little ankle boots with heels that raised her a good two inches towards his chin. When had she last cut her hair? The close crop had grown out and curls had begun to appear round her ears. They softened her appearance.

The jitters in his stomach receded. She was real, and she looked as nervous as he felt.

'Hi, Kate,' he managed to say as Wellington finally managed to bypass his legs to nose her crotch, his tail a flapping flag of ecstasy.

'Hello, Wellington!'

281

'I think he's pleased to see you.'

She straightened and smiled. 'Like the sweatshirt.' His wardrobe of sweatshirts came from the same stable as his tee shirts. Today's was dark green and simply read 'HARDY PERENNIAL'.

'Thanks. Like the, erm, top. Did it shrink on one side?'

Kate blushed. 'Okay, I know, it's a bit "ladies who lunch". Want to come in?'

His eyes never left her face. 'It's good to see you, Kate,' he said softly.

The blush extended from her face down her neck. He saw her swallow, then she whispered, 'And you.'

This wouldn't do. She'd made it clear that her marriage had to come first and Ibsen was no marriage wrecker. *Get a grip.* He stepped backwards. 'Let's look at the damage, shall we?'

She followed him into the garden. 'Did any of your dahlias survive?' she asked as they made their way towards the storm-hit willow.

'You remembered. Thankfully, all the tubers have been lifted and are safely in storage.' They rounded the corner of the house and he stopped dead. 'Oh dear.'

'Isn't it awful?'

She sounded teary. He said matter-of-factly, 'I did warn you it hadn't got long to live.'

'Yes, but to end like this—' Kate gestured at the bits of willow scattered twenty yards in every direction.

Ibsen stepped across one of the larger branches and bent down to examine the trunk. 'This is really interesting.' He beckoned her towards him. 'See this?'

She bent to look, so close that he could smell shampoo and some light fragrance. Damn. This was difficult. 'What?'

'When a tree is dying, it sometimes dies from the outside in. Most of any life-giving sap that's left is deep in its core.'

282

'So?'

'Lightning looks for the most conductive route – in this case, the moisture path. You had a direct hit, at a guess?'

'Yes. I saw it happen.'

'Must have been spectacular.'

'And scary.'

'The electric charge would have been unimaginably powerful. It found the moist core and simply boiled the water, like a pressure cooker, so that it exploded.'

'What, so quickly?'

'Instantly.'

'Good heavens.'

'The power of nature is fascinating, isn't it?'

'What do we do?'

'Sorry. I've read about this happening, I've just never had the chance to witness it first hand. Wish I'd actually seen it happen.' He stood up and looked around. 'I'll tidy everything up, you don't need to worry about it. I'll need to dig this out. Once everything's tidy and the ground is clear, you can replant if you want to.'

'When can you do it?'

'I'll make a start today. I should get all the debris cleared up and some other tasks done, like tying up the roses. Digging the trunk out will take longer and I might have to bring in help.'

'Do you need anything?'

'I've got a tool kit in the car, but if you can show me where you store yours they may be better suited.'

'Can I help?'

'Not in those clothes. But if you really want to get stuck in, we could set up a system. I'll do the heavy work, you can sort out the leaves and twigs.'

Later, over a mug of soup and some warm bread in her kitchen, he said, 'I heard there was some kind of trouble at work.'

283

The easy cameraderie of labour was gone in an instant and her eyes became guarded. *Damn.*

'News travels. They suspended me after that incident up at Bonny Brae Woods.'

'I saw the clip on the telly. It wasn't the way it happened.'

'Nope. But it looked bad. Anyway, I guess you're cheering.'

'Why?'

'One obstacle removed in the fight against Summerfield Wind Farm?'

He put his hands up to his face and rubbed the sides of his nose. 'You're wrong. I'm against the wind farm but there's no way I'd want you to lose your job. Besides, someone else'll just take over.'

'True.'

'And anyway—'

'Anyway what?'

'You haven't exactly converted me, I'd still prefer Summerfield to stay as it is, but I've been thinking a lot about it and – well, let's just say I'm less opposed than I was.'

Kate suddenly seemed to find the pattern on the cream granite worktop fascinating. He watched as she traced a white vein with her finger until it wound its way to the edge and became a beige puddle. 'O-kay,' she said, 'I'm happy with that.'

He nodded. Perhaps they could find a truce. 'There's a good movie on in Hailesbank on Friday. Fancy coming?'

Interest flared, then died as quickly. 'I'm still married, Ibsen,' she said softly.

'It's just a movie.'

'And I'm just another date, right?'

He shoved his chair back. It scraped harshly on the tiles. 'You took that comment all wrong.'

'Maybe. But you're a complicated man, and Christ

knows, I've got my own problems at the moment.'

'Complicated? Would you like to translate?'

'Come on, Ibsen.' She said it gently. 'You're never going to have another relationship till you've laid your ghosts to rest, are you?'

She was right. Dammit, he should never have told her about Violet. The first time he'd been honest with someone and look where it had got him.

She was saying, 'Anyway, Andrew and I might get back together. There's still a chance.'

'Oh, God.'

'A marriage is a big thing. No matter what he's done, I don't feel I should throw it away just like that.'

'No. You're right.' He was standing as stiff as a garden broom, legs planted apart, hands thrust deep into his pockets. 'I'd better get going.'

They stared at each other, tied by an invisible thread of emotion that vibrated and hummed and crackled with pent-up energy. If only he could—

She said, 'Thanks for coming. Let me know what it all costs.'

'I'll get someone to dig the stump out for you.'

He strode down the path with Wellington by his side, cursing his ineptitude. He'd handled that so badly.

286

Chapter Twenty-Seven

Kate's world grew small. Days that had been populated by whole offices full of people, who knew her name and what she did and who respected her skill and expertise, telescoped down to one house and not even one employee. The telephone seldom rang. Kate even missed her heavy breather. While she'd believed that the calls were a threat from someone campaigning against Summerfield, her conviction that the wind farm was a good thing and that everyone who disagreed was merely uninformed had carried her through on a wave of moral superiority.

Helena Banks came round. Odd to look forward so much to seeing a new friend.

'The thing is, I find myself starting to look for Ninian coming through the gates at the end of the afternoon,' Kate confessed, serving scones she had made in the morning. She was trying to master the basics of a new skill – baking. 'It's pathetic. I time my days between him heading off to school in the morning and coming back in the afternoon.'

'I'm sure most mothers look forward to their children coming home.' Helena tried to saw through the scone, failed, and put her knife down.

'But all the time he was a child, I was completely unaware of these comings in and goings out of the tide. Now they define my days.'

'What's happening about the job?'

'I got a call from the HR department. They want me to go in next week for the hearing.'

'What does that entail?'

'They've been conducting a formal investigation into

my behaviour.'

'Ouch.'

'I know it sounds arrogant, Helena, but to be honest, I'm a better engineer and a better project manager than guys who are much more senior than me in that organisation. I just lost my cool at the wrong time and in the wrong place.'

'You think they're out to get you because you're a woman?'

'No, in fairness, I wouldn't say that. They're doing what they have to do. It just annoys me. I don't think I'd have been put in the invidious position of managing such a hot project on home territory if I'd been a man. Or—' she added in a fit of self-awareness, 'maybe if I'd been a man I would have stood up to my boss more and told them I wasn't doing it.'

'But you do want to go back?'

'Oh yes. It's what I do.' She smiled a pale smile. 'And I'm going to need the income. Besides, I can't stand being here, alone in the house. I put the radio on to kill the silence, but there's nothing I want to listen to. I switch on the telly for company, but I can't settle in front of it. I put on music, but everything reminds me of Andrew, or something we once shared.

Helena's dark eyes watched her thoughtfully. 'About Andrew—'

Kate was still adrift where Andrew was concerned. She couldn't bear the thought of him with Sophie and was still miserable at the prospect of life without him. 'I don't know what to think about Andrew, and that's the honest truth. If he broke off with Sophie and swore it was over – if he could convince me he still loved me in the old way – I'd probably have him back.'

'What's he saying?'

'To be absolutely honest, I think he's probably in as much of a mess as I am. He wants this viewed as a trial separation, but he's staying with Sophie and that's no way to sort things out between us. We've talked to Ninian and tried to explain, but how can you explain when you don't really understand everything yourself? We both feel guilty.'

'So what's stopping you from sorting things out?'

Kate put the image of Ibsen firmly aside. Ibsen was absolutely not a consideration. 'I'm still angry with him. Not just angry – he's really hurt me. I don't trust him any longer. On his side, Sophie's a factor, in a big way. I do get the impression she's clinging like a limpet.' She managed to raise a laugh. 'Sorry. Cheap to take pleasure in their problems, but I'm sure not everything's rosy there. Ninian's been round to visit and he tells me they snap at each other all the time. She's got a small flat and Andrew needs privacy when he's writing.'

'That would be temporary though, surely. They'd get somewhere bigger in time. Sorry – I'm just playing devil's advocate here.'

'I know. Don't apologise, it's useful to have someone to talk about things with. There are so many imponderables.'

Kate was sorry when Helena got up to leave. She said, 'It's been great to see you again. I'm so glad Ninian and Alice are still seeing each other. How's Elliott coping?'

Helena laughed. 'Surprisingly well. He's developed a passion for another girl in their year, which is very convenient all round. Listen, Kate, let me know how you get on. At work, I mean. And if you want to talk about anything – any time – give me a ring.'

'Thanks, Helena.'

Kate picked the post up from the mat as Helena drove away. There were half a dozen letters for Andrew, which she'd have to readdress.

She hadn't wanted to show Helena how much she really missed him. She ached for him in ways she had not thought possible, like not seeing his shirts hanging on the line in the garden. She missed his cooking – God, did she miss his cooking! She picked up the scone Helena had abandoned. It was as hard as a brick. She opened the bin and dropped the scone into it, then disposed of the rest of the batch.

It wasn't just the cooking she missed. Without Andrew beside her in bed, she felt less than complete. Sixteen years of proximity to his lean body were hard to blank away. She missed making love with him – even their latter-day, mechanical sex had been pleasant and in some measure satisfying.

In the hall, she stood by the study door. She had envied him possession of this room. Now that it was empty, she discovered to her surprise that what she missed most of all was hearing the clack clack of the keys of the computer keyboard as he wrote, and the conversations they'd had over meals.

'Martyne needs to discover that the abbot has a secret,' he would say, his brow knotted with the effort of concentration, 'but there's no-one he can trust to discuss his suspicions with.'

'Ellyn?'

'Ellyn is currently staying with her father, the chieftain. He has sent her there for safety because of the disease in the village.'

'Another farm worker?'

'There's no-one as clever as Martyne.'

'But doesn't he have any friends?'

'Friends?'

'Men!' she would laugh. 'Women operate within support networks, men discuss only football or politics. You're right to look puzzled, men don't have friends.'

Now her words came back to her painfully, because what friends did she have? Only Helena and Charlotte, and she hadn't spoken to Charlotte since she'd confessed to sleeping with Andrew.

One morning, she woke from the uneasy sleep that was becoming habitual, and was quite certain that there was someone in the house. Ninian had come in late and this was Sunday. He'd still be deeply asleep.

It was Andrew. She was sure of it.

She didn't know how she felt about him coming in unannounced. Part of her would welcome him, another part was furious that he could so take her permission for the invasion for granted. She tied her negligée round her waist and opened the bedroom door.

From the top of the stairs she glimpsed flowers, a magnificent vase of lime-green chrysanthemums and white gerbera, set off with roses as large as a hand and as dark as old claret. She drew in her breath sharply at their beauty and descended slowly, considering their meaning. Was he trying to woo her back? And if he was, did she want him? Was she prepared to forgive him for Sophie? For Charlotte? For all the other betrayals over the years that Charlotte had implied?

At the foot of the stairs, she turned towards the kitchen. Another vase of flowers – wide-open pink stargazer lilies, heavily scented and perfect – had been placed on the small table between the kitchen door and the living room door and the spot had been switched on to light it.

She could smell coffee. And bacon. Andrew was cooking.

'Hello?' She ran her hands through her hair, which was growing unchecked because she had not been near the hairdresser. She wished she had stopped to wash her face and put on some make up. 'Andrew?'

She turned into the kitchen. A man was standing by the cooker, turning bacon in the frying pan. But it wasn't Andrew, it was Harry.

'Hi.' He turned and smiled. 'Hope I didn't wake you. I

wasn't sure when you'd get up.'

Kate said, breathlessly, 'Hi!' and sank onto one of the tall stools at the breakfast bar, so stunned that she could hardly speak.

'Thought I'd give you a treat.' He indicated the frying pan. 'Hope that's okay?' He was looking a little anxious, the astonished look on her face must have worried him. 'I was going to call, then I thought maybe I'd just surprise you instead.'

'You've certainly done that. I didn't know you had a key.'

'Dad gave me one ages ago. You don't mind do you? I didn't mean to scare you. I reckoned that no sane burglar would cook bacon.'

She had to laugh. Still, it did seem a bit like a dream. Harry? Cooking breakfast? For her? Kate blinked, but when she opened her eyes again he was still here, in the kitchen. She hadn't seen Harry, or heard from him, since the night he and Jane had descended on them, eager to share the news that Sophie had confessed all. She had no idea how he felt about Andrew's departure from her life, though she was sure he would be pleased. Yet here he was – with flowers – and coffee – and bacon.

'Did you bring the flowers?'

'I hope you like them?'

'They're beautiful. Really beautiful.'

'Good.'

He broke two eggs into the frying pan and set plates to warm. Forks appeared, and knives. Butter, a small bowl brimming with marmalade, toast. Breakfast cups, the ones she particularly liked, the huge round bowls they had brought back from France, laughing because they had had to pack them full of dirty washing to protect them, then coax them into over-full suitcases.

He dished out the cooked breakfast and sat down opposite her. She stared down at her plate and blinked again.

'Aren't you hungry?' he asked anxiously.

'Ravenous.'

'Then eat.'

Between mouthfuls of pork and leek sausage, bursting with flavour and dripping with egg yolk, and great gulps of fresh coffee, she surveyed her stepson as if she had never seen him before.

He said, a little tentatively, 'I wanted to find a way of showing you how terribly sorry I am about all this.'

Kate swallowed.

'I'm not great at words. Well, obviously, you know that. But Jane and I – well, we're devastated really.'

'I thought you'd be pleased.'

'*Pleased?* Good God, why?'

'Well, you know. I mean, you were always so terribly against me when I fell in love with your father.'

The surprise on his face seemed genuine. 'Against you? No. I was a bit protective of Mum, I suppose, at first but, to be honest, she was quite happy to see the back of Dad, their marriage had been going down the tubes for ages and she didn't have the courage to tell him to get lost.'

'*What?*' Kate's fork clattered onto her plate.

'You didn't know?'

'I thought he'd broken her heart, and all because of me.'

'Well, you're right in part. I guess he did break her heart, but it had happened before you came along.'

Harry, square-faced and stocky, had more of his mother's character than his father's. He was careful and unadventurous, as well as notoriously unimaginative. It occurred to Kate that Andrew had perhaps never understood his son and that some of that incomprehension might have transferred itself to her. She said, 'You hated me.'

To her surprise, Harry flushed. 'No, Kate. Quite the

293

contrary. I fancied you.'

'You *fancied* me?'

He smiled, patently embarrassed by the confession. 'Give me a break. You were a looker, well, you still are of course, you had bags of personality and you were my age, not Dad's. If I was angry with anyone, it was Dad for finding you first and making you fall in love with him.'

Despite the shock of this revelation, Kate's lips twitched with amusement. Harry had pulled at one end of a misconception and all at once, half a lifetime of guilt was being unravelled.

'What? Don't laugh at me.'

'I'm not laughing at you, Harry, I'm laughing at myself. I never guessed. Was that why you were so awkward around me?'

'Was I awkward? I suppose I was. I had a crush on you for years, if you must know. Plus, I really was mad at Dad. And now I'm furious with him all over again for treating you like this.'

The corners of Kate's mouth began to lift. She couldn't help smiling. She felt like jumping up and bouncing round the kitchen. It was the first time she'd felt good, really good, for months.

'Jane says—'

'She does know you're here?'

'Of course. I wanted her to come too, but she thought it would be better this way.'

'She's a clever girl, as well as a pretty one.'

'I know.'

'You're not like Andrew at all, are you Harry?'

'Not one bit. Surely you knew that?'

'Yes. I knew it. I guess I just didn't appreciate the good things about the differences between you.' She took his hand in hers and couldn't help being just a little gratified when he blushed again. 'Thank you, Harry. For doing this. For your honesty. And for your support.'

'It's a small enough thing to do.'

'But it means the world to me.'

'Really?' He looked shy, but pleased.

Harry and shyness? How well did she know him? All she had ever known of Harry was a hostility that was apparently more perceived than real. Charlotte had told her, *You don't know anything about other people's lives, Kate. You've never taken much interest actually, have you?* That had hurt, but now she wondered if there'd been some truth in it.

She laid a hand on Harry's arm and smiled.

'Really,' she said.

There's a painting, 'The Card Game', in a gallery in Madrid by the artist Balthus. It's an unsettling picture, almost medieval in feel, but in other ways very contemporary. A girl is seated at a table, holding some cards. Her expression is sweet and untroubled, but somehow very knowing. A boy, opposite her, half stands, half leans across the table, his shoulder hunched upwards awkwardly. He's looking not at her, but out of the canvas, at the painter, and he's holding a card behind him, out of her sight. His face is sly.

One picture. Four people looking at it. Each sees something different.

They'd gone to Madrid, as a family, when Ninian was about nine. Harry had not yet met Jane and was footloose. Kate was exhausted and overworked and Andrew, high on record-breaking advance sales for *Martyne Noreis and the Cuckoo in the Nest*, had suggested a family break, his treat.

In the gallery, trying to teach Ninian about art, all he did was snigger at the painting. 'He really wants to win, doesn't he?'

Harry wanted to move on. 'I like the colours, nice big blocks,' he said. 'The guy's shoulder looks strange, though, doesn't it? Just a couple of teenagers, playing cards.'

Andrew was excited. 'Look again, Harry. There's a world of meaning in there. I could write a whole book on the basis of that one scene alone.'

Kate was the only one who looked at the girl's face and saw power. She was calm, assured and knowing. Whatever the youth did, she knew she was going to win. He was going to try and cheat, but she was going to deal with it. She looked like Kate felt at work – always right, always in charge.

Harry's revelations reminded her now of that picture, and of their reactions. They had all been playing out their lives from parallel perspectives. All these years, she and Harry had looked at the situation they were in and had seen in it only one dimension, whereas in fact many dimensions had existed. That realisation gave her strength and hope.

In the village, though, people still avoided her. As she'd predicted, Mrs Gillies had spread the news of Andrew's departure more speedily and with more deadly accuracy than an Exocet missile. Many villagers resented the fact that he'd left and some weren't shy about telling her it was all her fault. Forgie revelled in the fame that came to the village through their local celebrity and Kate had always been a nonentity, at least until the Summerfield project had brought her to their attention for all the wrong reasons. *You're hardly the life and soul of the village*, Andrew had said, callously, and she'd felt hurt. She knew now, though, that there had been more than a grain of truth in what he'd said.

The end of the year was approaching and the weather was dull and damp. The protestors were still encamped in Bonny Brae Woods, she knew, but she had heard that their numbers had diminished. The amateurs and hangers-on had drifted off with the chillier nights and only the professionals were left, doggedly determined. This was, though, a lost cause, and they knew it as well as she did. Even the press had lost interest. As soon as another suitable project presented itself, the eco-protestors would be off – hoping, no doubt, that it might be in a more temperate southerly zone, Kent, perhaps, or Surrey. Few of those Kate had heard talking at the encampment had had Scottish accents.

The walk through Bonny Brae was still denied to her, for obvious reasons, but there were plenty of other walks to choose from. Most days she found herself retracing the route round the back of Forgie House and up the hill to where she'd encountered Ibsen. She told herself it was because she was pondering the logistics of the Summerfield Project in case she was reinstated as manager, though she knew in her heart this was not really true.

Once, she saw his asthmatic van disappearing round the corner, farting hazy fumes behind it, and once she met Cassie. She was walking, as she had taken to walking, with her head down, so it was Daisy Rose, the baby, she saw first, in her stroller. Daisy waved a tiny fist at Kate and blew happy bubbles from the corner of her mouth. Little feet kicked energetically with excitement.

'Hello!' Kate stopped impulsively and bent to offer her a finger. 'My, you've grown.'

'I'm sorry, I—'

She looked up. The family genes were unmistakeable in the tilt of the head and the humorous glint in the eyes, as blue as a loch under a cloudless sky. 'You must be Cassie.'

It was the nearest she had come to contact with Ibsen and she wasn't sure how to handle it.

'I guess you're Kate.'

Kate's heart lurched. Cassie knew who she was. She held out a hand. 'Hi.'

'Ibsen's talked about you.'

'Really?'

297

She grinned, in the family manner. 'You're the power behind the wind farm,' she said, 'and the garden.'

Kate smiled ruefully. 'Actually, neither now. I've been suspended by my company, and the garden needs nothing doing now it's nearly winter. I'm in no-man's land.'

'Sounds uncomfortable.'

'It is.'

'That garden,' Cassie said, pushing the stroller to and fro with little, reassuring movements to keep Daisy Rose happy, 'has been the making of Ibsen.'

'Really?'

'He spends hours on those drawings of his. Planning stuff. Going to meetings.' She guffawed. 'Meetings! Ibsen!'

'He was a real natural with the volunteers.' Kate's heart swelled as she spoke the words. It was good to talk about him.

'It's been a bit of a surprise to all of us. It hasn't been easy for Ibsen since—' Her voice tailed away.

'He told me about Violet,' Kate said softly.

Cassie was clearly shocked. 'He did?'

Daisy Rose decided she was bored and started to wriggle and grizzle, and the grizzling turned into a whimper and threatened to become a cry.

'I'd better go. Nice to meet you.'

'And you.' Kate bent to the baby. 'Bye bye, Daisy Rose.' *Give my love to your uncle*, she wanted to say, but she couldn't utter a word. She opened her mouth to ask Cassie to pass on her good wishes, but nothing came out. 'Bye, then,' she muttered lamely, and continued her walk, head down, ears burning.

Chapter Twenty-Eight

The disciplinary hearing took place in an impersonal meeting room at the AeGen offices. Kate felt her unfamiliar high heels sink into the dark green carpet as she strode across the room to the table. It was strange to be in tailored business wear again. She'd contemplated getting a haircut, but was rather enjoying her new-look longer-length style. It softened her appearance, and in the circumstances, she decided, that might be not be a bad thing. She wore the houndstooth check Burberry scarf she'd been wearing the day Mark told her she'd be managing Summerfield. It seemed a fittingly symmetrical choice. To complete the outfit, she'd pinned the suffragette brooch Andrew had given her onto her jacket, a flash of brilliance that lifted the black. Only she understood its message of defiance, but that was all that mattered.

The florid-faced Alan Weatherstone, Director of Human Resources, formally opened proceedings. 'We're here, Kate, to review the matter of your suspension.'

'Yes.'

'You know everyone here, I think?'

Simon Thomson, AeGen's Director of Operations was the other man present. He was the most senior man in the company, other than the chief executive, which instantly underlined the seriousness of her position. Kate had her own representative, Judy Fulham, from her trade union.

'Yes.'

Alan said, 'Let's start then. First, I'd like to apologise for the length of time it has taken to conduct the inquiry, but you'll appreciate how important it was that we do things by the book.'

'Of course.'

'The issue under investigation led to a charge of gross misconduct – that is, that on the day in question, you caused the good reputation of AeGen to be brought into disrepute as a direct result of your behaviour towards members of the public, in an incident that was filmed and later reported in the media.'

Kate remained silent. Her case had been prepared on her behalf and this was not the time to start arguing. The facts would emerge.

'You asked us to speak to a number of people, including your line manager, Mark Matthews, other members of your team, in particular your assistant Jack Bailey. Correct?'

'Yes.'

He patted the thick file in front of him. 'We took evidence from fourteen people in total. In addition, other salient facts were taken into account, in particular the position you had been put into when the AeGen management asked you to take charge of a controversial project in your own village. The pressures you were under were borne out by the threatening emails you received on your computer, and which you had filed.'

Thank God she had filed them.

'There are two other important mitigating facts. First, that you claim you had asked Jack Bailey not to include the route through Bonny Brae Woods on the plans to be shown at the public exhibitions, and second, the fact that your son was present at the time of the incident.'

Kate had battled discrimination and inequity all her life, but she felt intimidated by the formality of the proceedings, even though Judy had run through what would happen and they had rehearsed their responses. She hated being here in disgrace – in these offices, where she had been an important player with ambitions to reach the

300

top. She didn't even have a pass, only a visitor tag. She steeled her nerves.

'First, let's run through the facts of the incident itself—'

The whole hearing took almost an hour. The overwhelming weight of evidence was on her side, and they seemed to have been very fair. Alan Weatherstone smiled and said, 'I think that concludes things from our side. Have you got any questions?'

'No. Thank you.'

'No? Then can I suggest you go and find yourselves a coffee? I'll get someone to take you down to the canteen and we'll come for you once we've reached a decision.'

'Thank you.'

When the door of the meeting room closed behind them, Kate was about to speak when Judy gave her a warning glance and nodded at the back of the girl who was leading them down to the canteen. Kate closed her mouth again. When they were finally alone, Judy turned to her and said, 'Well? What did you think?'

'Tough but fair, I suppose. I was a bit shocked to see myself on that video again, I'd forgotten I'd been that forthright – even if it was meant to be a private conversation with my son. How do you think the decision will go?'

'Hard to tell. On balance, I think it'll probably be all right.'

'I hope so. I don't want to lose this. I don't deserve to lose.'

They waited a full, nail-biting hour before they were summoned back upstairs. Alan Weatherstone placed his hands together on the file. He looks, Kate thought, like a judge about to pass sentence.

'We've reached a decision, Kate. There were, of course, incontrovertible errors of judgement and behaviour on your part,' he paused, his face impassive, then broke into a smile that seemed quite genuine and went on, 'but on balance we found that the circumstances weighed against these. We are, therefore, going to reinstate you.'

'Thank you.' It was what she'd hoped for – what she had expected – but she was relieved nonetheless.

'However,' he continued, hardly giving her time to speak, 'although you have the right to be reinstated in your role, we are bound to give you a formal warning. You understand that?'

The relief receded. 'I— I suppose so. Yes.'

'In addition, you will be expected to report every day to your line manager, Mark Matthews.'

'Report? I don't understand.'

'You must give Mark a brief written report each evening before you leave the building on the main activities and decisions you have been engaged in during the day.'

'Like a school work experience child, you mean?' Kate said incredulously.

'It's just a safeguard.'

'You can't be serious?' she shot back at him, her impulsive reaction so strong that she had no time to weigh her words. 'Safeguard against what?' A shaft of sunlight, sneaking in through the blinds at the window, caught the faceted diamonds in her brooch and sent up a rainbow. *The suffragettes had beliefs. They fought for a cause and they fought with passion.* Fight!

She slapped her hand on the table with such vehemence that it stung. She saw the men jump with surprise. Good. That had got their attention!

'Forgive me for pointing this out, but I'm one of the most experienced engineers in the company. I've project-managed some of our biggest wind farms, on time and to budget. I've achieved more on the ground than many more senior managers in this company have ever done – don't you agree? Alan?' She stared intensely at the HR manager.

302

'Simon? You know my record.'

Neither man looked her in the eye.

'I think you'd find it very hard not to acknowledge the truth of what I'm saying. And yet—' she paused again, while they shifted uncomfortably in their seats, '—and yet you want Mark to crawl over every decision I make?'

Judy's foot pressed warningly against hers under the table, but the stress she'd been under over the past few weeks was threatening to explode like an Icelandic geyser. *I mustn't lose my temper,* she thought. She couldn't give them the satisfaction of seeing her again as she had appeared on television, shrewish and uncontrollable.

In fact … she wouldn't let them have the satisfaction of seeing her again, full stop.

She said, before she had time to change her mind, 'I'm sorry, but I think your judgement is flawed and your decision-making woeful. I have no wish to work in such an environment, or to work for people for whom I have little respect. You'll have my formal resignation in the morning.'

She picked up her briefcase and stalked out. Judy ran after her.

'Kate! Are you sure you mean that? After all this effort?'

'I'm sure.' Kate was walking so fast that Judy was almost having to run to keep up with her. 'The whole thing has just made me see what a grim place this is.' She stopped and gestured at the carpet. 'Forest green. Environmentally friendly. Care for employees. "Our people are our greatest resource",' she quoted sarcastically. '"We stand for respect and integrity and we listen to our people". Ha!'

Judy panted, 'But we've won. You've got your job back. The reporting restriction will be lifted in time. Don't you think—'

They'd reached Reception. Kate wrenched off her

Visitor tag and threw it down on the front desk. 'I know you think I'm just being hot tempered, Judy. And I do appreciate all your work on my behalf. But I'm not going to change my mind. I couldn't go back in there and be patronised and demeaned by those people. I've got too much self respect.'

They spun through the revolving door and out into the car park.

'I'm as good as they are. Better. And do you know what? It's the first time I've felt *good* for weeks.'

The feeling of euphoria, perhaps surprisingly, lasted for some time. Andrew phoned.

'How did it go? Did they give you back your job?'

'Yes.'

'That's great news, well done. I always had faith in you.'

'I told them to stuff it.'

'You did what?'

'They were so condescending.'

'You've given up your job on a principle?'

'Yes. The principle of self-respect. Aren't you proud of me?'

'I think you're as bloody-minded and impulsive as ever. How are you going to manage?'

'I haven't thought about it yet.'

'Oh, Kate.' The reproach in his voice was multi-faceted and she could name its planes – irritation, exasperation, concern, displeasure, and ire. Was the concern for her wellbeing, she wondered, or for his wallet? 'We have to talk.'

Kate felt bruised. All the things that had defined her as a person had been put through the mill and ground to powder. Being a wife: fail. Motherhood: half marks? Friendships: fail. Her work: fail, fail, fail. She clamped the phone between her left ear and her shoulder. Would it be such a bad thing to mend things with Andrew, put a small tick beside the box that said Marriage? Might it ever be possible to rebuild her trust of him? Should she try, for Ninian's sake if not her own?

He was saying, 'I'll come by tomorrow.'

A faint sense of alarm stirred. She needed time for her new situation to settle in her mind. 'Not tomorrow.'

'The day after then? I'll take you out for lunch.'

She tried to think rationally. She needed to understand what and who she was in this new world of hers. Perhaps talking to Andrew might help. She'd have to talk to him sometime anyway, to think about what to do with Willow Corner. 'Lunch then,' she said, twisting her wedding ring. 'On Thursday.'

In the small world of renewable energy engineering, news travels fast. Before teatime she got a call from an engineer she had trained with.

'Keith Devlin here. Remember me?'

'Vividly. Puking into a plant pot after a crazy night out, as I recall.'

'Ouch. Can we never put our student years behind us?'

Kate laughed. 'Only when the grey cells die in the last one standing. It's nice to hear from you, Keith. How's things?'

'Mad. One of our project engineers has been put out of action. Heart attack.'

'I'm sorry to hear that. I hope it wasn't stress.'

'He's a man who likes his pies and beer. The stress was all in his arteries.'

'He's all right, I hope?'

'He's alive. But he was coming up to retirement anyway and his wife's insisting he stops now, on medical grounds.'

'That's understandable. Listen, Keith, sad as I am for your man, what's it got to do with me?'

'I heard you're on the market for work.'

'What?' Kate was astonished. 'Where did you hear that from?'

'You know how it is. Are you?'

'I don't know. Possibly.'

'You've left AeGen though, right?'

'Almost. My resignation will be with them in the morning. I still don't know – who's your mole?'

'Just the jungle tom-toms.'

'What might you be offering?'

'Not a permanent job. Not as yet, anyway, we've got a head count limit. A contract. We need a project manager to take over from Tommy.'

'Where?'

He named a site in the Borders. 'Know it?'

'I've followed its progress, yes.'

'Think you could handle it?'

'Of course. But Keith—'

'Yes?'

'Everything would depend on whether they try to put any restrictive covenants on me. I won't know for a few days probably.'

'Fair enough. We're desperate though. You could just about name your price, though I shouldn't be telling you that.'

'How long's the contract?'

'Around a year to going live, bit of wind-down after that. Interested?'

'Definitely.'

'Give me a bell, then, soon as you know your position.'

'Will do. And Keith—'

'Yes?'

'Thanks for thinking of me.'

She sat staring at the phone. Work: fail, fail, fail? Maybe not.

Chapter Twenty-Nine

Harry called early. Kate wiped sleep from her eyes and tried to clear her brain.

'Dad tells me you're meeting him for lunch.'

'I am, yes. Why?'

'I can't talk now, Kate, I've got a meeting but I'll be through by midday. I'd like to see you before you meet Dad. Can you fit me in?'

Kate was ridiculously pleased to be asked. It was the first time, so far as she could remember, that Harry had ever asked her to meet him. 'I don't see why not. Was there something in particular?'

'It'll be easier to explain when we meet.' He named a cafe near the restaurant where she was seeing Andrew. 'See you then. You will come, won't you?'

'Of course I'll come,' she answered, surprised.

'Good. Bye, Kate.'

'Bye, Harry.'

He cut the call and she stared at the phone, puzzled. It rang again at once. It was Lisa Tranter.

'I'm in the car park,' Lisa said in a low, quick voice. 'I just wanted to say how sorry we all are. You know. About you leaving.'

'Oh. Right.' They knew already?

'No-one wanted you to go, you know.'

Kate wanted to say, *Not even Jack Bailey?* but she held her peace. 'Thank you for telling me that, Lisa. I appreciate it.'

'By the way, we just heard – all the readings from the Met mast are great. We'll certainly be pushing ahead with the full planning application.'

'When did you hear?'

'Just this morning. I'm so sorry you won't be running the project. It was fun working with you.'

'Thank you, Lisa.'

'Anyway, I'd better go. Could I buy you a drink sometime? I'd like to.'

'I'd like that too. What a lovely suggestion.'

So Summerfield would probably happen after all. Kate had always been confident it would. However, it would be Jack who took it forward, not her, and she couldn't say, hand on heart, that she was sorry about that.

With more time on her hands than she had ever had, it would have been reasonable to assume that she would be better organised than in the days when she'd been out all hours. Oddly, this proved not to be the case – she discovered that she was clean out of coffee. Unable to function without a strong brew of freshly-ground coffee, she put on her coat and set off for the village shop. A hundred yards before she reached it, she came across Frank Griffiths on a small folding stepladder, reaching up a lamppost to cut down one of the many protest placards that had been put up round the village. Georgie was with him.

Kate stopped.

'Good morning, you two,' she said brightly. 'What a lovely day. Was The Herons okay in the storm the other day, Georgie? Did you see the lightning?'

'Brilliant, wasn't it? I couldn't sleep.'

'It hit our old willow.'

'Is it all right?'

'No, sadly, it's not. A spectacular strike destroyed it completely, there's nothing left but the stump.'

'Oh no!' Georgie seemed upset. 'But it won't be Willow Corner any more.'

'We still have one tree left,' Kate pointed out, 'and I'll probably replant.' She looked at Georgie. 'Are you all right, Georgie? Shouldn't you be in school?'

'I didn't feel well this morning. Stomach cramps,' she looked meaningfully at Kate. 'Mum said if I felt better later I could go round with Grandpa to collect the posters.'

'So you do feel a bit better?' Kate said sympathetically.

'Much better, thank you. But I'll probably stay off all day. Mum says I need to get some colour in my cheeks.'

Frank had snipped the plastic clips on the card and he tossed the placard into the sack Georgie was holding. He climbed down from the small steps. 'Another one done. How many's that, Georgie?'

'Twelve. How many are there?'

'There should be forty, in Forgie and Summerfield.' He eyed Kate steadily. 'So. It looks as though the wind farm will go ahead.'

'What have you heard?'

'We were notified yesterday that a full planning application is to go in.'

'Can I ask why the posters are coming down?'

Frank looked embarrassed. 'Actually, the Community Council has decided to withdraw its protest.'

'Really? What's brought that about?'

'AeGen did a really good job on the Council,' he said, plainly piqued. 'First they sent us someone who gave us more detail about the size of the turbines and the sight lines. If we can believe them, we shouldn't see too much from Forgie once the landscaping is complete.'

As I explained, Kate thought, amused.

'And your Community Benefit Manager – Gail? – came and told us we could apply for funding to renovate the village hall.'

'That's a great idea.'

Frank tilted his head to one side as if to gauge her reaction, then shook it slowly from side to side. 'Blood money. That's what I called it, and that's what I still believe. But the Community Council voted by a majority to withdraw our opposition, so I'm obliged to accept that.'

Kate felt sorry for him. For all his faults, Frank had fought for what he believed. She tried to soften the defeat. 'Twelve turbines is quite a small wind farm, Frank. And what you were told about visibility was correct.'

'Eight.'

'Sorry?'

He beamed. 'It looks as though we'll probably succeed in one thing, at least, we've managed to negotiate down from twelve to eight turbines.'

'Right.' Kate suppressed a smile. She knew that AeGen had always assumed the proposal would have to be scaled back. 'Well, there you go. That's good news. And the village hall does desperately need an upgrade.'

Frank's attitude changed abruptly. 'We are where we are. I'm sorry,' he said, 'about your situation. You know – work, and—'

He left the sentence unfinished. It was obvious that he didn't want to discuss her private affairs with Georgie present, but he laid a hand on her arm, the gesture solicitous.

'Thank you.' Kate felt herself getting emotional, but choked her feelings back determinedly. She hadn't entirely given up on Andrew, and the work situation was looking amazingly bright. It was too early, though, to talk about either.

He removed his hand. 'Come on, Georgie, more placards to take down. Nice to see you, Kate.'

'And you.' She meant it. She had not liked the angry Frank. Rage had done him little justice, it had outweighed fondness, and courtesy, and intelligent discussion. All the kindnesses he had shown her over the years had been swamped by pique. She hoped they could learn to manage their differences more moderately. On impulse, she stood

310

on tiptoe and kissed his aged cheek, and was pleased when he looked gratified.

She tucked her arm into Georgie's and walked a little way down the street with her as Frank strode on ahead. Georgie said in a low voice, 'Do you know why Mum's so miserable, Kate?'

Kate glanced at her sharply. 'What do you mean?'

She glanced anxiously at Frank's rapidly receding back. 'I didn't want to say anything in front of Grandpa, but she's really snappy, and she never laughs. Frankie says she's drinking loads, too.'

'Drinking?'

'She seems to open a new bottle of wine every evening, and Dad's not even around at the mo.' She tucked her long hair behind her ear and looked sideways up at Kate. 'I don't mean to be cheeky, but have you fallen out with her? We haven't seen you in ages.'

'I'm sorry.'

'Will you come and see her? Please?'

Frank stopped at a lamppost and swung round. 'Here we are, Georgie. Number thirteen?'

'Yup.' She looked at Kate and mouthed, 'Please?'

Kate smiled and gave her a hug. 'I'll do what I can,' she murmured, wondering if she was telling the girl the truth. She wasn't sulking, it was just that she was still too hurt by Charlotte's admission to be ready for closeness again.

She met Harry at one of the small Italian coffee shops on George IV Bridge in Edinburgh. Harry was already there when she arrived, sitting on the edge of his chair at a small table in the far corner and nursing a tall latte. He stood up as soon as he saw her. 'Thanks for coming, Kate, especially at such short notice.' He bent and kissed her cheek. 'How are you?'

'As well as can be expected, considering I'm now

311

unemployed.' She took off her jacket and draped it over the back of the chair, where it dripped despondently onto the tiled floor. Outside, it was wet and bitterly cold, but the café was almost uncomfortably warm.

'Unemployed? What happened? Surely the hearing didn't go against you? They must be mad to let you go—'

'That's very sweet of you, Harry, but actually, I resigned.'

Harry blinked at her.

Kate explained the situation. 'Do you understand how I felt?' she asked.

'Absolutely.' His conviction was heartening. 'They're idiots, obviously. You're so bright and efficient they shouldn't be risking you going to the opposition.'

'Thanks. Andrew thinks I'm mad to resign.'

'Ah. Dad. That's what I wanted to talk to you about. Did you order coffee?'

'I think this is it coming now.'

A young waitress put a foaming cappuccino down in front of her and asked with a marked Italian accent, 'Is that everything? I can't tempt you to some torte? Or Pannetone? We've baked our own for Christmas.'

Kate shook her head and smiled. 'I'm having lunch in an hour, though it sounds terribly tempting.' When the waitress had gone, she said, 'So you've seen your father?'

'We met for a pint last night.' He cleared his throat, then stirred his latte. 'He wants to come back to you. I get the impression things aren't entirely going well with Sophie. Don't take him back, Kate.'

'Don't—?'

'He's an idiot. He's done this before and if you take him back, I'm sure he'll only do it again.'

'He's done this *before*?'

'He's had two or three affairs since you were married.'

Is the wife always the last to know? 'Why the hell didn't you tell me?'

312

'Would you have believed me?'

Kate stared at Harry, dumbfounded. He was right, of course. If he'd come to her with tales of Andrew's infidelity, she'd have thought he'd been provoked by resentment or spite.

'Why do you think it's taken me so long to get married myself? Because I saw the way Dad behaved and I didn't want to be like that. It's just taken me a long time to understand that I'm not programmed like him. When I met Jane, everything changed. I knew that there was no-one else I wanted to spend my life with.'

'I thought you'd be on his side.'

Harry grimaced. 'I love Dad, of course I do – but it's in spite of everything. I hate the way he behaves around women, particularly young women. I despise it.' He glanced at his watch. 'I'm going to have to go. Sorry. I just wanted to say, I love the way you fight for things, Kate, but I think if you decide to fight to save this marriage you'd be fighting for the wrong thing. Dad's not worth it.'

He stood up.

'Sorry. Perhaps I shouldn't have said anything, but I couldn't have rested easy if I hadn't told you how I felt. I'll get the coffee.'

Kate stood too, raking a hand through her unfamiliarly long hair. 'Goodness. Wow.'

Harry smiled. 'Whatever you decide, can we still be friends? I would hate to lose you just as we've begun to talk.'

'You won't.' Harry picked up his coat and briefcase and turned away. She called after him, 'And thanks for being so honest.'

Outside, frost had been replaced by rain, a biting, wind-driven, bone-chilling kind of wetness. Kate put her head down and marched through it to meet Andrew. In the next hour, she supposed, her future would be decided.

Andrew tried to impress her by taking her to The Tower, high in the Museum of Scotland.

'Hello, darling.' He bent to kiss her, but she turned her face away, so that his kiss landed awkwardly near her ear.

'Hello.'

They sat by a window, in a high eyrie with normally spectacular vistas – but today, Edinburgh was looking gray-cauled and sorry, a charcoal city in a pale mist. It had been raining all morning and now damp droplets slid off dark slates and landed in over-full gutters. Far below them, stone-slabbed pavements gleamed in cold light and pedestrians scuttled hopelessly, heads down, hoods up, wanting only to reach their destinations and better cheer. Trees in a nearby graveyard stood barren and black. It was winter, and dismal.

'Lovely day.'

He smiled at her irony. 'Nature's cycle. Without rain there is no life, after winter comes spring.'

'You're very jolly.'

'Wine?'

'I think it's absolutely necessary, don't you?'

He pulled his glasses out of his pocket and slid them onto his nose. It was an affectingly familiar gesture. The lenses were smeared and dusty and she fought the impulse to take them off him and clean them on a handkerchief.

'Viognier all right?'

'Perfect.'

How long had it been since she'd told him to go? Four weeks? Five? Six? She searched his face for change, but saw nothing. A faint strain round the eyes, perhaps, but no more than he showed when he was struggling with a novel.

'How's the writing?'

He winced, then tried to cover it by whipping off his glasses and playing with the leg, twirling the frame irritatingly to and fro in his hand. 'All right. Sophie's flat is rather small.'

314

'But temporary, I assume?'

The spectacles twirled again. He laid them on the table, swapped spectacles for wine and tilted the glass away from him, then sideways, then the other way, watching as sugary legs streaked down the glass. 'If things work out, I guess.'

'Oh?'

He took a quick sip, followed it with a sizeable gulp, then another. 'The thing is, Kate, I'm not altogether sure about this.'

'The wine? We can ask for something different.' She was being naughty, but couldn't resist teasing.

'Not the wine. You know I'm talking about Sophie.'

'Andrew, you can afford a bigger flat, surely. You could probably afford quite a big house, if it comes to that. Especially when we sell Willow Corner.'

He looked shocked. 'Sell Willow Corner?'

'You'll recall that I'm currently unemployed.' No need to tell him about the offer of contract work, not yet. 'The mortgage payments are high and I can't expect you to go on paying them. And you'll need capital yourself for somewhere bigger.'

'But you love Willow Corner.'

He was right. It was more to her than a house. Kate had always felt the connections to her home's past keenly and she knew she'd miss her muslin-draped eighteenth-century predecessors in their shawls and bonnets, and the nineteenth-century women of the house in their stays and corsets. *Stay with us,* they seemed to call to her, *don't abandon us.*

'It's a house,' she said, stubbornly ignoring them all.

'The thing is,' Andrew said slowly, looking at her over his wine, 'Sophie is – well—'

'Demanding? Broody? Jealous?'

'—very young.'

That brought her up short. 'Oh. Well, you knew that.'

315

He pursed his lips.

'Charlotte told me that young flesh fed your vanity.'

His mouth fell open. He dropped the wine glass onto the table, where it toppled precariously. Kate shot out a hand to steady it.

'She said *what?*'

'Was she right?'

His eyes were wide with shock. 'That's a terrible thing to say.'

Kate leaned forwards and stared at him intently. 'But was she *right?*'

'Kate, where's this going? I asked you here today because I wanted to tell you that I think I've made a mistake.'

'Who's having the salmon?' They both swivelled abruptly. A waiter was standing by the table, a steaming plate in each white-gloved hand.

'Here.' Kate indicated the space in front of her. The waiter placed an immaculately arranged dish of salmon in front of her, then presented Andrew with a sumptuous-looking bowl of braised beef. 'Thank you.'

'Will there be anything else?'

She smiled sweetly. 'Nothing. Thank you.'

They stared at each other across the food. Neither of them picked up a fork.

Andrew said, 'Your hair suits you like that.'

She ran a hand through the curls. Allowed to go untrimmed for more than three months now, the old cropped style had grown luxuriant and untamed to below her ears.

'It's more like when we met. Do you remember that day?'

'Of course I do, it was just like this. Wet and miserable.'

'You looked so beautiful.'

'You looked horribly tempting.'

316

His conker-brown eyes were hooded and sensual. 'Kate, I—'

'Stop.'

'I wanted to tell—'

'No. Stop, Andrew. It's no good reliving the old days. Everything has changed. You know that.'

'For better or worse? I thought you, of all people, would fight for your marriage.'

'Vanity is a terrible thing, Andrew.'

'I didn't mean— As a principle, I meant, that was all. I'm not so vain as to think you'd love me unconditionally. I just meant ... because you're a fighter. It's what I've always loved in you.'

'Has this just been a game, then? To watch me chase after you? To test me against Sophie?'

'*No!* You're twisting everything I say. I didn't mean that, either.'

'You're the one who's meant to be good with words. You'll have to be clearer.'

'I've made a terrible error of judgment. I never meant things to go this far.'

'No.' Kate lifted the linen serviette on her side plate and spread it across her knees. 'I don't suppose you did. You just thought you'd have a nice, comfortable fling, like you have done before, then when you got tired of it, I'd still be there, waiting for you. Trusting you.'

He hung his head, his finger tracing imaginary patterns on the tablecloth. 'It's not like that.'

Harry's words were fresh in her mind. 'I think it is. How many women, Andrew? Hmm? How many?'

'Don't. It was always you, sweetheart. No-one else meant anything.'

'Then why do it? Did those women mean so little? Did you afford them no dignity?'

His lips were tight. He looked much older today than his fifty-seven years. His skin was grey and there were two

317

loose folds under the chin she had never noticed before. He was becoming gaunt, and it was not a good look.

He swallowed hard. 'Sophie is a very insistent person. I suppose ... I confess I was flattered, at first. She's fine-looking, she's a little mysterious, you know? But I soon discovered that she's very needy.'

He looked straight at Kate. 'Not like you, Kate. You're so brilliantly sure of yourself. So capable. I admire you enormously.'

'But you still betrayed me.'

'I've been unutterably stupid. I suppose you're right about vanity. At the end of the day, that's what it is, isn't it? Having someone young and beautiful look at you adoringly is deeply gratifying.'

That acknowledgement was a start – but could Andrew really change? If he gave Sophie up and came back home, would suspicion gnaw at her for ever?

She thought of Harry's words. *You'd be fighting for the wrong thing. Dad's not worth it.* 'Nothing can ever be the same between us, Andrew. Even if I did say you could come back, every time you left the house in the future, I'd think it was to go to Sophie – or Rachel, or Jess or whoever the hell you'd got your eye on.'

'It wouldn't be like —'

'If you smiled at a woman, I'd think you were screwing her. If you even *wrote* about a pretty girl, I'd draw parallels and imagine you were indulging in some secret liaison.'

'I've told you before that fiction and reality are two very different things.'

This was the moment of choice. In front of her were two paths. One was familiar and would remove many uncertainties. She would be able to stay in Willow Corner, she would work to rebuild trust with the man she had fallen so deeply in love with, the man she had believed she would spend her life with. The other turned a corner and

318

was unmapped, its destination uncharted. She would travel it alone and there would be many difficulties along its course. Two days ago she had walked away from her job to salvage self-respect. Should she abandon her marriage for the same reason? She took a shaky breath.

'Stop. Enough. It's over. You know it is. We've both got to face it. Perhaps we should both just be grateful that our marriage has lasted sixteen years.'

'Kate—'

'No!' She threw her linen serviette onto the table. 'I can't do this. You made a choice. You've made a lot of choices over the years and most of them didn't fall out in my favour.'

She pushed back her chair and stood up. Andrew jumped to his feet and caught her arm. 'Don't go. Please. You haven't even eaten yet.'

'I've lost my appetite.'

'She's not right for me, Kate. You are. I love you.'

She gazed at him steadily. 'You should have thought of that before.'

'Please. Let's talk. There's Ninian—'

'Don't! Don't you dare use your son as a tool.'

She'd thought her job was the most important thing in her life, until she'd discovered that her family meant more to her than her work. She'd thought her love for Andrew was unassailable until she found that he had demeaned it. Now all that mattered was Ninian, and being true to herself. And in her current situation that meant discovering, all over again, who she was and what she really cared about.

'Sophie—'

'Yes, *you* need to think about Sophie. You owe the girl some honesty. But don't think about her in the context of your marriage, because that is over.'

She picked up her handbag and walked out. The maitre d', at the doorway, called after her, 'Is everything all right?

319

Madam?' Behind her Andrew stood, helplessly.

She emerged into a pale and watery sunshine. Seeing Andrew had been difficult, but her reaction to his feeble complaints had told her all she needed to know about their marriage. She hadn't lied to him. No more prevarication. No more fooling herself that maybe, 'for the sake of Ninian'...

She knew it really was over.

Chapter Thirty

The run-up to Christmas – a time when Ibsen normally found himself at something of a loose end – was exceptionally busy this year. He hadn't been back to help Kate clear up after the storm. Instead, making the excuse that he had too much to do in the community garden at Summerfield, he'd asked one of his pals from college to help her.

The story about the garden had the merit of being partly true, at least, because there was to be a carol concert in the garden on Christmas Eve, and as it was its very first official event, he wanted the place to look the best it could look at this time of year.

Ibsen hated computers and had no patience with texting – his fingers were too big and the phone was usually somewhere inaccessible. He relied on Nicola Arnott, therefore, to help him organise the volunteers, and at the end of November she circulated an email calling for as many as possible to turn out for a last push before the lights were brought in and staging set up.

He didn't expect Kate to come down.

Kate, reading Nicola's plea, was nudged by pangs of conscience into action. She hadn't volunteered in the garden for weeks. Too busy getting to grips with the new work, she excused herself – but was she really? She could easily have come to help for an hour or two.

Bracing herself, she wrapped up warmly and answered the call for help.

Nicola greeted her with an excited hug. 'Isn't it terrific?

It's been really full on, but I can almost see the end now. Look, the paths have all been delineated and some of them have been laid already.'

'What a change,' Kate said, her admiration tempered by guilt.

'Hi Kate, no' seen you for a while,' came a nicotine-husky voice from near her shoulder. It was Maisie, the volunteer she'd befriended. 'Afraid o' hard work, are we?'

'Not a bit of it.'

'They paths, they're buggers.'

'Really? Why?'

'Got to mark them then dig down four inches. Backbreaking. Then compact the lot o' it, then add wee stanes and compact again. That Jodie, mind her delicate hands?' Maisie cackled. 'One big blister.'

Guilt hit the heights. 'Oh dear, have I been slacking?'

'No worries, hen,' Maisie chortled, 'there's still loads tae do.'

Kate glimpsed Ibsen from a distance, but someone slotted her into a team at the far side of the garden, so she put her head down and got on with the work.

Maisie was right about the blisters – she could feel one coming up after half an hour. It felt good to be working here again though, she had missed the physical labour as well as the community spirit, which was fantastic. When it was time for a break, she rummaged in the basket she'd brought.

'Cookie anyone?'

'What kind?' Maisie asked, poking a grubby finger into the basket.

'Three-chocolate. I made them myself,' Kate said proudly.

'Nae bad,' grunted Maisie, wolfing one down.

There were some left. Why not use them as an excuse to find Ibsen? Maybe breaking a biscuit with him would also serve to break the ice.

She stood up and stretched. God, she was getting stiff. The light was beginning to fail too, they wouldn't get much more work done tonight.

She spotted Ibsen at the very far corner of the garden, leaning against the old apple tree, barely recognisable under a vast coat, his ponytail covered by a black beanie.

When she got to within five paces, she called a cheerful, 'Hi!'

'Hello.'

He sounded guarded. He didn't move towards her.

'How are you doing?'

'Pretty good. You?'

'Great.' She paused. This was unexpectedly hard going. They'd always been able to crack a joke and share a smile – what had happened to him? Had she really offended him so deeply? She waved her biscuit tin in the general direction of the garden. 'This is looking fantastic. You must be very proud.'

'Aye.'

Monosyllabic barely began to cover it.

'Would you like one of my biscuits?' She held out the willow basket.

'No, you're all right. Thanks.'

He seemed unwilling to move.

'I made them myself.' Her laugh emerged more as a nervous giggle. 'Your mother would be proud of me.'

'Terrific. But I'm not hungry.'

'I thought things would have quietened down once the digging was finished.'

'There's always something to be done in a garden.'

'I guess so.'

'You haven't been down for a while.'

'I've got a new contract. It's keeping me busy.'

'That's good.'

'Yes. Ibsen—'

She took half a step towards him and he pulled the

323

greatcoat more tightly around himself. Kate looked at him puzzled. His usual heart-warming smile had been replaced by a look of flat resignation. Under his coat, something wriggled. She glanced down. He appeared to have two pairs of legs – and one pair was definitely a woman's.

He followed her gaze and grimaced. 'Rumbled, Mel. Come on out.'

He opened his coat and the unmistakeable auburn hair of Melanie McGillivray appeared, followed by heavily-mascara'd emerald eyes and a mouth twisted into what could only be described as a smirk.

'She was cold,' Ibsen explained.

'Right,' Kate said, finding it impossible to keep the sarcasm out of her voice.

Melanie smiled smugly. 'And he's *so* warm and cuddly.'

Kate shifted from one foot to the other. How foolish she had been to think that Ibsen might still harbour any feelings for her – if he'd had any in the first place, that is.

'Well, I can see you're going to have a Happy Christmas,' she said, her voice raw with disappointment. She turned away.

For one hopeful second she thought she glimpsed movement – was he coming after her? – but all she got was a flat, 'And you,' from Ibsen and an arch 'And a *great* New Year,' from Melanie.

Holding her emotions firmly in check, she lifted her chin and headed for the gate. Holding onto her dignity seemed more important than retrieving her flask.

Melanie opened the passenger door of Ibsen's van and started to climb in.

Ibsen said, 'I'll drop you home.'

'I thought—'

'I've got things to do.'

'—you and me—'

He started the engine. In the dog cage at the back, Wellington barked. 'There's no you and me, Mel. I told you, remember?'

He was furious that Kate had caught him like that. It was the first time he'd even seen Mel since that night at the pub, but Kate would think they were together. The look on her face was something he'd prefer to forget.

'Come on Ibs, you don't mean it.'

She leaned across the gear lever and laid a hand on his arm. He shook it off, slammed the van into reverse and jolted off.

'I sent in an application for that job.'

Melanie thumped back in her seat so that her head banged into the headrest. 'Oh, shit, I thought you were kidding me. What's your family say?'

Ibsen didn't reply. He hadn't told them yet.

The thought of Christmas filled Ibsen with dread. They'd never had a single Christmas with Violet, she'd died in mid December. They'd both gone mad with the presents – how stupid can you get? Why buy a baby Christmas presents? It'd be another couple of years before she'd get excited, be able to rip open the wrapping papers, brandish some pretty pink hat or rattly toy—

Still, they'd done it anyway. The inevitable cuddly reindeer as well as a musical snowman; a white porcelain night light in the shape of a dog (from Wellington); a super-soft pram blanket; a My First Christmas photo album; a door plaque with Violet beautifully painted on it and adorned with tiny purple pansies that Lynn had ordered from a Christmas Fair. It arrived the day after Vi died.

He'd no idea what had happened to the gifts. He couldn't bear to have them near him. Had Lynn sent everything to some charity? Had his mother tactfully dealt with them? The only item he'd kept was a Peter Rabbit moneybox, because he'd been determined to give something back to the Lullaby Trust, the charity that tried to help them both to deal with their loss. He hadn't been able to say thank you at the time. Now he put all his change into the moneybox every night, and when it was full he sent off a cheque for the amount to the charity. It was surprising how quickly it filled up.

'We'll have a family Christmas,' Cassie promised, hugging her brother as she said it.

She must knew how difficult it would be for him, with Daisy Rose replacing Violet as the first baby in the family to celebrate Christmas.

The only thing Ibsen wanted to do was slip into a sleigh bed with Kate Courtenay and play jingle bells all night long – but the look on her face when she'd seen Mel under his coat said it all. He'd messed it up again, just when she looked like she might be prepared to talk.

His phone rang just as he was leaving for Frank Griffiths' house the following morning.

'Ibsen Brown.'

'Morning, Mr Brown, this is Anne in Northamptonshire.'

'Hi Anne.' Ibsen's interest quickened. She was calling from the office of the estate where he'd applied for the job.

'We'd love you to come for a final interview.'

He had to strain to understand her flat vowels. 'Sorry, I didn't quite get that—'

'A final interview. I know it's almost Christmas and really short notice, and it's a terrible time to ask anyone to travel, but there's a cottage in the grounds that's free, it goes with the job and our man has already left. So if you did happen to want a few days' break with your family, you could certainly use it.'

'I'll be there. Thanks.'

He cut the call. Great. He wouldn't be taking any family, but a few days in a cottage, away from everyone who knew him, was just what he needed. He could be back in time for a last Christmas with his folks.

Predictably, Cassie gave him a tongue-lashing when he told her. 'What about Mum and Dad?' she demanded, her sky-blue eyes glinting with anger. 'It'll break their hearts if you move away, Ibsen, you know that.'

'Just for once, I need to do something for myself.'

'Just for once? Who sat with you night after night when Vi died and after Lynn left? Who cooks meals for you and makes sure you're—'

'Don't, Cassie.'

His tone must have been forceful, because she shut up. But he knew what she thought, all right. And even though his parents, when he broke the news, were completely uncritical of his decision, he knew exactly what they thought too.

Still – what was the point in staying here?

Kate went to see Charlotte.

'I couldn't let Christmas go by without putting things right between us,' she said as Charlotte led her into the kitchen at The Herons.

It was almost twenty years since she'd first met Charlotte and for nineteen and a half of those years they'd been best friends. Much as she valued her new friendship with Helena Banks, there was nothing that could replace the thousands of moments they shared.

'What will you drink?' Charlotte asked, letting her into The Herons.

'A cup of tea would slip down rather well. How's Georgie?'

'High as a kite.' Charlotte appeared in the doorway. 'James has become attentive.'

'James? The boy she fancied?'

'That's the one.'

327

She sighed. 'Ninian's besotted with Alice. I can't believe our children are old enough for all this.'

'Lurve? Scary, isn't it?'

'Another three years and Ninian'll be the age we were when we met.'

'Life's passing quickly.'

Kate took the tea from Charlotte and laid it in front of her. 'That's why I've come, Char. We can't let it roll on and not make up.'

Charlotte pulled a face. 'Are you willing to forgive me? You thought I was the perfect wife, but I tried to tell you it wasn't true. I'm just a flawed human being.'

'You—'

Charlotte went on as if Kate hadn't interrupted. 'I was jealous. You were the clever one. You got all the boys, everything came so easily.'

'That's not true. I lost my Dad, I don't get on that well with my mother. You lived in Forgie, you had a lovely family—'

'Perhaps we all wish for what we don't have. I never thought much about Forgie or my family.'

'It seemed so idyllic. Why do you think I ended up here myself?'

'And then you finally realised Dad isn't exactly idyllic after all.' Charlotte looked at her and started to splutter with laughter.

Kate grinned. Soon they were both giggling, just like the old times. When they finally stopped, Charlotte said, soberly, 'It was years and years ago, Kate. I'm really, really sorry.'

'Years ago? Andrew you mean? I don't care any more about Andrew.'

'And me? Can you forgive me?'

'I only wish I'd known. That's all.'

'Would it have changed anything?'

'Maybe. Who knows?'

328

'Friends again?'

'We've always been friends. We're just wiser and sadder now.'

'Wiser? Maybe. Sadder? Let's not be, Kate, let's not be.'

Chapter Thirty-One

Kate strode briskly back from Charlotte's, her heart eased by making up with her, but her head a jumble of thoughts about a gardener who had found his way under her skin.

Was he back with Melanie because she had refused to go out with him? That was the question that haunted her most. Had she been an idiot? Had he? She couldn't work out how, as things now stood, to put things right with him.

She was still chewing this over as she turned into the drive at Willow Corner, and she was half way up it when she realised there was a car on the gravel.

She stopped abruptly. A small figure was huddled on the front doorstep.

'Hello, Kate,' Sophie said.

'Well. Sophie.' Kate was too surprised to be cutting.

Sophie had been crying, that much was obvious. Her pale skin was blotchy and her eyes red-rimmed. She wasn't wearing anything on her head, Kate noticed with surprise. It was the first time she had seen Sophie's hair, which she'd dyed purple, but then neglected so that the roots showed brown. She wore no make-up and the avid, excited look that had always characterised her had been usurped by something more desperate. *He's left her,* Kate thought with a surge of exhilaration, which quickly subsided. It might be gratifying to know that Andrew and Sophie had run into problems, but it was too late to save her marriage. 'Can I ask what you're doing here?'

Sophie gulped and she lifted her chin, as if grasping for defiance.

'I— I suppose you hate me.'

'Put it this way, you're not exactly on my Christmas card list.'

'You have every right to hate me.'

'I guess I do.'

Sophie sniffed. The girl looked ridiculously young.

'It's all right, Sophie, I won't bite. Come in, it's cold.'

As Kate unlocked the door, she found her consideration repaid by aggression. 'You broke his family up too, remember?' Sophie said with savagery.

'I don't think the situation was quite the same,' Kate said, but without conviction.

'I really fell in love with him, Kate.'

'I expect you did.' *Or thought you did.*

'He told me he loved me.'

'Sophie, I'm not sure I really want a blow-by-blow account of your relationship with my husband.'

'But you have to understand!'

Kate had never dealt with a daughter. She'd struggled with a stepson older than herself, and a son, whose transition to adulthood was being made more problematic by his parents' behaviour. Might a daughter have turned out like Sophie, over-excitable, self-obsessed and dangerously volatile? Never. There were no traits she could discern in this girl that resonated in any way with herself nor, so far as she could see, with Andrew. In fact, she could see nothing in Sophie at all – apart from the obvious attributes of prettiness and youth – that would engage Andrew's affections for much longer than it took to peel an onion.

'I found his latest draft,' Sophie said, clearly working hard to keep the wobble out of her voice, but failing.

'Ah. Now I get it. Andrew's still using Martyne Noreis as a way of venting his feelings.'

'Has he done it before— Oh! Then you'll understand. Here. I printed it off.' She opened her large velvet embroidered shoulder bag and took out a well-thumbed sheaf of paper.

Kate sighed. 'Sit down.'

Sophie subsided onto a chair in the kitchen, but Kate didn't follow suit. Instead she filled the kettle.

'Aren't you going to read it?'

'I'll read it. But I need coffee. Would you like one?'

'I don't drink coffee. Have you got any herbal tea?'

'Sorry, no. Andrew can't stand the stuff.'

The response was sheer reflex, she had not meant to be tactless – but after years of living with Andrew, she knew pretty much everything about him. He was her right glove, she his left. She remembered how she used to curl round his corkscrewed body with easy intimacy and felt weak with regret because she would do so no more. You can stop loving someone, but you can't just stop knowing them. She still knew all Andrew's likes and dislikes, his endearing habits and his irritating ones. She knew he could recall a face in a crowd and construct a whole back story around the image, and that he read obsessively until he found just the right historic hook for his plot. Had Sophie discovered these things yet? What would she think of the way Andrew could read deep into the night if he was pursuing a will-o-the-wisp thought? Would she find the cold place in the bed where his body should be as irritating as Kate had? How long would it take her to discover that he was tone deaf, or that he hated gadgets? Would she learn to live with his obsession for order and tidiness?

'I know he can't,' Sophie said. It was almost a wail.

There was no need for tact, she owed Sophie nothing. 'I have hot chocolate? Or tea?'

There was another sniff. 'Hot water will be fine. Thank you.'

Kate made her coffee and presented Sophie with a mug of water from the kettle. She saw chipped red fingernails as the girl pushed the sheaf of paper across to her with a feverish movement. The Sophie she had seen a few

333

months ago would never have allowed her nails to chip.

She picked up the top sheet and read.

'Martyne strode along the beach with Syme at his heels. The wind had risen and a storm would come. He could feel it in his bones. If he was to kill Ethelinda, tonight would be the perfect night to carry out the deed.'

Kate glanced up. 'He's planning murder?'

This time Sophie wailed in earnest.

'He had thought the whole thing through. Tonight, Ethelinda would be travelling along the cliff path to her uncle's house in the next village, with only her maid for company. There was a place where the trail became treacherous and recent rains had made it more so. The earth had slid to the sea so that the way was narrow. A nervous pony might lose its footing. There would be no need to touch her, or the horse, only to startle it. A small stone lobbed from behind the bush just past the point would be all that was needed – and if that failed, he could let loose the two birds he had caught and caged. The sudden flapping of wings right in front of the pony would cause it to rear and throw his pregnant mistress. She was not a good rider and the bulk she carried made her even less assured. The maid would be walking. If she chanced to see him after her mistress had fallen, one push would be all it required to send her down the cliffs to certain death. If she ran the other way, back to her own village, which was the more likely, he could make his escape through the darkness and be back with Ellyn before the alarm was raised.'

'What,' Kate asked, 'does Andrew say about this?'

'I haven't asked him. I was too scared.'

'Scared? You surely don't think—'

She should have chosen waterproof mascara, Kate thought heartlessly as she handed the girl a handkerchief. Small wonder that Andrew had wanted to come home. Sophie McAteer was no maneater, as Ninian had liked to characterise her. On the contrary, she seemed young for her age. She had no sophisticated wiles, she was just needy. Once the novelty had worn off, Andrew would hate the claustrophobia of being needed – he liked on-demand attention all to come his way.

'Andrew's no monster, Sophie. At least, not in that sense. You must know that.'

The girl dabbed at her eyes and sniffed. 'I do know. It's metaphorical though, don't you see? He wants to kill off our relationship.'

'It's just a novel,' Kate said, using Andrew's argument.

'Is it though? Is that what you think?'

Kate said, exasperated, 'What are you expecting me to do?'

'I want you to help me. Please?'

Kate laughed out loud. 'You can't be serious.'

'I know it's a cheek. I'm sorry. I didn't know who to turn to.'

What do you say to a young girl who has seduced your husband and who comes to you for advice? Kate thought of the misery she had been put through in the past months because of Sophie MacAteer and her first instinct was to tell her to go to hell. Then she thought of Andrew, systematically working his way through a procession of young women across the years and of her own realisation – far too late – that she should have talked to Val.

'If I tell you my views,' she said, 'you'll think my advice is biased.'

'I know he's not really going to kill me. He's just got tired of me already,' Sophie said, her eyes brimming with tears. As Kate watched, a couple escaped and rolled down marble-white cheeks.

Kate picked up another sheet of Andrew's draft.

'Martyne could see Ethelinda and her maid now, perhaps a mile away. Darkness had fallen, but the night was clear. He knew now that he wanted Ellyn more than

335

he ever had, that his passion for the younger girl had been nought but a mad dream. Was it too late to set things right? Was killing the gypsy girl the way out of his troubles? He had solved many a murder case, he knew how to cover his tracks, he would never be caught. The way before him was clear.'

She said, 'Haven't you got any friends, Sophie? Surely there are other people you can talk this over with?'

Sophie blew her nose noisily. 'I need you to tell me the truth.'

'About Andrew?'

She nodded.

Kate said, 'I think you know the truth, don't you?'

'He's done this before, hasn't he? And he'll do it again.'

So she might be immature, but she was not stupid. 'Well, I've got to admire your courage.'

'You think I'm brave?'

'You know the truth, don't you? And you've decided to face it. I think that's brave, yes.'

Sophie shuddered, but pinched her lips together and lifted her chin. 'What should I do?'

Kate shrugged. 'You're young. Just make your decision and stick with it, then get on with the rest of your life.'

'You think I should throw him out.'

'I didn't say that.'

'You do, though' Sophie insisted.

But Kate had grown weary of her. 'Do what you want, Sophie,' she said tiredly. 'I'm sorry to tell you that I don't really care one way or the other.'

She watched Sophie turn the car and drive off. She could not pretend that the visit had been a welcome, or even a pleasant one, but it had served one important purpose – it had reinforced the fact that her time for being in love with Andrew Courtenay was well and truly over.

336

Chapter Thirty-Two

In the middle of the eighteenth century a young girl called Miss Louisa Chalmers, who lived in Lily Cottage in Forgie High Street, kept a diary. This diary, beautifully illustrated with tiny, jewel-like watercolours, was discovered a hundred years later in a tin box that had been buried under an ash tree at the bottom of the garden. What Miss Louisa's motives had been in burying it could only be guessed at, but the diary excited interest, found a publisher, and became a small but steady seller for the next hundred years.

Miss Louisa's enchanting entry for Advent Sunday read, '*And so to the Hall, where the first Advent candle was lighted and hot wine was taken. Mother brought sweet bread with raisins, Aunt Julia a sponge cake with last season's raspberry jam. Much fun was had by all.*'

The tradition, which had apparently lapsed by the middle of the nineteenth century, had been revived around the Millennium, and the ceremony of putting up the village Christmas tree and the Hall decorations, now took place every Advent Sunday, with 'hot wine taken'. It was a good tradition, Kate thought as she leafed through a recipe book trying to decide on what to take to the party. She had always hated the dark days of winter.

Kate pulled a hardback from the shelf where Andrew kept his cookery books. Maybe Sophie did the cooking now, because he had not come to collect them. She flicked through the pages. Dundee Cake: too rich. Madeira Cake: too plain. Victoria Sandwich: too ordinary. *Jumble Cake.* Her hand hovered over the page and held the book open. It seemed to be basically a sponge cake with chunks of chocolate, lumps of sugar, and dried fruit.

Kate had discovered a passion for baking during the weeks of her suspension. She found it therapeutic, and although the scones she'd made for Nicola Arnott had been heavy and hard, she was beginning to be quite good at it, so long as she followed the recipe to the letter. This approach suited her training and inclination. Cooking dishes where the chef's instructions read 'add a handful of this' or 'throw in some of whatever' left her apprehensive and uncertain.

Jumble Cake it was then. Ideal.

Two hours and a slightly messy kitchen later, she took the cake out of the oven and placed it on a wire tray to cool. *Make sure,* she read, *that the centre bounces back when pressed.* She smiled. 'Bounces back when pressed.' How apt. She'd been under considerable pressure herself recently and was rather proud of how she was bouncing back.

As she dressed for her outing, though, Kate realised that a mask of confidence was harder to assemble than the ingredients for a cake. For someone who had never been seen to lack conviction, she found that facing the inhabitants of Forgie took a considerable amount of courage. To many she was still the ogre who was inflicting an unwanted wind farm on them, to others she was the bitch who had driven away their most famous resident. Either way, she knew she was far from popular.

Her apprehension was borne out when she arrived at the village hall. The place seemed busier than ever this year and no-one made way for her as she struggled to reach the cake table. There were no friendly platitudes and very few smiles. She squeezed past May Nesbitt from Forgie House with the cake almost above her head. It was nearly sent flying by Myra Carr from the tennis club.

'Oops, sorry,' Kate muttered, though it was Myra who

hadn't been looking.

She spied Charlotte, trying to find space for her own cake on an overflowing table. 'Here,' Charlotte said with a grin, 'let's dump Myra's ghastly pancakes onto this plate of rubbish brownies. They're all obviously shop-bought and don't deserve to be displayed.'

Kate began to feel better as they giggled conspiratorially.

Talking at this end of the hall was nigh on impossible. By mutual consent they edged through the crowds and towards the door. There was a large poster pinned up in the front porch. Kate hadn't spotted it when she came in, she must have been concentrating on protecting her cake.

'"Village Hall Refurbishment Plans." What's this?'

Charlotte chortled. 'You wouldn't believe it, Kate, but Dad's fairly changed his tune. He says he's still against the wind farm, but now that they know they're likely to get a load of money by way of compensation, he's adopted the refurbishment scheme like a new child. What do you think of the drawings?'

Kate studied the artist's impression. This was more than renovation, it was a full-scale extension, featuring a glass atrium to the rear of the old Victorian building that housed a large hall, with what looked like a number of meeting rooms and possible offices round the northern side. It was very contemporary, but stylish.

'Ambitious, but I like it. Do you think they'll get permission? This is a conservation village.'

Charlotte grinned. 'Dad's a man on a mission.'

Kate groaned. 'Thank God I'm not on the Council Planning Committee.'

'I know. They're no sooner rid of him camping out on their doorstep about the wind farm than he's back, campaigning for this.'

'This time,' Kate smiled, 'I'll be on his side.'

'He'll be delighted about that. Genuinely.' Her voice

changed. 'Look, there's Mike, talking to Ian Grant.'

'Ian—?'

'You remember me telling you, he's Ibsen Brown's brother-in-law. He works with Mike on the rigs.'

At the mention of Ibsen's name, Kate caught her breath. 'Ah yes, there's Cassie now, with the baby,' she said with a lightness constructed to mask her churning emotions. She surged forward to greet them, praying that Ibsen and Melanie weren't here too.

Cassie was carrying Daisy Rose in a sling. 'It's easier than a buggy in crowds,' she explained. 'I'm so pleased to see you. Ian insisted that we come but I didn't think I'd know anyone.'

'Is this the famous Daisy?' Charlotte had always been gooey-eyed about babies.

Daisy Rose kicked pink bootees delightedly and a conversation followed that Charlotte and the baby seemed to enjoy, but which was completely unintelligible to Cassie and Kate. Daisy seized Charlotte's hair and started winding it round her tiny fingers with glee. Above her head, Cassie said, 'Ibsen's leaving today. Did you know?'

Kate said, 'Leaving?'

'He applied for a job as head gardener at one of the big country estates in Northamptonshire and they've called him down for a final interview. They've pretty much told him the job's his.'

'Ibsen's leaving?' Kate repeated for a second time, stupidly. 'But why? What about Daisy Rose? What about his cottage? What about the *garden*?'

'I know. We're devastated, all of us. Nicola Arnott doesn't know what she'll do.'

Ibsen Brown was leaving, and the smidgen of hope Kate had not even known she was nurturing was extinguished in a blink. 'I can't believe he'd do that. Everything was going so well for him.'

'He's never got over Violet. You know what he's like,

he won't talk about it, but we think – all of us – that that may be why he's going.'

What about Melanie? 'You'll miss him terribly.'

'Yes.'

'When did he go?' *To hell with Melanie. What about me?*

'He left this morning. Trouble is, he's exactly right for the job.'

Daisy Rose abandoned Charlotte's hair and started to grunt. Her face grew red and a small frown of concentration appeared between her eyebrows. 'I think she's— Oh. She has,' Charlotte said, laughing and stepping back as a pungent aroma spilled from Daisy's vicinity.

'Oh, Lord, I'll have to find somewhere to change her.'

'There's a loo at the back of the hall.'

'Right. Thanks. I'll be back soon.'

As Cassie disappeared into the crowd, Charlotte looked at Kate and said, 'So tell me about Ibsen Brown, Kate.'

'What about him?' Kate couldn't bring herself to meet her friend's gaze.

'I thought he was madly irritating, an obtuse wind-farm protestor, a—'

'He is.'

'But?'

'But what?'

'Why are you so upset that he's moving away?'

'Did I say I was upset?'

'Oh come on, Kate, I've known you for years, remember? You're one unhappy woman right now. You should have seen the way your face changed when Cassie told you.'

'It did not.'

'It did.'

'It did n— anyway, you were busy playing with Daisy, how would you know?'

'I peeked.'

Kate looked away. Charlotte knew her too well.

Adapt or die was Kate's new philosophy. Adaptation is a natural state in human beings and she'd been working hard at reshaping a life without Andrew, without AeGen, and without Mrs Gillies. She had become a housekeeper, a single parent, self employed. She put the rubbish out and she vacuumed. She dusted and ironed and cooked for Ninian and herself. She had turned her back on a career ladder and was focusing on survival in the freelance jungle. She thought she was adjusting to a life without love – but Cassie's news pulled out a vital peg in the foundations of the edifice she had constructed and sent her spinning into a void.

'Nothing good can come of lying to yourself,' Charlotte said quietly. 'You taught me that.'

Kate's head whipped round. '*I* did?' she asked, wide-eyed.

'I lied to myself about Andy. I told myself it didn't matter, that what you and Mike didn't know wouldn't hurt you blah, blah, blah – but it nearly destroyed our friendship, didn't it? And it was eating away at me so much that it was getting in the way of my feelings for Mike too. Since I talked to him—' She leaned towards Kate and gripped her arm, '—it wasn't easy, actually it was hellish, but everything's a hundred times better than it was. Honesty is the key. Believe me. If you have feelings for Ibsen, go tell him. Don't let him just leave.'

Kate didn't move. Uncertainty gripped her. 'I think he's started seeing Melanie again.'

'Really? You sure about that? Why's he going away, then?'

'He's – I don't know. His private life is complicated.'

'And empty?' Charlotte studied Kate's face. 'I think I'm right, aren't I? There has been something between you.'

'There was,' Kate admitted. 'Once. But he doesn't love me.'

'Who's talking about love? Not everyone falls in love at first sight, you know.'

'Like me and Andrew, you mean?' Kate grimaced wryly.

'Love can take ages to develop. But don't be frightened of showing you care, just because you've been hurt – because sometimes, just knowing that someone gives a damn can turn your life around.'

Kate pursed her lips. 'You told me once that I didn't know anything about other people's lives, Char. You said I never took much interest.'

'So prove me wrong.'

Kate's voice tightened with anxiety. 'But he's gone already.'

'Maybe not. It's only midday.'

'But what if he has?'

'Kate! Shoo!'

Kate turned and ran.

Behind her, she heard Myra Carr's outraged voice complaining loudly, 'Someone's dumped my pancakes on top of a load of *brownies!*'

The gates into the Forgie House estate were never closed. Today, someone had shut them. She leapt out of the car and ran to slide back the bolts. They were heavy and unwieldy and half rusted, and her small hands struggled to shift them. The last one finally slid back, protesting, and she raced back to her car. She'd never realised how far Ibsen's cottage was from the gates. At the final corner of the road, she skidded on black ice and wrestled with the wheel as the car threatened to spin out of control. *Not now, damn you, not now.*

Then the cottage was in front of her, its blank windows staring sightlessly into the distance. It looked abandoned

343

and Kate's heart sank. He obviously wasn't there. She'd made a comprehensive mess of everything. She opened the car door and jumped out. The sound of her knock seemed to bounce backwards, skimming across the frozen grass to hit the cold stone walls of the estate, so that it reverberated back towards her as a spooky echo. There was no answer, to knock or to echo. Leaving the front door, she ran to the garden gate and barged in. The side door, he uses the side door, idiot.

She battered on the side door.

Silence.

She hammered again.

Nothing. Behind her, he had left neatness and order, but the small patch of garden was featureless and uncultivated. There would be no dahlias next summer to brighten the brown earth.

'Ibsen's gone.'

Kate whirled round.

'I saw your car,' Tam Brown said. 'He's gone. You've missed him.'

He was standing at the garden gate, looking heart-stoppingly like his son, with his sky-blue eyes that drilled into you, his weathered, kindly face, his stocky, strong build.

'When?' she demanded. 'When did he leave?'

Tam glanced at his watch. 'Best part of an hour ago.'

'His phone's off.'

'He'll be driving.'

'What way did he go?'

Tam shrugged. 'Up through Bonny Brae, if I know Ibsen, it's a pretty drive from there to the main road. He'd go on down through Lauder and Jedburgh I expect. You wanting him for something?'

Making love in a blanket of stars. Confidences given, behaviours misunderstood, wishes made and then ignored as they drowned in life-draining emptiness. Did Kate want

344

him? Like a dahlia needs nurturing, like a wind farm needs designing, like the world needs love and compassion to make it turn around the sun. Made mute with an indefinable sense of loss, she could only nod.

Tam smiled. 'You never know,' he said, 'what is intended for you. Go after him. Run.'

Kate ran.

She passed Bonny Brae Woods a few minutes later. The gritters had been out and the worst icy patches had been salted, but she took care nevertheless. On the left, she recognised the grassy bank where she had pulled over to avoid the protestor's dog. That had been the day she'd so stupidly rushed to the encampment. She slowed as she passed it, and fancied there was still evidence of the tyre marks she'd left as she screeched away from the fracas. That day, a thick autumn mist had lain across the ground like a blanket, lending an air of mystery and menace. Today, the air was so cold and clear that every blade of grass seemed to be visible, a palette of straw yellows and barren browns and dark, spent greens that lurked with intent. Ibsen had helped her to get away. He'd put himself at risk. Why hadn't she recognised that?

Kate pressed her foot down on the accelerator. It would do no good to linger among memories.

Through the woods, the road wound up past the back of Summerfield Law. She could see the fragile latticed skeleton of the Met mast, dark against the pale blue sky. All that was Jack Bailey's problem now, thank goodness.

Far in the distance, she could see the sea. 'I blame you,' she'd told Andrew in one of their recent bitter exchanges, 'for robbing me of my sweet memories.' But it wasn't true, she realised, a surge of optimism filling her as she pressed forwards. The memories were still there, nothing could change those. She cherished many moments in the life they once shared, it was merely time to move on. Bizarre though it had been, Sophie's unexpected arrival at

Willow Corner had taught her one thing – that she'd already started to put her life with Andrew into a filing cabinet marked 'Experience' and had opened another drawer, labelled, 'My New Life'. Now she just needed to fill it.

She was high now, and the car was still climbing. The temperature gauge had fallen from three degrees down in Forgie to one and a half at the edge of the wood and was now showing just half a degree above freezing. Grassland turned into moorland, pasture into wilderness; it was a frost-rimed, bleak landscape that had its own wild beauty.

Kate's emotions were intense. It was as if the cold glare of the winter sun was shining on the frost and refracting a dazzling spotlight back onto her. Under its beam Frank Griffiths' passionate opposition to the wind farm suddenly made absolute sense and she knew, with a comprehension that was deep and visceral, why Ibsen loved these rugged acres.

'I like things,' Ibsen had said, *'the way they are.'*

He was allowed to feel that. In her passion for her craft, Kate realised now that she had been slow to acknowledge this. She would defend her turbines to anyone, but perhaps she should learn to recognise, much more than she had, how deeply people wanted to protect a world that was changing inexorably around them.

Now she was on the bleakest part of the moor. It was December, it was freezing, and this was a desolate part of the country.

And it was the worst possible place to skid on black ice and slither helplessly into a ditch from which she could not possibly get out.

Chapter Thirty-Three

Christmas Eve. Frost hung on the trees, thickly sprinkled like icing sugar on a peppermint cream. When darkness had fallen, their cold ghostliness had faded – but now it burst joyously centre stage as headlights became spotlights and illuminated their denuded branches. Harry and Jane's car had just swung into the drive.

Kate poked her head out of the front door, waved a welcome, then pushed it hurriedly closed again so that the freezing air didn't percolate inside.

'Muffle up well, you two,' Kate called up the stairs. Ninian had taken down his death threat poster and transformed his room since his relationship with Alice had deepened. Gone were the random socks and tee shirts littering the floor. Kate had taught him how to load the washing machine and set it to the right programme. He pulled the vacuum cleaner out and used it with reasonable regularity. He kept his room tidy. It was now a room suitable for receiving visitors – and one visitor in particular. Kate recalled thinking that when Ninian lost his gaucheness and remembered where he kept his charm hidden, he would become a magnet for the girls. He'd certainly forged a deep bond with Alice Banks.

Ninian's bedroom door opened and Alice appeared. She called, 'Have Harry and Jane arrived? Are you ready to go?'

'They're here. Are you ready? Parking won't be easy. You have got gloves, Alice?'

Russet hair swung round slim shoulders. She was wearing a flimsy tee shirt. A *tee shirt*! In the middle of the

347

coldest snap for years! What happened to turning down the heating and putting on a sweater?

Ninian bounded downstairs. She could swear his shoulders had broadened and filled out in the last few months. 'Have you got the mince pies, Mum?'

Kate was proud that she had made her own and that they didn't look too disastrous. She waved a willow basket at Ninian. 'They're in here, warmed through and wrapped in dozens of tea towels to keep them that way.'

'And the mulled wine?'

'In there,' she gestured at a hessian carrier bag, 'in a couple of vacuum flasks. Can you take everything out if you're ready? I'll be there in a sec. Just need to pull on my boots.'

As Ninian and Alice fled into the cold, their laughter hung behind them in the freezing night air, tiny frozen bubbles of exuberance. Kate stood for a moment on the doorstep, savouring the sound of their happiness and thinking of everything that had happened in the last few months. Her world had turned upside down. She had lost her job, but fallen happily into new work. Ninian had gone through a period of self-doubt and anger, but had found Alice. She had learned who her friends were, and who they weren't. Her marriage had ended and— and nothing.

She hauled on one fur-lined boot, then steadied herself with one hand on the bannister.

She thought of Ibsen often. She liked him a great deal – far too much – and yet she always seemed to rub him up the wrong way. He'd peeled back a hard, protective layer and let her peep underneath to the rawness he battled with, and she had chosen to focus instead on the sticking plaster that was his lifestyle. He'd asked her to a movie, and she'd retreated into a sulk.

Kate shoved her other foot into the second boot and banged it on the floor to get it to slide in.

Enough.

348

Bang.

I'm doing all right.

Bang.

I can live without Ibsen.

'Mu-um!'

Ninian's voice leached impatience.

'Coming!'

She pulled the front door behind her and double locked it. Time to go.

Behind her, the lights on the tree in the window glistened like red berries. It was going to be a perfect, picture book Christmas.

Nicola Arnott was full of excitement. 'Isn't this wonderful? It's the first event at our community garden and look at it – there must be a hundred and fifty people here.'

Kate hugged her, infected by her excitement. 'You've done wonders. Look at this!'

And it *was* wonderful. She was standing on one of the paths she'd helped to make and even in the darkness she could make out some of the areas Ibsen had planned – the friendship garden, for example, just to her right. Once the plants started to grow, it would become a delightful, intricate labyrinth.

He hadn't come back from Northamptonshire – or if he had, she hadn't heard. She'd been silly to think she could ever persuade him to change his mind – but what a loss he would be to Summerfield.

She tried not to feel sorry for herself. She was on a long road, she would just have to find her own way.

'Here Mum, take this,' Ninian appeared and handed her a chunky red candle, its flame already flickering.

Kate looked around. While she'd been dreaming, the garden had become a bobbing, flickering, dancing sea of candlelight. She caught her breath. 'Oh! How lovely.'

349

Ninian slid his arm around Alice. Their eyes shone in the light of a hundred flames. *They look so happy*, Kate thought, with a pang of envy, but with genuine pleasure in her son's contentment.

'They're going to start the carols soon,' Alice said, her cheeks rosy with cold.

Harry said, 'I can't believe this patch of waste has been transformed like this. It was your idea, wasn't it, Kate? You must be very proud.'

Kate was glad that the darkness hid the tears that sprang to her eyes. Harry's praise meant a great deal to her.

Across the garden, Nicola Arnott jumped onto a low dais that had been placed at the top end, near the school. An electricity supply had been run out from the building to power a microphone and a couple of small lights. 'Hello everyone!' she called, her voice used to commanding attention. 'Hello,' she said again, as soon as the chatter stilled, 'and welcome to the Summerfield Community Garden for our very first carol service. We'll start our carols shortly, and after that there'll be a ten-minute interlude. The pupils have suggested that you use this time to introduce yourself to someone you've never met and exchange a cake with them, in a gesture of friendship. We'll have the switch-on at nine o'clock precisely.'

There was an excited murmur.

'Quiet please, quiet!' The murmur dropped. 'Before we start our carol service, can I just say a couple of brief words of thanks? First to Kate Courtenay, whose idea this garden was—'

Kate felt her face grow hot as people clapped, and was glad that the darkness concealed her.

'—and of course, to Ibsen Brown, who has designed the garden and co-ordinated all the many volunteers who have been working so hard to get the garden into shape. What?' she paused to listen to a shout. 'Oh yes, with the able assistance of Kylie Tolen, of course.'

There was much laughter. Kylie, the ten-year-old daughter of the forthright Mary Tolen who served on the Community Council, had developed a reputation as a powerhouse of persuasion. She'd worked so hard for the garden that she'd been chosen to switch on the lights.

'Now— please welcome the Summerfield Primary School Choir!'

Twenty small children filed onto the dais, a chord was played on a keyboard, a teacher raised her hands ready to conduct, and the heartbreakingly beautiful voice of a young boy rang out with perfect purity, 'Once in royal David's city—'

I can't be the only one, Kate thought, to have a lump in my throat. She tried to wipe away a tear that was threatening to escape down her cheek and was reassured to see a few handkerchiefs out. It was perfect. Freezing feet and scarlet noses and fingers, a sea of glimmering candles, the old apple tree with its charming decorations and a choir of little angels. And, above all, a community of people who might never otherwise have come together, drawn here in a spirit of harmony.

There was a sniff beside her and Maisie grinned happily. 'No' bad, eh?'

Not bad. Not bad at all.

'Mum, try this chocolate log,' Ninian said, 'and can you give me some of those mince pies?'

'Jane's brought a flask of hot chocolate spiced with a little rum,' Harry said through pastry and mincemeat, 'and by the way, these mince pies are pretty good.'

'I made them myself.'

'What, even the pastry?' Jane asked.

'Even the pastry.'

'Stunning.'

'I let Andrew take charge in the kitchen for far too

351

long. It was easier to let him cook because he was good at it, but it meant I never tried. Actually, I'm rather enjoying it. It's very therapeutic.'

'We'd better circulate,' Harry said, 'we're meant to talk to someone we don't know.'

'Here—' Kate gave him a cardboard box full of warm mince pies, 'distribute these. And Jane—'

'Yes?'

'Your hot chocolate is divine.'

'Thanks!'

They disappeared into the darkness. Ninian and Alice had already been swallowed up in the throng. Kate picked up her basket and started to walk. She found Jodie-of-the-blisters and accepted a rather heavy sausage roll in exchange for one of her pies. Mary Tolen gave her a slab of brandy-laden Christmas cake and her excited daughter, swathed in scarves and barely visible under an oversized bobble hat, traded an iced biscuit in the shape of a star.

Something thumped her in the back of the knees and almost knocked her over.

'Wellington!' His tail was a blur of excited greeting and Kate's heart raced from nought to sixty in three point four seconds. 'Hello, boy! Hello!'

If Wellington was here, his owner must be here too. She looked up.

Ibsen was standing a couple of yards away, the same – but somehow different.

'Your hair!' Kate gasped, 'What the hell have you done with your hair?'

The ponytail had gone and instead his hair had been shorn to a neat crop.

'Don't tell me.' She smiled. 'Melanie turned into Delilah and cut it all off one night to drain your power.'

There was no answering smile. Kate surveyed him critically. He was wearing a sweatshirt with the slogan 'TAKE THE LEAP' alongside a stick figure jumping a chasm. 'You look jolly cold.'

'Probably,' he said, 'because I've got no hair.'

'Why *did* you cut it off? Assuming my guess was wrong, that is.'

'I was going for a job interview. I thought it would look smarter.'

'Cassie told me. She was upset. She thinks you're running away.'

'Cassie's upset because she's losing a push-over babysitter.'

'You know that's not true. *Are* you running away, Ibsen?'

'What would I be running away from?'

They were talking. Never mind how difficult it was, they were talking. She said with great gentleness. 'Violet. Lynn. Memories.'

He said, 'No. I wasn't running away. There was nothing for me in Summerfield.'

'There was Melanie.'

'Melanie is a mischief maker. She had merely attached herself to me for warmth that night. Your timing was bad.'

'Oh.' There was a few moments silence, then she said, 'I've been thinking about it a lot – I'm sorry about the wind farm.'

'Summerfield? We scattered Violet's ashes up there. That's why I felt so strongly about it.'

'Oh God, I didn't know. That makes it even worse.' She took a step towards him, but he moved away and she stopped at the rebuff. 'I really am desperately sorry.'

'Don't be. It's taken a long time, but at last I've come to accept that it's immaterial – Violet will always be in my heart and that's the only thing that matters.'

'So why leave? Why the job?'

'Lynn wrote to tell me she may be getting married again. And the only woman I've really had feelings for since we split, turned me down. It seemed like a good time

353

to make a complete break.'

Kate's sense that she was about to lose everything was overwhelming – then his words sank in. *The only woman I've really had feelings for since we split, turned me down.* She gasped. 'Ibsen—'

His expression was bleak. Where was the twinkle that had drawn her to him? What was it Charlotte had said? *Sometimes, just knowing that someone gives a damn can turn your life around.*

She said, 'It's been a strange, winding road for me this past year, but across the crazy months, one night stands out.'

Not a muscle in his face moved.

'I wanted to make a little magic, but instead I found I had been enchanted.'

'Kate—'

'Shush. I'm talking.'

She saw his face crease, briefly, in amusement. That was better than lifelessness, a damn sight better, so she ploughed on. 'Charlotte tells me I've never taken much interest in other people's lives. I think that's a little unfair, but it's true that recently I haven't had much energy left over to cope with someone else's problems. And I guess when you've just been battered around the heart you get rather sensitive.'

Ragged with apprehension, she said, 'You shared your demons with me once, but I didn't fully understand how much your confidences meant. Will you let me support you now?'

Her heart hammered as she waited for his reply, but it was a long time coming.

Finally, Ibsen shook his head, a strange, unfamiliar, ponytail-less shake. 'No.'

Her head fell forward and she stared at the ground. Someone had obviously been smoking here, she counted five cigarette butts stamped half into the earth. So. This

354

was it. The fag end of her life, and she had only herself to blame for losing everything.

'I'd only want your support,' he went on, 'if you thought you might be able to give me your love too. Maybe not right now, maybe not this moment, but—'

He never finished the sentence, because she crossed the space between them and threw herself into his arms before either of them had time to think about it too much.

Instantly, Wellington objected. A cold, wet nose thrust itself between them so that passion turned to laughter. 'Behave, dog,' Ibsen growled.

Kate's teeth were starting to chatter. 'He's j-jealous.

'Kate?' He put a cold hand under her chin and tilted her head up so that he could look into her eyes. 'This isn't a game? You think you and I—?'

'Let's see.' She pretended to count on her fingers. 'Does it add up? I'd be swapping a man who wears shirts of finest cotton lawn for a man who has a taste for tasteless tee shirts—'

'A man with a sense of fun rather than one who's up his own—' he protested.

'I had a man who supported me in my career and I'd be getting one who detests wind farms—'

'But is prepared to be tolerant—'

'Really?' She looked at him surprised, but ploughed on. 'One who took himself seriously instead of one who—'

'Takes *you* seriously. Is this a job interview, Kate? Because I should tell you that I've just had one of those and I found to my surprise I was rather good at it.'

Kate stared at him in horror. 'Oh Lord. The job! What are you going to do?'

'You and I will have to negotiate compromise, if we're to be together. We'll need to learn to love our differences.'

'Ready everyone?" Nicola's voice boomed over the loudspeakers. 'Kylie Tolen, our year six pupil who has worked so hard on the Garden Committee, is going to

355

switch on the tree lights. Let's count down, shall we? Ten, nine, eight—'

Everyone joined in. '—four, three, two, one—'

Kylie pressed the switch and the old apple tree became a glittering mass of sparkling light, gold, silver and white. There was a collective gasp of appreciation and a round of applause.

In the spring, the bulbs they'd planted would begin to poke their heads bravely into the world and the garden Ibsen had designed would take life. Kate slipped her arm round him. She said, 'You should know that compromise isn't a word I understand. Not where love is concerned, at any rate.'

The unfamiliar, newly-shorn Ibsen chuckled. 'I've heard you argue about a lot of things, Kate Courtenay, but that's the first thing you've said I definitely agree with.'

She laughed and rubbed her hands through the short, unfamiliar hair, then eased herself away so that she could study him. 'You know,' she said, 'I rather like being able to see more of you.'

The slogan on his sweatshirt registered.

'TAKE THE LEAP'

She put a hand on his chest. 'Shall we, Ibsen? Take the leap, I mean?'

'That's why I turned down the job.'

She gasped. 'Why, you—'

The familiar face-splitting grin was back as Ibsen bent his head and stopped her indignant response with a kiss.

And this time, not even Wellington's howling could interrupt them.

THE END

Author's note:

Thank you for taking the time to read *Face the Wind and Fly*. If you enjoyed it, please consider telling your friends or posting a short review. Word of mouth is an author's best friend, and much appreciated.

Loving Susie

She thought she knew her husband, but he's been keeping a secret ... about her.

1

Susie Wallace pokes one foot reluctantly out from underneath the duvet, senses a chill in the air and pulls it back hastily. Ten seconds later she tries again. On the third attempt, she has to force herself to pivot her body through ninety degrees until she's sitting on the edge of the bed. Behind her, a rumpled form stirs as the duvet settles uneasily back into place.

'You off?' mumbles the formless shape under the covers.

Susie switches on her bedside lamp. 'Oh sorry, darling, didn't mean to disturb you.' She watches her husband Archie hunch upwards. 'I've got an early telly interview. Will I bring you tea?'

'I'll get up.'

His hair is white these days, but to Susie's biased eye, Archie's face hasn't changed in all the years she has known him. She steals a precious moment to contemplate her husband.

'What?' He pauses in the ritual scratching of the scalp, his hand hovering above the thick thatch of hair, his blue eyes paler, perhaps, than they used to be but even at this ungodly hour still swimming with tenderness and wisdom and laughter – all the things that she's always loved him for.

'Nothing. Just thinking how amazing it is that I still fancy you thirty years on.'

'*Christ.*'

'Did you forget?' She isn't angry, merely amused. Of course he's forgotten. Archie isn't a man for remembering birthdays, anniversaries, little landmarks of celebration. Why would he remember their thirtieth wedding anniversary when he has unrepentantly forgotten all the

361

others?

'Just joking.' His grin breaks through, boyish as the day they met. 'I've booked The Shore for dinner.'

'Really?' Susie is astonished. 'Am I free?'

Life has changed. As an actress, she'd snogged Colin Firth, flown the wires as Tinkerbell and delivered a twenty-minute monologue naked in an off-West End theatre. Now she's no longer in theatre, she's a politician – and in the two years since she was elected to serve the people as a member of the Scottish Parliament, Archie has had to learn to negotiate diary time with her assistant.

He yawns. 'I negotiated a seven o'clock slot with Karen.'

'How lovely.' She stoops and kisses him, responding involuntarily to the familiarity of his early-morning smell, then pulling herself away reluctantly as she senses his interest quicken. 'Sorry, darling, must hurry.'

Archie pulls a face and she smiles as she turns towards the shower. How close she'd come to messing everything up, in those crazy days of their early marriage – and how right she'd been to stay with him. She slips off her nightdress, but it's not just the sudden chill that makes her shiver – it's the thought of what might have happened if he'd come to hear of her folly.

Her life may have changed but Archie, thank heaven, is as important to her as ever. The thread of security and intimacy that binds them together is a precious treasure in the madness that has become her daily life.

Archie watches his wife pat her hair dry. She has never quite tamed her hazelnut curls with their glorious russet highlights and he hopes she never will. They define her. Open any newspaper in the land and Susie Wallace is likely to be there, a flame-haired beacon for her causes. She always was passionate about some perceived injustice – it's what he loves most about her. A progression into politics was probably inevitable.

She reaches for the drier and he swings out of bed. 'I'll put on the kettle.'

'Will you, love? Thanks.'

Downstairs, Prince's tail thumps excitedly on the stone flagstones of the kitchen floor. He's growing old now, a little prematurely, as Labs tend to, but doggy affection is so completely undemanding that its rewards are sweet. Archie bends to pat him.

'Hello, old boy. Another morning, another day of mayhem.'

He marches to the sink to fill the kettle, then glances at the old school clock on the wall above the range. Six thirty already. Susie will have to shift – she's due at the BBC studios in Edinburgh in an hour and the drive from the cottage on the outskirts of Hailesbank can take all of that on bad days.

As the kettle begins to steam, Susie comes into the kitchen.

'That was quick.'

'I wanted to share five minutes with you before I rush off. Jon home?'

'I'll take a look.'

He pulls aside the heavy curtains that mask the door into the cobbled courtyard. Outside, a battered Volvo has been strategically abandoned, as if its owner was too tired to park it neatly into its corner. And that'll be the truth, Archie thinks, guessing that their twenty-three-year-old son arrived home in the small hours. He says, 'His car's here, so yes.'

'Good. Sorry I won't see him today, but Mannie's popping in for lunch at the Parliament. I don't suppose she'll linger though.' Their daughter Margaret-Anne is a sales director for a hotel chain and lives almost as frenetic a life as Susie herself.

'Give her my love. And drive safely. I'll watch you.'

'Thanks. I'll call you after.'

'And I'll see you in—' he glances at the kitchen clock, '—twelve and a half hours.'

'Hell's bells! I'm off.'

But there's frost on the car and she has to spend seven precious minutes clearing it.

An hour later, Archie makes his second cup of tea and settles in front of the television. Susie will be on in a few minutes and he doesn't want to miss her. Prince settles himself heavily across his feet as the interviewer says, 'And in our studio we have communications specialist Brian Henderson to tell us how he believes morale could be improved at the troubled firm. Brian—'

Prince snores and his weight shifts. Archie reaches down and pats the dog affectionately. When he looks up again, a middle-aged businessman is talking. 'The key to good employee relations lies in communication—'

There is nothing remarkable about the man, yet for some reason Archie's attention is caught. He stares at the round face and receding hair.

'A culture of secrecy breeds a culture of suspicion—'

His grey suit is unremarkable, though his tie is loud. There's something about the hazel eyes that looks familiar.

'—while openness, by contrast, helps to build trust.'

Archie watches, riveted. It's more the mouth than the eyes. There's a peculiar mobility to the mouth, a certain twist to the smile, a way of moving the lips, that he has seen before.

'It takes time, naturally. It's impossible to turn a culture around in a matter of days or weeks—'

'Are you saying that—?'

Archie's heart begins to race. He thumps the mug onto the table so hard that tea rises in a great wave and splashes onto the wood. He knows where he has seen that mouth before – or one very like it.

Jesus! Surely the secret he has kept safe for so long is not in danger of getting out now? Panic grows. Is the man in the studios with Susie? Will she see him? Will she make the connection she has just made?

And then the interview is over and the presenter is introducing his wife.

The panic slowly subsides. There's no problem, he tells himself, the man must be in the Glasgow studio, Susie is in the remote in Edinburgh, there's no chance of them meeting. And anyway, he must be mistaken, it's just a coincidence.

The BBC's remote studio in Edinburgh's Tun is hardly inspiring. There's a rather tired-looking backdrop of an Edinburgh scene that has nobody fooled, and the monitor is set below the camera, so that it's all too easy to look down at the interviewer instead of engaging through the lens. Susie sets her plastic beaker of coffee down on a side table and settles onto the chair.

She isn't really nervous. She has done this dozens of times, it's no big deal – but today's a little different because she's going to go directly against her Party's policy. It's definitely not a good career move and she's conscious of her heart rate picking up as she waits.

'—The Government will today announce cuts in its funding for the teaching of music and drama in schools. One backbencher, however, disagrees with her own Party's policy. Good morning, Mrs Wallace.

She's on air. 'Good morning,' Susie says brightly. 'You're right. I believe there's absolutely no case for axing funding.'

'It's easy to say that, but when there's a choice to be made between health care and—'

Susie interrupts the interviewer passionately. 'Don't you see? Sometimes I wonder if it's only politicians who are unable to understand that music and drama can be

365

powerful ways of preventing ill health from happening in the first place.' She leans towards the camera, her eyes aflame. 'Art, music, drama, poetry all help people to make contact with places deep inside themselves where difficult emotions can fester and explode and turn these into something joyful and exhilarating. It's something they can share with others, do with others.'

'But don't you think—'

'The performing arts and literature aren't only ways of fulfilling our creativity, they also require us to work with other people. And wherever you come from, whatever your home life is like, these things can be immensely rewarding.'

'Are you saying that the arts can keep us out of the GP's surgery?'

'Yes. That's exactly what I'm saying.'

'Susie Wallace, thank you very much for joining us this morning.'

'It's been a pleasure.'

'And congratulations on "Home, Where My Heart Is". You must be pleased the series has finally reached our television screens again after all these years.'

'Oh. Yes. Thank you. I am. We all are – the cast, I mean.'

'That was Susie Wallace MSP, talking about arts funding in schools. We did, of course, ask for a government spokesperson on the issue, but no-one was available.'

Susie watches until the red light goes out, then takes a deep breath.

'Fabulous as ever, Susie, thanks,' comes the producer's voice.

'No problem. Thanks for inviting me on.'

She collects her handbag and briefcase and walks out of the studio. Outside she dials Archie. 'Was I all right?'

'Darling, you were magnificent. Susie Wallace in full

flow is a force to be reckoned with. I was terrified.'

She laughs. It's infectious – passers-by turn their heads and smile. She nods at a sunken-cheeked man hurrying towards the newspaper offices opposite, his legs stick-like and bony, like a bird's. A freelance journalist – what is his name? Justin something. Justin Thorneloe. 'Right,' she says dryly, into the phone. 'Like I could terrify you.'

'You scared me into marrying you.'

'Stop teasing, you're a wicked man.'

The sound of his chuckles keeps her smiling all the way into the nearby Parliament building.

Some people might think that Susie is the stronger one in the Wallace marriage, but she and Archie know otherwise. She is an unrepentant social being, she can work a room like a pro, though the difference between her and many others is that she genuinely loves talking to people and sorting out their problems. Where she is loud, extrovert, and passionate, Archie is thoughtful, balanced and diplomatic. He's her rock, her anchor and her strength, and she very much doubts if she could scare him into anything.

Her heels click clack on the polished granite floor as she passes into the Garden Lobby, adrenalin still pumping from the interview. The sun streams through the boat-shaped windows high above her, illuminating the face of a lean terrier of a man who is striding across the great empty space of the Lobby towards her. It's Tom Coop, her chief whip. He slows and opens his mouth, his stare steely – but another colleague arrives, eager to buttonhole him.

Susie breathes again. Good. She has no doubt he'll be mad at her, but at least her wigging is deferred.

She swipes her pass to gain access to the Member Only office area and steps into the lift. She has an hour to hour to deal with her emails and get her papers in order, a blissful hour before the next public pressure has to be faced.

Just another normal day.

For further news, please visit my website

The Heartlands Series

Jenny Harper

For more information about **Jenny Harper**

and other **Accent Press** titles

please visit

www.accentpress.co.uk

http://www.jennyharperauthor.co.uk